MAINE
Brides

THREE ROMANCES ABOUT SOCIETY'S CASTOFFS
REDEEMED BY LOVE

SUSAN
PAGE DAVIS

BARBOUR
PUBLISHING

The Prisoner's Wife © 2006 by Susan Page Davis
The Castaway's Bride © 2007 by Susan Page Davis
The Lumberjack's Lady © 2007 by Susan Page Davis

ISBN 978-1-60260-106-2

All scripture quotations are taken from the King James Version of the Bible.

This book is a work of fiction. Names, characters, places, and incidents are either products of the author's imagination or used fictitiously. Any similarity to actual people, organizations, and/or events is purely coincidental.

Cover image: Randy Wells

Published by Barbour Publishing, Inc., P.O. Box 719, Uhrichsville, Ohio 44683, www.barbourbooks.com

Our mission is to publish and distribute inspirational products offering exceptional value and biblical encouragement to the masses.

ecpa Member of the
Evangelical Christian
Publishers Association

Printed in the United States of America.

Dear Reader,

Writing about the early days of Maine was a joy. I was born in Waterville and grew up in the small town of Belgrade, where my father's family had lived for seven generations before me. My parents were avid readers, and my father had a special love for history, which worked its way into my heart as well.

While writing *The Prisoner's Wife*, I took three of my children to visit the Olde Gaol in York, Maine. Viewing this historical structure helped solidify the story growing in my mind. Jack Hunter's town is not York, and his prison is not exactly like the Olde Gaol, but they have a similar feel. I hope you'll enjoy Jack and Lucy's struggle as they begin their marriage at the darkest moment of Jack's life.

For the second story, *The Castaway's Bride*, I chose a real setting—the city of Portland in the year Maine became a state. Researching this story included a trip to the Maine Historical Society in Portland and a great deal of reading and poring over old maps and accounts of Portland's growth. The only "real" person in this story is Ann Frazier King, wife of Maine's first governor. For Edward Hunter, returning to the burgeoning city after years in isolation is a shock but not as big as the shock his former fiancée gives him.

In the third story, *The Lumberjack's Lady*, I once more created a town. Readers who know Maine will learn from the context that "Zimmerville," where the lumber company's headquarters are located, lies near Fairfield and Waterville, along the Kennebec River. This is the love story of a poor lumberjack who dares to love the boss's daughter.

My three heroes, Jack, Edward, and Étienne, all start out at a disadvantage. The women who believe in them and pledge their love to them must draw on their faith for inner strength. I hope you enjoy this journey with Lucy, Deborah, and Letitia.

I love to hear from my readers! Come visit me at my Web site: www.susanpagedavis.com

THE PRISONER'S WIFE

Dedication

To my dad, Oral D. Page Jr., who inspired in me a love of history and family. Thank you for giving me the ideal childhood in a godly home. Thanks for staying in Maine and for all the stories about those who came before us.

Chapter 1

Coastal Maine—June 1720

Jack Hunter was putting the last rail of his pasture gate in place when he heard footsteps. Looking up, he saw two men—farmer Charles Dole and Ezekiel Rutledge, the tavern keeper—marching up the path that connected his homestead to the lane. A prickle of anxiety tingled the back of his neck. Shunned by many of the town's residents, he seldom had visitors. The sight of the town's two constables paying a call together was ominous. Jack took a deep breath.

"Good day, gentlemen," he called.

They met him halfway across the dooryard, between his pole barn and the modest house. Stopping a couple of yards from him, they eyed him silently. Rutledge, the tavern keeper, had a prosperous air, from his powdered wig to his neat blue breeches and long waistcoat. Dole eked out his living much as Jack did, farming on a small scale and cutting firewood for others in winter. He was twice Jack's age, and gray streaked his hair and beard.

"You'll be coming with us, Hunter," Rutledge said at last.

"How's that?" Jack asked, his apprehension rising.

"You heered him," Dole said, loud enough that the young calf inside the fence jerked away from its mother's side and stood splay-legged, staring at the men.

Jack glanced at Dole then focused on Rutledge.

"What is it, sir?"

"We'll need you to come with us."

"What for?"

"Here, now, you're addressing the law!" Dole stepped toward him, his hands extended to grasp Jack's arm, but Jack stepped back, raising his hands in defense.

"I said, what for?"

Dole caught him by the shoulders, and Jack shoved him away. In an instant Dole leaped on him, carrying him backward onto the turf near the fence. Tryphenia, the spotted cow, grunted and sidestepped.

"Get off me, you oaf!" Jack gasped, struggling against Dole's weight.

"Hold on, Hunter. Calm yourself." Rutledge stood over them and hauled Dole backward. The grizzled man squatted, panting and eyeing Jack malevolently.

Jack stood and brushed off his clothing. "What do you want?"

"As if you don't know," Dole snarled.

"I don't."

"Right. You've been feuding with Barnabas Trent for years, and you wouldn't know anything about what befell him this morning?"

"What are you talking about?"

"Easy, now," Rutledge said. "Just come along with us, Hunter. We'll discuss this in town."

"And if I say no?"

"Then we'll have to arrest you, boy."

Jack stared at him for a moment, but Rutledge didn't flinch. A dozen disjointed thoughts flitted through Jack's mind. He was in trouble, that was certain, but why? He hadn't done anything. Most likely it was simply because he was who he was—Isaac Hunter's son. Whenever anything bad happened in the area, the law used to come looking for his father. But Isaac Hunter was dead now, so the next best suspect was his son. No matter that he was now a grown man of twenty-four and had never caused any trouble. The name was enough.

He saw there was no use in resisting. "Will we be long?"

"Might be." Dole cackled. "Might be a long, long time after what you done."

"Quiet, Charles," said Rutledge.

A wave of mistrust and fear swept over Jack, but he looked the tavern keeper in the eye. "Are you accusing me of something, sir?"

Rutledge drew a deep breath and looked off toward the pasture.

"You mentioned Goodman Trent," Jack prompted.

"Trent was found dead this morning," Rutledge said.

Jack held his gaze straight. "I. . .I'm sorry to hear that."

"It were murder," Dole said with relish.

Jack swallowed. Trent was a near neighbor. They'd had their disagreements, but Jack would never consider harming the man, much less killing him. "I didn't have anything to do with it."

"That's fine, then, boy," said Rutledge. "Just come along and tell us all you know." He stepped forward and took hold of Jack's arm.

"I don't know anything."

"We'll see about that." Dole sounded downright gleeful.

∽∾∾∽

Lucy Hamblin stood in the cottage doorway and watched her six students skip down the lane toward their homes. Seven-year-old Betsy Ellis turned and waved at her, and she smiled and waved back. Betsy took her little brother's hand and led him away.

When the children were out of sight, Lucy turned back to the house and hurried about, straightening the main room. Her mother had been gone all morning, and there was nothing cooking for dinner. She quickly put away her speller and slate, then tied on an apron.

Corn bread and bacon again, she decided. It was monotonous, but there was no fresh meat in the house, and no time to come up with something more creative. Perhaps in the garden she would find a bit of chard mature enough to pick, though it was early in the season for fresh greens.

She prepared a creditable meal. She was beginning to wonder if she would have to eat it alone when the door opened and her mother trudged in. Alice Hamblin set down her basket with a sigh and looked over Lucy's preparations.

"Bless you, child. It's good to come home to hot food."

"How is Mr. Barrow?" Lucy asked, filling her mother's cup with tea.

"He'll mend in time. The bull wasn't kind, but it missed his liver. I think he's out of the woods now."

"Goodwife Barrow must be relieved."

"Oh, yes, indeed. I told her to send the eldest boy if she needs me, but I expect they'll get on all right now." Alice hung her shawl over the back of her chair and took a seat at the table. "She gave me a chicken breast, and she said they'll bring us a bushel of apples when they're ripe."

Lucy sat opposite her and said a brief grace for their food.

"There's been a murder in the township," Alice said as she reached for the cream pitcher.

Lucy nearly dropped her fork. "No."

"That's what Goody Walter says. She came to commiserate with Goody Barrow and brought her some greens and the latest gossip."

"Who was it?"

"Barnabas Trent."

Lucy winced. She knew Trent. He lived about a mile away, on the other side of the Hunters' farm. His older son had died in the Indian war a few years back, and the younger one went south as soon as he was grown. Goodwife Trent had been dead several years, and Barnabas had a reputation among Lucy's young scholars as a curmudgeon who yelled at any hapless children who cut across his pasture on their way to school. His dog was just as bad, barking fiercely at every passerby. Most of the children avoided Trent's property. Lucy felt sorry for him. She had always figured he would die a lonely old man.

"What happened to him?"

"I didn't hear particulars, but likely we'll learn more soon."

"Could it have been Indians?" Lucy asked with a shudder.

"Goodness, child, I hope not."

The area had been peaceful for a few years, but the threat of violence from the natives was never far from mind, especially among the elders who had experienced savage raids in the past. Trent's farm was closer to the town and the garrison than was the Hamblins'. If Indians were striking the outlying homesteads, the farmers would have to evacuate to Fort Hill.

A quick tapping at the door preceded a child's voice calling, "Goody Hamblin! Miss Lucy!"

Lucy jumped up and opened the door to find Betsy Ellis gasping on the doorstep.

"What is it, child?"

"It's Mama. She said to get Goody Hamblin quick!"

Alice stood and reached for her basket. "Likely it's her time. I'm coming, Betsy. You go ahead and tell your marm I'll be along in less than no time."

As the little girl fled down the path, Alice turned to her daughter.

"Can you get me some tea and a bit of maple sugar, please? Likely the Ellises don't have any, and it will be a treat for Sarah when she feels up to it."

"Finish your dinner before you go," Lucy suggested.

While Alice hastily finished her meal, Lucy scrambled to restock the basket her mother always carried when going to act as a nurse, packing a few extras in case an overnight stay at the humble Ellis cottage proved necessary.

Her mother was out the door in five minutes. "If I'm not here by dusk, don't look for me till the morrow," she called over her shoulder.

Lucy was used to being alone nights. Her mother's services as a midwife and nurse were much in demand in the growing community. Lucy kept school in the forenoon when the weather was fair but enjoyed other pursuits in the afternoons, especially in summer. She would spend an hour in the garden most days, then put in the rest of the afternoon at her loom, while the light was good.

She hummed softly as she tidied the room and banked the fire, then went out to the garden to hoe her cabbages, corn, turnips, and beans. She had learned slowly the painful lesson of contentment. Living here with her mother was not the same as having her own home and family, but it was not so bad.

Lucy never allowed herself to think about Jack Hunter for long anymore. Never would she cook at his hearth or bear his children. Her love for him, while not cold, was carefully banked beneath the outward calm of her present life, as the glowing coals were hidden beneath the ashes in the hearth.

Day by day she kept house for her mother, taught school, wove, prepared meals, and kept the fire burning. She was useful, and that was something.

The image of Jack's face was never far from her memory. His gray-blue eyes that looked deep inside her, his solemn demeanor, his neatly trimmed brown beard. He was a handsome man, and back in the old days, when he showed a preference for her, it took only a smile from him to send tremors down her spine.

She realized she had stopped hoeing and was standing between the rows, leaning on her hoe and thinking about Jack, though she'd sworn she wouldn't.

She took a deep breath and determined yet again to forget him. Suddenly she remembered her mother's words about Barnabas Trent. She looked toward the woods and shivered. Perhaps she had chopped enough weeds for today. She lifted her hoe and headed back to the house, where she could bar the door and work at her loom.

Jack stood before the table in the dim hall of the big, barn-like jail. With his wrists shackled, he struggled to remain on his feet.

"You can't keep me here," he insisted.

"Whyever not?" Dole asked with a satisfied smile.

"I have my chores. I hadn't even turned all my stock out this morning. I've got two oxen fretting in the barn. If you keep me here till evening, they'll be hungry, and my cow will need milking."

Dole looked at Rutledge, his eyebrows raised. "Mayhap we should bring his cattle to my place until this is settled."

"No need for that, Charles. Surely one of Hunter's neighbors would do his milking for him tonight."

Jack thought of Samuel Ellis, his nearest neighbor. Jack had helped Sam out before in a pinch, and Sam would do the same for him if need be. But he didn't say anything. Sam had a large family to care for, and besides, Jack didn't want the constables to think he was resigned to staying at the jail overnight.

"If you'd just admit what you did, Hunter...," Rutledge began.

"I've done nothing, sir!"

Rutledge sighed. "We've sent to Falmouth for the magistrate. As soon as he gets here, we'll get down to business."

"And when will that be?"

Rutledge grimaced. "We were hoping he'd be here by now. John Farley left this morning to fetch him, just after we brought you in. He must have been delayed for some reason."

Jack swallowed hard. "I give you my word, when he arrives I'll come back here and answer his questions."

Rutledge looked away. "This is a capital case, Hunter."

"A what?" Jack stared at him.

"And you're the most likely suspect we have."

"How can I be a suspect?"

Dole's lips curled in a maniacal sneer. "Because we found the murder weapon near Barnabas Trent's dead body." He crossed to a small bench with a tarp on it. Lifting the canvas with a flourish, he revealed a blood-encrusted ax. Jack's ax. "Look familiar?"

Jack's stomach lurched, and he reached for the edge of the table to steady himself.

"Like as not we'll be hanging you at dawn." Dole's grin was almost canine.

They kept him on his feet most of the morning, questioning him. At noon the jailer's wife, Goody Stoddard, came in from the jailer's family quarters with a plate of stew for his dinner, and they allowed Jack to sit and eat it. Then the interrogation began again.

Dole grew more impatient by the hour. Jack figured it was only Rutledge's even temper that kept the foul man from attacking him physically.

They brought in the jailer and several of the town's upstanding citizens to try to reason with him, as Rutledge put it, but Jack would not confess to something he didn't do.

"I'll go see if there's any news on Farley," Rutledge finally said, seeming to tire of Jack's constant denial of any wrongdoing. He exited the room, leaving Jack alone with Dole. The only light came through a small window and the open doorway, but Jack could make out the gray-haired man's sneer and glittering eyes.

"You may as well admit to your crime, boy," Dole said, coming closer and peering straight into Jack's face. "It won't make no difference in the sentence, but you don't want to meet your Maker with a lie on your conscience as well as a murder."

Jack said nothing. Dole's foul breath sickened him, and he looked away from the gap between the teeth in the older man's jaw.

"You're nothing but a rogue," Dole said. "Stubborn. Just like your pa."

Jack bristled, tempted to respond, but thought better of it. He didn't trust Dole one whit, and he didn't want to say something he would regret later. Besides, it was true that his father had been a scoundrel. There was no point in defending him.

Dole squinted at him and gave a sage nod. "You'll regret it if you don't own up to it."

"The only thing I regret is letting you bring me here, you dog," Jack said through clenched teeth.

Dole's quick fist caught Jack just below his ribs, and he doubled over, gasping. Dole followed up with a punch to his temple.

Jack raised his chained hands in defense. "Whatever happened to the law?" he choked.

"We are the law," Dole snarled. "So don't you be striking an officer." He shoved him hard, and Jack stumbled off his feet, his skull thudding against the rough wall.

Chapter 2

Here, now!" Rutledge's voice rose in distress as he entered the hall, followed by Reuben Stoddard, the jailer. "Charles, what's the meaning of this?"

Dole wiped his chin with his grimy sleeve. "Young Hunter be disrespectful of the law."

Rutledge grunted and walked over to where Jack was sprawled and extended his hand. "Here, get up, boy."

Jack still felt a bit dazed. There was a knot on the back of his head for sure, and when he tried to catch his breath, his stomach hurt. He took Rutledge's hand and staggered to his feet.

"We'll have to keep you here, Hunter," said Rutledge. "Stoddard's got to lock you up."

"I don't understand."

"You heard the evidence. It looks black for you. I can't let you go."

Jack shook his head, then winced at the pain it caused. "I didn't do anything to Trent, I swear."

"Careful about swearing, now," Dole put in.

Rutledge silenced him with a scowl, then turned to Jack. "I've sent my oldest boy to get some word on the magistrate's whereabouts. Just settle down in the cell here for the night. I'll have Goody Stoddard bring you some supper later on, and we'll get someone to tend your stock this evening."

"Mr. Rutledge, please. Just because my ax was used to kill a man, that's not enough evidence to condemn me."

"Most folks think otherwise." Rutledge's face was grave. "That's why we'll let the magistrate decide."

The jailer led them through a dim passageway and opened the door to a cramped cell. Bars formed a barrier in the small window high in the thick oak door.

Jack stepped unwillingly into the dim room. A damp odor filled his nostrils, and he blinked, trying to make out the details. The amenities seemed to consist of a pile of straw in one corner. The one tiny window was recessed the length of his arm into the thick stone wall. He whirled to face Rutledge. With a large key in his hand, Stoddard was already closing the door. Jack reached out to steady himself and touched a cold stone wall. His head was spinning. "Wait! Please!"

Stoddard paused with the door still open a few inches.

"I'd best get some boys to start setting up for the hanging," Dole said.

Jack fought back his fear. "Goodman Rutledge, please tell him to stop saying that." The peril of his situation struck Jack with awful force. This might be the end of his short life. His struggles to outlive his father's bad reputation, his hard work building up the farm these last few years. . .it was all worthless. In a short while, he would stand before a judge. What could he say to defend himself? No one believed he was innocent. They would hang him for certain. The thought was too terrible to contemplate.

Rutledge squinted at him. "You'd best be making your peace with God tonight. Would you be wanting to see the parson?"

Jack stared at him. "I. . .no."

Rutledge's cold stare told Jack he had said the wrong thing. Undoubtedly the senior constable was doubly convinced he was a heartless killer with no conscience.

Stoddard closed the door and turned the key in the lock. Jack raised his hands, the shackles clanking as he grabbed the bars in the window opening. Rutledge and Dole stood back. Rutledge held the lantern, obviously intending to take it away with them and leave him in darkness.

"Wait!"

"I'm sorry, Hunter." Rutledge's tone was rueful. "We don't face something like this often, thank God. Why, I don't think there's ever been a murder in this township. Not counting Indian troubles, of course. We've got to hold you, boy. It's the only thing we can do."

"We could hang him now and save the judge a lot of trouble," Dole said.

"Hold your tongue," Rutledge told him.

Raging panic rose in Jack's throat. "I won't run away, sir. I give my word. Let me go home, and I'll return whenever you say."

Rutledge gritted his teeth. "You've got no family. Nothing to keep you here. I can't risk it."

"Is my word worth nothing?" Jack yelled as the constables turned away.

"That's right," came Dole's cackle. "The word of a murderer is worthless."

Their footsteps faded, and Jack heard a door close. He reached out and felt the rough wall. Leaning heavily against it, he bowed his head.

Dear God, help! Is there no hope for me? Tears formed in his eyes, and he swallowed hard.

Jack had gone to church every Lord's Day with his mother when he was a boy. The minister had railed from the pulpit against drunkenness one Sunday, and his mother's face had paled. She sat still throughout the long sermon, her shoulders back and her chin high. When Jack asked her why the minister preached against his father, she'd told him the parson was only telling what the Bible said about all drunkards, not anyone specifically.

Isaac Hunter had died when Jack was thirteen, but he and his mother were still treated as outcasts. The closest neighbor, Samuel Ellis, was one of the few who offered comfort. He'd helped Jack haul out logs and chop a firewood supply for the winter. The minister had visited once, but only to remark that Isaac was no doubt receiving just payment for his evil deeds.

Jack wanted to stop going to church after that, but his mother insisted they continue to attend. They always timed it so they arrived as the service began, sat in the back, and slipped out at the last "amen," often without speaking to a soul.

The other women of the village would not accept his mother into their circle, and that hurt Jack. He wondered how she escaped the bitterness that mounted inside him, but his mother seemed to accept it as her due. She had been foolish enough to marry a ne'er-do-well, and she paid the consequences. The Hunters lived a life of seclusion, and he had few friends.

Except Lucy.

The thought of her made him feel weak, and he slid slowly down the wall and sat on the cold stone floor. What would Lucy Hamblin think when she heard he'd been hanged for murder?

Lucy.

How he had loved her. Four years ago Lucy had deigned to notice Jack. She'd spoken to him in a civil manner several times, which had shocked him. Finally Jack got up the nerve to sustain a conversation with the golden-haired maiden. For months he found excuses to walk past the Hamblins' house. It was amazing how often seventeen-year-old Lucy was at the well or in the garden when he passed. She would come to the gate and speak to him, and they found many common interests. At last he dared to ask if he might court her. The smile she gave him that day was a treasured memory. She was willing! His heart sang. Until he approached her father.

Jack bowed his head against his chest. Lucy's father had made it clear what he thought of Isaac Hunter's son. Thomas Hamblin was furious at the idea that a miscreant like Jack would dare think of courting his daughter. "If you loiter about my property, I'll put the law on you," he'd said.

Jack stopped walking past the Hamblins' house after that. In fact, he made long detours to avoid it. He saw Lucy only occasionally, from a distance. Her eyes were always lowered. Only once had he caught her eye, and she'd returned his gaze for just a moment, a troubled frown crossing her sweet face.

She was the youngest of the Hamblins' six children, and she stayed in the home, the dutiful daughter. She had never married, though Jack was sure several young men in the village had hoped at one time or another to win her hand. Jeremiah Hadley, who drilled in the militia with Jack, had commented one day that Lucy Hamblin would never marry. She was as cold as the ice on the river in January. "Colder," young George Barrow had agreed. "A man couldn't touch her without risking frostbite."

Jack had wanted to thrash them both but managed to keep his temper. No sense laying himself open to new humiliations. It bothered him, though, that people were beginning to speak of her as a spinster. She must be twenty-one now, and more beautiful than ever, but the young men all agreed she was aloof and unapproachable.

Jack had never stopped loving her. When he heard about her father's death last winter, he'd wondered if she might consider accepting his advances again. That was inconceivable, his brain told him. She'd submitted to her father's edict and closed the door on their fledgling romance. She was older now, and she understood that allying herself with Isaac Hunter's son would only cause the villagers to despise her. Jack's loneliness and bitterness grew.

He hadn't spoken to her in four years, and now the dream was destroyed for good. He would face the hangman in the morning.

Chapter 3

Jack raised his head. He saw a small patch of light at the end of the tunnel leading to the one window in the outside wall. The light became fainter, and he knew the daylight was waning. He was wasting his last hours on earth in self-pity. Hadn't he learned anything in the past six months? Jack Hunter might be despised and ridiculed, accused and, yes, even convicted of a crime he did not do, but God was still in the heavens.

He rose and paced the tiny cell, three steps to the far wall and three steps back to the door. He had to stop pining for Lucy and feeling sorry for himself. Surely God expected more of him.

Heavenly Father, he prayed, raising his eyes toward the ceiling of the dark cell, *I don't want to die for something I didn't do. Please, if You can see Your way clear to help a nobody like me, show me what to do.*

They'd found his bloody ax lying beside Trent's body. The ax he'd chopped wood with just yesterday. Jack was sure he'd put it in the barn when he finished the task. He peered through the tiny barred window in the oak door then paced the small cell again, mentally listing all the people who might have access to his barn. It amounted to the whole township.

He heard footsteps. Reuben Stoddard entered the hall outside his door.

"Has the magistrate come?" Jack asked through the barred window.

"Not yet," Stoddard replied. "But the constables are keeping enough men ready to act as a jury when he does arrive."

"You mean they'd hold the trial tonight?"

Stoddard shrugged. "What's the point in waiting? Trial tonight, sentence carried out in the morning, like as not. I'd be on my knees if I were you." He opened the cell door and handed him a wooden platter with a tin cup of water, a chunk of brown bread, and a bowl of samp, then closed the door and strolled away.

Jack sat on the dusty straw pallet and ate the bread but took only one spoonful of the bland corn mush.

Perhaps he should ask for the parson after all. The officials were determined; he might as well be condemned already. He mulled it over, then got up and approached the door.

"Goodman Stoddard!"

"What do you want?" The jailer shuffled toward his cell door.

"I want to see Captain Murray."

"What do ye want with the captain?" Stoddard eyed him suspiciously.

"It seems the whole town is against me. The captain is a fair-minded man. I thought to seek his advice."

Stoddard frowned. "I'll send someone to see if he'll come. But the sun's getting low. I expect the captain is busy and won't want to trouble himself with the likes of you."

Jack slid down the wall and sat limp, leaning against the rough stonework. He was exhausted, and his head throbbed where Dole had hit him and where he had crashed into the wall. His ribs were sore, and his left cheek felt puffy and tender.

He hoped his bid to see the captain would bring some prospect of justice. Jack had joined the militia at age seventeen, and Captain Murray was one of the few men who seemed to accept him. The huge bear of a man encouraged him when he did well at drill, and Jack looked up to him, trying to emulate his confident air and posture. But he couldn't consider the captain a friend. Right now it seemed no one would take his part.

He closed his eyes. He was used to being alone, bereft and rejected. But desperation was a new feeling. He had always believed that if he worked hard enough, he could overcome the sorry lot he'd been dealt at birth.

After Isaac Hunter's death, Jack had improved the farm his father had neglected. Sam Ellis taught him to use tools and raise a productive garden. He'd made the hut the family occupied into a comfortable little house for his mother, built up the herd of sheep, and sold enough firewood to finance his purchase of a yoke of oxen and a cow. Jack saw his farm begin to thrive as a result of his hard labor and determination.

But now he was powerless. "God, help me," he whispered. "No one else will."

Half an hour later he heard boots thumping on the stone floor. He pulled himself up, clutching the bars. At once he recognized the huge man accompanying the jailer.

"Captain Murray! Thank you for coming."

Stoddard unlocked the cell, and the captain ducked his head as he entered, blinking. Stoddard fixed a torch in the iron bracket on the wall and swung the door shut. "Ten minutes, Captain."

Murray eyed Jack and stroked his full black beard. "What can I do for you, Hunter?" His stern expression didn't give Jack hope.

"Sir, I didn't harm Goodman Trent, but no one will listen to me. They're talking about hanging me. I don't know what to do."

Murray stood silent for a moment, then drew a deep breath. "The mood in the village is not favorable, Hunter. Most folks believe you're guilty. They're clamoring for your just punishment. It's getting downright ugly out there."

"But, sir, I haven't been tried! They found my ax, but anyone could have taken it and used it against Trent. I've never been at odds with the law. If I had someone to speak for me—"

18

"Not many lawyers in these parts," Murray said, shaking his head.

"But, sir, if you would vouch for me . . ."

"How could I do that? I don't know that you're innocent. They say the apple doesn't fall far from the tree."

Jack felt light-headed. He sat down on the straw. "Sir, please. You know I pull my weight with the militia. Have I ever refused to do my part?"

The captain shook his head slowly. "No. But Dole is claiming they caught you with blood on your hands."

"That's an outright lie."

"Your father was a bad 'un, Jack."

"I'm not my father!"

"True. But folks have long memories hereabouts. Isaac Hunter did a lot of mischief in his day. Stealing, brawling, you name it. And now—well, it was your ax. You don't deny that, do you?"

"No. I saw it. It's mine. But it wasn't me who did in Barnabas Trent. And if I did, I wouldn't be stupid enough to leave my ax there."

"Your pa started a fight with Trent twenty years past, over where the boundary was. Plenty of folk remember that."

"I know, sir, but—"

"Some say you've had words with Trent yourself, and not so long ago."

Jack stopped as the realization of his plight hit him anew. "That's so, but it was words only, Captain. I wouldn't strike a man." The memory of Dole's blows came back. "At least, not unless he struck me first."

"Did Trent strike you?"

"No! I never even saw him today, or yesterday, either."

The captain spread his hands. "Well then. If not you, who did it?"

"I don't know."

"That won't be enough to sway a jury in this township. The men are worked up, and their women are scared. They want to string up the murderer and be done with it."

"That's foolish! If they hang an innocent man, the murderer will still be among them. Can't they see that?"

Murray ran a hand through his thick black hair. "Apparently not."

Jack slumped forward, his chin on his chest. "Isn't there anything I can do to help my cause?"

Murray sat beside him in the musty straw. Jack took mild hope from his pensive gaze.

"Trent wanted my property," Jack said. "That's no secret. My father got title to the land next to his twenty years ago, and Trent always resented it. He'd hoped to buy it himself."

"How did your father get the money for the land?"

"His father-in-law left it to him. Buying that farm was the only wise choice he ever made, as near as I can tell."

Murray nodded. "Well, you've worked hard since the old man died, I daresay. Took care of your mother her last few years."

Jack bit his lip.

"I'd make a will if I were you."

"A will?" The thought startled Jack. Neither of his parents had made a will. He'd never even seen one.

"Do you have any kin?" the captain asked.

"No, sir."

Murray grunted. "Well, a will won't do you much good if you have no one to inherit."

"What will happen to my house and my livestock—all my things, if. . ." Jack felt a knot in his chest constricting his breath.

Murray cocked his head to one side. "If you're convicted of murder, the commonwealth will probably seize your property."

The thought of Dole getting Tryphenia and her calf infuriated Jack. Who would be plowing with his stout oxen next week? Who would harvest the barley and corn he had planted?

"I'll do anything to keep unscrupulous men from taking what I've built. Even if I'm not around to enjoy it, I don't want them to have my property!"

Murray scratched his chin. "You want to sell your place?"

"What? Right now, on the spot?"

Murray shrugged. "Someone would buy it, I'm sure."

"You, sir?"

The big man shifted uncomfortably. "I don't think Katherine would be pleased if I gained from another's misfortune."

"Well, I won't sell to Charles Dole."

"He wouldn't have the money."

Jack leaned back against the wall. "If I sell my place, and they kill me, someone else would take the money. The court or the constables."

"Likely so." Murray let out a long, soft sigh. "Of course, if you was married, that would be different."

"How?"

"They wouldn't turn your wife out."

Jack's mind raced. "If I were married, my wife would keep my estate if they hung me?"

"I expect so. Part of it, anyway, if you stated so in your will. And if she were a good woman, the court might look more favorably on you, allow you to bring character witnesses, that sort of thing. Though not many in this town would speak for you, I'm afraid. Most have made up their minds."

"Would you put in a word for me, sir?"

Murray hesitated. "Is your soul right with God, boy?"

Jack nodded. "I was bitter when my mother died, but that's changed, sir. I've been attending services since last February."

Murray peered into his eyes. "What brought about the change?"

Leaning back against the damp wall, Jack sighed. "You recall the storm?"

"Aye."

"For nearly a week, I was cooped up in my house. I dug a tunnel to the barn to tend the stock, but I never saw a soul for days, and I began to wonder if the snow would ever melt."

Murray's wry smile told him the captain understood.

"One night," Jack went on, "I thought I'd go crazy without someone to talk to or something to do. We had but one book—my mother's Bible. I was desperate, sir, and I began to read." He smiled. "I read the whole book of Job. Once I got started, I couldn't stop. When I ran out of lamp oil, I kept throwing logs on the fire so I could see."

Murray chuckled. "There's no better pastime than reading God's Word."

"True enough. By the time I finished the book, I realized how wretched I was. It was no use going on the way I had been. I. . .I knelt there on the hearth and begged the Almighty's forgiveness."

The captain nodded. "Glad to hear it."

Jack stretched out his long legs and sighed. "Over the next few weeks I kept reading, and pretty soon I began to see how God wanted me to live. It was like my pride was stripped away, one layer at a time."

"You were a rebellious lad, I expect."

"Yes. All my life, I kicked against authority—my father, the pious villagers, even Reverend Catton and the church."

"Still feel that way?" Murray asked.

Jack shook his head. "Now I just want to be like Christ." He glanced at the captain to see if the older man found him ludicrous. He'd never been so open with anyone.

Murray was nodding. "That's the best move a man can make."

"So I started going to meeting again," Jack said. "I knew they all thought me an infidel, but I had to make a beginning somewhere."

The captain clapped him on the shoulder. "I'll speak for you. I can tell the court you've been faithful in your duties to the militia and you were a good son to your mother."

"Thank you."

"It won't change the verdict, I fear."

"But it might make them more favorable on the distribution of my estate?"

"I don't know. I'm not versed in law."

"If they're set on hanging me and there's no way to stop it, I know how I'd like things to end up."

"How's that?"

Jack inhaled deeply. "I started working on my house again this spring. I was thinking. . .if things went well. . ." He smiled sheepishly. "There's a young lady I thought to court, sir."

The captain's eyes glittered. "Ah."

Jack ducked his head. "Her father didn't like me, but he's dead now. I prayed for the Lord's guidance and decided to work hard this spring and get the house ready. If God allowed it, then I'd speak to her."

"But you haven't spoken yet?"

"No, sir. It's been a dream of mine. A longing, you might say." Jack swallowed hard. That dream could never be realized now, but perhaps he could show his esteem for her before he died. "Do I get a last request, sir?"

"You mean like a last meal?"

"No, I mean like. . ." Jack took two deep breaths. "They sent for you when I asked. If they'll let me, I'd like to request another visitor."

Murray nodded. "I'll tell the jailer, and we'll see what he says about that."

⌘

Lucy jumped at the peremptory rap on her door. It was nearly sunset, and she had laid down her shuttle to prepare the evening meal. Neighbors came to fetch her mother at all hours, and normally she wasn't afraid. Still, if there was a murderer loose in these parts. . . She went to the door and cautiously lifted the latch.

On her doorstep stood Gideon Rutledge, the constable's youngest son. The boy favored his mother, with fair hair and freckles. She judged him to be about twelve, too old for her school.

"Excuse me, miss." The lad looked at his shoes. "But my father sent me to say you're wanted at the jail."

Lucy stared at him. "Is someone in need of healing? My mother is the one—" Lucy glanced toward where her mother's basket usually sat, ready for when she was urgently summoned to the bedside of an ailing neighbor or an expectant mother.

"No, ma'am, it's not that. The prisoner asked to see you."

"Prisoner?" Prickles of apprehension began on the back of her neck.

"Jack Hunter," Gideon said.

"Jack Hunter is in the jail?" Dread and incredulity assailed her. "Whatever for?"

"For the murder of Goodman Trent, miss."

Lucy's mouth went dry. "Are you making up tales?"

"It's true." The boy's face was grave. "Mr. Trent was found hacked to death this morning."

She leaned against the doorframe. "I'd heard he was dead."

"Father says it were Jack Hunter's ax that done the deed."

"I don't understand." She felt ill. Could this really be happening? She didn't want to walk nearly two miles to the jail, and she didn't want to find out that the boy was telling the truth. She didn't want to see Jack confined and accused of a heinous crime.

The boy eyed her anxiously. "Father said I'm supposed to bring you back."

Lucy took a deep breath, weighing her options and trying to grasp what Gideon had said. All afternoon she'd been imagining that a savage Indian or a maniacal cutthroat had slain the surly farmer. But Jack? It was unthinkable. She knew him better than to believe that. She also knew she could not forego the chance to go to him when he'd asked for her in his time of distress.

"Give me a moment." She hurried to bank the fire, trying to think what she could take to the jail that might be useful to Jack, but nothing came to mind. It was nearly dusk and the moon just past new. It would be very dark when she started home again. She stuffed a short candle and two pennies into the pocket tied around her waist and grabbed her knit shawl from its peg by the door.

What good could she do Jack in this muddle? No matter. He'd asked for her. She was going.

Chapter 4

Jack heard other prisoners come in, one or two at a time, all evening. They were ordinary men who had fallen into debt and were serving their sentences. They were generally allowed the freedom of the village during the day so they could work to pay off what they owed, but had to report to the jail at sunset and were confined every night. They were herded into the more comfortable cells upstairs. Jack didn't mind being denied the company of his poor neighbors. He didn't want to talk now. He wanted to think.

He went to the recessed window in the outer wall and peered out. At the end of the square tunnel in the stonework he could see the barred opening, and beyond it the twilit sky. He inhaled deeply and caught the smells of wood smoke and the mud flats at low tide.

Although a death sentence had not been formally issued, the constables had made it clear that it was only a matter of time. Murray's pessimism had further weighed him down. Even his captain, who was a fair and honest man, was sure Jack was headed for the gallows. The flicker of hope Jack had felt while Murray was with him gave way once more to a heavy hopelessness.

The prospect Angus Murray had held out to him was not a possibility of saving his life. But perhaps he could have a say in the matter of who claimed his farm after he was dead. That was not much consolation, however. Jack felt the constricting panic threaten to engulf him again.

There were people who wanted his property, he was sure. Trent had openly coveted the homestead, and he'd seen the way Dole eyed his sturdy barn and snug house that morning. And Tristram Drew, whose land abutted Jack's on the other side, had approached him and his mother a few years back and asked if they didn't want to sell out.

If Murray's plan worked, Jack could give something of value to the only woman he had ever loved. Lucy wasn't destitute, but he was sure she could make use of his possessions. Much better her than someone else.

But what if she refused to see him?

He closed his eyes in prayer and waited.

❧

Lucy stopped on the threshold of the jail. She looked around to speak to the Rutledge boy, but he was fading into the darkness, heading for home, no doubt. She took a deep breath, opened the door, and stepped inside. Reuben Stoddard rose from a bench by the wall. The big room was drafty, but beyond him was an open doorway through which she could see a cheerful room, where a woman stooped before the fire burning on the hearth.

"Well, now. Good evening, Miss Hamblin."

She nodded, unable to speak past the lump in her throat. She'd never been inside the building and found the experience unnerving. Jack was here somewhere, locked away in some remote corner of this cold, dark place.

"Here to see the accused murderer?" Stoddard's face was grim as he reached for a large ring of keys.

"Y–yes. Mr. Rutledge's son said Goodman Hunter asked for me."

Several flickering candles illuminated the room, and she saw a large man sitting in the far corner, whittling. Lucy recognized Captain Murray at once. No mistaking the huge man. He said nothing but tended to his whittling as though it were the most important thing in the world. A long clay pipe protruded from his lips, and he sent a lazy puff of smoke out the corner of his mouth. It floated toward the ceiling and hung there. She supposed he must be here to help guard the prisoner or to keep the angry townspeople from forming a mob and menacing the jailer.

Stoddard scowled. "I must say I'm surprised you agreed to see a dangerous man like Jack Hunter."

She swallowed hard. "I wasn't aware Goodman Hunter had been tried and found guilty already."

She saw Captain Murray throw a quick glance their way. His dark eyes glinted, but he remained silent.

"He'll stand trial soon enough," Stoddard said. "Come on. There's nothing you can do to help that one. But I suppose there's no sense trying to tell you it's foolish to see him."

He unlocked a door in the side wall and picked up a candlestick. Lucy saw a shadowy passageway beyond. Before she ducked through the door behind Stoddard, she noticed movement in the corner. The captain rose, shoved the small stick he'd been whittling into his pocket, sheathed his knife, and headed for the front door.

The jail smelled damp and earthy. Lucy shivered and gathered her shawl about her.

Stoddard led her into the darkness and stopped before a dark door. The closed portal had a barred window about a foot square just above her eye level. "Ho, Hunter," the jailer cried.

"I'm here." Jack's low voice was so near that Lucy jumped.

"You've got another visitor."

Lucy heard a soft movement beyond the bars and peered through them. She could see a dark form but couldn't make out his features.

"Can we speak in private?" she asked Stoddard.

He grunted and placed the candlestick on a rough bench beside the doorway. "Not long, miss. Ten minutes, same as I gave the captain."

Lucy gulped in the musty air. So the captain was here as a visitor. She hoped that meant he was displaying support for Jack. "Thank you."

The jailer turned to go, and Jack called urgently, "Wait! Goodman Stoddard, can't you let the visitor in?"

Stoddard looked back. "That's not a good idea, Hunter."

"You let Captain Murray in here."

"Captain Murray is. . .the captain. I can't let a woman in there with you."

"Why not? She's only here to speak to me." Jack leaned close to the barred window in the cell door as he spoke, and Lucy caught the glint of his eyes in the flickering light.

"Sure, and it would only take you a second to strangle her, now, wouldn't it?"

"Mr. Hunter is not a violent man," Lucy protested.

Stoddard grunted and turned away, muttering under his breath.

When he was out of sight, she peered at the door, trying to see inside the dark cell. "Jack, I'm so sorry. How did this happen?"

"I don't know."

"They can't believe you killed Trent. That's senseless."

"Ah, Lucy." Jack gave a deep sigh and grasped the bars in the window. A chill ran down Lucy's spine as she heard the clink of chains against the bars and realized he was fettered. "Thank you for saying that. You must be the only person in the province of Maine—no, in all of Massachusetts—who doesn't think I'm guilty."

"But why?" She stepped closer and squinted up at him through the small window.

"They say they found my ax beside the corpse. Lucy, this is a nightmare. I've done nothing."

She retrieved the pewter candlestick from the bench and held it closer to the window. At last she could see his mournful face. There seemed to be a bruise around his left eye, or was it just shadow? His eyes were filled with sorrow.

In spite of their surroundings, she drank in the sight of him. It had been years since she'd been this close to him. He'd matured, and very nicely, she thought, except for the anxious, haggard air that clung to him.

"What can I do to help?" she asked.

Jack sighed. "I. . ." He lowered his head.

"There must be something." She tried to insert normalcy into her tone. "Do you need anything? Have they fed you tonight?"

"Yes, I've had food, and they've given me a wool blanket."

"They're keeping you overnight, then?"

He hesitated. "I believe that's the plan."

"But they'll release you in the morning."

"They've sent for a magistrate," Jack said.

"That's good. He'll straighten this out and release you."

He didn't answer.

"Jack?"

"I don't think they'll let me go, Lucy."

"But you didn't do it."

"No, of course not."

"Then why. . . ?" She couldn't give voice to the terrible thoughts that were bombarding her mind.

"Lucy," he whispered.

She caught her breath and looked up through the hole in the thick, oaken door. Jack slipped his hand between the bars, as far as the short chain would allow. She leaned toward him. His cold fingers touched her cheek, and a thrill shot through her.

"Will there be a trial?" she asked.

"Of sorts, I suppose."

Her pulse pounded. "Jack, you are an Englishman. Surely they'll let you defend yourself."

He winced. "I'm told things look bad, Lucy. Most folks are determined I did it. They want. . ."

"What?"

"They want to see me hang."

"No!"

He ran his finger along her jaw and tipped her chin up so that they looked directly into each other's eyes. "It's true, I'm afraid. Charles Dole is making preparations. They expect the magistrate to pronounce sentence." He retracted his hand. "Dole, Stoddard, and Rutledge have it all planned. They say it's to be in the morning."

"Not. . .tomorrow morning?" Her voice squeaked, and she gasped for breath.

Jack leaned his forehead against the bars and closed his eyes.

Her knees felt weak, and she reached for the doorjamb. "They can't."

"They can."

She swallowed hard. "I saw Captain Murray out there."

"The captain thinks nothing I can do will help. I'm doomed, Lucy."

Her eyes stung with tears. "I can't believe this." She took a deep breath and asked the question that had plagued her since Gideon Rutledge showed up on her doorstep. "Jack, why did you send for me?"

He looked away for a moment. "I don't want to upset you. Perhaps I shouldn't have asked you to come."

She raised her hand, then drew it back, frustrated by the thick door between them. "Don't say that. We're friends, Jack. I'm glad you sent for me. If it's only to say good-bye, though, I shall be disappointed. There must be something I can do for you. Is anyone caring for your livestock?"

"Rutledge promised he'd ask Sam Ellis to tend them tonight. After that. . . well, I'm not sure."

"I could go over in the morning," she said. "I could milk the cow and—"

He shook his head. "You've enough to do at home."

"There must be something. . ."

⌘

Jack watched her for a long moment, knowing the minutes were fleeting. One moment he was ready to blurt out his request, the next he was certain it would be unconscionable to make such a proposal.

He took a deep breath, weighing his words. She waited, staring at him with tear-filled eyes, her breath rapid and shallow.

"Lucy, if it hadn't been for your father, would you have married me four years ago?"

She waited so long his heart began to pound.

At last she whispered, "Yes, Jack, I would have."

Relief swept through him. "Thank you." At least he would have that assurance to savor through the night.

"But that was a long time ago," she said softly. "I've put all that behind me."

He sighed, his lingering hope and flame of desire for her squelched once more into a smoldering bit of ash. "You still have the school?"

She nodded. "I teach classes in the mornings. But that doesn't mean I can't do a few chores for you."

Jack speculated that she was a pleasant tutor.

"I don't think we could take your stock to our house," she said with a frown. "The old fences are in terrible shape. We've let them go since Father died. You have oxen, don't you?"

"It's all right, Lucy. Don't fret about that."

"But what will happen to your cattle?" she whispered, her brow furrowed in anxiety.

He shrugged. "Dole said some of the neighbors can take them temporarily, but. . .well, it's looking like I won't get out of here, and. . ."

Her hand came timidly through the bars and rested lightly on his sleeve, ever so tentative, like a hovering butterfly alighting on a blossom, ready to take wing in an instant.

He stared at her slim fingers. "Lucy, this is the end for me." He turned away, unable to face her, knowing she would see his fear.

"I don't want to believe that."

"You must. Will you pray for me?" He looked at her through the bars. A tear fell from her lashes and streaked down her cheek.

"Of course." Her voice cracked.

Jack's heart wrenched. He bit his lip as he gazed at her, trying to gauge the depth of her feelings for him. She still had faith in him. Of all the people who knew him, she was the only one who truly believed him innocent. He took a deep breath.

"Lucy, will you marry me?"

Chapter 5

Lucy gasped and stared at him in disbelief.

"What did you say?"

Jack felt his cheek muscles twitch. "I'm sorry. I shouldn't have said it like that. I just. . .Lucy, we don't have much time."

"But. . ." Her gaze remained riveted on his face. "Jack, you just proposed marriage."

"Yes."

"But if what you say is true, there can be no marriage."

"You're right. We would never be able to share a life together. But the captain told me that if I were married, the officials would have to let my widow inherit my estate, or at least part of it. I don't want them to take the farm, Lucy. If I've got to die tomorrow, I'd at least like to go knowing someone I care about has my property, not some greedy land grabber."

Her lips quivered, and he wondered if this was a huge mistake. Had he destroyed his last shred of hope? *No*, he told himself. *It's impossible for things to be worse than they are.* Still, a tiny voice told him that if Lucy rejected him now and walked away, his last hours would be spent in the worst mental anguish possible.

Her chin came up, and she sniffed. "Jack, I don't need your farm."

"I know you don't. It's just. . .I can't stand the thought of Dole having it. I didn't know widows could be heirs, but Captain Murray says they can."

She nodded. "My brothers were my father's heirs. They have to let Mother live on the farm as long as she wants to. But they took all the livestock and Father's tools. We don't have much, but as long as Mother's alive, we have a roof over our heads."

"Murray says there's a way to make it legal to name you as my heir. You may not get everything, but if they force a sale of the farm, you would at least get a portion of the proceeds."

"Jack—"

"Please. I want to do this."

"Why? To thwart the constables? To pay them back in small measure for the way they've treated you today?" Her voice was steady now, and his heart ached with a longing for things to be normal so he could court her the proper way.

"Not that so much as. . .Lucy, I. . .I think about you a lot. About what passed between us earlier. I've always regretted. . ."

"What, Jack?" She leaned close, and he could smell the soap that she used on her clothing.

"Not standing up to your father."

"Don't feel that way. We did what was right in abiding by his wishes."

He sighed. "I suppose you're right. Still, I've always hoped I could make things up to you someday, and. . .Lucy, I want to make amends for any hurt I caused you, and this is the only chance I'll have to do that."

"Oh, Jack." She bowed her head. The candlelight threw shadows from her long eyelashes across her cheek. "You don't need to give me anything. I don't regret loving you."

She said it so low he barely caught her words, but his heart tripped. If only he'd acted sooner, perhaps the embers of their romance could have been fanned into flame once more. He longed to embrace her and try with his last bit of strength to give her comfort.

"I've worked hard over the years to make something of that sorry homestead my father left. I don't want it to go to waste. Bequeathing it to someone is my only way to salvage some of that hard work. And I want to bequeath it to you. But unless we're married, they won't let you inherit from me. Please let me do this."

She took a deep breath. "There's no one else for an heir?"

"I've no family now that my mother and father are dead."

"You know I wish it were otherwise for you."

"Aye. The officials won't like it, but this is what I want to do. Please grant me this as my last request, Lucy."

She blinked up at him. "Will they let us get married with you in prison?"

She's considering it! Thank You, Lord! "The captain thought so. He said he'd fetch the parson after you came, without telling him my purpose. If you say no, I'll let him think I wanted him to come and pray for me. But if you say yes. . . Lucy, will you?"

Swallowing seemed to take great effort on her part. Her pupils were large, reflecting the candlelight. The door opened down the hall, and the flame fluttered in the breeze as booted feet tramped toward them.

Jack held his breath, and Lucy's lips parted.

"Yes."

Five men came—the jailer, the two constables, the minister, and Captain Murray—each bearing a lantern or a candlestick. Lucy looked them over quickly then lowered her eyes against the bright light and the open stares of the men.

"Your time is expired, Miss Hamblin," Stoddard said, examining his bunch of keys as he walked.

"What news, Goodman Stoddard?" Jack called.

"My son says the magistrate will be here on the morrow. He gave instruction for the process to be carried out speedily."

Jack cleared his throat. "I'd like to see the parson now."

Dole's smug smile showed the gap in his jaw where a tooth was missing. "So this miscreant wants to shrive his soul after all."

The preacher, with his white hair tied at the nape of his neck, cut a grim figure in his black frock coat, breeches, and vest. He stepped close to the cell door, and Lucy moved aside, darting an anxious glance toward Jack.

"They tell me you stand before the gate of eternity, Hunter. Are you ready to meet God?"

"Yes, sir."

"You are?" Parson Catton appeared puzzled. He handed Dole his lantern and shifted his Bible from under his arm. "I assumed you had a confession to make."

"No, sir, I've done that. The Lord and I are square."

"Then why. . . ?" The parson gazed at Murray, who had slouched onto the nearby bench. "You told me Hunter had need of me, Captain. If he won't hear my counsel—"

"He has a different sort of need, Pastor." Murray stuffed the bowl of his pipe with tobacco.

Stoddard held up the key and said with a bit of impatience, "Miss Hamblin, you'll have to leave now."

Jack stood tall. "Miss Hamblin and I would like to be married, sir."

The men all stared toward the barred window, then exchanged confused glances. The parson's eyes widened. He looked at Lucy then at the captain. Lucy took a wobbly step toward the captain, and Murray stood.

"It's the prisoner's last request," he said. "Surely it's reasonable."

The parson licked his thin lips. "I don't know about this. I was told the prisoner was to be executed in the morning."

"All the more reason to perform the ceremony," Murray said. "It's Hunter's dying wish. Do it quick, before Dole or Rutledge makes up a new rule that says you can't."

The constables scowled at him but said nothing. Stoddard stood with the keys in his hand and his mouth hanging open.

Sorrow filled the parson's features. "Miss Hamblin, does your mother know about this?"

Lucy straightened her shoulders, feeling suddenly proud and determined. "No, sir. She was not at home when I was summoned. But I am of age. This is my decision."

"I see," Catton murmured. He arched his eyebrows in Rutledge's direction.

Lucy's heart raced. She sent up a swift prayer. *Lord, please don't let them deny Jack this one consolation.*

The constable shrugged. "It's not customary, but I'm not aware that it's illegal. If this young couple wants to be tied before Hunter meets his end. . ."

"There's just one thing," Murray said.

Lucy caught her breath.

Murray reached inside his doublet and pulled out a sheet of parchment. "This contract will allow Jack Hunter's widow to own and distribute his property after his death."

The other men stared at him.

Dole was the first to react. "You can't do that, Captain."

"Why not?"

"He's a murderer!" Dole sputtered.

"That has not yet been proven," the captain bellowed.

"Let me see that." Catton reached for the paper. "Is this an attempt to thwart the law?"

"Of course not." The captain bristled with offense, and the parson withdrew his hand. Murray glared at the constables. "This is a legal process, and you both know it. The relict Chadbourne is now owner of a prime piece of property to dispose of as she pleases because John Chadbourne signed such a document before they were married. His ship went down, and now she is the richest woman in the province."

Rutledge nodded. "That's true."

"This is mad." Catton raised his hands. "For this young woman to bind herself to a murderer on the eve of his execution! I don't know as I'll allow it."

Rutledge took the parchment from Murray and scanned it. "I'd say you've no choice."

"I don't have to marry a couple if there is question as to their piety."

Murray frowned. "Surely you're not questioning Miss Hamblin's spiritual condition."

The parson's cheeks colored above his beard. "She's always seemed a most demure and obedient young lady. . .until today. Hunter is another matter. He's forsaken public worship."

"He's been in church every Sabbath these past four months," Murray said.

Jack held the bars and leaned close to the window. "Pastor, it's true I turned away from the Almighty for a time after my mother passed on, but I've sought God's forgiveness for that and other waywardness. My conscience is clear."

Catton hesitated.

"What about this little matter of killing your neighbor?" Dole muttered.

Jack sighed. "I'll save my pleas for the magistrate."

Murray cleared his throat. "Perhaps it's time to open the cell door and sign this contract."

"We can't open the door of a felon's cell with a lady present," Stoddard argued.

Murray smiled. "She's about to become his wife, Reuben, and I doubt he'll try to escape his nuptials. But if it will ease your mind, I'll stand between Hunter and the exit."

Stoddard looked to Rutledge. The constable nodded.

The jailer unlocked the door and swung it open. "All right, Hunter, step out here."

Jack complied, and Lucy caught her breath. His left cheekbone and eyelid were a deep purple, and his lower lip had cracked and bled.

Dole frowned. "Should you put irons on his feet?"

"I won't run," Jack said.

Lucy felt as if her heart would burst. His gaze rested on her for a long moment, and the intense gratitude in his eyes overwhelmed her. She would not cry before these men. As it was, she and Jack were giving them months' worth of gossip to bandy about the village.

Rutledge handed the document to Jack. "Have you seen this?"

"No, sir, but I asked the captain to have it drawn up proper."

Rutledge nodded. "Stoddard, we'll need a quill and ink."

"I'll fetch it," the jailer said.

"Perhaps we should move to the outer room, where the light is better," Murray suggested.

Stoddard turned in the doorway. "There be plenty of light in here, and I'll not take a chance of losing the prisoner before the magistrate comes." He gave a brusque nod and hurried out of the room.

Murray advanced to stand at Jack's side. "If you wish it, I'll witness that contract for you, and the wedding, as well."

"I'd be honored, Captain," Jack said.

The jailer's wife came in with him when he brought the pen and ink, and the contract was quickly signed.

Lucy slipped her hand through the crook of Jack's arm, barely touching his sleeve. He laid his other hand on hers and pressed her fingers. When he looked down at her, she managed a smile, but her insides felt like pudding.

She straightened her shoulders and faced the dour minister. Goody Stoddard squeezed in beside her. "Your mother will want to know a woman stood by you," she explained.

"Thank you, ma'am." Lucy smoothed the skirt of her threadbare gray dress and wished she had stopped to put on her Sunday gown. This would have to do. It was the linsey she wore day after day around the house, at her loom, doing chores, teaching the children. Her wedding dress.

Pastor Catton rested his Bible on the bench and blinked at them. "Dearly beloved," he began, and Lucy found it hard to breathe.

This is it, she thought. *I'm going to be Jack Hunter's wife.* She refused to dwell on the fact that she would hold that position for only a few hours.

The minister's words echoed in the passageway, leaving her befuddled. The flickering light, the smell of the tallow candles and oil lamps, the haze of smoke in the air, and the stench of unwashed bodies in the confined space combined to make her a bit dizzy. She glanced up at Jack, and he squeezed her hand.

This is real, she told herself. She thrust her shoulders back and took a deep breath. *I won't faint at my own wedding!* By the time the parson called on her to state her commitment to the groom, her voice was steady.

"You may kiss your bride, Hunter," Catton said.

Lucy looked up at Jack from beneath her lashes. She hadn't thought about this. Their first and last kiss would be accomplished before these witnesses. He shot a glance at the constables then stooped toward her. She closed her eyes. Jack's lips brushed hers for an instant, feather soft; then he straightened.

Her cheeks were crimson, she could tell from the heat of them, but no one seemed to care.

"There, now," said Goody Stoddard. "Not an ostentatious wedding, but very nice."

"Thank you," Lucy choked.

"All right, Hunter," said Rutledge. "Back inside."

"Oh, really!" Captain Murray said. His deep, full voice startled Lucy. "Let's have a piece of cake or something."

"It's not like this is a happy occasion." The stiffness in Rutledge's voice made Lucy blush even deeper, this time for shame. If only she'd had the courage to defy her father and marry Jack four years ago! But even as the thought came, she dismissed it. She had tried to live in obedience to God, which also meant obedience to her father while he lived, and she could not regret that, even though it meant giving up the time she might have had with Jack.

The jailer stroked his chin. "I seem to recall my wife was cooking something this evening."

"Yes," Goody Stoddard cried with a wide smile. "I've a gingerbread in the bake kettle. It's just the thing to celebrate this union. I'll be back in a trice." She hurried down the passageway toward the jailer's family quarters.

"I suggest we all move out to the main hall," Murray said. "Give the happy couple a few moments alone."

"We can't—" Stoddard stopped and looked up at the captain, who towered over him with a menacing frown. The jailer gulped. "All right, but just a few moments. And, Hunter, you must give me your word. No tricks."

"I give my pledge," Jack said, looking into Stoddard's eyes.

"Well then," said Rutledge, "let us go get some cake." He threw Jack a sharp glance.

Murray stepped toward Lucy and said in a low tone, "I shall wait for you, Goody Hunter, and see you home."

She felt her cheeks warm as she savored her new title, and she realized the man cradling her hand in his was now her husband.

"Thank you," Jack said to the captain.

The men all headed down the hallway, with Dole going last and casting an acrid glance over his shoulder.

Chapter 6

J ack watched the men go. They left behind two lanterns. When the door to the outer chamber closed, he turned and grasped Lucy's hands. "I cannot thank you enough."

She swallowed hard. "You're welcome, Jack."

His heart pounded as he looked down at her. At last he had his greatest longing fulfilled, only to be snatched away from him. "We've got to be realistic."

"God can do a miracle."

He shook his head. "There's no hope for me, Lucy. I'll swing before sunset tomorrow."

"Don't say that!"

"We have to face it. That's why you agreed to this, you remember?"

"Yes," she whispered, blinking back tears.

She was doing the noble thing, giving a dying man peace of mind. Was that the only reason she had made her vows? He knew it wasn't his only motive. Warm, tender feelings transcended his desperation. Should he tell her how much he loved her, or would that only distress her more when he was dead?

"We haven't much time," she said. "Tell me what I should do with the farm."

"Do as you wish. If you want to keep it, do so. Move your mother there if you like. If it's of no use to you, then sell it, but for my sake, don't sell to anyone who witnessed our nuptials, unless Murray offers. Sell it dear, and enjoy every penny you receive."

She smiled through tears. "Have no fear. But I shan't take any action until I've received word of your. . .on the outcome of your trial."

"Dear Lucy! Don't cling to false hope." He squeezed her hands and smiled at her, wishing he dared pull her into his arms. But the reserve of four years' estrangement between them restricted his movements beyond what the shackles did.

"Tell me about the livestock," she said.

"The sheep can stay out to pasture. In the morning you'll want to feed the oxen. Since I won't be plowing, they ought to be turned out. Can you manage?"

"I think so." Her doubtful expression belied her words. "I'll do my best anyway. They're not fierce, are they?"

"Nay. And if you have any trouble, ask Sam to help you. And be sure to give Tryphenia a little extra corn."

36

"That be your milch cow?"

"Aye. You may as well let the calf stay on her, unless you be needing the milk. I was going to wean it this week."

He felt suddenly that he was in danger of losing control of his emotions. He sat down hard on the bench beside the wall and buried his face in his hands.

"Jack?" He felt Lucy's hand, warm and gentle on his shoulder.

"It doesn't matter now, does it? Do whatever you want with the stock. Sell the oxen right away. Keeping them would be too much for you."

She bit her lip. He knew the enormity of his situation was settling in on her heart, as well.

"We could use a bit of milk," she said softly.

"Then take it. The cattle are yours, Lucy." He looked up, forcing a smile. "Take them to your place if that's easier."

"I can stay at your house tonight."

"Your mother—"

"She went to Goody Ellis this morning."

"Ah, number ten."

"Yes." The chuckle that escaped her was more of a sob. "She may not be home at all tonight."

"Sam might be busy the next few days, tending the young 'uns while his wife is confined." He stood and reached for her hands once more. "All right, then, stay at my place tonight and feed the livestock on the morn." He searched her face intently, looking for the strength she would need over the next few days. He thought he saw it there, in the resolute set of her chin and the earnest fire in her blue eyes. "One more thing."

"What is it?"

"You ought to stay at my house tomorrow, too, just to be sure. . . ." He broke off and stared at his boots. "I don't know what they would do to my place, and my things, if no one were there. But if you are in residence as my wife. . ." He drew her hands up to his chest and caressed them with his thumbs. "It comforts me to know you'll be there to take possession and keep the vultures away."

"I will, Jack. I'll see that your estate is settled."

Tears spilled over her eyelids and ran down her cheeks. Jack reached out and caught one on his finger. "Don't weep for me, Lucy."

"It's not the first time."

A bittersweet craving washed through him. He lightly stroked her jawline with his fingertips. "Don't tell me I broke your heart."

"Into tiny slivers."

"You never showed it. All this time, you never once gave me an indication that you cared."

She looked past him toward the pierced tin lantern that hung beside the cell door. He wished she would tell him her thoughts. He would be dead tomorrow. Would it hurt her to tell him how she felt? If she were agonizing over losing him again, she would say so, wouldn't she? It must be that she didn't care beyond friendship and fond memories, or else she would speak.

At last she whispered, "Jack, I'm so sorry. I wish I could do something to change this."

He was quiet for a moment, trying not to grieve over the fact that she did not speak of love. He raised his chin. "It's all right. I don't understand why God let this happen, but I suspect He knows what He's doing."

She eyed him sharply. "The Jack Hunter I knew wouldn't accept such an unjust blow with resignation."

"The Jack Hunter you knew wasn't certain God was always wise in His dealings. I know better now. If this is His time for my end, then so be it."

She brushed the wet streaks from her cheeks, and he felt the sting that preceded tears in his own eyes. "I've made you feel horrid. I'm sorry."

She flung herself at him, throwing her arms about his neck. He stood in shock for a moment, then slowly pushed her away far enough so he could raise his manacled hands and lower his arms around her. She was so warm and soft. He held her, breathing in the scent of her hair and reveling in her nearness.

"Don't be coming around here in the morning, Lucy," he whispered.

She leaned back to look at him in question.

"I don't want you here. You understand, don't you? As my wife, grant me this wish."

"All right."

"Good. Now, the sheep. They'll need shearing soon. You ought to be able to hire William Carver to do that. Sell what wool you won't use yourself. And take what you want to weave to the carding mill."

"That costs money. I can comb my own wool."

"It will save you a lot of time to have it done, and you'll be able to afford it." He glanced toward the door and leaned down toward her until his lips were close to her dainty ear. "Under the clothespress, I've hidden some coins. You'll have to tip it over—"

She looked at him and frowned. "What—"

The door at the end of the passage swung open, and he raised his arms quickly, allowing her to duck outside their circle.

Stoddard marched toward them with his keys in hand. "Time's up, ma'am."

She looked at Jack. He squeezed her hand with a smile that he hoped would give her courage. He tried to fix her lovely face in his mind. Her delicate features, framed by golden hair, sent a dart of wonder through him. He'd married the most beautiful woman in the village. Her lustrous blue eyes tugged at his heart, causing a dull ache beneath his breastbone.

"Good-bye, Lucy." He didn't move to touch her again.

She raised her chin. "Good-bye, Jack."

She turned and hurried down the dim passage.

꙯

When Lucy stepped out the front door of the jail, Captain Murray rose from the step and sheathed his whittling knife. The smile he bestowed on her looked rather mournful.

"I'll escort you home, Goody Hunter."

"Thank you. I'll be going to my husband's farm, if you don't mind."

"Why should I mind? It's closer than your mother's house."

"Indeed." Lucy took a deep breath and smelled turned earth, salt water, lush June vegetation, and a hint of manure. She wished Jack could get his lungs full of that air instead of the damp, foul atmosphere of the dungeon. She tried to match her steps to Murray's, but his long legs forced her to scurry to keep up. When she skipped a few steps, he slowed his pace.

"Congratulations," he said.

"Thank you."

His thick eyebrows nearly met as he frowned.

"Captain Murray," she asked, "why have you been so kind to me and Jack tonight?"

He sighed. "It's six or eight years now since the lad started drilling with my company." He glanced at her and shrugged. "His mother made a mistake in marrying that wretch Isaac Hunter. It's not Jack's fault. Whatever he's done, I just want to see that he gets a fair shake."

"Do you think he will?" Lucy asked.

Murray took his clay pipe from one of the pockets of his voluminous jacket and placed it between his teeth but made no move to light it. "If he's guilty, he will."

"But he's not."

"So say you and your husband."

"If you don't believe he's innocent, why are you helping him?"

"I believe in the law, ma'am. I was afraid things would get wild tonight. A lot of folk have smelled blood and are thirsty for a hanging."

Lucy clamped her lips together to keep them from trembling.

He took the pipe from his mouth. "Jack asked for my advice. I knew I couldn't save him, but it seemed reasonable to help him do what he could to go with an easy mind." He waved the pipe toward the common area they were passing. Only a few pedestrians lingered in the evening air. "The townsfolk seem to have settled down for the night. I expect Rutledge let it out that the trial will take place tomorrow, and they're satisfied for now."

"All is quiet," she agreed, peering at the citizens from the corner of her eye.

"There was some concern earlier that a mob might form."

Her heart skipped a beat. "They wouldn't break a man out of the king's prison to lynch him, would they?"

"I've seen men do some strange things."

She shivered.

Murray walked in silence for a moment. "I hope word of your marriage doesn't get out tonight, or there may be some who feel the need to go to the jail and protest. Then again, I guess things can't get much worse for Jack. If they hang him now or hang him at dawn, what's the difference?"

She shuddered, and he took her elbow.

"Forgive me, Goody Hunter. I shouldn't have shared that sentiment."

"Do you know much about oxen, sir?"

He chatted amiably about farming for the rest of their walk to Jack's doorstep.

"Would you like me to step in and build your fire up, ma'am?"

"I can do it. Thank you. For everything."

Chapter 7

The light was fading as Lucy mounted the stoop. It didn't creak and give when she stepped onto it, the way the one at home did. The door was set into the low, thatched part of the house. This was the original cottage Jack's father threw together hastily twenty years ago. The addition Jack had built later looked more substantial, with its roof shingled in cedar strips. The chimneys of the house's two sections rose back to back in the center of the building.

She tried to picture the room that lay beyond the door. Three years ago she'd come here with her mother and several other neighbor women to lay out the body of Goodwife Hunter. Jack had kept away while they performed the ritual washing of the body and dressed her in her best gown.

Lucy recalled the simple, dark wool dress Jack's mother was buried in. She could still picture the delicate features of Abigail Hunter's thin face. Jack had his mother's kind eyes, but his hair was thick and unruly. It must be like his father's, for his mother's tresses were fine and limp. Lucy didn't remember Jack's father; the notorious Isaac Hunter had died when she was only seven, and she was sure her parents had done whatever was necessary to keep her from seeing much of him.

This is my new home if I want it to be, she told herself. She took a deep breath and lifted the latch, then pushed open the door of sturdy pine planks. It didn't make a sound. Jack must have greased the strong, black iron hinges. She sniffed. The air inside felt cool and fresh, though it carried faint whiffs of wood smoke, cooked meat, and balsam.

Suddenly she felt an unexplained dread. It seemed that someone or something was watching her from the darkness.

She whipped around and stared toward the barn then the fence of the sheep's pasture, then down the path to the lane. All was still. Too still. The crickets had quit chirping. An old ram had lifted his head from grazing and was staring toward the woods.

Lucy fought down the panic that assailed her and stumbled into the house. She closed the door, then stood gasping in the darkness. There was no glow from the fireplace, though the smoky smell of the hearth was stronger now.

After a long moment she could make out the pale rectangle of the one window in the room. Soon she would be able to see well enough to find a candle and a tinderbox. They would be on the mantel, of course.

She fingered the inside of the door and found the strong crossbar. With trembling hands, she eased it into its cradle then tested the latch to make sure it was secure.

Taking a deep breath, she turned to the fireplace. No time to stand about imagining phantoms when there was work to do. She felt along the edge of the stonework and jumped when a poker clattered from its peg to the hearth.

"Lord, give me Your peace," she whispered. Her heart hammered, and her breath came in short spurts, but she knelt and cast about until she located the poker, then used it to delve deep in the ashes. She was rewarded by a faint orange glow from a tiny coal that still smoldered.

Ten minutes later she had a candle burning and the beginnings of a cook fire. In another ten there would be a cozy blaze going, and she would make some tea. Then she would have time to think about what she had done this day.

She raised the rough shutter that hung below the window to cover the opening from the inside. Then she turned the wood blocks along the edges that held the shutter in its frame. Feeling more secure, she reached for larger sticks of firewood from the nearly full box.

Jack's hands had split these maple logs and laid them here. Her husband's hands, using his ax. The one that had killed a man.

As the flames leaped higher, she looked around. The room was neat, with shelves built along two walls. A small table and two stools occupied the middle of the puncheon floor. She sank into the one chair with a back, which sat close to the hearth. This must be where Jack relaxed in the evening. His bullet mold rested on the mantel, alongside several other implements. His musket hung above the door—she could see it in the firelight and felt comforted. If need be, she could handle that gun.

She spied a full wooden bucket and dipped some water from it into an iron kettle. When she had set the water to boil, she resumed her survey of her new house.

A couple of dark, nondescript garments hung on pegs behind the door. Jack's mother's dishes gleamed on the shelves beside crocks and tins and sacks. It was a homey room, one where a woman could be happy while she prepared the meals for her family. But she and Jack would never have a family.

She leaned back and closed her eyes. What would her mother say?

She hadn't allowed herself to think it, but now the question leaped unbidden into her mind. She gritted her teeth. "I wonder if I haven't been foolish this day," she said aloud.

The water burbled in the kettle. There must be tea somewhere. Or did Jack drink tea? She didn't even know something that simple about him.

She checked the shelves and found a tin. Pulling off the lid, she lifted the tin to her nose to sniff its contents. Dried parsley. A larger tin sat next to it, and she opened that. Ah, good black tea. She took her mother-in-law's teapot from the shelf with great care and went about the familiar task of making the brew.

Her decision today was right, she decided. Whatever she and Jack once had or would never have, she'd made the only choice she could. She refused to regret it.

⤚⤜⤚

Lucy awoke in darkness. Something wasn't right. Her heart pounded, and she lay still.

It came to her then. She was at Jack's house. In Jack's bed.

She drew in a deep breath. Part of her heart longed for daylight so she could see the unfamiliar room and reassure herself that all was well. The other part dreaded the dawn that would bring her husband's execution.

"Lord, have mercy on him," she whispered.

One of the logs that composed the walls creaked, and she jumped. She could make out thin fingers of grayness around the shutter. Daylight must not be far away. She rose and made her way to the fireplace in the wall that separated the bedchamber from the kitchen. She'd made a fire in both rooms last night, craving the light and extra warmth.

After much fumbling, she located her supply of kindling and the poker then knelt on the cold stone hearth, shivering in her shift. After she had a good blaze going, she gathered the three candles in the room and lit them all.

"Lord, I'm so frightened," she confessed. "Please give me Your peace, and give Jack peace, as well."

She pulled the patchwork quilt off the bed and sat on the low stool beside the hearth, extending her bare feet toward the warmth.

This room had been Jack's mother's, she was sure, but after her death Jack must have moved his things down from the loft and started sleeping here. She had begun to explore it last night but stopped after opening the clothespress. His shirts and a doublet hung there, and as the smell of him wafted to her, she had been unable to hold back her tears. She'd taken a wool flannel shirt from its peg and crushed it to her breast. It smelled like Jack did when he held her close that evening at the jail, for one fleeting moment.

"Show me what to do, heavenly Father," she prayed. "Should I live here now? I'm jumping at shadows. How can I be a property owner if I'm scared to live alone? And how would I keep my school if I had to care for Jack's animals and property?"

She sighed and bowed her head. "Please, Father, please be merciful. Do not let my husband die for this crime."

⤚⤜⤚

As dawn broke, Lucy rose and quickly donned her stays, pockets, overskirt, bodice, and cap. She sat on the edge of the bed and pulled on her stockings and shoes. It was a comfortable bed. She had slept well for several hours before waking and giving in to her sorrow and fear.

She lifted the edge of the linens and smiled. A feather tick and two straw ticks rested on the taut ropes that crisscrossed the wooden frame. She wondered if Jack had built the bed.

She let the hearth in the bedchamber cool but started her kitchen fire. Next she took the bucket and opened the door. Looking out at the fresh, early summer morning, she was almost able to chide herself for her panic in the night.

"It's a very neat farm you have, Goody Hunter," she told herself. She wanted to smile at that, but her lips trembled.

Lucy strode toward the well, determined not to break down again. She was a true housewife now, and she had chores to do.

The sheep were taking care of themselves in the pasture, but she knew she couldn't leave them out every night. They would make tempting morsels for wildcats and wolves. She would have to pen them each evening.

She drew a bucket of water and put the teakettle and a portion of cornmeal on to simmer over the fire, then headed with resolve toward the pole barn.

One of the oxen lowed as she opened the door.

"Good morning," she said, trying to sound confident. She would lead Tryphenia and the calf out first, for practice.

"Hello." The deep voice startled her, and she turned in the barn door, her pulse racing as she looked toward the lane. Jack's nearest neighbor was ambling toward her.

"Goodman Ellis, you frightened me."

"I beg your pardon, Miss Hamblin. I didn't expect to see you here."

Lucy swallowed hard and stepped toward him. "I was going to try to turn the cattle out."

"Allow me to do that." He eyed her with frank curiosity.

Lucy wondered if she should just blurt out her new state. Instead, she asked, "Is your wife well?"

Samuel grinned. "She's as fit as can be expected. We've a new little lady at our house."

She smiled. "A girl! Betsy and Ann must be pleased."

"Dreadful happy."

"My mother, be she still at your house?"

"Aye. She said she would stay the day if need be, but I told her she could go as soon as I..." He frowned. "I don't mean to pry, miss, but..."

Lucy tried to smile, but the strain was too much for her. "I...I saw Jack last night, sir. He...he asked me..."

"Surely he didn't ask you to come do his farm work?"

"Not exactly." Lucy bit her lip. "He asked me to marry him. I am his wife now."

Ellis's jaw dropped.

～⊗～

Lucy kept busy all morning. Samuel Ellis permitted her to milk the cow while he tended the other livestock. He showed her how to drive the oxen to the pasture and where Jack kept his tools for cleaning the barn, but he shoveled the manure out for her.

She thanked him as he prepared to leave, assuring him she could manage all right that evening. He had his own chores to do and his large family to take care of.

He leaned the pitchfork against the wall. "Perchance I'll stop by tomorrow to see how you fare, ma'am."

"Thank you, sir."

Ellis hesitated, then pulled off his hat and wiped his sleeve across his brow. "Is there any news of Jack? I don't wish to distress you, but what I heard last night..."

"I've had no word," she said, staring at the ground. "I am praying for his acquittal."

He nodded. "I shall add my prayers to yours."

When he left, she went inside and swept the floor of the front room. Though it was not dirty, a few chips and pieces of bark had fallen from the firewood. She found an apron hanging near the broom, put it on, and sat down to eat her samp.

Poking about Jack's pantry shelves, she'd found a good supply of cornmeal and wheat and barley flour. She could bake, but for whom?

She wandered outside and looked at his garden. The shoots were coming along, despite the rather chilly nights they'd had. Before the summer was over there would be a bountiful harvest of peas, corn, pumpkins, beans, cabbages, carrots, turnips, and beetroot. Near the back of the house was a small herb garden, and she recognized dill, basil, rosemary, and several other plants she and her mother grew at home. She went to the barn and found a stout hoe. Gardening was something she could do well.

The sun passed the meridian, and still she'd heard nothing. Would anyone come and tell her when her husband was dead?

The thought of Jack's predicament made her angry, and she worked with fury. At the end of the last row, she stopped and leaned on the hoe.

"Dear God, what should I do? Should I seek word of the proceedings? Should I go home to my mother's to get some of my things and come back here to stay the night? Should I install myself here as Jack's widow?"

A breeze ruffled the young leaves of the corn, mocking her words.

She heard a sound in the woods and turned toward it. There was no path on that side of the garden, just trees. Maple, hemlock, pine, and birch. An involuntary shiver beset her. Was someone watching her? Was someone biding his time to take over Jack's property?

Another sound reached her, and she whirled around, then relaxed. Her mother was coming up the path from the lane.

"What are you doing here?" Alice called.

"Goodman Ellis didn't tell you?" Lucy hurried to meet her.

"Nay. I saw him return this morning and start his own chores, but several goodwives came to help out with the housework, and Goody Ellis told me to go on home. I didn't speak to her husband again before I left."

"I see." Lucy swallowed hard. "Then how did you find me?"

"I came home this morning to an empty house and a cold hearth. Then Patience Rankin comes to my door and tells me my daughter has pledged to marry that murdering Jack Hunter."

"No, Mother." Lucy lowered her gaze. "It's worse than you think in one way, but better in another. I'm not promised to Jack; I'm his wife now. But he's not a murderer. My husband is innocent."

They stood for a minute, each woman taking the measure of the other.

At last Alice sighed. "Romance, child. It's not all it's rumored to be."

"I didn't do this for romance."

"And what did you do it for?"

"To give Jack peace of mind, mostly."

Alice shook her head. "Well, the town will say you've done it to get his land and his house and his mother's fine furniture."

"All of which Jack built with his own hands." Lucy drew herself up tall. "Mother, this is my home now. I'll be over later to get my things."

"Think, child."

"I have. All night and all day. If I'm to live out my days as the widow Hunter, so be it."

"This is not right."

"What Father did to Jack four years ago was not right. This is the best I can do."

Alice's face contorted, and her eyes sparked. "I should have known. I always thought you gave him up too easily. You never complained or sniveled. It was unnatural, if you really cared about him."

"Father wouldn't have stood it if I'd let my true feelings show. I tried to be a good daughter."

Silence simmered between them; then her mother said grudgingly, "You were. All this time, even since your father passed, you've been good to me, child."

Unable to hold back a sob, Lucy raised her apron to mop at the tears that bathed her face. She felt her mother's hand, light and tentative, on her shoulder.

"I'm sorry," she gasped. "You're right. I married him for love. We wasted a lot of years, Jack and I, and this was the only way I could have him, in the end. It helps him to know I'm here."

Alice nodded slowly, and Lucy thought she saw a glint of tears in her mother's eyes. "Goody Rankin said they'd likely hang him today."

Lucy pulled in a shaky breath. " 'Tis what they told him last evening. He forbade me to go today. He wants me here, in case someone tries to take his possessions."

"Don't bother to come home, then. I'll bring your things over later."

As her mother strode toward the path, Lucy gathered her wits and followed her. "You needn't come back today, Marm."

"Nonsense. You'll need your workbasket, and your apron is filthy."

Lucy swallowed hard. "There's another of Jack's mother's aprons in the clothespress."

"Still, you'll want your comb and extra stockings."

"Take tea with me later, then."

"Perhaps I shall."

A movement at the edge of the woods caught Lucy's eye, and her pulse raced. A dark shadow slunk from one tree to the next. "What's that?"

Alice whirled and stared. "Looks like a mongrel."

Lucy sighed when she recognized the animal. "It's Goodman Trent's dog."

"He looks hungry."

Lucy and her mother stood still, watching the mutt slink closer, his head drooping.

"Maylike you should feed him," Alice suggested. "There's no one to feed him over to his home. And he might be company for you."

Lucy wavered, remembering her fear in the night. "I suppose I can find him something, but I don't like to waste Jack's food."

Alice winced. "Likely Jack won't be needing it, child. Give the dog a soup bone now and then, and he'll stay by you always."

Lucy took a deep breath. "You're probably right. I'll see if there's not a bit of something I can spare."

"I'll be around later."

"Mother, if you hear any news of my husband, you won't spare me, will you? I need to know."

"I'll see what's noised abroad when I go to the Bemises' to check on their wee one. I'll see you soon, Goody Hunter."

Lucy smiled through her tears.

Chapter 8

"T here's no reason you couldn't keep your school here, should you decide to stay," Alice said that afternoon, looking about the kitchen at her daughter's new home. She poured a bit of tea into her saucer and sipped it. "It would be closer for the Ellis and Rowe children, but farther for some." Lucy picked up half a biscuit, looked at it, and put it down. It was a perfectly good biscuit, light and brown. She'd found that her mother-in-law's bake oven heated evenly, but her appetite had strayed today.

Her mother showed no such languor. She took a second biscuit and smeared it with apple butter. "I'd no idea Goody Hunter had such fine tableware."

"I never thought to have such," Lucy admitted.

Alice held up her knife and squinted at the delicate design cast on the handle. "I'll not believe her husband bought it for her. Jack must have furnished her kitchen for her when he grew to a man."

Lucy sipped her tea. The more her mother came to appreciate Jack, the easier their relationship would be in the future. Just seeing the interior of the comfortable house seemed to have tempered Alice's opinion of her son-in-law.

An unspoken knowledge passed between the two women as they waited for word of Jack's end. Lucy watched the shadows lengthen and listened for footsteps. Surely someone would bring her the news.

"Of course, you must sell those huge oxen immediately," her mother said.

Lucy refilled their cups and offered the plate of corn fritters to her mother.

"You may even decide to let the property go. We've been comfortable together, you and I."

Lucy said nothing. Until they knew for certain that it was over, she could not make any decisions that would change things. Jack had asked her to take control of the property when he was gone. Was he dead, even now?

The thick, burning sensation that accompanied tears assailed her. "I found a wool wheel and a small hand loom in the loft."

Alice nodded. "Aye. Abigail Hunter spun wool, and I daresay she wove the gray Jack's Sunday coat is made from. But I don't recall her ever spinning flax or weaving linen. If you're going to continue that, you'll want your small wheel over here. Unless you come home, of course."

Lucy couldn't meet her inquisitive gaze. "I can't say yet what I'll do, Marm. I...need time to think about it."

"The Ellises know not to send their children to you until you give the word, and I asked Samuel tonight to send the eldest boy around to tell your other pupils."

"Thank you."

Lucy rose to remove the dishes but froze when she heard a male voice calling outside. She rushed to the door and threw it open. Captain Murray strode up the path.

She ran to meet him, not caring that her hair jounced and a few strands escaped her mobcap.

"What news?" she panted as she jolted to a stop a yard from him. She gazed upward to his somber face, searching for anything other than distress.

"Your husband be still at the jail," he said.

Lucy let her breath out in a puff and wrapped her arms around herself. She stared at the ground and swayed from one foot to the other, trying to absorb his news.

"Tell me," she said, raising her chin.

Murray reached for her arm and turned her gently toward the house. "Come sit down, ma'am."

"My mother is with me. Will you join us and tell us all?"

He guided her along the path, holding her elbow as though afraid she would crumple to the earth. Alice Hamblin stood in the door, watching, but stepped back as they approached.

"What's the word, Captain?" the midwife asked.

"Better than I expected to bring, Goody Hamblin. Young Hunter still lives."

"Praise be!"

He pulled off his hat as he entered, and they sat at the table. Alice fetched a cup and poured the last of the tea into it for Murray. "Have you any sugar?" she asked Lucy.

"I don't know," Lucy confessed.

"No need," Murray said. He took a gulp, then set the cup down and wiped his mustache with the back of his hand. "The magistrate arrived midmorning. He heard some petty cases first: pig stealing and slander."

Alice's eyes shone bright and eager. "I heard tell Sarah Wait threatened to take Rebekah Castle to the courts for slander."

"Yes, but His Honor threw them both out," Murray said with a wry smile. "He told them to tend less to their neighbors' business and more to their housewifery. At last they brought Jack out." He eyed Lucy warily. "Be you ill, Goody Hunter? Ye look pale."

Lucy made herself take slow, even breaths. "Nay. Please proceed."

Her mother came around the table and placed one hand on Lucy's brow. "Perchance you should lie down, child."

"If I'm ill, it's from anxiety," Lucy said, "and the captain can remedy that. Pray go on, sir."

Murray nodded. "Well, they brought Jack out, and the magistrate called a hearing."

"A hearing, not a trial?" Lucy asked.

"Yes. The magistrate said the accused should have counsel. Rutledge said we haven't a lawyer in town, and His Honor said to send to Falmouth and get one. He heard Dole and Rutledge give evidence, then Goodman Swallow—"

"Jacob Swallow?" Alice cried. "What has he to do with the matter?"

"He found Trent's body," the captain said. " 'Tis a crucial bit of testimony. He told how he saw the ax lying there on the ground next to Trent."

"Did he say it was Jack's ax?" Lucy hated the way her voice trembled.

"Nay, but Dole and Rutledge did."

"Did they make my husband testify?"

"Nay. The magistrate told him he'll have a chance to speak for himself at trial. He will hear the case when he comes next."

Lucy pulled in a deep breath. "And when will that be?"

"The next new moon."

"Nearly a month!" Alice wrung her apron between her hands. "Lucy, daughter, 'twill be weeks afore you know the outcome of this!"

Lucy smiled. "But this is good news, Mother. The magistrate didn't sentence Jack. He even said he'll have a chance to prove his innocence."

"I thought it was all settled last even." Alice raised her eyebrows at Murray. He shrugged. "So it seemed. But cooler heads prevailed this day."

"Praise God," Lucy whispered.

The captain stood and offered her his hand. "It gives me pleasure to see the joy in your face, ma'am."

"I'll warrant there be some who aren't so happy," Alice noted.

"Aye. But they will have to abide by the magistrate's word."

"I must go to Jack." Lucy jumped up and fumbled with her apron strings.

"Surely not tonight," her mother said. "It will soon be dark."

"Wait until daylight," said Murray. "I told Jack I'd see you this eve and let you know."

"All right. I thank you for that, and for coming."

"It's nothing. Now let me bring your livestock in and feed them for you, and I shall be off."

Lucy rose early the next morning. Her heart felt light as she went about her kitchen chores. She was not a widow. Not yet. By God's grace, she had a month at least to be a married woman. She would show her husband that he had not made a bad bargain in choosing her.

She went out to the barn to tend the stock but stopped short in the path.

The barn door was unlatched. Surely the captain had closed it tight the evening before. Cautiously she pushed the heavy wooden door inward and peered inside. Nothing seemed amiss. Tryphenia gave a prolonged moo, and the calf bawled.

Lucy shook off her unease and went in, stooping for the milk bucket.

After she had milked the cow, she turned the cattle out to grass. The bigger ox, Bright, gave her a start when he changed course outside the fence. But she ran around to his far side and yelled, "Get, now!" To her amazement, he obeyed and waddled through the gap in the fence. She hastened to put up the rails that made the gate, before Bright could change his mind.

She found only two eggs, which surprised her, as she'd gleaned six the previous day. Two hens were brooding, and she left their nests undisturbed but took her two eggs and half pail of milk to the house.

She sang as she moved about the snug kitchen, baking seed cakes and stewing some dried pumpkin with spices. She found that she did, indeed, have sugar—half a large cone. Would the jailer let her take her husband sustenance? If not, she would appeal to Stoddard's wife.

Lucy added one of Jack's clean shirts and a pair of light wool stockings to her basket. As she left the house, a flicker of movement at the corner of the barn caught her eye. She stood still, her heart thumping, then smiled. The dog was back.

"Here, then," she called softly. "You're looking for another feed, aren't you?"

She hurried back inside. Since her arrival she'd cooked no meat, but if the dog was hungry he'd eat a biscuit. She took one from the tin she'd stored the leftovers in and went back outside. The dog was lying beside the doorstep. She tossed the biscuit to him, and he snapped it down in one gulp.

Lucy stroked his head. "You're starving, aren't you? Have patience, and I'll find you something more later on." She started down the path, then lifted her skirt and whirled to look at the dog once more. "And don't you get any ideas about those chickens!"

The shaggy mutt rose and trotted toward her.

Lucy laughed. "Come on, then."

❧

"It's not fair!" Jack's spunky new wife insisted.

He couldn't help smiling. "Don't vex yourself over it."

"But they should let you have the food I fixed for you."

"Perhaps they will another time. I'm thankful they let you in, and that they allowed you to bring the clothing."

She sighed. "Do you think Goody Stoddard is upset? She seemed to think I cast aspersions on her cooking and was saying she didn't feed you well."

Jack shrugged. "Perhaps."

Lucy frowned and stamped her foot, and he laughed outright.

51

"It's wonderful to see you."

Her features relaxed. "I'm glad I was able to come, but they ought to let me in the cell, now we're married."

"Nay. I don't want you in here. It's dark and smelly and not at all suitable for a lady."

"I'll bring you another blanket if they'll let me."

"No, Lucy. Don't come here again."

She frowned. "Jack—"

"Please."

She took a deep breath, then sighed. "Did I promise to obey you?"

"I think you did. The vows are a bit hazy in my mind, though."

"Mine, too. Well, if I did, I shouldn't have. I shall come every day to see you."

An unaccustomed joy pierced him. She wanted to be near him. In spite of this pleasant revelation, his better judgment schooled him to dampen her spirits. "It's better if you don't."

"How is it better?"

"Lucy." He grasped the bars in the tiny window, pulling himself closer so he could see her better.

"They still have you in irons!" Her face blanched as she stared at his wrists.

"Lucy, this is far from over. Just because the magistrate gave me this short reprieve doesn't mean I'll ever be free again."

He watched her sweet face as she struggled for composure. Her lips quivered, and she blinked rapidly. She put one fist to her mouth. "I didn't mean to make light of your circumstances."

"I know."

"I shall trust God for your deliverance."

"You mustn't count on it. Expect the worst, or you're apt to be disappointed."

"Nay. Expect the best, and rejoice in God's working."

He couldn't argue with her. But did she really want him delivered from the gallows? It wasn't at all what he'd led her to expect. What sort of life would they have together if by some miracle he survived? He whispered, "Continue to pray, wife."

She looked away as she answered, "No fear. I pray for you constantly."

"And I for you."

Her lips turned up in satisfaction. "No matter what happens, Jack, some good has come of this."

"Yes," he whispered. "I thank God. Not that I'm in here; I can't get round to being thankful for that yet, I'm afraid. But I thank Him for. . .other things." *For bringing you back into my life,* he wanted to say. *For drawing me closer to Him.* But he couldn't bring himself to voice those thoughts.

She moved her hand as though to touch his through the bars but let it fall back to her side. "I shall visit you every day, as long as they let me."

He slumped against the doorframe. "I don't like you coming here, and I don't like to think of you walking all that way alone."

She brightened at that. "We have a dog now."

"We do?"

"Yes. I call him Sir Walter."

Jack laughed.

"It's Trent's dog," she confided.

His amusement fled, leaving a cold, hard knot in his stomach. "I'll not have you adopt that cur."

"But—"

"That mongrel is vicious, and he steals food. Trent would have liked it if he'd attacked me."

"But I feel safer with him there." Her huge blue eyes pleaded with him.

Jack looked away and took a deep breath.

"I won't waste your supplies," she whispered, "but I'll be less lonely at night if I have a dog."

Jack closed his eyes and considered this small blessing God had sent to Lucy in her fear and confusion. If he had been hanged yesterday, as he had expected, what would he care if she nurtured his adversary's dog?

"All right," he said. "At least if you're feeding him, he won't be after the chickens."

Her smile shot arrows of hope into his heart.

"And his name is Battle," Jack told her.

She sobered. "Nay. His name is Sir Walter."

Chapter 9

Lucy woke that night and lay still, holding her breath. What had waked her? There it was again—soft footsteps on turf. Then came a low creaking. The dog stirred. She had let him sleep on the rag rug beside the bed, and she reached down and stroked his flank. He gave a little shake, and his skin rippled.

"Hush now, Sir Walter."

She stole from the bed to the shuttered window and peered through a crack, but the overcast sky made for a dark night. And this side of the house faced the pasture and the wood beyond, not the barn.

She padded into the front room in her bare feet, halted by the door, and listened. All was quiet. She jumped as the dog's nose connected with her thigh.

"You be still, now," she whispered. She slowly lifted the bar and opened the door a crack. She stared toward the barn, waiting for her eyes to adjust to the change in grayness. She couldn't be sure, but it looked as though the barn door was open.

Sir Walter gave a low growl, and she laid her hand on his head. "Shh."

The dog's ears were as high as her hip, and his presence made her feel somewhat more secure. Should she send him out into the night? Perhaps he would bark and frighten away the intruder, if there was one. Should she light a lantern and go out to see if the barn door was indeed open? That seemed foolhardy. She kept her place.

The dog tensed and growled again. Lucy wondered if he could hear something she couldn't. She stood unmoving for several minutes but caught no noise or flicker of movement. Perhaps she'd been hearing the hoofbeats of a deer as it crossed her yard.

Dear Lord, she prayed, *protect us!*

At last the dog relaxed his position and yawned, then turned away. She closed the door and barred it once more, then built up the fires and with great caution took down Jack's musket. It was loaded and primed. She carried it into her bedchamber and climbed back into bed. Sir Walter settled on the rug once more.

She tried to stay alert but soon fell into an exhausted sleep.

⌘

"What is it like outside today?" Jack asked.

Captain Murray sat on the three-legged stool the jailer had brought in a few days earlier, and Jack sat on the straw pile that was his bed.

"It's fine out," Murray said. "I ought to be fishing or cutting hay."

"Why aren't you?"

The captain smiled and reached for the sheath at his waist, but it was empty.

"Took your knife away?" Jack asked.

"Yes." Murray brought his pipe from his pocket and stuck it in his mouth. "Forbade me to smoke in here, too."

"Well, I'm thankful for that," Jack said. "The smoke would never clear in here."

Murray sucked on the cold pipe. "I came to see if I could strike a bargain with you."

"What sort of bargain?"

"I want to clear some new ground. Next spring I'd like to plant rye. Thought perhaps I could take your oxen for a month and use them to pull stumps. I'd give you a barrel of salt fish and a load of hay."

"Better speak to Lucy, but it sounds fine to me. It would help her by taking Bright and Snip off her hands. If she doesn't need the hay and fish, she can sell them." Jack smiled. "But if I know her, and I believe I'm beginning to, she'll feed some of the fish to that mongrel dog she's adopted."

Murray nodded. "I thought you'd agree. Shall I tell her you've approved my proposition?"

"Nay. Ask her what she thinks, and let her handle the transaction herself."

Murray studied him. "Training her to be independent, are you?"

"I've got to."

"She'll do fine, lad. She's jumped right into the farm chores, and I heard she's opening school again Monday week."

"Yes." Jack couldn't suppress the pride he felt. "She's a hard worker and a good businesswoman, I'm finding."

"If she has a chance, she'll be a good wife to you, as well."

Jack felt his face flush but trusted his beard and the poor lighting to hide it.

Murray stood and stretched. "I'd best move along. I'll hike out to your place and see about the oxen."

"She comes every day about this time," Jack said. "If you wait, you'll see her."

"Faithful in her visits, is she?"

Jack stood and walked with him to the cell door. "I tried to discourage her, but she's come every day since the magistrate was here."

"That bodes well for you if you are acquitted."

"Do you think so?"

"Of course! A wife who can cook and keep her house clean is a blessing, but one who dotes on you is a treasure."

Jack frowned. "She wouldn't listen when I forbade her to come."

The captain threw back his head and laughed. "Better and better." He clapped Jack on the shoulder. "I miss you at drill."

"No trouble with the Indians, is there?"

"Not lately, but I rather expect some this time of year." Murray bowed his head to look out the barred window. "Hey, Stoddard!"

A moment later the jailer unlocked the cell door. "Hunter, your missus is here again."

"Is she coming in now?" Jack asked.

"After she's done raking my wife over the coals."

"What's that?" Murray cocked his head to one side.

"She's raising a ruckus about the food," Stoddard explained. "My wife gives this man three meals a day—good, plain fare—but Goody Hunter wants to bring in sweets and such."

Jack smiled. "I hope you'll forgive her, sir. She only wants to keep my spirits up. I've told her the board is adequate here."

"I should hope so," the jailer growled.

"Can it hurt a prisoner to get a little extra food prepared by loving hands?" the captain asked.

Stoddard sighed. "I told my wife to let her bring it. Just cut it up in small pieces so we're sure she's not baking any contraband into her apple flan."

Murray's laugh roared out, echoing in the passageway. "As if Lucy Hunter would try to slip her husband a knife or a file! You know she's as honest as the sea is wide."

"I know no such thing, not when it comes to the wife of a desperate man." Stoddard closed the cell door. "I'll bring her right in, Hunter."

Murray laid his huge hand on the jailer's shoulder. "Reuben, this couple's been married a week now and not allowed to see each other but through that sorry little window. Can't you let Goody Hunter spend an hour alone with her husband?"

Jack's heart lurched, though he knew what the answer would be.

Stoddard's spine straightened, and he looked into the captain's face. "We do not allow such in the king's prison, Captain. Not even for a man I esteem as much as I do yourself. And certainly not for Isaac Hunter's boy."

ॐ

Lucy hummed as she hurried home from the jail. She had made her point, and the jailer had allowed her to take two of her tarts to Jack in his cell. Never mind that they were cut into niggling pieces.

His eyes had fairly glowed when he tasted them. She wanted to think part of that glow was for herself, not just her cooking.

The dog trotted alongside her, foraying off now and then to explore new scents at the edges of the lane. In her mind, Lucy catalogued the provisions in her larder and made a list of treats she could bake for Jack. If her cooking was the only one of her skills Jack was permitted to enjoy at the moment, she would become the best cook in all of Maine.

The dog barked, and Lucy looked ahead, gasping when she saw a man emerging from the path to her house. She didn't think she was acquainted with him. He came toward her at a leisurely pace, and she kept walking, wondering whether to turn in at her home or keep going toward the Ellises' farm. She recognized his long blue jacket and spotted kerchief as the clothing of a sailor.

"Good day," he called as she came closer, sweeping off his cap.

"Good day." Sir Walter stood beside her, growling.

"I be looking for the goodman what lives yonder. Hunter, is it not?"

Far down the lane, Lucy saw an oxcart approaching. Relieved that she was not alone with the stranger, she said, "I be Goody Hunter. May I help you?"

He grinned. "There, now. Don't tell me young Jack Hunter's married?"

"Yes, sir."

"Imagine that! I knew Jack when he was just a boy."

"Indeed."

He bowed slightly. "Forgive me, ma'am. I should have introduced myself. I'm Richard Trent."

She caught her breath. "So...Barnabas Trent was your father."

"That's right. I've been away some time now, nigh on ten years. I got word three days ago that my father had expired, and I've come to close his estate."

Lucy weighed that in her mind. "To what purpose did you wish to see my husband?"

"Why, to see if I could borrow a few tools, ma'am. My father's cottage seems to need some repairs."

That was an understatement, Lucy thought, but she would never say so. "And what do you know of the circumstances of your father's death?"

Trent's tanned face contorted into a grimace. "I received a letter saying he was killed. It didn't say much else."

"And who sent the letter?"

"One of the constables. Rutledge, I believe. Doesn't he live over by Fort Hill?"

"Aye," said Lucy.

"I suppose I should go around and see him," Trent said with a frown, "but when I arrived I found the doorstep rotted and the hinges sagging, and I thought I'd do some work first." He gave her a wistful smile. "I stopped at the churchyard and saw the new mound where they buried him next to my mother, and then I came straight here. But I should go see Goodman Rutledge right away. He would have the inventory of my father's goods, I suppose, and he could tell me more about what transpired."

Lucy nodded. "That is probably best."

The oxcart came closer, and she saw that Goodman Littlefield walked beside the near ox.

"Perhaps I can come by later and call on you and your husband," Trent said.

Lucy cleared her throat. "My husband is not the one you should borrow tools from, sir."

"I'm sorry. I meant no presumption."

"Nay, I'm sure you didn't." She gritted her teeth. He would learn the truth soon enough. She straightened her shoulders and looked him in the eye. "You see, Mr. Trent, though he be innocent, my husband stands accused of murdering your father. Good day."

The oxcart was nearly abreast of them, and she nodded to Goodman Littlefield, who trudged beside the team. He lifted his cap and nodded, then stared at Trent. Lucy marched up the path toward her house with Sir Walter padding along beside her.

She sobbed as she reached the doorstep. The dog looked up at her with trusting brown eyes and whined. Lucy shifted her basket to her other arm and stroked his glossy head. She had bathed him and combed out his matted hair so he made quite a presentable companion for a lady.

"Perhaps it was wrong of me not to tell him that you were his father's pet," she conceded. "But you're mine now, and I think you enjoy being such. Besides, I think he's got enough to think about this day."

Chapter 10

Lucy trudged wearily to the jail. A month had come and gone, but the magistrate had not.

"He were called to Biddeford last week," Reuben Stoddard had told her the day before.

"When will he return?"

"No one knows."

She supposed she ought to be thankful. Each day's delay meant Jack lived twenty-four hours more. But the uncertainty wore on her, and it took its toll on Jack, too.

He coughed now, too much for a healthy man. Although it was hot outside during the day, it was cool and damp in the dungeon, and he admitted to feeling a chill at night. His appetite fled, and her baking no longer tempted him. He ate the dainties she took him, but some days she was sure it was only because she was watching him. Instead of seizing hope from the postponement of proceedings, he had grown morose. The passion had left his eyes, and he seemed not to care anymore what the man appointed to defend him was planning.

The lawyer had visited the village once, spending about an hour with Jack in the outer room of the jail, during which the prisoner was kept fettered and heavily guarded. Then he went away, saying he would return when he was notified that the case was to be heard. Lucy found the lawyer's apparent apathy scandalous, but she could think of no way to advance Jack's cause.

Stoddard escorted her down the dim passageway to the felons' cells.

" 'Ey, now, missy!" a man cried as they passed the door to another cell. Lucy jumped and crowded against the opposite wall.

"Hush," Stoddard shouted. To Lucy he said, "Sorry, ma'am. We got a couple of new prisoners in today. A cut-purse and a public drunkard." The jailer shook his head. "Ladies oughtn't to come here, that's certain."

Lucy inhaled deeply and followed him to the door of Jack's cell.

"Hunter!" Stoddard called. He nodded at Lucy, then ambled away down the hall.

She stood on tiptoe to see through the window. Jack rose from his straw pallet and ambled toward the door. His face was thin, almost gaunt. "Hello, Lucy."

She forced a smile. "Good day! I've brought you a raisin bun and some fresh peas from the garden. Goodwife Stoddard will bring them in with your supper. She promised."

"Thank you." He slumped against the doorframe, his eyes nearly closed. His melancholy demeanor made her spirits plummet.

"I'm going to Mother's this afternoon," she went on. "Richard Trent wants me to weave him some linen, and I need to use the big loom."

Jack looked at her with dull gray eyes. "He's still here?"

"Yes. He's decided to give up the sea and work his father's land."

"Odd," said Jack. "Ten years ago he couldn't leave fast enough."

"Perhaps he's had enough sailing," Lucy said, trying to keep a lightness in her tone.

"His father used to beat him, you know."

"No! Really?"

"It's why he ran off."

Lucy tried to fit that with gossip she'd heard in the past. "He did say he hadn't been back home for a long time. Yet when his father died, he received the news within days. Said he'd been living in Portsmouth."

"So he wasn't across the sea," Jack said. "He was just down the coast a ways."

"You don't think. . ."

"What?" Jack's gaze met hers.

She followed the thought to its logical conclusion, but she didn't like it. "That he's been around close when he says he hasn't?"

Jack's knuckles whitened as he gripped the bars. "You mean, he could have come around and seen his father a month ago?"

"Jack, we mustn't say such things. It's evil."

"Someone did evil the day Trent was murdered. I don't want you having anything to do with him."

"But. . .he wants me to weave him enough yardage for a pair of breeches. He says he'll trade me firewood for it."

"You don't need firewood, at least not for this year. I stacked plenty."

"I could sell it, or keep it against next year's supply."

He shook his head grudgingly. "Don't you be alone with him for a second." Lucy noted that a spark lit his eyes for the first time in weeks.

"He seems a decent man. A bit crude, but I suppose that's how sailors are."

"I don't trust him. I wish you hadn't made a bargain with him."

"I'm sorry." She looked down. The last thing she wanted was to give Jack something to worry about. She'd thought bartering for firewood and other commodities would make her more independent and let Jack see that she could take care of herself. Still, this development seemed to have prodded him out of his listlessness.

"Don't fret about it," he said. "Just be careful."

She bit her lip. "I will."

"How is school going?" he asked.

"Fairly well. I lost two pupils, though. It's too far for the Howard children, their mother says." Again, she was glad he showed an interest. Lately it had seemed he didn't want to think about anything outside the jail. She'd wondered if he was deliberately shutting out life and preparing himself to leave it. "That little Betsy Ellis is a quick one," she said with a smile. "I'm proud of her reading, and she helps the younger ones learn their letters."

"And the farm?"

"The sheep are all sheared. Goodman Carver took the wool to the mill for me. And the garden is coming along splendidly. The corn is up to my waist!"

"It sounds as though you're faring well, Lucy. I'm glad."

"You made good provision." They were silent for a long minute, and she wondered if Jack had thought about her at all as he planted the garden and cut next winter's firewood. Or was it all done just because those were the things a farmer did? Everything seemed well planned. Of course, he'd done things for his mother for years, but there were things that seemed to go beyond that.

His vegetable crop would be far larger than one person would need, for instance. Of course, he might have thought to trade some of his produce. Then there were the bunches of dried herbs that hung from the beams in the great room. He'd harvested them last fall, she was certain, and this spring he'd tended the kitchen garden and the wide selection of herbs his mother had used. Had he kept up the herb bed hoping another woman would use it one day?

"Remember, if you ever need hard money, you've only to retrieve it," he said softly.

She glanced down the hallway to be sure no one was within earshot. "I remember where you told me to look."

Jack hung his head. "Lucy, I'm sorry I've put you in this position."

"What?"

"I never expected you to have to wait so long to be rid of me."

"Stop it!"

"You're working too hard, trying to do everything. The chores, the school, your weaving. You don't have to keep up the farm."

"Our farm."

Exasperation sparked in his eyes. "Your farm."

"Maybe someday, but for now it is ours, and I'll not abandon it or sell it, so hush."

"The work is too hard for you."

"I'll get someone to help with haying and harvesting the wheat field. Don't worry about that."

He sighed. "I don't want you to wear yourself out trying to keep things going for my sake."

"What do you want me to do, Jack?"

She thought she saw the ghost of a smile on his lips.

"Would you have me close the school?"

"Nay." He shuffled his feet. "Do exactly as you wish, Lucy. I mean it. Now and. . .after. Just. . .take care of yourself."

She squeezed her eyelids shut for a moment, determined not to cry. They'd had a month's grace. Now Jack was falling back into despair and hopelessness. For a minute, she had routed his gloom, but it sat heavy on him once more. She feared his thoughts were even blacker when he was alone in the cell.

"Listen, Goodman Hunter, you stop feeling sorry for yourself."

He cocked his head toward his shoulder. "How should I feel, then?"

Lucy pulled in a breath. "I can only tell you how I feel."

"Which is?"

"Terrified, and. . .blessed."

"Both?"

"Aye. I keep thinking God should take away my fear. But it's always there. Still, I'm grateful. To Him. . .to you. Thank you, Jack."

She heard Stoddard unlock the door to the passageway. Jack gazed at her with mournful gray eyes.

"Good day, husband," she whispered.

The next day, Lucy had just started out for the jail when Gideon Rutledge came running toward her from the village.

"What is it?" she called as he approached.

"Father says you aren't to come to the jail." The boy stopped a few feet away and bent over with his hands on his knees, panting.

"Whyever not?" She bristled at the idea that Ezekiel Rutledge was interfering in her life once more.

"The magistrate is come."

Her anger gave way to a sick apprehension. "Be they holding court today, then?"

"Aye. Father says it is likely they'll hear Goodman Hunter's case later."

"But. . .the barrister." She stared at the boy. "Did your father say anything about my husband's attorney?"

"I don't know, ma'am. But he said you're to stay away, at Goodman Hunter's order."

Lucy opened her mouth, then closed it. What would be the good of defying Jack now? If she appeared, her presence would only distress him. Yes, and humiliate him, since the entire town would know she had come against his express wishes.

She stood facing Gideon Rutledge in the lane, weighing her course of action. "Will you take a message to my husband for me?"

His eyes widened. "I be not permitted to speak to the felons, ma'am."

"All right, then, your father. Will you deliver a message to Constable Rutledge for me?"

"Aye."

She nodded. "Tell him, please, that I wish my husband to know I am at home praying for him."

⁂

Lucy sat in the ladder-back chair, unable to stop picturing Jack's handsome face wreathed in sorrow. She wrenched out fractured prayers as she stared into the fire. Suddenly a hand touched her shoulder, and she jumped, whirling to see her mother.

"Ah, Marm, you startled me."

Alice set her basket on the kitchen table and sat on one of the stools. "I'm sorry, daughter. I thought perchance you could use some company."

Lucy nodded. "Thank you."

"Have you eaten anything?"

Lucy brushed her hair back from her forehead. "Not since breakfast. I was going to eat dinner after...after I took Jack some blackberry pudding."

"Well then, we shall partake together." Her mother lifted a small covered crock and a pottery bowl from the basket, then took out a linen towel and folded it back to reveal fresh corn pone. "It's not fancy, but good, hearty food. Stew and such."

"Thank you, but..." Lucy turned away with a tremulous sigh.

"It could take days, you know," Alice said.

"Do you think so?"

Alice waved one hand through the air in dismissal. "You know how men are."

"Do I?"

"Goody Walter says they've sent to Falmouth for your husband's lawyer, and the magistrate is hearing other cases today."

"What if the lawyer doesn't come?"

Alice hesitated only a moment. "We shall see. Sit up here and eat with me."

Lucy fetched pewter plates and forks for both of them, and a dish of butter. After her mother offered a prayer of thanks for the food and a brief supplication for Jack, they began to eat.

Alice attacked her meal eagerly. "Ah, that's good stew. I was out all night, sitting up with Granny Sewall, and I was afraid my kettle would go dry, but not so."

Lucy made herself take a bite of the cornbread. It crumbled in her mouth, flavorless. "How is Goody Sewall?"

"She'll recover. Let's have some of that maple sweetening of yours."

Lucy jumped up, grateful for the excuse to escape her mother's eye for a moment.

"Goody Walter says the magistrate took a room at the tavern and paid for three nights," Alice said.

"Three?"

"But you know how things get exaggerated. Likely she got it wrong."

"Yes." Lucy sat again, setting the jug on the table. Staying at home and trying to analyze the meager scraps of information that came her way was maddening. If only Jack had not forbidden her to attend court.

Alice sighed. "That's not the maple syrup, child. That's treacle."

"Oh." Lucy hopped up again.

"Never mind," said Alice, but Lucy went to the larder again and came back with the small jug that held the syrup.

"I'd tell you not to fret, girl, but I know my breath would be wasted."

"He is my husband. You wish me to be indifferent?" Lucy looked at her plate.

"Pining for him will change nothing."

Lucy felt an unwelcome flush in her cheeks. "I'm not pining. I know what to expect."

Alice nodded. "Perhaps we'll hear something this evening."

But there was no word that evening. Alice stayed the night, and Lucy lay awake beside her on the rope bed, staring into the darkness while her mother and Sir Walter snored.

The morning dragged after the chores were done. By noon Lucy was beside herself, pacing the front room from the door to the fireplace to the east window and back to the door.

"Put your hands to something, child," her mother said. Alice had made better use of the morning, pounding a sack full of dried corn in Lucy's samp mortar, then sifting the meal and storing it away in a big crock.

Lucy sighed and wrung her hands. "I suppose I should be about the garden."

"Yes," said Alice. "Your turnip patch is full of weeds. Bring me some beans to snip, and pick a few beet greens for supper."

The sound of steps on the path caught Lucy's ear, and she rushed to the door. She saw Goodman Bemis walking toward the house.

"What news, sir?" Lucy called.

He swept off his hat. "I was told I could find Goody Hamblin here."

Lucy sagged against the lintel. "Mother, you are needed."

Alice bustled toward them. "Is it the wee one?"

"Aye. He's feverish again. Can you come?"

"Of course." Alice untied her apron. "Have you heard anything about my son-in-law's case?"

Bemis glanced toward Lucy. "No, ma'am. But I hear they fined Solomon Whittier for letting his dog savage his neighbor's chickens."

At dusk Lucy was still alone. No one had brought her news or comfort. She fed the livestock and laid in wood and water for the night, then called the dog to her and barred the door.

She sat for a long time in the chair by the hearth, staring at the flames and trying to form a coherent prayer. At last she moaned and buried her face in her hands.

"Heavenly Father. . .it cannot end like this. Please let them acquit my husband." She choked on a sob. "I didn't even get to tell him a proper good-bye, Lord. I never told him. . .I love him."

Sir Walter leaped up from the floor and barked toward the door, his ears pricked and his legs stiff.

Lucy stood and listened. She heard the creak of a cart and the slow tread of oxen coming up the path.

She ran to the door, and the dog went with her, renewing his barking when she lifted the bar and flung open the door. Darkness had fallen, but the moon was near full, and she recognized the bulky forms approaching. Captain Murray walked slowly beside Jack's oxen, and his farm cart creaked behind them.

Lucy's heart surged with relief. Murray wouldn't come all this way for nothing, and knowing the worst would be better than this agonizing ignorance.

"What news?" she called, lifting her skirt and running down the path toward him.

"Whoa," Murray boomed. Snip and Bright stopped in their tracks, snuffling and twitching their tails. "Goody Hunter, I've brought your husband home."

Chapter 11

S o it was over. Lucy's knees buckled and the breath whooshed out of her lungs. She reached toward the captain but grasped only a handful of the air between them. She swayed, and he caught her in his brawny arms.

"Please, sir," she gasped, "let me down."

He stood there uncertainly, measuring her with anxious eyes in the moonlight. "Forgive me, ma'am. I didn't mean to shock you."

He set her on her feet, and she grasped his arm while regaining her balance.

"Tell me where you want him, and I'll carry him in."

"I didn't realize they would. . .send him home after." She looked apprehensively toward the cart, wondering if her mother and Sarah Ellis would come to help her lay out her husband's body.

After a moment's silence, Murray seized her by the shoulders. "Dear Goody Hunter! Pardon my clumsiness. You didn't think—dear woman, your husband yet lives."

She stared up at him, stunned. Her mouth seemed to have ceased working. "Jack. . .is alive?"

"Yes, yes! Oh, how could I have been so careless? I've shocked you awfully, haven't I? Please, ma'am, accept my apology. Your husband will require some nursing, but there's no call for the undertaker."

Lucy stared at the oxcart. "How can this be? They. . .didn't finish the job?"

Murray shook his shaggy head like a gruff but gentle bear. "They didn't hang him, ma'am. The magistrate said the evidence was not sufficient to convict a man. They let him go two hours past."

"Two hours? I don't understand." Why had she not heard? And where had Jack been in those two hours?

"Let me bring him inside, and I'll tell you what I know."

"Of course."

He walked to the side of the wagon, and she followed. Murray stooped, then rose with a lank form cradled in his arms. Lucy heard a low moan, and the sound brought the reality home to her. Jack was not dead! And she, his wife, must care for him. Joy and anxiety assailed her.

"This way, Captain. Put him in his bed, in the back chamber. I'll go turn the coverlet back."

She raced into the house and grabbed a candlestick, then dashed to the

66

bedroom. The captain followed close behind her.

When she had set down the candle and drawn back the bedclothes, she turned to help him. She gasped at what she saw.

The skin around Jack's eyes was blackened and swollen, and below them were bloody lacerations. One arm hung limp as the captain lowered him to the featherbed. Murray straightened Jack's legs, and he groaned again.

"Tell me," she commanded, looking up at the big man. "Who did this? Surely not the jailer."

"No." Murray wiped a hand across his brow. "There was a lot of shouting and drinking after court was done. I asked Jack if he'd be all right getting home. He said yes, so I left him. An hour later, I passed the tavern, and. . ." The captain stroked his beard and paused.

"What, sir? You must tell me all."

"I saw a form lying in the alley between the tavern and the wheelwright's shop. I thought it was a drunkard, but when I went to see who it was. . .well, it was Jack."

"My husband does not take strong drink." Lucy drew herself up, daring him to challenge that.

"No, he doesn't. But a lot of people were angry when the magistrate let him go. I thought the crowd had dispersed, or I'd never have left him to walk home alone. I'm sorry. As near as I can tell, several men jumped him and beat him in the alley."

Lucy steadied herself against the bedpost. "I cannot thank you enough, sir."

"Is there anything I can do?"

"I don't like to ask it of you, you've been so kind, but could you fetch my mother?"

"Of course."

"She may not be at home. She left this noon with Goodman Bemis. I thought she would be back ere now."

Murray nodded. "I shall find her. Might I leave the team here while I go? 'Twill be faster."

"Of course."

He left her, and Lucy scrambled from bedchamber to kitchen and back several times, fetching a basin, linen, water, and salve.

She built up the fires in both rooms and put a kettle of water on to boil over the cook fire. At last she stopped her frantic activity and stood at the bedside, looking down at Jack. He hadn't moved since the captain laid him there. The thought came to her that he might have died while she made her preparations. Her pulse accelerated, and she held her breath as she watched anxiously until his chest rose and fell in a gasp.

Lord, thank You!

She set to work once more, bathing his disfigured face. His nose had bled profusely into his beard, and she surmised his nose was broken. His hands were wounded, too, she noticed. He must have tried to defend himself. She hoped he'd given the blackguards cause for regret. Her tears flowed as she saw the raw chafe marks on his wrists that could only have been caused by the manacles he wore so long.

Jack moaned, and she rinsed her linen cloth in cool water, then continued tenderly blotting his face. His beard had protected him to some extent, she realized, but his lips were torn and bleeding. What else had they done to him?

Her hands trembled as she unbuttoned his vest and shirt. It was the blue linsey shirt she had washed last week and taken back to him at the jail. She laid the material back and bit her lip. His left side was bruised from his chest to his waist. They must have kicked him. She put out one hand and touched the purple skin. He did not flinch but moaned. Sir Walter crowded in next to her and stuck his nose over the edge of the bed. He stayed there, his chin resting on the linen sheet.

"Oh, Jack." How could anyone be so cruel? Gently she probed his rib cage. "Broken ribs, I expect." She wondered how much internal damage he had. Her mother had more experience and would tell her what was best to do, but Lucy thought she would probably recommend binding up Jack's chest with strips of cloth. She had best find something suitable.

Knowing the hours of labor that went into weaving a length of material, Lucy hated to see fabric torn, but her thoughts were only on her husband now. There was a chest of old clothing and linens in the loft. She would sacrifice some of Jack's mother's garments to bandage his wounds.

∽◈∽

Lucy heard the door to the outer room open, and she rushed out of the bedchamber.

"Mother! I'm so glad you're here." The tears she'd held back as she worked burst forth.

Alice gathered her into her arms and held her. "There, now. Calm yourself, daughter, and let me take a look. Has he wakened at all?"

"Nay. I tried to spoon some broth into his mouth, but he choked and spit it back out, so I quit. I've washed him up, but I need to change his clothes."

"Was there any blood in his spittle?"

"I don't think so, but he'd bled a lot before he came, and it's hard to tell what is fresh." Lucy glanced toward the barred door. "Where is the captain?"

"I sent him home to his family, but he promised he or one of his men would come around in the morning to do the barn chores."

"He's been very kind."

Alice followed her into the bedchamber and surveyed Jack's inert form. Her grim face made Lucy lose heart.

"You don't think he'll die now, do you?" she whispered. "After all he's been through! We've got to save him, Marm."

Alice bent over Jack and lifted one eyelid. She ran her fingertips lightly over his jaw then down to his ribs.

"I think his right arm is broken," Lucy said.

"Aye. Fetch me two straight sticks of kindling. We'll have to splint that before we roll him over."

"They must have beat him with a stick, or kicked him." Lucy blinked hard.

"Murray said there was a faction who were sure your husband was guilty, and they weren't pleased with the judge's ruling. They must have followed Jack from the jail, or met him on the street later."

Lucy shook her head. "I can't believe the magistrate set him free, and then this happened."

"The captain said it's partly due to you that Mr. Jewett freed him."

"Jewett," said Lucy. "Why do I know that name?"

"He knew your father," Alice said, wringing out the cloth Lucy had left in the basin on a stool beside the bed. "The captain said that when the magistrate learned the accused had married Thomas Hamblin's daughter, he began to sway toward favoring Jack and believing his tale of innocence."

"Because of Father?" Lucy whispered.

"Aye. You should be proud of that. Now fetch me the sticks and some strips of linen."

"I'll have to sacrifice one of Goody Hunter's bedsheets, I fear, unless you think the remains of her mourning gown will do."

"Child, I don't care what color the material be for bandages. And if we're clever and God is merciful, you won't be needing a widow's weeds."

Lucy ran to the kitchen and sorted through the wood box for the best pair of sticks to use for splints, then climbed the ladder to the loft above the bed-chamber once more. She set her pewter candlestick on the floor by the chest of old clothing and pulled out a black dress.

She quelled the stab of guilt that hit her. It was not disloyal to use these things to benefit Jack. She dropped the dress over the edge of the loft to the kitchen floor and hurried back down the ladder.

As she cut the skirt into narrow strips, she lifted her heart to God. *Thank You, Lord, for restoring my husband to me, and for allowing my father's good name to aid Jack, though in Father's lifetime he had nothing good to say of the Hunters.*

When she returned to the bedchamber, Alice turned to her with a sober nod.

"I think his legs are sound, though he has some deep bruises on them. It's his innards I'm most worried about. I'll splint the arm. Then we'll turn him over. I need to see what the back of him looks like, if his spine is injured, and how extensive the bruising be."

"What shall I do to help?" Lucy asked.

"For now, start a tea of willow bark for pain. He'll need that. And a poultice. Set some leaves of comfrey to steep. Then tear more strips of cloth. Have you any yarrow?"

"Yes, I believe some dried flowers hang in the kitchen."

"Good. If not, go out at daybreak and pick some. I've mustard with me, and flaxseed."

They worked side by side for nearly an hour. Lucy cringed when they rolled Jack on his side and she saw that the bruises extended around his lower back.

"Wicked men," Alice muttered as she applied the poultice and began to bind Jack's ribcage with strips of linen. "No good ever comes when men usurp the law."

At last Jack lay, pale and still, with all his wounds tended to. Alice gently fingered his jaw. "I don't believe any teeth are broken. Some of that blood was from his tongue, though. Likely he bit it when they struck him."

Lucy sank onto the stool beside the bed. "You do think he'll recover, don't you?"

"What, a strong young man like this?" Alice smiled, but Lucy noted the anxious look in her eyes as she glanced back toward the patient.

"There's never a guarantee, I know," Lucy said.

Alice sighed. "Well, child, you keep him clean and apply the remedies as best you can, and you pray, and you wait. That's the method for healing a broken body."

Lucy nodded. "Thank you, Mother."

Alice straightened and pushed her fists against the small of her back. "I believe I could use a cup of tea."

"Of course."

When she returned a few minutes later, her mother was sitting calmly on the stool, knitting. "Is there another bed?"

Lucy handed her the steaming cup. "Nay, but there's a straw pallet in the loft."

Alice sighed. "Can you bring it down by the fire in the kitchen?"

"Surely," said Lucy.

"Good. We'll rest by turns, then."

"You don't have to sleep here, Mother. Your own bed would be more comfortable."

"So it would, but I feel my place is here, if you want me."

Lucy felt tears spring into her eyes. "Thank you."

Alice sipped her tea. "I warn you, I'm watching two women who are near their times. I could be called at any moment for a birth."

"I understand. I'll drop the straw tick down from the loft. I don't think I can sleep just now, so you should take the first rest."

❦

In the predawn darkness, Lucy let the candle burn out and kept her vigil by the soft glow of the coals in the fireplace. Jack stirred only occasionally, when his hands would twitch and he would give a low groan. Lucy sat forward then and sponged his brow, whispering to him that all would be well.

So, she thought, *I am to be Mrs. Jack Hunter after all, not the Widow Hunter.* What would this mean to her? How would Jack take the news? She wished she'd been in the courtroom and had been able to speak to him. Perhaps she would have an inkling of how he perceived their future.

She leaned forward and rested her weary arms on the edge of the bed, lowering her head onto them. For four years Jack had shown not a speck of interest in her. Would he ever have proposed to her if he hadn't thought he was about to die?

Some time later she raised her head. Fingers of light pierced the cracks in the shutter, and she rose to lower it. Light flooded the room. One of the captain's men would come soon. She'd better see if her mother was awake.

She glanced toward Jack's bed and froze. He was staring at her from beneath half-closed eyelids.

Lucy stepped to the bedside and bent over him, her breath coming in shallow gasps. "Jack? Can you hear me?"

A frown settled between his eyebrows as he studied her. His swollen lips moved, and he blinked.

"Lucy," he whispered.

Joy flooded her heart. "Welcome home, Jack."

Chapter 12

"Why doesn't he waken?" Lucy asked her mother the next day.

Alice shook her head and bound a fresh poultice over Jack's abdomen. "He spoke to you once. That's a good sign."

"But then he went back to sleep, and he hasn't opened his eyes since," Lucy protested.

"Don't fret. True, his situation is grave, but I believe he will heal in time. He had some blows to the face and a bump on the back of the head, but I can't feel any fractures in his skull. Perhaps seeing you and realizing he'd got home was all he needed to let him rest awhile longer. This be a healing sleep."

Lucy tried to accept that, but she found herself questioning every little movement. Her mother was skilled, but was she skilled enough? Were the infusions and poultices they used the best remedy, or was there something better? Should she get out some coins and ask someone to send for a doctor?

"You should sleep while you can," her mother urged, but Lucy found it impossible to relax her tired muscles and stop worrying. What if Jack suddenly stopped breathing, and she wasn't at his side?

In the early afternoon, Sarah Ellis paid a call. She carried her baby girl and brought young Betsy with her.

"I cannot stay," she said as soon as Lucy opened the door. "I only came to bring you a bit of gingerbread and tell you my husband will come by tonight at chore time. We're praying for you and Jack."

"Thank you." Lucy seized her hand. "I appreciate all you and Samuel have done."

"We don't mind. Jack has helped us plenty." Sarah hiked her little daughter higher on her hip. "How is he faring?"

"He's still unconscious, but my mother hopes he will mend."

"If Alice says it, then it is probably true."

"I shan't be able to keep school for at least a fortnight," Lucy said.

"I'll spread the word. Now don't fret. Just take care of him and mind your own health."

Sarah's comforting smile cheered Lucy a little. After she'd gone, Lucy let her mother persuade her to sample the neighbor's gingerbread.

Goodman Woodbury came in the midafternoon to fetch Alice to attend his wife, and Lucy wondered how she would carry on alone. With her mother there, she'd felt competent, but alone? How would she know if she was doing everything she could?

"Just keep on as we have been," Alice said. "If he wakens, give him some broth and tell him all is well."

"You said he needs more liquids, and it's so warm today. What if he won't drink?"

Alice frowned as she gathered her basket, shawl, and packets of herbs. "The sooner you can get him to take a little water the better. Wet his lips with a clean cloth now and then. Just do your best, child. I'll return when I'm able."

At sunset there was a rap on the door, and Lucy opened it to Goodman Ellis.

"Good evening. How is Jack?"

"About the same," she said. "Thank you for coming, sir."

Samuel shrugged. "I was going to milk your cow, but I see it's been done."

"What?" Lucy stared past him toward the barn. "I haven't milked her this evening."

"Is it possible someone has been here before me?"

"I didn't hear anyone."

He frowned. "The calf, then?"

"Nay. I took the calf off her near a month ago." Lucy stepped outside and looked toward the pasture. The calf stood grazing among the sheep. "Where is Tryphenia?"

"In the barn."

"I didn't put her there. And I doubt my mother went out to the barn before she was called away."

"This be strange," Ellis said.

Lucy looked up at him. "It's not the first time," she admitted.

"Oh?"

"Sometimes it seemed the cow gave only a scant bit of milk in the morning, and a few times I've found no eggs. The chickens usually give six to eight eggs a day, but some days there are none."

"Perhaps a skunk got at them in the night."

"And once I thought the barn door was off the latch."

Ellis looked toward the barn. "I'll check the premises, just to make sure things are secure."

She went inside and sat by Jack, waiting for Samuel to report to her. She hoped nothing was amiss, for her hands were full with her injured husband. She couldn't think about prowlers and petty thievery.

When he came back, he gave her a reassuring smile. "I've found nothing untoward, Goody Hunter. All your stock is bedded down for the night. I'm sorry there was no milk for you."

Lucy waved her hand in dismissal. "She gives more than I can use most days."

"We'll be making cheese next week," Ellis said. "Sarah mentioned that I should send you a piece of rennet, if you wish to make cheese yourself."

"I'm not sure yet how my husband will be, but if I can spare the time, I'd like that."

"Well, if your cow gives plenty of milk, it might be better if I carried it home and my wife made a cheese for you."

"Oh, I can't ask her to do that. She has her hands full with all the children."

Ellis smiled. "One more cheese won't matter. But I'll ask her if she's up to it."

"Wait here," Lucy said. She climbed the ladder to the loft and picked up a small pile of folded cloth from beside the hand loom.

"These be for Sarah," she said when she came back down to the kitchen. "I was working on them last week. I wanted to have a full dozen to present to her, but I've only seven finished, and I mightn't have time for a while, but she should have them now, and. . ." She stopped, realizing she was rambling. "They're clouts for the baby. Linsey-woolsey, but I used more wool than flax, to make them soft."

Ellis smiled, and when he spoke, his voice was husky. " 'Tis a splendid gift, and much needed. The little one seems to need changing every minute. Thank you."

"I wish we could grow cotton here. Babies need soft material against their skin. But it's so expensive."

He nodded. "Let me know if you need anything else. I'll come by again tomorrow."

"No need. Captain Murray has arranged for one of the militia men to come every morning until I tell the captain we don't need them any longer."

His eyes widened in surprise. "That's fine. I'll just continue the evening chores then."

"I'm grateful there are so many who are willing to help. It means that not everyone thinks my husband a monster."

"I know Jack better than that," Ellis said.

"Hearing you say it warms my heart."

"Aye, well, I'll say it to any who will listen. Jack Hunter is no murderer."

Jack slept on. Lucy turned him onto his side twice, and every hour she put a wet rag to his lips and squeezed a few drops into his mouth, but other than that she let him be. Jack stirred and moaned occasionally, but for the most part he slumbered. She kept her watch with waning hope that he would awaken. *Dear husband,* she cried in her heart. *You mustn't leave me, now that we are together at last!*

That evening she dragged the straw pallet into the bedchamber and lay down on it. She was so weary she could barely keep her eyes open, but she didn't want to miss hearing him if he wakened and called out. The dog slunk in after she blew out the candle and nestled down on the edge of the pallet. Lucy thought about making him leave but instead reached out and caressed his back.

The next morning, she moved the pallet to the outer room and left the house for short periods to tend to the garden but kept checking on Jack every few minutes. At noon she stopped working and ate a light meal, then carried her flax wheel into the bedchamber and spun an impressive pile of flax fibers into thread.

Her mother stopped in before sunset, on her way home from overseeing the prolonged labor and difficult birth at the Woodbury house.

"There's no change in Jack's condition," Lucy said. "Isn't there something more I can do for him?"

Alice examined the patient. "You're doing fine. Just keep on as you have, child. I can stay if you like."

"Nay," Lucy said. "You need a good rest. Go on home, Marm."

Again that night she slept on the floor near the bed, but she lay awake a long time, praying silently and listening to Jack's even breathing and Sir Walter's sighs and snuffles.

She woke to the sound of Tryphenia's lowing and heard a man's voice in the barnyard. Lowering the shutter, she saw one of the captain's men leading the cow to the pasture gate.

Lucy reached for her stays. She must dress quickly, for the man would soon bring her the pail of morning milk. She laced them on over her shift, then seized her pockets, tied them about her waist, and grabbed her bodice. Her gaze lit on Jack, and she gasped, then clutched the bodice to her chest.

He was awake.

She took a faltering step toward him, then held back, glancing at her skirt that still hung on the peg by the door.

Jack started to raise his hand, then moaned and looked down at his splinted and swathed arm. "What. . ." His gaze met hers once more, and he whispered, "Am I really home?"

Lucy laughed with joy. "Yes! Let me get you some water. Your throat must be parched."

She started toward the stool that held the basin and water pitcher, then halted once more and looked at the bodice in her hands. She felt her face go scarlet.

"Please excuse me for just an instant." Snatching up her skirt, she ran with the garments into the kitchen. *Lord, don't let him lose consciousness while I make myself decent.* She glanced toward the front door, hoping the militiaman would not choose this moment to bring her the milk.

At last she was covered by both bodice and skirt. Her hair was uncombed, her feet were bare, but she didn't delay another moment. She raced back to the bedroom doorway and stood panting as she eyed her husband.

He lay watching her, and his lips seemed to hold a hint of amusement.

Lucy stepped forward. "I'm pleased to see you awake. May I bring you something to eat?"

"Water first," Jack said, his voice gravelly.

"Aye." She scurried to the bedside and poured water into a tin cup, then offered it to him. Jack struggled to elevate his head. "Let me help you." She hastened around to the other side of the bed, where she could get her arm under his head and lift him.

Jack drank the entire cup of water, then lay back. "What's wrong with my arm?" he asked.

"You broke it."

"How did I manage that?"

She opened her mouth, at a loss for an explanation. "I should have said it was done for you. Rather thoroughly."

He barked a short laugh, then winced and gritted his teeth. "I don't seem to remember yesterday. Was I flogged?"

"Nay, Jack." Lucy bit her lip and carefully removed her arm from beneath his head. Being so close to him hadn't agitated her while he was unconscious, but now that he was awake, she found it disconcerting in the extreme. She stood back a pace and looked down at him. "It wasn't yesterday, though. This be the third day since Captain Murray brought you here."

"Aye?" He closed his eyes for a moment, then opened them again. "I don't think they hung me. My neck is the only thing that doesn't hurt."

She stifled a laugh, but it came out as a low sob. "Nay, it wasn't done at the jail. The captain said some wicked men caught you and. . .and beat you afterward." She swallowed hard, wondering if she'd just added to his misery by recounting what he might perceive as a humiliation. "Anyway, he brought you here, and. . .and Mother said you would live, so I've been keeping care of you."

He stared at her with solemn gray eyes, then lowered his eyelids. "Thank you."

Lucy waited, fearful that his eyes would stay closed. Should she rouse him? He needed nourishment if he was to regain his strength. She cleared her throat, and his eyes opened. He looked at her from beneath the thick lashes.

"Do you have much pain?" she asked.

He ran his tongue over his lips. "Aye."

"Where? I mean, what's the worst?"

"My. . .stomach, and my arm."

"Could you take some broth?"

"Perhaps."

She nodded. "I'll fetch it and some comfrey tea."

As she hurried to the kitchen, a knock came at the door. She opened it to find Murray's man there, holding a bucket more than half full of warm milk.

"Here you go, ma'am, and I've four eggs in my pockets."

"Bless you," Lucy said. "Would you like some of the milk? It's too much for me to use today."

"I expect we could use a drop."

She poured half of it into a jug for him, wondering how she could get word to her mother and Captain Murray. "Will you see the captain?"

"I doubt it. He were going out to fish the morn."

"That's all right, then. Thank you very kindly."

He put his hand to his brow in salute. "I'll send the jug back to ye."

⁓⊛⁓

When her husband regained consciousness, Lucy began sleeping in the kitchen once more. Two days later she told Samuel Ellis and the militiaman who came to do chores that day that they need not continue.

Jack still slept most of each day, but his periods of wakefulness grew longer, and he advanced from broth and medicinal teas to gruel, then solid food.

Lucy rejoiced inwardly as he grew stronger. She saw his embarrassment at having her tend to his most intimate needs, but she persevered, trying to accomplish the more distasteful tasks, such as removing the chamber pot, while he slept. They managed to go on in this way, avoiding direct mention of the menial chores she performed.

By the fourth day, Jack was well enough to sit up and debate with her the wisdom of hiring someone to harvest the flax field and lay the plants to dry.

"I can do it," Lucy insisted.

"It's too heavy labor for you."

"I've done worse."

"I won't have my wife pulling flax."

In the end she hired Richard Trent to do it, a solution that irritated Jack.

"He's close by, and he's willing," Lucy said.

"I don't want you to deal with him."

"I'm already weaving him a length of linen. He said if I'll double it, he'll pull my flax and clean it."

"Don't do more for him. Let him do the flax for the cloth you first said you'd weave him. Take his work instead of the firewood he promised."

Lucy grudgingly agreed to revise the bargain the next time she saw Goodman Trent.

"Do you be weaving his cloth on my mother's little loom?" Jack asked.

"Nay. I went a few times to my mother's house to start it on the large loom, but I haven't been back there in a week."

Jack frowned.

He's angry with me, Lucy thought. She wished she hadn't implied that his injuries kept her from her routine. Being married was going to be different from being unwed, she could see that. She could no longer make decisions or take on barters without consulting her husband.

Her prayers became convoluted. Instead of simple pleas for Jack's life and health, she begged for wisdom and discretion, but it came down to one thing in the end. *Lord, teach me to be a good wife.* She knew it would be the hardest lesson she had ever set herself to learn.

Chapter 13

Jack lay on the featherbed, feeling helpless. His wife was in the barn, milking the cow and feeding the livestock, and he was lying about like a sluggard. It wasn't right. Lucy was working herself to a shadow, doing a man's work as well as a woman's.

He moved to sit up and fell back against the pillow. It seemed like the pain would tear him in two. *If I just move through it, I'll be fine.*

He pulled in a deep breath and braced himself, then pushed his body upward and swung his legs over the side of the bed. An involuntary groan escaped him, and he clutched his side with his good arm. The pain was so intense he thought he might retch. His arm ached, his ribs throbbed, and the searing in his belly was agony. He was shaking, and beads of sweat dripped from his brow.

He pushed harder on his side, and that seemed to help a bit. His breeches. . .where were they? He looked about the room but couldn't spot them. They must be in the clothespress. It was at least two steps from the end of the bed. He bit his lip and measured the distance in his mind. Lucy wouldn't like it, that was certain, but it was time he stopped being a burden to her.

He gathered what strength he could muster and pushed himself up off the bed. Immediately his knees buckled, and he fell back with a stifled cry, landing half on and half off the bed.

"And just what are you doing?" Lucy's eyes snapped in anger as she surveyed him from the doorway.

Jack groaned and covered his eyes with his good arm.

"Ah, Jack." She hurried to him and grasped his shoulder. "Come on, now. Back in bed."

"It's time for me to be up and about."

"Oh, yes, surely." She scowled at him. "Maybe in a fortnight."

He set his teeth and let her help him ease back up toward the pillow, then lay gasping, staring up at the ceiling.

To his surprise, Lucy sat on the edge of the bed.

He continued to stare upward.

"Healing takes time. I know this is difficult for you, but let me do what I must, and don't make things harder. If you overdo now, you'll have a setback, and then I shall be longer getting you well."

He nodded.

"Jack."

It was a whisper as soft as lamb's wool, and he couldn't help looking at her. She was so beautiful! She oughtn't to be worked like a servant. She squeezed up her face for an instant, and he was afraid she would cry, but instead she reached for the pitcher and cup.

"Drink this." After he complied, she said, "I'll have your supper soon." She rose, straightened the coverlet, and turned away.

"Wait," he said.

She looked back, and Jack hesitated.

"I recollect the court now."

"Do you?"

He nodded. "Lucy, they didn't acquit me."

"So the captain told me. The magistrate said the evidence was insufficient to try you on."

"But they could arrest me again. Did he tell you that?"

Fear leaped into her eyes. "Nay, but. . .if there's not enough evidence. . ."

"We can't count on anything," he said. "I wasn't tried for the crime, but many still suspect me."

She came a step nearer. "What does this mean, Jack?"

"I don't know."

The sheen in her eyes told him tears were near.

"We keep on, I guess, and hope the sentiments in town die down." Even to him it sounded inadequate. What if some other bit of trumped-up evidence surfaced? Would he have to go through the accusations and abuse again?

Lucy licked her lips and wadded her apron between her hands. "Jack, there's something else. I didn't want to worry you, but. . ."

"What?" Her hesitance and unsteady voice alarmed him.

"It may be nothing, but. . .well, sometimes I think someone's been about the barn."

"Is anything missing?" he asked, thinking of the way his ax had been taken and used.

"Nothing except a few eggs and a little milk. And one day last week the beans were stripped and the turnips thinned, but I didn't do it, and I certainly didn't eat the vegetables." She shrugged. "This evening, as I was milking. . .I felt as though I was being watched."

Jack frowned. It was probably nothing. Normal edginess for a woman who has been forced to rely on herself. But he had approved her dismissal of the men who had come to do the farm chores. He was glad they'd helped and shown their support, but he didn't want it to go on to the point of the Hunters being beholden to others.

"Keep the dog with you when you go outside," he said.

"I shall."

Jack's mind raced as she left to start supper. It was his place to protect his wife and to perform the heavy work about the farm, not lie here weak and helpless.

The dog came and laid his chin on the edge of the bed, staring up at Jack with huge brown eyes. Even that mongrel dog was a help to Lucy. But her husband was useless—no, worse than that. He was a hindrance and the cause of extra work for her. Did she regret the marriage? It crossed his mind that an honorable man would offer to let her put the marriage aside and return to her mother's home if she wished, but that was the last thing he wanted.

Sir Walter whined, and Jack scowled at him.

"Go away."

The next Sunday, Lucy rose early to do her chores and fix breakfast. Jack had insisted the evening before that she go to church. The fact that he wasn't able to attend didn't mean she should neglect public worship. She looked forward to mingling with the other parishioners, but at the same time was nervous as to what their attitudes would be. Before Jack's release, many of the church members had offered their pity to the soon-to-be widow. But would they accept her as the wife of Jack Hunter, accused but walking free?

She put cornmeal, salt, and water to simmer over the fire and headed for the barn with her milk pail. She was nearly there when she saw that the barn door was open several inches.

"Sir Walter," she called.

The dog trotted out of the sheep pen.

Lucy stroked his broad forehead. "Good dog."

She stepped toward the barn door and pushed it open. "Go in," she told Sir Walter. He looked up at her, then scrambled through the doorway. She stepped in cautiously and watched him sniff about. He snuffled a pile of straw, then crossed to the calf's stall and exchanged stares with Tryphenia's young one. The calf bawled, and Sir Walter moved on to sniff the oxen's empty stalls, then stopped before the cow's tie-up and yipped. Tryphenia turned a large eye toward the dog and mooed. Sir Walter pranced back toward Lucy.

"If anything was wrong, you'd tell me, wouldn't you?"

Just to be sure, she latched the door and shook it. The latch stayed in place; it wasn't likely the wind had blown the door open.

She shook her head and went about feeding the animals. After milking Tryphenia, she led her to the pasture, then took the calf out and released the sheep from their small pen into the larger fenced field.

At last she was able to gather the eggs. She found only one. She took it and her milk into the kitchen.

When she was ready to leave for church, she peeked into the bedroom.

Jack lay drowsing against his pillow but opened his eyes and smiled when he saw her.

"Good," she said. "You finished your breakfast." She picked up his empty dishes, knowing he was watching her and feeling inordinately pleased.

"You're going with the Ellises?" he asked.

"Yes, they said they would stop for me. I'll be going out to the lane to see if they're coming now."

He smiled. "You look fine."

Disconcerted, she shrugged. "I look as I always do on the Lord's Day." She felt her cheeks redden under his scrutiny.

"I hope. . ." He frowned and adjusted the sling that kept his fractured arm immobile.

"What?" she asked.

"I hope folks won't turn against you because you married me."

"No one has been unkind. In fact, several families have helped me and inquired about your health."

"I'm glad. Lucy, I. . ." She waited, but he just smiled and waved his hand. "You should go. Don't keep the Ellises waiting."

❦

The next week flew by as Lucy settled into her new activities. She soon found that she could no longer keep Jack confined to bed. Ten days after the captain hauled him home in the oxcart, Jack limped to the outhouse while leaning on her shoulder. After that, he insisted on dressing every morning and joining her in the kitchen for meals. Before long he was shelling peas for her and casting bullets, though he still could not lift more than a trifle or perform strenuous work.

"I believe I shall be able to milk the cow soon," he said one morning. He sat on a stool in the kitchen while she clipped his hair.

"Perhaps," Lucy said. She tried to maintain a balance between encouragement and restraint. So far his wounds were healing well, but his tendency to attempt harder labor each day concerned her. "We don't want you doing much with that arm until the bones have knit."

His ribs worried her, too. She saw him grimace when he shifted his weight, and he became short of breath whenever he expended any effort.

Jack put his good hand up to feel how short she was trimming his unruly locks. "I've gotten rather shaggy, haven't I?"

She chuckled. "I didn't want to say so, but I hardly recognized my husband." She ran her hand through his hair, holding out the strands she would cut next. Jack sat very still, and suddenly the intimacy of the moment struck her. She finished the job as quickly as she could, not looking into his eyes as she worked around the front, where the hair wanted to fall over his eyebrows.

"Perhaps you should take up barbering," he said.

"Nay, I don't think I would like that."

"Oh? I was hoping you would, and I'd have you trim my beard, as well."

"Surely you can do that better than I." She put the handles of the scissors in his hand.

"Don't you think you'd be ashamed to have anyone see me after I trimmed my own beard left-handed?"

She hesitated, then took the scissors back. "I've never done this before, you know. Perhaps I shall do a worse job than you would with either hand."

She clipped away timidly at first, then with more confidence, at last standing back to eye her work critically. "There. Not a perfect job, but you'd pass in a mob."

His eyes twinkled. "Next time I'm in a mob, I'll recollect that."

Lucy fetched the broom, swept up the clippings, and tossed them into the fire.

"Not saving it to stuff a pillow?" Jack asked with a smile.

She stared at him. "I stuff my pillows with feathers, if you please."

He stood slowly, using the chair back for leverage. " 'Tis what my mother did when I was a lad. That little embroidered cushion yonder is filled with my baby hair." He nodded toward the bedroom door.

Lucy blinked, unsure how to answer. At last she said, "Well, she was a doting mother."

"Yes, and I was her only child to survive infancy."

"Then we can't blame her for being a mite smothery, can we?" Lucy said. "Now, I must get back to my loom."

She hurried up to the loft. Why did her heart pound so? It was only a haircut, and a badly needed one at that. Was it because a bit of quiet fire had returned to his eyes, and more and more he resembled the young man she'd fancied four years ago? All those years she'd longed for Jack to notice her again. One glance would have satisfied her, she'd told herself. And now, here she was actually married to him and still craving his notice. But when he did look at her and attempt to tease her, panic filled her breast.

As she moved her shuttle back and forth, she considered his words. Was he merely trying to ease the tension between them so their odd marriage would seem more normal? Or could it be he hoped to woo her again? She knew she didn't want to go on as they were, living as brother and sister might, sharing the work of the farm, each benefiting from the other's labor. She'd had as much with her mother.

No, she would be very disappointed if things did not change soon. But was it her place to instigate change? Or was that what Jack was trying to do this morning? As the shuttle flew back and forth through the warp, she renewed her prayers for wisdom and discretion in her marriage, but added a meek plea, if the Lord so willed, for a bit of passion.

When she came in from milking that evening, Jack was leaning on the table, and on it lay a quilt and a lantern.

"What's this?" she asked.

"My bedding. I shall sleep in the barn tonight."

Lucy stared at him. "To what purpose?"

"Why, to protect our property, and to. . .to give you back your bedchamber." His stare came across as a challenge.

Lucy felt her annoying blush return. It seemed that whenever Jack looked at her for more than a moment, her cheeks flushed.

"That's not necessary," she said. "After all, it's your bedchamber, and was before I came here. I am comfortable out here on the pallet, and you need to have your healing rest each night."

"I'm much better now, and I'll not have my wife sleeping on the floor one more night. Please don't fight me on this, Lucy."

She pressed her lips together and studied his face. How important was this to Jack? Would it set him back to sleep on the straw pile in the barn? She supposed not, as long as he had clean bedding to lie on. The nights were warm, and lying on the straw, while not as comfortable as a featherbed, might ease his mind enough to let him sleep peacefully.

She had no doubt that Jack's full recovery was dependent on his keeping his pride intact, and occupying the bed while she slept on the floor threatened it. Moving to the barn seemed to be the answer he'd found, and he was set on it.

"Fine." She set down the bucket of milk and began her supper preparations. Jack said nothing, and after a minute she looked over at him.

He was watching her and gave a nod when she caught his eye. "That's settled, then."

"Yes, Jack. But I doubt you are ready to split wood or swing a scythe, so please don't try it." She began cutting the tops off a bunch of carrots.

"I should be haying."

"We'll trade work with Sam Ellis, or buy hay."

"I'll not buy hay when I've fields begging to be mowed."

"Then we'll hire someone. Will Carver, perhaps."

He scowled. "In a week I'll be ready to do a full day's work."

Lucy stopped chopping the vegetables. "Perhaps yes, perhaps no. You mustn't go too quickly."

"I don't like having you haul water and firewood and hoe the corn."

She shrugged. "That's as it must be for now. It won't last." But she could tell by his expression that he was still not content. All right, she would give in to him on the sleeping arrangements, though it wasn't at all the next step she'd hoped to see in their relationship.

"At least we'll know if anyone pokes about the barn at night." She chopped the carrots into pieces and tossed them into her stew kettle.

"If someone's pilfering from us, we'll soon know it."

"Perhaps. . ." She turned to face him. "Perhaps you should take your gun with you."

"Oh, I don't think this phantom is desperate. He's only been taking a bit ⟨of⟩ food."

"You don't think it's something more sinister?"

"What do you mean?" He walked over to stand beside her, and Lucy wa⟨s⟩ keenly aware of his nearness.

"Nothing. It's just that. . .well, while you were in the jail, I wondere⟨d⟩ if perhaps the person who killed Barnabas Trent was lingering about th⟨e⟩ neighborhood."

Jack frowned. "This petty thievery doesn't seem to fit in with violen⟨t⟩ murder."

"No, but. . .at least take Sir Walter with you."

Jack laughed. "Nay, the dog is your comfort. Keep him with you." H⟨e⟩ limped to the table and picked up the bedding. "I'll take these things to th⟨e⟩ barn and look around."

"Supper will be ready in a bit."

She watched him go, holding back her impulse to advise him to take th⟨e⟩ stick he'd been using as a cane while hobbling about the house and dooryar⟨d.⟩ Jack was as loath to surrender his independence as she was, it seemed.

She set the kettle on a pothook over the fire and opened her bin of whea⟨t⟩ flour. Biscuits tonight. Jack liked her biscuits. As she kneaded the dough, sh⟨e⟩ glanced toward the corner where she'd been leaving her straw pallet during th⟨e⟩ day. Sir Walter was curled up on the edge of it.

"Aye, you can have that bed tonight," she said, pounding the dough extr⟨a⟩ hard. What had she expected? That she would move from the pallet on th⟨e⟩ floor into her husband's bed with him? Apparently that was another thing Jac⟨k⟩ was not ready for, and she would certainly not be the one to broach the subject.

Would she ever have a real marriage? She had bound herself to Jack, and i⟨n⟩ so doing had helped save his farm and perhaps his life. Did his feelings for he⟨r⟩ go beyond gratitude, as she hoped they would? He was free now, not only fro⟨m⟩ prison; he was free to establish a family and give her the warm, loving hom⟨e⟩ she had always craved. But Jack seemed interested only in getting on with th⟨e⟩ farm work. Did he regret his impulsive decision to marry her?

She prayed as she rolled and shaped the dough. *Lord, I need Your grace. Hel⟨p⟩ me to be the best wife he could want. And someday, if it be in Your plan, let me trul⟨y⟩ be his wife.*

At supper Jack talked about the livestock and his plans for haying and har⟨-⟩ vesting the grain crops. Lucy smiled at his eagerness and forced herself not t⟨o⟩ protest when he suggested that he would be back to full strength soon.

"Do you want to open your school again?" he asked as she refilled his cu⟨p⟩ with milk.

Lucy hesitated. "We've been so busy, I'm not sure. What do you advise?"

Jack smiled, and she felt her heart contract the way it used to when sh⟨e⟩

knew he'd walked a mile out of his way just to see her.

"Do as you wish, but I'll give you the same advice you gave me: Don't do anything too soon. If you need your strength for harvest and preserving and weaving, perhaps you should not hold school just now."

She nodded. "Thank you. I'll think about it."

When he rose to go to the barn, her disappointment again assailed her. He hadn't changed his mind. "Won't you take the dog?"

"Nay. If our egg stealer came around, that hound would scare him away before I got a good look at him."

Chapter 14

The hour was late, and Jack's eyelids drooped with weariness. He stirred, grimacing at the pain that still lanced his side too frequently. What good would it do to stay awake any longer? No one was prowling about. Lucy had imagined it. Perhaps the men who had done chores for her had taken a few eggs and sneaked a few vegetables from the garden.

He'd sat in the barn doorway for the better part of an hour, to be sure Lucy had gone to bed. He'd seen the light of her candle go from the front room to the bedchamber. After a few minutes, it was extinguished.

Good, he thought. *She'll be comfortable tonight.*

He hadn't really wanted to distance himself from her. In fact, while she'd stood so close to him that morning to cut his hair, he'd wanted to sweep her into his arms and kiss her. Her gentle touch was almost a caress, although to her he supposed it was nothing, only another chore.

But those ten minutes had told him that he couldn't keep sleeping in the house. He didn't want his wife sleeping on the floor any longer, now that he was recovering, and he was certain she wouldn't sleep in the bedroom while he was there, though he couldn't help longing to have her beside him. What other solution was there?

He inched his aching arm into a marginally better position. He was married to a beautiful woman, yet he was sleeping in the barn.

Don't think that way, he chided himself. *Be thankful. The loveliest woman in the district is in your house. So far, she's been willing to stay with you. She hasn't mentioned leaving. She's humbled herself to nurse you.*

But then, Lucy would probably do that for anyone. It was her nature to be kind and to give of herself. She came here as a favor to him, and he wouldn't ask more of her. He'd already asked too much. How had he ever thought he might ask her to share his life with him? He was amazed that she was willing to go on living here now.

Perhaps someday, Lord, You will allow us to form a true family. Give me strength to wait for that time. And, if possible, please allow Lucy to see me as a man who can provide for her and who is worthy of her love.

The door creaked on its hinges. Jack froze.

He held his breath and tensed, seeing a dark form silhouetted against the gray sky. He waited for the intruder to come closer. The door thumped softly shut. Jack determined to put all of his hoarded energy into his attack.

Lucy awoke to Sir Walter's fierce barking. The dog flung himself against the closed bedroom door and scratched its lower panel, alternately barking and whining.

She lit the lantern with shaking fingers and grabbed her shawl from its peg, throwing it about her shoulders. When she opened the door, Sir Walter catapulted to the front door of the house and repeated his frantic performance.

"Steady," she cautioned, reaching over his head to lift the latch. She hadn't barred the door, lest Jack decided to return to the house for something. As soon as she drew the door in a few inches, Sir Walter raced off in a straight course to the barn, yowling as he ran.

Lucy stumbled after him, holding the lantern high. As she approached the barn door, she heard a muffled cry and a thud, followed by the clatter of a tool falling to the floor.

"Jack?" she called.

The barn door stood open, and the dog was already inside. His barking had lowered to a menacing growl punctuated by yips. She wished she'd brought the musket.

"Jack?"

"Here," he panted. "Bring the light."

She crept forward toward the cow's stall, where she saw her husband kneeling over a twitching form. Jack held the intruder down with his knee squarely in the other's back, but he clutched his right arm tight against his side, and his face was lined with pain.

Lucy hurried toward him and gasped when she saw his captive's face. "Why, it's a boy!"

"Is it?" Jack sighed. "I'm grateful. Any bigger or stronger, and he'd have bested me. I'm weak as a kitten."

The lad squirmed, and Jack pushed his head into the straw with his good hand. "Lie still if you know what's good for you. My wife's a terror, and she'll kill you if you move."

Lucy opened her mouth to protest, but Jack looked up at her, still panting, and winked. Gingerly he moved off the boy's body and sat on the floor. "Now, what's your name?"

The boy raised his head, throwing Lucy an anxious glance. "Simon. Simon Brady."

Jack frowned. "I don't know anyone named Brady."

"My father lives up the coast."

"Ah. And what are you doing in my barn, Simon Brady?"

"I. . ." He looked down and bit his lip.

"Come to forage for your supper, eh?" Jack said.

"Aye, sir," the boy whispered. "I'm sorry."

"It's a bit late to repent of your stealing. You've been at it for some time."

Simon hung his head, and Lucy thought she saw the glint of tears in his eyes.

"And why have you left your father's house and become a criminal, eh?" Jack's stern voice made Lucy feel sorry for the boy, but she said nothing.

Simon sniffed and looked at Jack from the corner of his eye. "I thought to join the militia, sir. I heard the captain here is a fine man to serve under."

"And what did your father think of that?"

The boy's mouth worked for a moment before he said, "He forbade me."

"So you ran away."

"Aye," Simon whispered.

Jack let that hang in the air for a moment before asking, "So did you see Captain Murray?"

"Yes, sir."

"And did he take you into his company?"

Simon's head sank lower. "Nay. He said I'm too young."

"Ah."

Simon darted a glance at Lucy, then raised his chin and looked at Jack. "He said I might come back when I'm sixteen."

"And how long will that be?" Jack asked.

Simon slouched once more. "Three years."

"Did you think to live off my eggs and milk for three years?"

The boy said nothing.

Lucy cleared her throat. "Shall I fetch the constable, husband?"

Jack looked up and frowned. "Not just yet." He turned to Simon. "Boy, I'm going to consult with my wife about what to do with you. We could have you put in irons and flogged for this."

Simon sniffed, and his shoulders trembled. He didn't look at either of them.

"You stay right here," Jack said. "Don't you move so much as your little finger, you understand?"

"Aye."

Jack reached toward Lucy, and she gave him her hand. He groaned as he got to his feet, then stood still for a moment, wincing and holding his right arm close to his abdomen.

"Where is your sling?" she whispered, peering at his ashen face.

"Lost in the scuffle. I'll find it in the morning. Step outside with me." Jack sought out the dog. "Battle, keep watch!"

The dog growled and settled down on his haunches a yard from the boy. Simon cringed away from him.

Jack limped out the door, and Lucy followed, shutting it behind them.

"What shall we do?" she asked.

Jack looked up at the stars. "I'd hate to see the boy treated the way I was, although he deserves some punishment."

"I only said that about the constable to frighten him," Lucy admitted, "the way you said I might kill him."

Jack chuckled. "He's terrified of you now."

"Oh, Jack, I expect he's afraid to go home. Perhaps his father would beat him."

"That may be why he left home to begin with, although many a boy romanticizes about the military life."

"Shall we tell him he can sleep in the barn tonight?"

Jack frowned. "I want to make sure he had nothing to do with Trent's death first."

Lucy caught her breath. "He's a boy."

"Yes, and Trent was a mean old man. If he caught the lad stealing and came at him, who can say what might have happened?"

"All right, then, you talk to him. But let me know how it turns out."

Jack gave her hand a squeeze. "If it's not too much trouble, I think I'll be ready for some willow bark tea when I'm through here."

"Oh, Jack, you haven't cracked your ribs again, have you?"

"I don't think so, but I'm sore, and my arm aches." He held up his left hand and examined it in the starlight. "I expect I skinned my knuckles, as well. I hope I didn't hurt the lad."

❧

At the end of half an hour, Jack felt satisfied that he had the boy's entire story and that Simon was telling the truth. He bade the lad to lie down on his own blanket and promised to bring him some food, then left him in the barn with the dog.

He found Lucy sitting by the kitchen fire. She'd put on her outer clothing and had the tea steeping for him. She started to rise as he entered, but Jack waved his hand. "Sit."

"I'll need to check your injuries."

"It can wait." He settled on a stool across the hearth from her and clasped his hands together between his knees. "He's not a bad boy. He's been hiding in the woods all summer, making the rounds of farms in the night for food."

"Where has he slept?"

Jack sighed. "He lived in Trent's barn for a while, before Richard came. Most nights, though, he camped out under the stars. The weather's been warm, so I don't think he suffered much. But like all boys, he's always hungry. Hence, the thievery."

"I don't want to press charges." Lucy searched his face with an uncertainty that led Jack to believe she would follow his lead in this, whatever he suggested.

"Nor do I," he told her. "I asked Simon about Trent's murder, but he says he had nothing to do with it. In fact, he claims he didn't even know what happened for weeks. He did notice a lot of men at Trent's place one day—probably the day of the murder or mayhap when they took inventory of the estate. After that he never saw the old man again. But he swears he didn't harm Goodman Trent, and I believe him. Lucy, he's either an honest boy or the best liar I ever met."

She leaned back in her chair, a frown puckering her brow. Jack watched her, thinking how pretty she was in the soft firelight, with her hair hanging loose about her shoulders.

"What are you thinking?" he asked.

She hesitated. "Jack, you need help right now. If the boy were to stay on and give you aid with the mowing and the wheat harvest. . ."

He smiled. "I like the idea. With a strong boy to help, I'm sure I could handle the work that needs doing before cold weather sets in. I can get to know him better, and perhaps in time I can discern whether to contact his father. Yes, I believe I'll put it to him that he can work off his debt for the things he stole."

Lucy smiled, and Jack's heart flipped. "Drink your tea now," she said, rising and fetching his mug.

"Aye. And when I go back to the barn, I'd like to take the lad something to eat, if you can fix it. Not much, just enough to keep his belly from growling and keeping me awake tonight."

She stopped with the kettle in her hand. "You'll sleep in the barn with him?"

"That was my intention."

Lucy turned away, and he sensed that she was not happy.

"You're not afraid he'll cut my throat in the night after I offer him food and a place to stay, are you?"

She shook her head but kept her back to him.

"What, then?"

She brought a roll of linen from the blanket chest. "Let me bind up your arm again."

As she worked, he tried to assess her mood, but he couldn't read her expression. At last she stood back and surveyed the new sling. "Now, you mustn't do anything vigorous for a few days."

"Lucy," he said gently, "you don't want me to bunk with Simon. Why?"

"It's nothing. Only. . ."

"Speak, wife. Please." He laid his free hand on her sleeve.

She stepped away from him. "How will it look to a hired boy if his master sleeps in the barn?"

Once again, Jack tried unsuccessfully to read her expression. "Perhaps he'd think I don't trust him yet, which I don't."

She bit her lip and picked up his empty mug. "You know best."

Somehow Jack felt he had failed a test. Her words did not match her thoughts, he was certain, but what those thoughts were, he couldn't divine.

What did she expect of him? Surely she couldn't mean. . .

He eyed her as she straightened the dishes and banked the fire. There was no softness in her straight back and stiff shoulders. Nay, she couldn't mean she wanted a husband's caresses.

He stood and breathed slowly for a moment until the pain in his side passed.

She brought him a dish of cold stew with a slab of corn pone on top. "Take him that."

Jack started to speak, but she plucked a candlestick off the mantel and hurried into the bedchamber. The door closed softly, but with a finality that assured him his place tonight was in the barn.

He looked about for another blanket. A quilt his mother had pieced lay over the back of the chair. Lucy had hauled the straw pallet back up to the loft, he realized, but she'd left the quilt here. He picked it up and took it, with the dish of food for the boy, to the barn.

It was very quiet. When he entered, Battle—no, Sir Walter, he corrected himself—gave a low woof.

"Simon?" he called softly.

A snore greeted him. Jack sighed. If he set the food down, the dog would eat it, but he refused to stay up and guard the boy's supper. Still, he couldn't bring himself to waken the lad. He supposed he could take the dog to the house and return. Of course, when Simon awoke in the morning and found him there. . .

What does it matter? he asked himself. Who cared what a hired boy thought of his master and mistress?

At once he knew the answer. Lucy cared. She didn't want it getting about the neighborhood that she'd relegated Jack to the barn as soon as his wounds were healed. That's the way it would look, or at least she probably feared it would. He didn't want her to be anxious over more village gossip.

He set the dish beside the sleeping boy and gave a low whistle. "Come, Sir Walter."

The dog scrambled up and padded to him. Jack took him outside, closed the barn door firmly, and limped back to the house. He and the mongrel entered as quietly as possible. Jack hesitated a moment, staring at the bedroom door. No light showed from the crack beneath it.

"Go lie down by the fire," he whispered to the dog. "And mind your manners."

Jack slowly climbed the ladder to the loft, setting his teeth against the pain, and felt about until he found the straw tick. He was clumsy in the dark, stumbling against Lucy's spinning wheel and the clock reel that wound the skeins of yarn. At last he felt the rustic mattress and managed to unfold the quilt, pull it over himself, and sink in a weary heap on the pallet.

Chapter 15

Lucy rose early and dressed in the gray light of dawn, wondering if Jack had everything he needed in the barn. She scurried to the kitchen and snatched up the water bucket. During her quick trip to the well, she prayed that God would give her husband wisdom in dealing with Simon Brady.

She lugged the bucket of water back to the house and stepped over the threshold, then stopped when she saw Jack climbing down the ladder.

He gave her a sheepish smile. "Good morning."

"You. . .slept in the loft?"

"Aye. I've no wish to subject you to a boy's speculation or a town's gossip."

She stood beside her worktable. Was she supposed to thank him?

"Lucy. . ." The question in his voice needed a response.

She whirled toward him with a forced smile. "I'll get you some wash water. And you make that boy wash, too."

While Jack went to fetch Simon from the barn, she set out double portions of samp, along with a great quantity of sausage and applesauce. In moments, it all disappeared. The boy drank a full quart of milk to wash down all the food he put away.

Jack worked outside with him all morning. When they came into the house for dinner, Lucy learned that Simon had received instruction in using a scythe. He was a well-proportioned boy, taller than Lucy, though several inches shorter than Jack. Auburn hair and green eyes accented his tanned face. He was thin but seemed capable of a full day's work.

"He needs gloves," Jack said. "His hands are blistering. I believe I have a pair of doeskin gloves in the bottom of the clothespress."

Lucy found them, and after dinner the two went out again. She refrained from cautioning Jack against using his arm too much.

When she came in from an hour in the garden, she prepared to pickle a batch of beets. Going to the bedchamber for a large apron her mother had lent her, she noticed that all of Jack's clothes had been removed from the pegs and the clothespress. Frowning, she climbed to the loft. His things were folded in a neat pile on a stool beneath the eaves, on the other side of the loft from her hand loom and spinning wheel.

So he saw this arrangement as permanent. But it was silly to feel hurt, wasn't it? He wasn't rejecting her. He was only going on as he had for the past four years.

92

Still, she couldn't help remembering the moment in the jail when he had held her in his arms. They'd had that one glorious moment just after their wedding, a moment of desperate hope for a life together. At least it had been that way for her. What had it been for Jack? A moment of grim satisfaction, knowing he'd stymied Dole and Rutledge?

Lucy caught herself up short, realizing she was angry. *Lord, why do I feel this way? Let me be content with what You have given me.*

She resolved to submit to this humiliating turn of events. If her husband wanted to live apart from her, so be it. Tears streamed down her cheeks, and she mopped them away with the hem of her apron.

Give thanks in all things, she told herself. As she went about her work, her anger cooled, and she was able to list her blessings. *Thank You, Lord, for my husband. Thank You for this snug little house, and for a stout barn and a thriving garden. Thank You for bringing Jack home, and for his health. And thank You for sending Simon. May he be a boon to Jack.*

When the two came in weary and dirty at suppertime, she was able to greet Jack with a cheerful smile.

"You look happy." His voice held a touch of wonder.

She spoke the truth from the depths of her heart. "I am happy."

As she set the table and heaped their plates with food, she felt him watching her. The thanks she received from him and Simon were gratifying, but it was the spark in Jack's eyes that made her pulse trip.

On Sunday Jack walked to church beside Lucy, with Simon trailing along behind them. The boy had shown reluctance about going to service, but Jack had given him no choice. The Hunter family was going to church.

His mother-in-law greeted them with obvious pleasure, and several other parishioners spoke to Jack outside the church, telling him they were glad he was well enough to attend meeting. There were others who did not speak to him or meet his gaze, but all in all, fewer people shunned him than he had expected, and no one outwardly reviled him. Alice Hamblin even invited them to come and take dinner with her after church and bring the boy along. It was Jack's first meeting with her since he'd regained consciousness, and he was glad she showed no animosity toward him.

He sat between Lucy and Simon, listening to Parson Catton's homily on honesty and thinking how appropriate it was for the first sermon Simon had heard in months. Yet after a time, the truth of the scripture pierced his heart, and Jack began to feel guilty.

Was he being honest with Lucy? When he proposed to her in the jail, he hadn't expected they would have the opportunity to live together. He knew she hadn't, either. She seemed nervous now whenever he got too close, and he'd thought she was upset when he announced he would move to the barn. In the few days since Simon's arrival, she'd seemed more docile and content. Perhaps continuing to keep his distance was the best course.

Still, she was his wife. Wasn't a married couple supposed to be open and frank with each other? Or was there such a thing as being too honest? He tried to imagine Lucy's reaction if he told her how he truly felt about her. It would shock her for certain. It might even be enough to cause her to pack up and move back to her mother's cottage. He didn't want that to happen. No, he would bide his time and hope that eventually he could show her what she meant to him and they could start their marriage over, not as a business arrangement but as a love match that would last a lifetime.

He glanced at her. Lucy was watching the pastor, eyes forward. Jack wondered how she could concentrate on the parson so intently. He was barely able to breathe steadily when he peeked at her profile. The way her hair was pulled back sleekly above her ear tempted him to reach up and touch it. He knew how satiny it would feel and how beautiful she would be when she turned in amazement to stare a rebuke at him, her cheeks flushing at his boldness.

When had he acted like such a schoolboy? If Lucy could listen to Catton without being distracted, so could he. Just as he turned to face the pulpit again, Jack noticed a delicate pink blush flooding his wife's face. Her long, feathery eyelashes swept down and lay against her smooth cheek. Jack pulled in a ragged breath and stared at the parson.

After services, Captain Murray approached them in the churchyard. His wife, Katherine, came with him, and their two little daughters clung to her hands.

"Hunter, I'm glad to see you up and about," the captain boomed.

Jack shook his hand, then wished he hadn't. He'd left the sling off, and Murray was far too vigorous.

"Who's the boy with you?" Murray asked.

"That's my new hired help," Jack said. He beckoned to Simon, and the boy stepped forward but stared at the ground, digging a hole in the dirt with the toe of his shoe.

"I believe you've met Simon Brady," Jack said.

"Oh, yes." Murray looked the boy over. "I thought you'd gone back to Yarmouth."

Simon shook his head.

"Well, I think you'll make a good farmhand."

Jack nodded. "He's been a big help with the haying."

"Well, now, Hunter," the captain said in a jovial voice, "I've kept your oxen a fortnight longer than we stipulated. Suppose I return them tomorrow and give you a day's labor with the scythe."

Jack noticed that several men were watching them with unabashed curiosity, and he knew Murray had timed his offer so that a large part of the congregation would hear it and take it as his endorsement. This was not the time to refuse a friend's offer due to misplaced pride.

"I would appreciate that most kindly," he said.

Lucy's eyes glowed as Katherine Murray stepped forward and extended her hand.

"Goody Hunter, I haven't had a chance to congratulate you on your marriage."

"Thank you," Lucy said with a little curtsy. "If it's convenient for you, I wish you and your daughters would accompany your husband tomorrow and spend the day with me."

Jack continued to chat with the captain about the harvest, keeping half an ear cocked toward the women's conversation. It pleased him greatly that Katherine Murray was showing Lucy her favor.

"I seem to have far too many cabbages," Lucy said. "If you can bring a crock with you, we shall both have pickled cabbage when the day is done."

Isn't that just like Lucy, Jack thought, *sharing her bounty with others.* She was both compassionate and diligent: the ideal wife. She was frugal, too. All during his time in jail, she had managed on what she'd earned herself by teaching and weaving, never once needing to tip over the clothespress for the coins he'd hidden there against a day of need. Yes, he had chosen well.

Jack saw Alice greeting some of her many patients as she waited for them. "Pardon us," he said to the Murrays, "but we'd best be going. We are to be guests of my wife's mother for dinner."

⬱

Lucy was setting the table on Wednesday evening when Jack brought in the full bucket of foamy milk. "Where's Simon?" she asked.

"Putting up the oxen," Jack said. "Lucy, I need to talk to you."

"What is it?" She stopped with the spoons in her hand and studied his face. Jack seemed anxious, more agitated than she'd seen him since he'd been able to leave his sickbed. "Has something happened?"

He leaned on the back of the chair. "I've spent near a week with that boy now, and he's beginning to trust me."

"I've noticed that, though he's still wary of me."

"That's my fault, and I'm sorry. I've begun trying to rectify it by assuring him that you are actually a kind-hearted woman, if a bit strict. And you know he appreciates your cooking."

"Thank you. But what is it that has you so concerned?"

"He told me. . ." Jack glanced toward the door, then met her eyes. "He says he saw a man go into my barn early in the summer and come out with an ax."

She stared at him, her fear returning. "When?"

Jack winced. "Simon wasn't sure of the day, but from what he told me, I believe it was about the time Trent was killed. Perhaps the day before I was arrested. He said he stayed hidden for a while after the man took the ax, and he saw me come out of the house not long after and hitch up the oxen. I broke some ground with my team the day before Dole and Rutledge came for me."

"Could Simon describe the man he saw?"

"He did, but his account was vague. At first it sounded as if he were describing Barnabas Trent himself."

Lucy caught her breath. She hadn't considered that. If Goodman Trent had come and "borrowed" the ax without permission, then whoever visited him at his cottage would have found the weapon ready at hand.

"Could it have been he?"

Jack shook his head. "Nay. Simon knew Trent when I described him. He tried to pilfer some eggs over at his place one morning, and Trent nearly caught him. After that Simon stayed away from there until that day when he saw the gathering of men. The next day he went back out of curiosity and saw that there was no smoke coming from the chimney and the house was empty."

Lucy nodded. "So. . .what did he say about the man who took the ax?"

"Simon was about to sneak into my barn when the door opened. It startled him, and he hid 'round the corner. He watched the man come out with the ax and walk into the trees."

"Not down the path?"

"No. It sounded as though he took a shortcut from the barn to the lane."

"What did he look like?"

Jack scratched his chin. "Simon mostly saw his back. He was wearing a blue jacket, dark breeches, and a hat of some sort. The lad couldn't recall what the hat was like, but the fellow wore shoes, not boots.

"Half the men in town would fit that description. Was he tall or short? Old or young?"

"Simon thought he had brown hair and a beard, but he was a bit fuzzy on that. Said the ax caught his notice more than anything."

"Would he recognize the man if he saw him again?" Lucy asked.

"He thought he might." Jack was quiet for a moment, his expression pensive.

"You've formed an opinion, haven't you?"

He met her gaze. "It may be ridiculous, but I can't help thinking. . .could it have been Richard Trent who stole my ax?"

Chapter 16

Jack saw Lucy's blue eyes cloud with confusion. "How could it have been Richard Trent? He was in Portsmouth when his father was killed."

"Was he?"

Her lips thinned, then twitched. He drew a deep breath as pride surged through him. He'd married well. His wife was hardworking and intelligent. Not only that, she was striking, with her golden hair, creamy skin, and sweet features. Although her beauty had always held him captive, it was not the main reason he'd pursued her. No, it was the cleverness and courage she was exhibiting now.

"Richard does wear a blue jacket," she mused. "You're thinking he might have returned to the family farm before his father's death?"

Jack ran a hand through his hair. "Richard could have come back here without anyone in the village seeing him. If he had a fight with his father—say, over the property—killed him, and went away again. . ."

"And then, after the constables notified him of Barnabas's death, he resurfaced to claim the estate." Lucy nodded. "It's possible. I'm not saying I believe it."

"Not yet," Jack agreed. "It's only a theory, but I intend to put it to the test."

"How?"

"Have you finished weaving Trent's linen?"

"Nearly. I could be done with it tomorrow if I get to my mother's early."

"That's fine." Jack frowned. "Though it occurs to me you need a large loom here so you don't have to leave home to ply your trade."

"Mother says I can bring it here if I wish. She spins some, but she has no time to weave."

"Do you want it here?"

Lucy's eyes shone with eagerness. "I'd like that very much. I could help you more if I could weave here. It's a fine old loom, Jack, and more folks ask for my linen than I can supply. I enjoy making it, and if I didn't have to leave home to do so, I could accomplish so much more."

He smiled. "Then you shall have it. Now that I have the oxen back, there's no reason I can't haul the loom over here."

She clasped her hands together. "Where shall we put it?"

He hesitated. "In the loft?" Would there be room enough under the eaves for his pallet with the bulky loom up there?

"I suppose so," Lucy said. "It would take up too much floor space elsewhere."

97

"Fine." He would worry about where he would sleep later. Seeing her pleasure was worth being a bit crowded. "I'll move it as soon as I can. But finish Trent's order first."

"And then what?"

"Then Simon and I shall deliver his cloth."

When Jack came knocking at the door of Richard Trent's cottage, the young man stood back in surprise. "Goodman Hunter. How may I help you?"

Jack held up the bundle of cloth. "My wife is finished with your linen, sir. I believe this squares us."

Trent took the material with a nod. "Thank you. I'm sadly in need of new clothing. My father's few garments were threadbare. I don't suppose your wife sews for people?"

"No, she doesn't." Jack tried not to let his ire at the thought of Lucy stitching for this man show on his face.

"Good day, then." Trent started to close the door, and Jack realized that Simon, who had hung back behind him, might not have had a good look at the man yet.

"Oh, I say!" He reached out, and Trent paused, then opened the door wide again. "I hear you're keeping the property and taking up a farmer's life." Jack moved down off the doorstep, and Trent came forward into the doorway, just as he'd hoped. Jack glanced toward Simon and said, "By the way, this be my hired boy."

Trent nodded in Simon's direction without showing interest in the boy. "Yes, I've decided I've had enough sailing."

"Your father left you the farm, then."

"Oh, yes. I am his only heir. My sisters and brother were killed in the Indian raid of '98, and my mother, as well."

Jack frowned in sympathy. "I've heard tell about that year, but it was before my family moved here."

"My father took me with him that day into the village. We were one of the outlying farms then, and folks told him it was dangerous to live so far from the fort."

"Someone has to make a beginning, or this wild country would never be settled."

"Exactly," said Trent. "But after my mother died, Father wasn't the same man. He'd got this land for back taxes and hoped to build it up into a grand place, but. . ." He shook his head.

Jack eyed Richard with speculation. He recalled the many times his father had groused about his boundary disputes with the Trents, but Jack had never bothered to learn the details. Hesitantly he said, "There was bad blood between your father and mine."

"It's too bad they could never agree. My father had planned to buy the

98

adjoining land. But while he was grieving my mother's death, Isaac Hunter bought the land he'd been wanting, and he couldn't expand the farm."

"So that was what caused the rift," Jack said.

"Aye, that and general bitterness on my father's part." Richard gave him a rueful smile. "It didn't help that all the men in town ragged him for losing out to a ne'er-do-well. No offense to you, Jack."

Jack smiled. "We've both had our family problems, eh?" He looked around the yard and noticed that the bushes had been trimmed back and the roof mended with new shingles that stood out bright against the weathered ones.

"My father never forgave yours. Made his life difficult whenever he had the chance."

"I'm guessing he didn't make your life easy, either."

Trent's face darkened. "It's no secret Father and I didn't get along." He sighed. "Ten years I stayed away. Perhaps I should have come back; I don't know."

"You never made up your differences, then?"

"Nay, we were both stubborn."

Jack wondered if Richard was telling him the truth. He glanced at Simon, but the boy had wandered away a few steps and was watching a chipmunk scurry over the stone wall that bordered Trent's pasture.

"Funny, I thought my father hated yours because the old man got this land ahead of him," Jack said.

Richard came down the steps into the sunlight. "It were the other way around. My father was one of the first settlers. He was here a good many years afore you folk came."

Jack scratched his cheek. "I guess that's right, now that I think on it. Then it wasn't my father who defaulted on the taxes here."

Trent laughed and took a clay pipe from his pocket. "Nay, it was another fellow. But I doubt your father paid his taxes promptly, either."

"True enough. His creditors had him confined for debt more than once."

"Yes, and I recall my father had yours taken up for slander once, too." He pulled out a tobacco pouch and began to fill his pipe.

"Aye, he spent a day in the stocks for it," Jack said.

"That must have been hard for your mother. I was sorry to hear she passed on. She was a good woman."

"Thank you." Jack extended his hand to Trent with mixed feelings. "Well then, we're neighbors once again, Richard. And I haven't welcomed you back properly."

Trent took his hand. "Thank you. I know what they're saying about you, Jack, but I don't believe it."

Jack looked into Richard's eyes, searching for a hint of shiftiness but not finding it. Still, the man had been abroad ten years and could have learned to lie smoothly in order to protect himself. "Good day," Jack said.

He called to Simon, and the two headed down the path. As soon as they were out of sight of the cottage, Jack looked closely at the boy. "Well, was that the man who took my ax?"

"Oh, no, sir. Not him. He's too young."

"You said it wasn't an old man."

"Well. . ." Simon cocked his head. "Not all gray-haired like the one you say was him's father. But older than he, I'm sure, and not so leggy."

"All right. That's helpful."

⁂

"I'm glad it wasn't Trent's son," Lucy said when Jack told her what had transpired.

"So am I," Jack admitted, "but I'd hoped we could find out the truth and be done with this." He sank onto a stool by the kitchen table.

Lucy walked over to him and gently touched his shoulder. "This is wearing on you."

"Aye." Jack looked up at her, his eyes sparking. "And if Richard Trent asks you to sew for him, don't you do it!"

She stepped back, puzzled at his sudden animation. "Of course not. I've enough to do as it is."

"Good. Because if my wife makes breeches for any man, it should be me."

"Of course, Jack."

He turned back to the table, sinking his face into his hands. "Oh, Lucy, I'm so tired of this."

It tore her heart to see him in such low spirits. "Mayhap we should tell the constables Simon saw the ax taken."

"I don't trust Rutledge or Dole. They'd think I told the boy to say it in order to help my own cause."

Lucy sat on the stool opposite him.

Jack raised his head and gave her a melancholy smile. "We'll get on, wife."

"We must keep praying about this. I'm sure God will set things right in time."

Jack's gaze flew to the chest against the wall, where the Bible lay, then looked back at her. "I've been praying, but I've not been reading the scriptures as I ought."

"You can change that."

"Aye." He rubbed his right arm as he spoke, and Lucy got up to put some willow bark to steep. Her husband was growing strong again, but she knew that pain was never far from him.

"Perhaps. . ." Jack stopped.

She waited for a moment, then asked, "Perhaps what?"

"I thought we might read together. I always planned, if I had a family, to have devotion and family prayer."

Hope welled inside her. Such a course could only draw them closer. "I think that would be wonderful."

"I used to read Mother's Bible a lot, before. . ."

"I should have brought it to you at the jail."

"Nay. I asked Stoddard once, and he said they wouldn't let me have it. They allow the debtors books and all sorts of comfort, but not the felons."

"I read it sometimes, in the evening," she confided, pouring the tea into Jack's cup.

"Then we'll hold family worship after supper," he said.

A sudden thought came to Lucy. "Simon should hear the scripture, too."

"Yes, he should. I think the lad fears God the way he fears his father."

"I'm sorry to hear that."

Jack stretched his long legs out before him. "Simon is afraid to go home. He's certain his father will thrash him for running away and beat him even worse for not being there to help with the farm work this summer."

"And you feel his fear is justified?"

"He thinks his father is harder on him than on the younger children. Maybe it's true. He begged me not to tell his family he's here."

"Well then, we won't."

Lucy went about her work singing that afternoon. She could scarcely wait for supper to be over. When at last the three of them sat by the hearth and Jack took the Bible on his lap to read, her heart rejoiced.

He offered prayer and then read from Genesis, beginning with the Creation story. Simon paid close attention, and Lucy settled back in her chair. Jack had insisted she sit in the best one—his mother's ladder-back chair—and she reveled in comfort and contentment beyond any she'd ever felt.

When Jack reached the point where God created Eve for Adam, she felt her cheeks flush and studiously avoided looking at him.

" 'Therefore shall a man leave his father and his mother, and shall cleave unto his wife,' " Jack read.

He paused, and Lucy wondered if he was too embarrassed to go on. She knew the chapter ended, "And they shall be one flesh. And they were both naked, the man and his wife, and were not ashamed." He hadn't even read the words yet, but she felt blood suffuse her face, and she knew her cheeks were scarlet.

" 'Tis the best reason for a man to leave home," Jack said.

Simon looked up at him, his eyes troubled. "I left home, but not to marry."

"Aye," said Jack. "You be a bit young to think of taking a wife. But maybe you should think of sticking with your folks a mite longer."

Simon drew up his knees and wrapped his arms around them, resting his chin on them. "I miss Mam and Father."

"Are they so very cruel?" Jack asked.

Simon pressed his lips tight together. "Likely I'd be whipped, but. . ."

"I'm sure they miss you," Lucy said. "And what about those little brothers and sisters of yours?"

Simon blinked, then hid his face in his arms.

"Perhaps we've read enough for tonight," said Jack, glancing at the book in his lap.

Lucy stood. "Off to bed with you, Simon. I shall pray that God will soften your father's heart."

The boy stared up at her. "Would He do that?"

"I think He would, especially if you repent of your disobedience."

Simon took a candle and headed for the door.

"Douse the flame outside the barn," Jack reminded him.

"Aye. Good night, sir. Ma'am."

"Good night, Simon." Lucy smiled at him.

"Well," Jack said when the door was closed, "I expect we should turn in. The days grow shorter now."

Lucy nodded. "I must bank the fire."

"I'll do that."

She stepped aside to let him. When Jack had spread ashes over the hot coals, he stood and eyed her. Lucy wondered what he was thinking.

At last he said softly, "It comes to my mind that I've been remiss in our courtship, Goody Hunter."

Lucy pulled in a shaky breath. Her heart pounded and her lungs ached. "A married woman doesn't expect to be courted."

"Nay, but she ought to have had that before the wedding."

"It's hard for a man in jail to court a woman," she whispered.

"I'm not in jail now."

"No, you're not."

Jack reached toward her face with his left hand. Lucy closed her eyes. When his fingers touched her cheek and glided down her chin, she felt a jolt of anticipation.

"I believe I should court you properly," he said.

She gazed at him from under her lashes. How long had she waited for this moment? She wanted to throw herself into his arms, but that wouldn't be lady-like, and he'd just said he wanted things done properly.

"Perhaps tomorrow evening we can take a stroll together," he said. "There'll likely be a pretty moon to look at."

She swallowed hard, afraid that if he kept on she would soon be unable to breathe at all. "I should like that," she squeaked out.

He smiled and let his hand fall to his side.

"But you and Simon will be haying all day if the weather is fine," she protested. "You'll need your rest." At once she regretted having said it. Would he think she was trying to talk him out of paying attention to her?

Jack grinned. "I'll be sure not to tire myself too much so that my nurse will not object."

"In that case," she said, "I shall look forward to it." She turned toward the bedchamber with a pleasant fluttering in her stomach.

Chapter 17

"You stay here and churn for Goody Hunter this afternoon," Jack told Simon over dinner the next day.

Simon scowled. "I thought to help with the haying again."

"Nay. The field needs to dry one more day. And my wife has more need of you than I this afternoon. She must make butter, and you are just the lad to help her."

Lucy opened her mouth to speak, but Jack threw her a glance that silenced her. "You've got that special weaving order to do," he reminded her. "Set the boy up at the churn. He can do it."

Lucy nodded. Jack and Simon had gone to her mother's with the oxcart that morning, brought the big loom back, and set it up in the loft. Jack knew her fingers were itching to begin warping it for the new job they'd discussed—linsey-woolsey for a new jacket and breeches for Simon. The boy was outgrowing the clothes he'd come in, and they were getting ragged. Lucy had patched the breeches and given him an old shirt of Jack's, but he needed new clothes, there was no question.

When he went to the barn for his pitchfork, Jack looked toward the pasture. Clumps of evening primrose grew wild near the fence, and the sight of the bright yellow flowers made him smile. He wondered if Lucy had seen them. He paused only a moment, then hurried to pick a bunch. Feeling a bit silly, he carried them back to the house. When he opened the door, Simon was beating away with the churn dasher, up and down, up and down. His eyes widened as he spotted his master, but Jack put one finger to his lips, and Simon kept churning.

Jack raised his eyebrows in question, and Simon jerked his head toward the ladder. When Jack looked up, he saw Lucy, her back to them, working at her loom above, near the window in the little loft.

Sneaking forward, Jack laid the bouquet on the table and fetched a small jug. He dipped water into it from the bucket Lucy kept full near the hearth, then stood the flower stems in it.

Simon watched him, laughing silently. Jack shrugged and smiled, then hurried out to the barn. Let the boy laugh. If it were up to Jack to raise him, he wanted to show Simon that a man wasn't afraid to bring his wife a posy. Yes, and there were more things he wanted to do for Lucy, if she would let him. Tonight would perhaps clear the air on some things. He hoped he wouldn't be too nervous to speak freely with her.

He hurried to the hayfield that bordered the lane and began turning the swaths of hay with his long fork. He winced as he lifted a clump and flipped it. His arm was sound now, but he still felt a twinge of pain with each sideways movement. Well, Simon would help him put the hay up tomorrow. He'd wanted to save Lucy the drudgery of churning, and it wouldn't hurt the boy the way it would Jack to plunge the dasher up and down.

"Ho there, Hunter!"

Jack turned toward the voice and saw Charles Dole approaching him. The constable left the lane and walked across the hayfield, stepping through the drying grasses.

Jack lifted his hat and wiped his brow. What could Dole be wanting with him? Nothing good, he surmised. "Good day," he said.

Dole stopped a few feet from him, frowning. "I see you're back at your work now."

"And why shouldn't I be?"

Dole spat in the grass. "You think you can get away with foul murder, don't you? Everyone's coming 'round and saying you was innocent." Dole shook his head. "Oh, they may listen to the captain for now. Folks respect Murray. But the man's faith in you be misplaced. Someday they'll learn that fact."

Jack forced himself to stay calm as he met Dole's seething stare. "Goodman, I must get on with my work. I'll ask you to leave my property now."

Dole glared at him. "You'll hang yet, Hunter!" He spun around and stalked toward the lane.

❧

When the churning was done, Lucy sent Simon off to the field with a basket of fresh biscuits and butter and a jug of sweet cider. Once he was gone, she took a basin of water into the bedchamber, where she bathed and washed her hair, then put on her Sunday gown.

True, she liked to bathe on Saturday, but she usually waited until after the evening work was done and the supper dishes put away. And she certainly never wore her Sunday best to the table on Saturday. But tonight was special; she could feel it.

She took her workbasket out to the stump Jack used for a chopping block. It was behind the house, where there was no chance of the men seeing her from the hayfield, or passersby in the lane getting a glimpse of her with her hair unbound. As the fresh breeze of early September dried her tresses, she mended her stockings and put a button on Jack's gray linsey shirt.

Her husband had brought her flowers. The sight of them had startled her, and when she questioned Simon, he had admitted that the master had sneaked in with the posies just after dinnertime.

Lucy hummed as she secured the button with neat, tight stitches. Things were beginning to progress in her marriage at last. *Thank You, Father.*

After supper Jack again led the three of them in worship. It seemed to Lucy that his eyes strayed from the Bible to her face more often than ever, and as soon as they had read a chapter and offered prayer, he sent Simon to the barn.

"Wash well, mind you," Lucy called after the boy.

"Never fear," Simon replied.

Jack rose and set the Bible carefully on the chest. "Be you ready to stroll, Goody Hunter?"

Lucy smiled. "I am."

"It seems I'm walking out with the loveliest lady in Maine this night," he said, his eyes dancing.

Lucy ducked her head but could not suppress her joy.

"You'll want your shawl," Jack said, and before she could protest, he went to the peg near the door and fetched it, then wrapped it snugly around her shoulders.

He stood very close to her, and Lucy's pulse raced. "Thank you."

The moon was rising over the pasture as they stepped outside.

"You're leaving the sheep out tonight," she observed.

"Aye. Sir Walter has become a good shepherd. If any predators come around, he'll advise me."

She laughed. "With strident barking, no doubt."

Jack crooked his arm, and Lucy slipped her hand through it. "Would you like to walk to the creek?" he asked. "It's pretty by moonlight."

Lucy's heart sang as they ambled toward the little stream. Her hand felt warm in the bend of Jack's elbow.

He covered her fingers with his other hand. "Many a time over the years I've wished to walk thus with you."

Her stomach flipped, and she dared to look up at him. *My dear husband,* she thought.

Jack stopped at the edge of the water, where the creek widened and formed a pool. "I shall have to bring Simon fishing here one morning."

"Yes," she whispered.

After a long silence, Jack took her hand in his and walked along the edge of the water. She sensed that he was on edge and wondered if his earlier confidence had deserted him when he found himself alone with her.

"So," he said at last. "I want you to know. . ."

"Yes?" she prompted.

"You've made me very happy, Lucy."

She smiled up at him. "I'm glad."

"You've done everything I asked you to. You've worked hard and been frugal. You've never once complained."

"I have nothing to complain of."

He swung around slowly, and she realized with mild disappointment that they were heading back toward the house. When they came into the dooryard, Sir Walter raised his head and woofed.

"Hush," Jack said.

He opened the door, and Lucy stepped inside. She took off her shawl and hung it on its peg. Jack went to the fireplace and stirred up the coals, then dropped another log on them.

"Will you want a fire in your room tonight?" he asked.

My room, Lucy thought, once more disappointed. "Nay, I'll be fine."

"Very well, then."

She wondered how long this strained courtship would continue. She supposed she could put an end to it now by telling him to speak his mind or go up to his straw tick and leave her alone.

"Thank you for the flowers," she said.

"Oh, aye. I'm glad. . ." He halted and stooped for another stick of firewood.

"Jack. . ."

"Lucy, I want you to know. . ." He straightened and tossed the stick into the fire, then brushed off his hands. "I'm not doing this very well, but I had it all planned out."

"What, Jack?"

He looked into her eyes and caught his breath. "I wanted to tell you that if your father were alive now, I'd go and speak to him again. But this time I'd reason with him, and I'd make him see that I'm not the ruffian he thought me."

"Oh, Jack." She stepped toward him and touched his sleeve. "I think that if Father were alive, we'd find a way to let him see the true Jack Hunter. That doesn't still distress you, does it?"

"I suppose it does, some. I botched things badly with your father, and instead of trying to make amends, I—"

"That's past, Jack. Please do not speak of it again."

"All right." He eyed her anxiously.

Lucy wondered how they'd strayed so far from the cozy, romantic feeling she'd had earlier.

"So may I call upon you again tomorrow evening, ma'am?" he asked.

"Well, yes. . .certainly."

Jack's smile appeared far from assured, and she thought his hand trembled as he took her arm and guided her toward her bedroom door.

"Good night, then, Jack," she whispered, looking up into his eyes.

He placed his hands on her shoulders. Even in the dim light, she could see the troubled yearning his eyes held. "Lucy. . ."

Wondering if she was doing the right thing, she reached up and touched his beard. He stood very still and lowered his eyelids, as if waiting to see what she would do. With agonizing slowness, she furrowed her fingers into his beard and stroked his cheek. "I enjoyed this time with you, Jack."

"Oh, Lucy." He pulled her toward him and stooped to nestle his face into the curve of her neck.

Warm satisfaction swept over her. She slipped her arms around his neck and held on to him, eyes closed, soaking up the pleasant assurance she craved. She felt his lips on her cheek, feathering soft, sweet kisses toward the corner of her mouth. She turned her head toward him. Their lips met in a shock of culmination. His arms tightened about her, and she rested in his embrace, relishing the riotous exuberance that shot through her.

He released her at last and leaned back, breathing in ragged gasps. "Dearest Lucy!"

She smiled at the glow in his eyes and stroked the back of his neck, feeling suddenly languid.

"Tomorrow is Sunday," Jack whispered.

"Aye." She was a bit surprised at this turn of the conversation.

"We shall have to rise early to do the chores before meeting."

"So we shall."

He frowned. "And I'll have to put the hay in later. I expect Dole will come around and malign me for Sabbath breaking, but if I don't make this hay crop—"

She laid her index finger on his lips. "I don't fault you if you need to do some labor on the Lord's Day. Sometimes it is necessary. Even Christ said such."

"I'll only do what I have to, but if we leave the hay out and it gets rained on. . ."

Lucy nodded, wondering at his anxiety. "Do what you must, Jack."

He drew a deep breath, his eyes still fretful. Reaching up to his neck, he pulled her hands away gently and carried them to his lips. "So I'll court you again tomorrow, dear Lucy."

Ah, now she understood. He was saying a regretful good night, with a promise of something more on Sunday evening.

"I shall be waiting," she whispered.

He kissed her once more, a lingering, thorough kiss, and they clung to each other for one warm, sweet moment. Then he stepped away and climbed the ladder.

Chapter 18

Breakfast was a hasty affair between the chores and preparation to go to the meetinghouse. After eating, Jack washed up in the kitchen and Simon disappeared to the barn, both to don their Sunday clothes.

Lucy came from the bedchamber just as Jack finished dressing, and he surveyed her with pleasure. It was the first moment they'd had alone since their parting last evening, and she came toward him smiling. "You look fine this morning, Goodman Hunter. No one would know you'd been injured."

He pushed back a tendril of golden hair that peeked from beneath her bonnet. "I'm still amazed at how blessed I am. I'm walking to meeting with an angel."

"Hush," she said, turning her face away, but he noted both a blush and a smile on her face.

He wondered if he could steal a kiss this morning. It was a bit shocking to have such a thought, but after all, they were alone in their own house. He seized her hand and tugged her gently toward him. As she came willingly into his arms, a loud knock reverberated through the room.

Lucy stepped away from him, looking toward the door in confusion. "Who can that be?"

As though in answer to her question, a deep voice shouted, "Hunter? Be you in there? Open, I say!"

Jack's pulse hammered at the unfamiliar voice. Was some official coming to arrest him again and drag him off to prison? He sent up a quick prayer: *God, give me grace!*

He strode to the door and flung it open. The stranger on his doorstep stared at him, and Jack stared back without flinching. The man was between thirty-five and forty years old, Jack guessed, and the sun glinted on his reddish hair.

"I'm Jack Hunter."

"Where's my boy?"

Jack looked him up and down with mingled relief and chagrin. There was no doubt this was Simon's father—the stocky build, the green eyes, and the auburn hair were the same.

"And who be you?"

"I'm Edward Brady. The boy's father."

Jack nearly looked past him, toward the barn, but forced himself to continue looking Brady in the eye. "What is your boy's name?"

"Stop toying with me, you knave!" Brady's face grew red. He raised a fist and shook it in Jack's face. "I heered my boy is living in a murderer's household, and I won't have it. You give me back my son!"

It was all Jack could do to refrain from punching him, but he felt Lucy stepping up behind him. Her small, warm hand touched his shoulder.

"Mr. Brady," Jack said, "my wife and I were about to leave for church. Would you care to walk along with us?"

"I'll go nowhere with you! Don't try to deny that my son is here. Your village parson said the boy was at the meetinghouse last Sunday, and he told me how to find your farm. Now, where is Simon?"

Jack hesitated. He didn't want to betray the boy, yet he had to be honest with the man. He wished he had pressed Simon more on reconciling with his family, but he had delayed, hoping the lad would write to his father soon and reveal his whereabouts.

"I'll take you to him," Jack said.

Brady stepped back, and Jack went outside just as the barn door swung open.

Simon walked forward with a slow, wooden pace, but he came on his own. Jack felt a wave of pride and anguish. He didn't want to lose the boy, but if he must, he'd rather it be this way than by having to force Simon to show himself.

"I'm here, Father."

Brady looked his son over. Jack was glad Lucy had washed and mended the boy's breeches. He wished she'd had time to weave the cloth for a new suit. Jack's shirt was too large for the boy, but at least he was clean, and his hair was neatly trimmed.

The father marched toward Simon and stopped a couple of feet from him. "I should thrash you this instant."

Simon cringed but stood his ground. "I'm sorry, Father."

"Oh, are you? You ran away, breaking your mother's heart, and stayed away months on end. Oh, I've heard the tale. You wanted to join the militia but were turned away, so you found a berth in a murderer's house. What do you do here?"

Simon swallowed hard. "I work, Father."

Brady glanced at the structure behind Simon. "They make you sleep in the barn?"

"I'm comfortable there, and Goodman Hunter said when the nights get cold I can sleep in the loft of their house."

Jack threw an apologetic smile at Lucy. He hadn't had a chance to discuss that plan with her.

Brady glared at his son. "Well, you are coming home with me today. Do you have any things to gather?"

Simon shook his head. "Only my old shirt. Goody Hunter gave me this one."

"Get your old one and give this one back to her."

Lucy came down the doorstep. "There's no need, sir. Simon's been a good boy, and he's worked hard for my husband."

"For what wage?" Brady glowered at Jack.

Before Jack could speak, Simon said, "Goodman Hunter says he'll start giving me a penny a week soon."

Brady advanced toward Jack. "Here you are, a criminal who's somehow escaped the hangman's noose, making a slave of my boy!" He drew back his hand as if to strike Jack.

"I wouldn't do that, sir." Jack put steel into his voice and prepared to counter the blow if it fell.

Brady backed off a step. "Aye, from what I hear about you, it's probably best not to anger you."

"My husband is not a murderer!"

Jack started as Lucy leaped forward, placing herself between him and Brady. He reached out and took her arm gently. "Easy, wife. Let Mr. Brady take his leave in peace."

Tears streamed down Lucy's face. "Does Simon have to go?"

Jack wasn't sure if she was pleading with him or the boy's father, but he said, "Yes, I'm afraid he does."

"Don't you whip him," she cried.

Brady stared at Jack in mock horror. "You'd best study how to keep your wife in check."

"He is a good boy," Lucy said. "If you treat him well, he'll give you the same devotion and hard work he gave us."

Brady grabbed Simon's arm and pulled the boy with him down the path.

Jack and Lucy stood watching in silence.

"He forgot his shirt," Lucy said as they disappeared out of sight. She burst into tears.

Jack gathered her into his arms. "There, now, wife. We knew he couldn't stay."

"Did we?"

Jack stroked her back. "I thought to have him write and apologize to his parents, but. . ."

Lucy sobbed a bit more, then straightened and wiped her cheek with her sleeve. "I've mussed your clean shirt."

"It will dry."

"I wish. . ." She looked up at him.

"What?"

"I wish we had a right to keep him. I was getting rather fond of Simon."

"Aye. But we can't refuse to let his father take him."

Lucy grimaced. "I don't suppose we want any trouble with the law just now."

Jack pushed back a lock of her hair. "Perhaps one day we'll have a plucky boy like that." He looked deep into her eyes, and her face turned crimson.

"If we do," she said, looking down the path, "I hope his father will teach him not to run away or steal from folks."

He smiled. "I'm sure his mother will make him love his home so much he'll never want to leave it."

"Shall we go now?" Her voice quivered.

Jack considered their options. "We're already a few minutes late. Perhaps we should sit down and calm ourselves. I don't want you going into the meeting all distressed."

Lucy took a gulp of air. "I'll be all right."

He squeezed her and rubbed the top of her head with his chin. "The parson will call for a psalm in an hour. We'll go in then." He kept his arm around her waist and guided her into the kitchen.

"Do you want tea?" she asked.

"Nay, don't trouble yourself."

They sat at the table, and Jack eyed her uncertainly. "I. . .I've been wondering. . . if you've a mind to pray together."

"Yes, please!"

His heart leaped, and he reached across the table to take her hands in his. As he bowed his head, he sent up a silent word of gratitude for his wife.

"Dear Father in heaven," he said, "give us peace this day. I pray also for Simon, that You would calm his spirit and give him contentment so he may live with his family in harmony. And, Lord, give Your wisdom to Lucy and me. If there is anything further we can do to help that boy, please show us." He paused, trying to think if he'd left anything of importance unsaid, then whispered, "In the name of our Lord Jesus, amen."

"Amen," Lucy said with a sob.

Jack opened his eyes. Her sad smile moved him to leave his stool and kneel beside her. "Dearest Lucy. God has given you a mother's heart for that boy, and I am thankful that it is so. He has heard our petition for Simon."

"Yes," she whispered, leaning against his shoulder. "Oh, Jack, do you think he'll be all right?"

An authoritative knock rattled the little house. Brady's strident voice called, "Open up, Hunter!"

Lucy drew back and stared at Jack. The blood drained from her face. "What can he want? Surely he's not brought the constables to arrest you?"

Fear coursed through Jack's veins, but he pushed it aside and squeezed her hands. "God is in this, dear wife. Pray now."

He rose and went to the door. When he opened it, Brady's fist was drawn back to knock upon the boards again. He stopped with his hand in midair and stared into Jack's eyes.

"What is it?" Jack asked, noting with relief that Simon and his father were alone.

"The boy insisted we come back and tell you that he's seen something."

Simon pushed up next to his father. His green eyes glittered with excitement, and his face was full of anticipation and wonder.

"I seen him, Goodman Hunter! Just now. I seen the man what took your ax!"

Chapter 19

"You're certain it's him?" Jack asked.

He'd brought Goodman Brady and Simon into the house and seated them at the table. Lucy flitted about as the boy told his story, quietly preparing tea and getting out the apple cake intended for Sunday dinner. She set a plate and a pewter mug of steaming tea before Edward Brady. He did not refuse it.

"It were him, I'm sure, sir!" Simon's eagerness warmed Jack's heart.

"The boy told me a bit of what's gone on here as we walked back," Brady said. "It sounds to me as if this bit of knowledge might help your case."

Jack met his gaze and realized Brady was making a concession. It was not an apology, and he had not called Jack "sir," but it opened at least the possibility that he doubted Jack's guilt.

"Simon told me a few days ago that he saw my ax stolen last June," Jack said. "I hoped that he could identify the thief for me."

"Is that why you kept him here?" Brady asked, his eyes squinting.

"Nay. Simon had been with us more than a week when he told me. We like the boy, and he was welcome here, whether he could name the man or no."

"A week?" Brady asked thoughtfully. He blew on his tea and sipped it, then fixed his stern gaze on Simon. "You were not here all summer, then?"

Simon stared at the slice of cake Lucy had placed before him. "No, sir."

"Then where were you all this time?"

"I. . ." Simon swallowed hard. "I stayed about the town, sir, and. . .and the farms."

"Were you hiring out to farmers?"

"Nay," Simon whispered.

Jack wanted to defend the boy but kept silent. He glanced at Lucy and saw that she also waited to hear what Simon would say.

"Then how did you eat?" Brady roared, his red eyebrows drawing together in a frown.

"I. . .I took things." Simon hung his head.

Jack cleared his throat. "The boy and I came to an understanding, sir. He would work for me in haying time to pay back the bit of provender he'd taken. He would have repaid me by the end of this week. I told him I would pay him after that, and he could make restitution to the other farmers whose chicken coops and gardens he plundered."

Brady stared at Jack for a long moment.

114

"I'm sorry, Father," Simon whispered. "Truly I am, and I've told Goodman Hunter and. . .and God. They both forgave me."

Brady drew in a long, slow breath. "This is not the way I raised my son."

"I know that, sir," Jack assured him. "The boy felt desperate and justified his actions in his own mind, but now he sees his error. He's been a good lad since we found him out, and I trust he'll be obedient once you take him home."

"We shall see," Brady replied. "But what of this other matter?"

"Well," said Jack, "if Simon can identify the man who stole my ax, then I suppose we need to go to the law and tell them his name."

"I don't know his name," said Simon.

"A lot of folks were walking to the meetinghouse," his father explained. "All sudden-like, the boy says to me, 'Look yonder, Father! That man is a thief.' And I says to him, 'How so, son?' And he tells me, 'I saw that man steal Goodman Hunter's ax—the one what killed his neighbor last June.'"

Lucy stepped forward. "This man—the one who took the ax—he went into the meetinghouse?"

"Aye," said Simon, looking at her with wide eyes. "I don't recall seeing him there last Sunday, but he looked to be headed there today."

"I expect Goodman Rutledge is at meeting," Jack said.

"Who is that?" asked Edward Brady.

"He's the chief constable," Jack said. "Perhaps if we go to the meeting-house, we can have him called outside."

"Yes," Lucy said. "Then if the thief is in the meeting, we can wait until they're done, and Simon can watch as the people come out and identify him for the constable."

"It might work," said Jack, "provided we are discreet."

"I'm willing to go with you," said Brady.

⁂

An hour later the little group clustered beneath a large maple tree, waiting for the meeting to end.

"I don't know, Hunter," Ezekiel Rutledge said to Jack, shaking his head. "The boy saying someone took your ax doesn't prove that person killed Barnabas Trent."

"I agree," Jack said. "But won't it lend credence to my claim of innocence?"

"Aye, that it will," Rutledge acknowledged. "The boy seems honest to me."

"I raised him to be truthful," said Brady. He glanced at Jack, who nodded. If Brady feared he would tell the constable about the boy's pilfering, he could rest easy.

At last the service ended, and the people streamed out of the meetinghouse.

"Look carefully, son," Brady told Simon.

Rutledge put a hand on the boy's shoulder. "If you see him and you are certain, tell me."

Angus Murray and his family exited the church, and the captain glanced their way. He spoke to his wife, then walked toward them.

"Goodman Rutledge, Goodman Hunter. What's afoot?" The man nodded at Lucy and Simon, then eyed the stranger with curiosity.

Jack looked toward Rutledge, hoping he would make an explanation, but the constable only murmured, "Captain," and resumed watching the congregation coming down the steps.

"This is Simon Brady's father," Jack explained. Murray nodded, a question still scrawled on his face.

"I see him!" Simon squealed. He grabbed Jack's arm. "That's him, sir. The one with the blue coat."

They all looked toward the church door. Jack inhaled sharply. The man Simon indicated was none other than Charles Dole.

"Lucy," he said, "take Simon out of sight." Jack walked toward the church with Rutledge and Edward Brady. Captain Murray fell into step with him.

Rutledge halted at the bottom of the steps as Dole came down them.

"Charles," Rutledge said, "I've something to discuss with you."

Dole's gaze flitted from Rutledge to Edward Brady then to Jack. "What is it, Ezekiel?"

"Let us speak in private," said Rutledge.

Dole's frown became a scowl. "You can speak to me here. I suppose this reprobate has told you I stopped by his field and had words with him."

Rutledge shot a glance at Jack. "Nay. This concerns another matter."

Dole glared at Jack and Brady. Angus Murray stepped up beside Jack.

"If you insist on plain talk in public. . ." Rutledge said.

Dole sniffed. "I do. Get on with it."

Rutledge took in the small crowd that had gathered. "All right. A witness has come forth saying he saw you take Jack Hunter's ax from his barn last June."

Dole exhaled in a puff. "Nonsense. You know Hunter's a liar. He'd say anything to save himself."

"It's not Hunter who made the claim," Rutledge said.

Dole's eyes focused on Brady. "If this witness of yours thinks he has evidence, why didn't he come forward earlier?"

"Because he did not know the significance of what he saw. Come, Charles," Rutledge pleaded. "Let us walk over to the jail and speak about this in private." He laid his hand on Dole's sleeve, but the man shook him off in anger.

"What are you saying? Some friend of Hunter's claims I killed Trent?"

Jack prayed Rutledge would exercise wisdom and restraint.

"I'll have you up for slander!" Dole lunged toward Brady, but Captain Murray leaped forward and caught Dole by the shoulders.

"Not so, Charles," Rutledge said. "This man never met Hunter until today, and furthermore, he is not the witness I spoke of."

"Then who is it?"

"You'll have a chance to face the witness in court."

"Court?" Dole snarled. "You'll not take me to the jail." Dole tried to push past Rutledge, but the captain caught him once more.

"Shall I hold him, Constable?" Murray asked. He tightened his grasp on Dole's shoulders.

Dole winced. "Unhand me! Ezekiel, make this half-witted Samson let me go."

Murray's laugh boomed out over the churchyard. "Constable Rutledge, if there are to be charges of slander brought today, perhaps I should be the plaintiff."

Rutledge leaned toward Dole and lowered his voice. "Charles, this witness's tale rings true. You owned that farm before Trent. When you couldn't pay your taxes, you lost it, and Trent bought it. I know that's rankled you for twenty-five years."

Richard Trent pushed through the people on the steps. "Constable Rutledge, you spoke true. This man owned my father's farm once, but he defaulted on his taxes. My father bought it all legal."

"That were my farm," Dole snarled. "Weren't my fault I couldn't pay. They should have waited, but no! Trent comes along with ready coin, and they let him take half of it."

"Aye, and the rest of the land was sold a couple of years later to Isaac Hunter." Rutledge stared steadily into Dole's wild eyes.

"It weren't fair," Dole shouted. "First Trent, then Hunter, that scoundrel! They got my land, and I had to start all over. I never could get ahead on the stony ground I got south of town."

Dole twisted in Murray's grasp, but the captain held him in a tight grip. "Stay put, Dole," the big man growled.

Rutledge shook his head. "Did you think you could get the land back if you killed Trent, Charles?"

Edward Brady cleared his throat. "Pardon me, sir, but it seems to me a bitter man might connive something like this. He steals the ax of one man he hates and kills the other with it. If the one is convicted of murdering the other, then both of their properties are apt to become available."

Rutledge scratched his head and surveyed Brady, then turned to Dole again. "Is there truth to that? Speak up, Charles!"

"Yes," Murray roared. "Speak, Constable Dole!"

❦

The heavy rain pounding on the roof put Lucy on edge as she washed the supper dishes. There would be no stroll tonight. Would Jack continue his awkward courting? He built up the fire, then took the Bible and sat on his usual stool, leafing through the pages.

Lucy wiped off the table, then removed her apron and went to her chair.

Jack read a chapter, then closed the Bible with a sigh. "We have a good life Lucy."

"Yes, we do. But I'll miss Simon."

"Aye. Still, it's good that he was content to go home after he saw his father take my part this morning."

She ran her hand over her hair and wished she'd snatched a moment to comb it. "Did you hear Edward Brady tell his son how proud he is of him?"

"I did." Jack pressed his lips together.

Lucy leaned toward him. "They'll never take you up for Trent's murder again. Now that Dole has confessed to the killing, it's all behind us."

"It's hard to realize that it's over."

"But it is! We can rejoice and not fear the future."

"Let's give thanks," he said.

Lucy bowed her head and folded her hands in her lap.

Jack's prayer was brief but heartfelt. When he finished, he stood and came to her side. "I have so much to thank God for, Lucy. And not only having my name cleared of this crime."

"Aye." A rumble of thunder sounded, and the drumming of rain on the roof almost drowned out her voice.

"Well, we shan't have our walk tonight," he said.

"It's all right. At least your hay is under cover."

"Yes, thanks to Angus and Samuel."

"That's another thing we can be thankful for. . .good friends."

"Aye." He stood before her, as though waiting for something.

Lucy smiled then pulled in a deep breath. She was learning that sometimes her husband needed a slight prod. "So, Jack," she said softly.

"Yes?"

"If you were courting a girl, and it poured rain the evening you were to call on her, what would you do?"

He chuckled. "I suppose I'd go to her parents' house and sit and stare at her while she knitted." He drew his stool over and sat next to her, his knee almost touching hers.

"I haven't got my knitting," she said.

"Would you like me to fetch it?"

"Nay, I think not."

He seized her hand and looked into her eyes. "Lucy, are you truly happy here with me?"

Despite his gravity, she couldn't hold back her smile. "I've never been happier in my life."

"So you have no regrets?" he asked, still anxiously searching her face.

"None."

He reached up to caress her cheek. "I love you, Lucy."

It was almost painful to breathe. She couldn't break the stare, but she managed to whisper, "I love you, too."

He bent toward her and kissed her. She responded with a sweet longing in her heart.

"Lucy, dear, I wondered. . ."

"Yes, Jack?" She snuggled in against his shoulder.

"Are my things in your way up in the loft?"

She sat up and cocked her head, trying to figure out this turn of phrase. "In the loft?"

"When you do your weaving."

"No, I. . ." She stopped as his meaning became clear. "It might be a bit easier if your clothes were put away in the clothespress and. . ."

He lifted her hand to his lips. She closed her eyes, savoring his touch.

". . .and if the straw tick. . ."

"Yes?" He kissed each finger, and she shuddered with delightful anticipation. *Your husband loves you*, she told her herself. *He's only waiting for you to speak.*

"Well, if I didn't have to trip over it. . ."

"I'll put it away tomorrow." He stood, pulling her up with him, and swept her into his embrace. "I think. . . ," he whispered.

"What?"

He glanced toward the mantelpiece then looked directly at her with his pensive gray eyes. "I think we've done enough courting for a couple who's been married two months."

"Almost three."

"I do believe it's time we ended this courtship and. . ."

She swallowed hard, trying to still the fluttering in her chest.

". . .and I stopped sleeping on the floor."

She gasped as Jack stooped and lifted her in his arms.

"Can you pick up the candlestick, sweetheart?" he whispered in her ear. He swung her toward the table. She grasped the candle and held it with great care as he carried her toward the inner chamber.

Epilogue

Jack and Sam Ellis shed their linsey shirts as the late June sun beat down on them. Sweat poured down Jack's face as he swung his scythe over and over. After an hour of steady mowing, Sam called to him, and he stopped his rhythm and laid down the scythe. Sam walked toward him, drinking from the cider jug as he came.

"Here, you need a rest."

Jack took a swig of sweet cider. At least it was cooler than the air around him. They had sunk the jug in the shallow water at the edge of the creek when they began haying.

"I should be at the house," he said with an anxious glance toward home.

"The ladies will tell us when you're allowed," Sam reminded him.

Jack sighed. "She's working harder than we are, and it's too hot for this."

"She'll do fine, Jack."

"That's easy for the father of ten healthy youngsters to say."

A call reached them, and both men turned to stare up the slope. Sarah Ellis stood near the woodpile, waving her apron.

Jack thrust the jug into Sam's hands and bolted for home.

Before he reached her, he could see that Sarah's face was one huge smile.

"Lucy?" he gasped.

"She's fine, and so is your son!"

Jack laughed. "It's a boy?"

"A strapping, healthy boy."

"I thank you, Sarah." Jack ran around to the door and hurried to the bedchamber.

Alice Hamblin was bending over the bed, holding a bundle wrapped in flannel. "Well, well, here's Papa," she said with a smile.

Jack slowed his pace and walked forward, trying to control his panting. His heart flipped as he looked at Lucy. Her hair was plastered to her brow, and her eyelids were heavy with exhaustion, but her face radiated joy.

He sat on the edge of the bed and took her in his arms. "Are you all right?"

"Of course I am," she whispered.

He held her close.

After a moment, Alice said, "Well, Papa, do you want to see little Johnny?"

"Johnny?" Jack asked, blinking at her.

She nestled the bundle into his arms, and Jack looked down at his son. In spite of Sarah's description, the baby seemed tiny, and his face was red. Golden down grew on his head, and he opened his mouth in a huge yawn.

Jack laughed. "He's beautiful, Mother Hamblin, but didn't Lucy tell you? We're naming him for your late husband."

"That's right, Marm," Lucy said with a smile. "We'll save Jack's Christian name for next time. This is Thomas Hunter."

Alice bent over the baby, her eyes wet with tears. "Thank you. That's a wonderful gift you've given this old granny." She smiled and stroked the infant's head. "He looks like Lucy's brothers did when they were born."

"I don't mind." Jack grinned. "The Hamblins all be handsome."

"You must write to Simon tonight and tell him we have a boy," Lucy said.

"I shall."

The baby stirred and let out a little wail.

"What do I do?" Jack asked in dismay.

"Give him to his mama." Alice laughed. "Now, pardon me, and I'll go help Sarah fix dinner and do a bit of laundry. We'll bring you something to eat in a few minutes."

She left the room, and Jack passed the baby to Lucy, feeling clumsy in his new role.

"When I married you, I never thought I'd live to see this day," he said.

"Nor I," she admitted. She cuddled the baby close. "Most women would say their wedding day was the happiest day of their life, but that's not so with me."

"Nay, that was quite a grim day," he agreed. "Today is much happier."

She smiled at him over the baby's head. "Aye. Today is wonderful. But still, I think the very best day. . ."

Jack raised his eyebrows. "Go on."

She squeezed his hand. "The best day of my life was the day your name was cleared, Jack Hunter, and you stopped courting me."

THE
CASTAWAY'S
BRIDE

Dedication

To my sister Pam, always supportive, never predictable. You were brave enough to sleep alone in the Hired Man's Room for years. You brought us Moon Man and Ambercrombie Benson. Without you we'd all be a little more melancholy and provincial. Sisters forever!

Chapter 1

Portland, Maine, 1820

Edward Hunter hurried down the gangplank to the wharf, taking a deep breath as he viewed the city before him. In the five years he'd been gone, the docks of Portland had grown more crowded, and they bustled with business. Since the end of the war with England, commerce was good, and merchants in the brand-new state of Maine prospered. So many changes! Maine was no longer part of Massachusetts. What else would he discover today?

When he gained the street, he glanced south toward where his father's shipping company had its offices and docks, but he squared his shoulders and turned inland instead. Abigail first, then home.

As he rounded the corner onto Free Street, he felt the tug of his heart stronger than ever and picked up his pace. At last he would be with her again. His pulse quickened as he thought of Abigail. She'd been so young when he'd left. Had she changed?

He chided himself. Of course she had.

For the last five years, that question had plagued him. His fiancée no doubt believed him dead for most of the time he'd been away. Anything could have happened during that period. She would have matured, which was a good thing. When Edward first approached him, her father had considered her too young at seventeen for an engagement. Several months later, after many evenings spent in the Bowman parlor under the watchful eyes of Abigail's parents, the betrothal had been allowed.

Age would not be a problem now; she must be two and twenty. But how else had she changed? He didn't like to think she had pined for him, grief stricken all this time, but neither did he like to think she might have forgotten him. She could have fallen in love with another man by now. She could even be married.

That thought slowed his steps as he walked up the path to the Bowman house. He had tried to avoid thinking about such possibilities during his years of isolation and loneliness on a desolate island in the Pacific Ocean. In all those lonely days and nights, his worst fear had not been death. He had faced that and come so close it no longer frightened him. What he dreaded most was learning that Abigail had forsaken his memory and married another man.

Edward stood before the door for a moment in silent prayer. *Dear Father in heaven, You alone know what is to come, and You know what is best for me. You saw fit to bring me back from near death in the deep, for what purpose I do not know. But now I trust my future to You, Lord.*

He squared his shoulders and lifted the knocker.

⁓⊗⁓

Deborah Bowman broke off her humming as the door knocker's distinct thud resounded through the lower rooms of the house.

"Can you get that, Debbie?" Her mother's voice reached her from the kitchen, where preparation of the evening meal was underway.

"Yes, Mother!" Deborah laid down the stack of linen napkins she'd been distributing on the long walnut dining table and headed into the front hall. It couldn't be Jacob Price, her sister's fiancé. He was due in an hour and a half for dinner, and his business usually kept him until the last minute.

The hymn she had been humming stuck in her mind, and she resumed the melody, tucking an errant strand of hair behind her ear as she crossed the hall. She turned the knob and pulled back the heavy oak door. A tall, slender man stood on the doorstep, taller even than Jacob. Almost as tall as. . .

She stared at his sun-browned face and swallowed the blithe greeting she'd prepared to deliver.

"Ab—" He stopped and frowned as he studied her.

The air Deborah sucked in felt heavy in her lungs. She must be mistaken. Again she surveyed the man's handsome but anxious face. A new scar dipped from the corner of his right eye down and back toward his earlobe, and he was thin almost to the point of gauntness. But his dark hair and eyes, his firm chin, even the tilt of his head were the same. It must be him.

"Edward? It can't be!" Her words were barely audible, but the flickering response in his eyes told her she was not mistaken.

"Not little Deborah!"

Her cheeks burned as she felt blood rushing into her face.

"Yes, it's me. But. . .Edward, how. . .? You can't. . . ." She gave it up and shook her head.

"It's me." A glint stole into his eyes that assured her he was indeed the Edward Hunter she'd known and admired since childhood. The merry demeanor he'd sported as a youth was replaced by something more grave, but there was no doubt in her mind. Somehow Edward had returned from the dead.

"Praise God!" She seized his hands, then dropped them in a rush of embarrassment and stood aside. "Come in. I can hardly believe it's you. Am I dreaming?"

"If you are, then your mother is baking apple tart in your dreams."

Delight bubbled up inside her, and she grasped his sleeve. "Oh, Edward, do come into the parlor. I'll run up and tell Abby you're here."

"She's. . .she's here, then."

"Yes, of course." Deborah halted, anticipating the shock this revelation would bring her older sister. "I expect she'll need a moment to absorb the news." The thought of Jacob Price danced at the edge of Deborah's mind, and she firmly shoved it into oblivion. Edward was home! He was alive! Nothing else must get in the way of the joy his return brought.

She slipped her hand through the crook of his elbow and guided him across the hall into the snug parlor where her mother received guests.

"There, now. You just wait here."

"Thank you."

His strained smile sent a pang of apprehension through her. She longed to sit down beside him on the sofa and hear his tale, but that privilege belonged to Abigail. The pain and anxiety in his face transferred to her own heart. Should she tell him? No, that obligation, too, belonged to her sister.

There was one thing she, as the hostess greeting him, should ask.

"Your mother?"

"I haven't seen her yet." Edward's mouth tightened. "I heard about Father on the ship I took up here from Boston."

Deborah nodded, feeling tears spring into her eyes as she noted his deep sorrow. "I'm sorry, Edward."

"Thank you."

She took a deep breath. "Sit and relax for a few minutes. I'll tell Abby."

At the parlor door, she paused and looked back. Edward sank into a chair and sat immobile, staring toward the front windows. What was going through his mind? Five years! What had happened to him in that time? And how would his return affect Abigail?

She turned, lifted her skirt, and dashed up the stairs.

"Abby?" She careened to a stop in the doorway to her sister's room. Abigail was brushing her long, golden hair, arranging it just so.

"You shouldn't tear around so, Debbie." Abigail turned her attention back to the mirror.

"Abby, I have something to tell you." Deborah took two steps into the room. At least her sister was sitting down. "Something's happened."

Abigail's gaze caught hers in the mirror, and her hands stilled, holding a lock of hair out away from her head, with her brush poised to style it.

"Not Father?"

"Oh no, nothing like that. It's good news. Very good."

Abigail laid the brush down and swiveled on her stool to face Deborah. "What is it?"

"It's. . . Oh dear, I'm not sure how to say this."

"Just say it."

Deborah gazed into her sister's eyes, blue and dreamy like their mother's. For such a long time, those eyes had been red-rimmed from weeping. But recently Abigail had overcome her grief and taken an interest in life once more.

Her family had encouraged her to leave off grieving for the man she'd loved. He was dead and gone, and it was all right for her to go on with her life. That's what they'd all told her.

But what would happen now? Deborah didn't want to be the one to shatter her sister's peaceful world again. She ought to have told Mother first and let her break the news to Abigail.

"Debbie." Abigail rose and stepped toward her, clearly annoyed. "Would you just tell me, please? You're driving me wild."

"All right. It's. . .it's Edward."

"Edward?" Abigail's face went white, and she swayed. Deborah rushed to her side and eased her gently toward the side of her four-poster bed. Abigail sat slowly on the edge, staring off into space, then suddenly jerked around to stare at Deborah. "What about him? Tell me."

"He's. . . Oh, Abby, he's alive."

<hr />

Edward stood and paced the parlor to the fireplace of granite blocks. Turn. To the wide bay window that fronted the street. Outside was the Bowmans' garden and, beyond it, people passing by, bustling toward home and dinner, no doubt. So ordinary. So common. But to his eyes, painfully odd.

Five years! Dear God, everything is so strange here. How can I come back and pick up my life again?

He jerked away from the scene and paced to the fireplace once more.

He'd left the ship determined that the first woman he set eyes on in five years would be the woman he loved. Of course, he'd seen a few ladies from a distance as he walked from the dock to the Bowman house, but none whom he recognized. The city had grown in his absence, and new houses and businesses crowded the peninsula between the Fore River and Casco Bay.

His thoughts had skimmed over the surface of what he'd seen: a multitude of sailing vessels floating in the harbor, scores of people crowding the streets, freight wagons and carts, hawkers preparing to close business for the evening, and housewives hurrying home to start supper. He'd been thinking only of Abigail.

But the woman who opened the door to him had not been Abigail but her little sister, Deborah. Debbie had grown strangely mature and womanly. She was not the child—with the gawky limbs, bushy dark hair, and big, brown eyes so unlike Abigail's—that Edward recalled. Deborah favored Dr. Bowman's side of the family, no question about that.

She was no longer the awkward tomboy. She had moved with grace as she ushered him to the parlor. Her hair had tempered to a smooth, rich chestnut, neatly confined in an upswept coiffure. Her green gown edged with creamy lace was the attire of a lady, not a rambunctious adolescent.

He turned and walked toward the window once more. Abigail. She was the one he longed to see. His thoughts should be focused on her. It was only the strangeness of seeing Deborah grown up that had pulled his mind in a different direction. He tried, as he had so many times in the past five years, to conjure up the image of Abigail's face: her creamy skin, her golden hair, her blue eyes. He sighed and stopped before the window seat.

He would have sent a letter before him at the first opportunity, but as it turned out, he traveled back to civilization by the fastest means he could find. The ship that rescued him conveyed him directly to Boston, and there he'd found a schooner heading north and east the next day for Portland. No letter could have winged its way to his beloved any faster than he had arrived himself.

Would the shock of his appearance endanger her health? Deborah recovered quickly and welcomed him with joy. Still, Abigail had always been less robust than Debbie. Was he inconsiderate to come here first? Perhaps he should have gone to his mother first and sent advance notice to Abigail, then come round to see her in the evening.

He glanced out the window and saw that the shadows were lengthening. He'd lost his pocket watch four years ago in the roiling storm that shipwrecked him, but he could tell by the angle of the sun that late afternoon had reached the coast of Maine. His gaze roved over the lush trees shielding the house from the street. The full foliage welcomed him like the face of an old friend. How he'd longed for the shade of the maples in his parents' yard during the searing summers of the island, where the seasons were turned about and the hottest time of year was in January and February.

He'd kept meticulous count of the days, as nearly as he could reckon, and consoled himself in the hottest times by recalling the ice and snow of Maine winters. He'd tried to picture what Abigail was doing as he sweltered in exile. Ice-skating with Debbie? Riding to church in her father's sleigh? He would imagine her wearing a fur hat and muff, romping through falling snow.

He walked once more to the fireplace, where he leaned one arm against the mantel.

How would she receive him? What would she say? It seemed like he had been waiting for hours. What could possibly be keeping her? She ought to be tearing down the stairs and into his arms. Shouldn't she? Edward offered another silent plea for serenity, knowing that the next few minutes would determine the course of his life.

⤟⤠

"How can I face him, Mother?" Abigail sat on the bed, twisting the ends of her sash between her hands.

Deborah stood by, panting a little after her dash down the back stairs and up again with her mother.

"My dear, think of all he's been through. You must see him. You cannot send him away without hearing his story. Furthermore, you must explain your current state to him."

"Oh, Mother, must I?"

"Yes, I'm afraid you must. Break the news to him gently. He will understand, I'm sure, that you've grieved him properly and moved slowly in pinning your affections elsewhere. Your father and I watched you mourn and weep over that young man for three years. No one can fault you in your devotion to him. But now you've got beyond that."

"But, Mother, it's Edward." Deborah grasped her mother's arm, fighting the unbearable confusion that swirled inside her.

"Well, yes, dear." Her mother glanced at her, then back at Abigail. "Of course we're thrilled that he has returned, but your sister hasn't entered into this betrothal with Jacob lightly. It's not something to cast aside—"

"But she loved Edward first." Deborah saw the agony in her sister's eyes as she spoke and clamped her lips together, determined to say no more on the matter. This was Abigail's dilemma, not hers. Still, she couldn't imagine a better surprise than to learn that Edward, whom she'd always adored, still alive. Deborah had been only fifteen when the news of Edward's death came, but she had felt her heart would break along with Abby's. He was such a fine young man. Deborah knew that if she ever gave her love to a man, he would be a man much like Edward Hunter.

"Couldn't Father just tell him?" Abigail pleaded.

Mother frowned. "Really, Abby! I sent Elizabeth around to ask your father to come home as soon as he can, but he has no inkling of the situation. And he might not be able to leave his office for some time if there are a lot of patients. You mustn't keep that young man waiting."

Abigail stood and walked with wooden steps toward the looking glass.

"Your face is pale," Mother murmured. "Let me help you freshen up. Debbie—" She turned, and Deborah looked toward her. Mother's usual calm expression had fled, and her agitation was nearly as marked as Abigail's dismay.

"Debbie, go down and tell Elizabeth to take him some—no, wait. Elizabeth's gone to fetch your father. You help your sister finish her hairdo, and I'll go and greet Edward myself and see that he has a glass of cider. Don't be long now, Abby."

Mother swept from the room, and Deborah approached Abigail's chair.

"Would you like me to pin up the last few locks?"

"Oh, would you?"

Deborah reached for the silver-backed brush. Her gaze met that of her sister in the wall mirror. "Try to smile when you greet him, Abby. You look like a terrified rabbit."

"Oh, Debbie, I'm not sure I want to see Edward."

"That's silly. You'll have to see him sometime. He's home to stay."

Tears escaped the corners of Abigail's eyes and trailed down her cheeks. "But it's been so long. Debbie, I was seventeen when he left."

"I know." Deborah sank to her knees and pulled Abigail into her embrace.

Abby sobbed and squeezed her, then pulled away. "I'll ruin your dress."

"Here." Deborah reached for a muslin handkerchief on the dressing table and placed it in Abigail's hand.

"If only Mr. Hunter hadn't sent him away," Abigail moaned.

"You know he wanted his son to learn every aspect of the business before he began running it," Deborah said. "Edward was preparing to take over when his father retired. His commission as an officer on the *Egret* was intended to give him the experience he'd need to head a shipping company. The men wouldn't have respected him if he'd never been to sea."

"I know, but he'd been on one voyage with his father already. Why did Mr. Hunter have to send Edward on that horrid voyage to the Pacific?"

Deborah sighed. "Maturity, Abby. Experience. Look at Jacob. He was a lad, too, when the *Egret* left. But now he's a man, and he understands the business perfectly, so he's able—" She stopped and looked into Abigail's stricken face.

"What will happen at Hunter Shipping now? They've given Jacob the place Edward would have had if he'd lived. I mean, if he'd—oh, Debbie, this is too awful, and I'm confused."

"There, now, you can't keep crying. Your eyes will be puffy and bloodshot. And you can't blame Mr. Hunter. The news devastated all of us, and it was his own son who went down with the *Egret* in that brutal storm. Or at least, we all thought he did. Jacob and the other men in his boat survived, and we all praised God for that. You can't hold it against Mr. Hunter for taking his nephew into the office afterward, when he thought his only son was lost."

"Edward's drowning broke his poor father's heart."

"Yes." Deborah picked up the hairbrush and began once more to pull it through Abigail's tresses, then pinned her hair up quickly. "If only Mr. Hunter had lived to see this day."

"He would be so happy," Abigail whispered.

"He certainly would be. There."

Abigail examined her image in the mirror, blotted the traces of tears from her cheeks, and stood.

"I guess it's time."

Chapter 2

"Edward, what a joy to see you again!" Mrs. Bowman bustled into the parlor, and Edward jumped up.

"Thank you. I'm grateful to be here, ma'am."

She set down the tray she carried, took his hand, and smiled up at him. "Abigail will be right down. She was surprised at the news, of course. You understand."

"Of course." He sat when his hostess sat, perching on the edge of the upholstered chair, and accepted the cold glass of sweet cider she offered him.

"You must have been through a nightmare."

"Yes, ma'am. A very long nightmare." He wondered if he ought to launch into his story or wait until Abigail appeared.

From the hallway, he heard the front door open and close, and his hostess sprang up again. "That must be Dr. Bowman. Will you excuse me just a moment, Edward? I know he'd love to see you."

Edward stood up but said nothing as she hurried from the room. This was getting increasingly chaotic. All he'd wanted was a glimpse of Abigail's face and a moment alone with her, but he should have known he would have to wade through her family first.

The murmur of voices reached him, then Dr. Bowman's deep voice rose in shock and pleasure. "What? You don't mean it!"

Abigail's father strode across the threshold and straight toward him, his hand outstretched in welcome.

"Edward! What a wonderful surprise!" The older man shook his hand with vigor, and Edward eyed him cautiously. He hadn't changed much. Perhaps his hair held a bit more gray. His square face bore the interested expression that inspired confidence in his patients. Edward had always liked the physician but was somewhat intimidated five years earlier, viewing him as his future father-in-law. His persistence and diligent labor in Hunter Shipping's office and warehouse had finally convinced Dr. Bowman that he was acceptable husband material for Abigail. Her father had relented and permitted the engagement just before Edward left on his voyage.

"It's good to see you, sir."

"Sit down." The doctor waved toward his chair, and Edward resumed his seat, more nervous than ever, as Dr. Bowman took a place on the sofa.

Mrs. Bowman, who had entered the room behind her husband, gave Edward a nod and a smile. "You'll excuse me, won't you? I must go and give some instructions about dinner to the hired girl."

"You've moved your practice out of the house, sir?" Edward asked.

"Yes, I've got a small surgery down on Union Street now. Convenient for the patients, and it saves the family the disturbance of all those people coming to the house. The short walk there and back gives me some exercise."

"You look well, sir."

"Thank you. I can't say as much for you." The doctor looked him over with a professional eye, and Edward tried not to fidget.

"So, tell me: What happened to you when the *Egret* foundered? And better yet, what miracle has restored you to us now?"

Edward decided that an abbreviated version of his adventure was in order. He would probably have to tell the story many times in the next few days, but short of Abigail herself, Dr. Bowman might be his most important audience.

"Well, sir, we'd done our trading and were ready to start home. Almost four years ago it was. We hit bad weather, which is not unusual, but it was a wild gale. The storm buffeted us about, and we lost a great deal of rigging; finally the mainmast went down. The captain could see the ship was lost, and he urged us all to get into the boats."

The doctor placed his elbow on the arm of the sofa and leaned his chin on his hand, watching Edward with his avid dark eyes.

Like Deborah's eyes, Edward thought. *Always searching. Wants to know everything.*

"Your cousin Jacob told us how you had to abandon ship," Dr. Bowman said.

"I heard he survived. I'm thankful for that," Edward said. "Jacob led the first boatload, and they got away from the *Egret* in the yawl. I held the longboat near the ship until the captain came down. He insisted on seeing all the men down first. It was difficult. . . ." He closed his eyes for a moment, remembering the howling wind and the boat lunging on the waves. In his mind he saw young Davy Wilkes leap over the side of the ship and land half in, half out of the longboat, with his thighbone broken.

"Did the captain survive, too, then?"

Edward opened his eyes, shaking off the memory. "At first he did. We had eight of us in the longboat. Jacob had a dozen or more in the yawl."

"Fourteen came home."

"That many? I'm glad. I knew a few drowned in the storm, trying to get into the boats. And we lost four men from the longboat before we reached land."

"Starvation?"

"Lack of water, mostly. One boy died of his injuries, and we lost one man over the side in rough water the first night."

"Jacob told us that after your boats became separated during the night he and his crew sailed on for several days, and then another ship picked them up."

"God be praised," Edward murmured. He had often prayed for his comrades

133

and wondered whether they had escaped death.

A stir in the doorway drew his attention, and he realized that Deborah had returned. As he jumped up, she smiled at him, and again he felt the infectious warmth of her presence.

"Well, girls. About time," Dr. Bowman said.

Edward saw then that another young woman was entering behind Deborah, hanging back as though reluctant to break in on the scene. Her eyes were lowered, but when she glanced up as she came forward, he caught his breath.

"Abigail." His pulse hammered.

Deborah stepped aside, and Edward met Abigail in the middle of the room. She looked him in the eye then, her mouth a tight line and her eyelids swollen.

"Hello, Edward."

He reached for her hands, and she hesitated a moment, then let him take them. She hadn't changed, really, except for the shy, sorrowful air she bore. She was as lovely as he remembered. Thinner, perhaps, and more fragile. She had lost the gaiety he always associated with her. Indeed, Deborah exhibited far more pleasure at his appearance than Abigail did.

"I'm so glad. . . ." She turned away abruptly and pulled a handkerchief from her sleeve. "Forgive me," she sobbed.

Edward cleared his throat. "There's nothing to forgive. I realize this is a shock, my dear."

"There, now, sit down, girls," said their father. "Edward was just telling me how he and several others escaped the shipwreck."

"Do tell us," Deborah begged, guiding Abigail to sit with her on the sofa. Dr. Bowman took another chair, and Edward sat down again. "Your boat also was spared by the storm, then?"

"We drifted for two weeks." Edward glanced at Abigail, who was surreptitiously wiping away a tear.

Mrs. Bowman returned, and in the pause she asked, "Shall I bring tea?"

"Not for me, thank you," Edward said.

"Nor me," said the doctor. "It's too close to dinner."

The young women shook their heads, and she slipped into a chair near her husband.

"Please go on, Edward," his host urged.

"Well, sir, we had a small sail and a rudder, and we steered for the nearest land we knew of. We took on water constantly, and I was sure we would all perish. But finally we fetched up on an island."

"What island?" Dr. Bowman asked.

"A small one west of Chile, sir. Far west. It is called Spring Island after the water available there. It has been charted for many years, but not many go there, as it is off the usual shipping lanes."

"Four years!" Deborah stared at him, her lips parted and her eyes glistening.

"You stayed on that remote place for four years?"

He nodded. "Nearly. I hoped we would be rescued soon, but after a few weeks we grew discouraged. We were just too far off course for most ships. The one that finally came had also suffered damage and put in for fresh water and a chance to make some repairs before resuming its voyage."

"The ship that rescued Jacob Price and the others searched for your party," Dr. Bowman said.

"Aye. I expect they did. But we'd gone a long ways before we struck land."

"How many of you were there?" Deborah asked.

"Four of us were left when we first landed. But. . ."

"Some of them died?" the doctor asked softly.

"Yes, sir. Alas, I was alone the last two winters." Edward's throat constricted, and he wished they would not ask him any more questions. Eventually he would have to tell all, but for now he wanted only to forget the island and gaze at Abigail.

She had said nothing since they were seated, and Edward wondered at her reserve. She had never been boisterous, but neither had she cringed from him as she seemed to be doing now. This was not going at all as he had imagined.

He drew a deep breath.

"By God's grace, I was found a few months past and carried home again." He turned toward her father. "I don't mean to be forward, but might I have a word with Abigail, sir?"

Mrs. Bowman looked at her husband, and the doctor stood, smiling.

"Of course. I must change my clothes for dinner. Will you stay and eat with us, Edward?"

Abigail's gaze flew to her father, and her features froze as though she dreaded Edward's response.

Edward hesitated. Abigail was definitely not throwing him any encouragement.

"Thank you, sir, but I must decline. I have yet to see my mother."

"Of course," said Dr. Bowman. "Please convey our respects to her."

"I must go to the kitchen," Mrs. Bowman said. "Do come see us again, Edward."

He watched them go, puzzling over what Mrs. Bowman's words might mean to a man who was engaged to marry her daughter. Deborah was also rising, but Abigail shot out her hand and grabbed her sister's wrist.

"Please stay, won't you, Debbie?"

"Well, I. . ." Deborah glanced at him and back to Abigail. "I need to change my clothes as well."

"Please," Abigail whispered, so low Edward barely heard.

Deborah swallowed hard, tossed him an apologetic glance, and settled once more on the sofa.

Is she afraid of me? Edward wondered. He knew his experience had changed him. He was thin and run-down physically, but his love for Abigail was unscathed. *I must be patient until she realizes I am the same man she loved five years ago.*

Deborah looked hard at her sister. When Abigail did not speak, she said, "Edward, I would like to hear more of your ordeal sometime, if it is not too distressing to speak of it."

He nodded. "Perhaps sometime after I've settled in and gotten used to being home again. It was a time of great testing and hardship. The isolation. . ."

"I'm so sorry you had to go through that." Deborah glanced at her sister again.

Abigail turned her attention on him, but her smile seemed to strain every muscle in her face to the point of pain.

"My dearest," he said quietly, leaning toward her. "I do hope you'll forgive me for speaking so frankly before your sister, but I must know—"

She pushed herself up from the sofa, clapping a hand to her temple.

"I'm sorry, Edward, but I don't feel well. Would you please excuse me?"

Edward leaped to his feet, but before he could reply, she had dashed for the door.

◈

"Abby!" Deborah cried, but her sister was gone. Appalled at Abigail's behavior, Deborah turned back to face their guest. "Edward, I'm so sorry. That's not like her."

"She must be ill, indeed." He frowned, staring toward the empty doorway.

Deborah's heart went out to him. The forlorn dismay in his eyes wrenched every tender inclination she possessed.

"I'll go to her." She reached out and squeezed his hands. "Do, please, forgive her abruptness. I'm sure she wouldn't behave so if she were well. Perhaps you could come around again tomorrow."

"Yes, I shall. Please convey my apologies."

"You've nothing to apologize for."

Edward grimaced. "I'm afraid I must, or she wouldn't have reacted so. I seem to have lost my social graces. It would have been better to take a different approach rather than to shock you all." He took an uncertain step toward the door.

He looked so lost that Deborah gently took his arm and stayed beside him as far as the front door. He had no hat to retrieve, so she reached for the doorknob.

"Do come back tomorrow, Edward."

"Yes, I believe I will." Her heart ached as he turned his troubled eyes toward the stairs, then back to her. "But if Abigail is too ill to see me, you will tell me, won't you?"

"Yes, of course."

"Good. I don't want to be a bother."

His confusion and dejection made Deborah long to blurt out the truth. *Abby's promised to marry your cousin, but we still love you.* No, she couldn't say that. She glanced toward the stairway, wishing her father would appear to take over and tell Edward. Surely they shouldn't let him leave their house in ignorance. The whole town knew. Someone else would tell him. His mother, perhaps. He should not learn it that way.

But their father assumed Abby was doing her duty and explaining the situation to Edward herself. Perhaps Deborah should take him back into the parlor and beg him to wait while she fetched Father downstairs again. No, it was drawing close to dinnertime, and if Edward didn't leave the house soon, he'd still be here when Jacob arrived.

"Good day," Edward murmured. He was outside on the doorstep now.

What could she do? What could she say?

She caught her breath and stifled the words she wanted to shout. They nearly choked her. Instead, she managed to say, "I'm sure Abby will be all right once she gets over the jolt of your appearance. She ought to be able to receive you properly tomorrow."

He nodded and turned away, and she closed the door in misery, certain that she'd done the wrong thing.

❧

Edward walked slowly down the path toward the street. What did this mean? Abigail seemed anything but glad to see him. Her blue eyes had remained downcast during most of their interview, and when she looked up, he saw something like panic harbored in them.

But she was still here at home with her parents. That in itself was an encouragement. His fear that she might have married was unfounded.

Lord, show me how to approach her tomorrow, he prayed silently as he stepped through the gate. *You know my wishes, dear Father, but. . .Your will be done.*

He pulled up suddenly as another man nearly collided with him.

"Sorry." He jerked away, but the man seized his arm and stopped him.

"Edward? Is it you?"

He turned to look at the man. Sudden joy leaped into his heart, and he flung his arms around his cousin.

"Jacob! I'm so glad to see you at last. The Bowmans told me you and your men made it."

Jacob gasped and pulled away from him, his eyes wide in disbelief and his mouth gaping.

"I can't believe it! How can this be?"

Edward laughed, the first merriment he'd felt in a long time.

"It's wonderful to see you."

"But where. . .when. . . ?" Jacob shook his head and stood staring.

"I'm on my way home to see Mother. Come with me," Edward said.

Jacob looked longingly toward the house, then back at him. "I'm afraid I can't. I've a dinner engagement this evening. But perhaps I can get away early. You must tell me everything that's happened to you and the others."

"I'll be at home," Edward said. "We'll have a chance to discuss it soon." He wanted to get away, to have more time to think about his encounter with the Bowman family. And he must get to his mother right away. He'd sent a note to her as soon as the ship docked, but she would not forgive him if he lingered in the street, chatting with his cousin when he ought to be hurrying home to her embrace.

"All right," Jacob agreed. "Were you planning to go by the office tomorrow?"

"I might. Are you working there?"

"Well. . .yes. Listen, if you don't come in tomorrow, I'll come looking for you. I need to hear it all." He lifted the latch of the gate.

"You're going to the Bowmans' for dinner?" Edward asked.

"Well, yes." A flush washed Jacob's cheeks. "I say, Edward, have you been to see Abigail?"

"As a matter of fact, yes."

"Then she told you?"

Edward eyed him for a moment, then cleared his throat.

"Told me what?"

Jacob looked toward the house, then back at him. "Edward, I. . ."

Edward's anxiety mounted to paralyzing torment as he took in Jacob's pale features. Why should his friend and cousin sound remorseful?

"I. . ." Jacob straightened his shoulders. "We all thought you were dead, Edward."

"So I've been told." This was it, then. This was why Abigail felt ill when she saw him.

"Yes, well, it's been a long time."

"Four years since the *Egret* sank."

"Yes. And for the past year—oh, Edward, I didn't mean any disrespect to you or. . .or any presumption, but. . .well, you see, I've been courting Abigail."

Chapter 3

Deborah knocked softly on the door to Abigail's room. Even through the six-panel pine door, she could hear her sister weeping. She opened it a crack and peeked in. Abigail lay facedown on her bed, crying into her pillow.

Deborah tiptoed in and sat on the edge of the bed.

"There, Abby. Don't take on so." She rubbed her sister's heaving shoulders, and the sobs grew quieter.

At last Abigail rolled over, her cheeks crimson and her eyes awash with tears.

"I suppose you think I'm horrible." Abigail sniffed and her mouth twisted into a grimace. "Oh, Debbie, I know I was unkind to him—and I'm sorry—but I just couldn't tell him. How am I supposed to deal with this situation? It's unthinkable."

"No, dear. I'm sure other women must have faced similar problems before."

"I just want to die." Abigail broke out in weeping once more, and Deborah gathered her into her arms.

After several minutes, Abigail leaned back and blew her nose on the clean handkerchief Deborah offered her.

"Look at me! I'm wretched, and Jacob will be here any minute for dinner. Maybe I should stay up here and not eat tonight."

"Don't you dare."

"But what do I say to him?"

"Well, that depends." Deborah sat back and studied her face. "Do you love Jacob?"

"Yes, of course, or else I wouldn't have agreed to marry him."

"And do you still love Edward?"

Her heart sank as Abigail hesitated.

"I'm not sure. I mean, I loved him when he went away, but he seems like a different person now."

"You were only in his presence a short time," Deborah chided. "What changes did you see in him?"

"Well..." Abigail smoothed her skirt and frowned. "Besides his looking a bit shaggy, you mean? And that jacket!"

Deborah smiled. "I expect someone cut his hair and found him a razor on the ship, and those were probably borrowed clothes."

"You're right, of course, but I found it disconcerting. Why didn't he go home first and—"

"I expect he didn't want to wait to see you."

Abigail drew a ragged breath. "There's more than that." She seized her sister's hand, her eyes pleading for understanding. "I think I'm a little afraid of him, Debbie. He's not nearly so docile as he was before."

"Docile? Honestly, Abby, I saw great longing and love in his face when you came into the room. He still dotes on you. I dare say he's been dreaming of this reunion for five years."

Abigail sobbed and put the handkerchief to her lips. "I want to do the right thing, but what is the right thing in this case? Though I didn't intend to, I find myself engaged to two men. What sort of hoyden would do that?"

"There, now, don't vex yourself. No one is going to think ill of you. You waited far longer than most women would to set your affections elsewhere. For three years after his disappearance, you mourned Edward. Even then, when Jacob began calling on you, you held him off for a long time. No one can fault you for your conduct on that score."

"Thank you. It means a lot to hear you say that." Abigail squeezed her hand. "But what should I do now? Should I break off my engagement to Jacob, or should I tell Edward things have changed and I am now committed to Jacob? What is the honorable thing to do?"

"I don't know. If it's not clear to you, you must pray and seek God's will about your dilemma. But I do know one thing."

"What is that?"

"You must tell Jacob tonight, and when Edward comes round tomorrow, you must be honest with him."

"What if he doesn't understand?"

"Did he understand you five years ago?"

"Well, yes, I thought so, but—we were so young, Debbie. Perhaps Father was right to urge Edward and me to put off an engagement until he returned from his voyage."

Deborah's heart twisted. How could Abby consider not marrying Edward now? He was the brightest, finest young man she'd ever known. They'd all mourned his loss with Abby. Yet they'd all felt relief this past year when she'd finally put aside her sorrow and risen from her anguished grief.

Deborah put her hand to her sister's cheek and wiped away a straggling tear. "Pray hard, then, and speak your heart to both men."

A soft rap sounded on the door, and Mother looked in. "Jacob has arrived, girls. Your father is entertaining him in the parlor. You'd best come down and greet him, as dinner will be served shortly."

Abigail stood and inhaled deeply. "I suppose I must go down and tell him that Edward has come back."

Her mother sighed. "You can stop worrying about that. He knows."

"But how—"

"He arrived a bit early, and he learned it when he saw his cousin leaving the house."

"He saw Edward?" Abigail grabbed the bedpost and clung to it.

Concerned that her sister would swoon, Deborah leaped to her side.

"Please, Mother," Abigail wailed. "Let me stay up here. I'm not hungry."

"None of that, now. It's bad enough you seem to have let Edward leave without explaining your situation to him. You mustn't neglect to speak to Jacob."

Deborah slipped her arm around Abigail's waist. "You'll feel better after you discuss it with him. Jacob is a reasonable man."

"Not to mention a very handsome one and devoted to you," her mother added. "Come, now."

During dinner, Deborah sensed that everyone was on edge. After a timid, "You've heard about Edward," from Abigail and Jacob's response that he was indeed aware of the marvelous news, the conversation grew a bit stilted. Deborah ate mechanically as she strove to find topics that would put them all at ease. Her father launched into a story about one of his patients, and the tension subsided.

As soon as the meal was over, Dr. Bowman said, "Jacob, will you join me in my study for coffee?"

"If you don't mind, sir," Jacob replied, "I'd like to speak to Abigail privately." He looked anxiously at his fiancée.

Deborah expected Abigail to find an excuse to decline, but instead, her sister said, "I will take a short stroll with you if Deborah accompanies us."

Her mother frowned. "Are you sure you are up to it, dear? You've had a shock today."

"I—" Abigail glanced at Jacob, then looked down at the linen napkin crumpled in her hand. "I think Mr. Price and I need a chance to discuss today's events."

"You're right," said Dr. Bowman. "With Debbie along, I have no objection. Just see them home early, young man."

"Thank you, sir." Jacob rose and pulled Abigail's chair out for her.

Deborah found the prospect of chaperoning while Abigail bared her heart to her suitor distasteful, but she knew that if she refused, her sister would probably put off clearing the air with Jacob. Resigned to the outing, she fetched her shawl and headed toward the harbor with the couple.

As they walked, Jacob kept to mundane remarks about the weather, not broaching the subject that concerned them all until he found a bench overlooking the water. They sat down, and he reached for Abigail's hand.

"Abigail, dearest," he began.

Deborah turned away and stared studiously at a sloop anchored beyond the cluster of fishing boats nearest the shore. It was not fully dark yet, and other people passed them, ambling peacefully along in the warm June evening.

"I must know how things stand with you and Edward," Jacob continued. "Surely you understand my turmoil. I know you pledged your love to me in good faith, but you also pledged yourself to my cousin. I shan't be able to sleep tonight if I don't know that you still love me and plan to become my wife."

A prolonged silence followed, and Deborah felt Jacob's distress. Even more, she felt Abigail's anguish. Her sister's shoulders began to shake, and the bench quivered. Deborah whirled and put her arms around Abigail.

"Really, Jacob, can't you be more considerate?"

Jacob coughed and stared at Deborah. "Forgive me, but my future is at stake here. Surely I have a right to know where I stand."

"And what about Abby? Hasn't she any rights?" By the shock in Jacob's eyes, Deborah knew she was coming at it a bit strong, but she couldn't help it, seeing her sister crushed by the weight of the decision that lay before her. Suddenly she wondered if her own secret preference for Edward was influencing her to fight so fiercely. Was she more committed to seeing Abigail have time to make a rational decision or for Edward to have time to make his case? She wouldn't think about that now. "Abby has had a severe shock, and a gentleman shouldn't clamor so urgently for answers."

Jacob sat back, his spine rigid against the bench.

Deborah stroked Abigail's hair and whispered, "There, now, dear. You need some time to think everything through and pray about it."

Jacob produced a clean handkerchief. Abigail took it with a murmured, "Thank you," and dabbed at her eyes.

Jacob sat forward, clasping his hands between his knees. He shot a sideways glance at Abigail, and when he caught Deborah's eye, she favored him with a meaningful glare.

He cleared his throat. "I suppose your sister is right, my dear. You are as startled and confused as I am. Would you say that a week is time enough for you to sort out your feelings on the matter?"

Abigail gulped and raised her lashes, meeting his gaze in the twilight. "A week?"

"Yes." Jacob reached for her hand, and Deborah turned away, feeling even more the unwanted companion.

"Abby, dearest, I love you more than life itself. When you grieved for Edward, I admired that. I saw your tender heart and your faithfulness to the man you loved. And I longed for that. I craved to have that devotion turned my way."

Abigail let out a soft sigh. "Oh, Jacob! I do care for you. You know that."

There was a soft smacking sound, and Deborah assumed he was kissing her hands. She turned even farther away, her cheeks flushing, and wished she were anywhere but on that bench.

"Oh, darling," Jacob said, "if your earlier attachment to Edward is stronger, then I suppose you should honor it. It's not in your character to deny it. But in my heart, I can't help hoping you will choose me. Edward is an honorable man, and I love him, too. I promise to hold no bitterness toward you whatever your decision."

"Thank you." Abigail's voice broke, and Deborah foresaw another deluge of tears. She jumped up and faced the startled Jacob.

"I believe it's time we returned to the house, Mr. Price."

"Oh, certainly."

Abigail stood and gathered her cloak about her, and they strolled away from the harbor, back toward the residential neighborhood. Deborah noticed that her sister kept her hand tucked through Jacob's arm as they walked.

They reached the Bowmans' door, and Jacob caressed Abigail's hand before releasing it. "Might I come to call again Sunday, Abby?"

"I. . .well, yes."

He nodded. "I'll see you then. Good night."

Deborah opened the door, and she and Abigail stepped into the hall. She hung up her shawl and turned to face her sister.

"Oh, Debbie, they are both fine men. Whatever shall I do?" Abigail burst into tears again.

⌘

"My dear, dear boy!"

Edward submitted to his mother's ferocious embrace. "I love you, Mother. I'm so sorry I wasn't here for you when Father was ill."

She stepped back and devoured him with her eyes. "It was a trial, but your sister was a great comfort to me. The Price family, too. Jacob and his parents helped me with everything, from the burial arrangements to finding new household help when the hired girl left to be married. And Jacob has kept the business running as smoothly as a sleigh on ice. Thanks to him, I have not wanted for money."

"I'm glad he's taken care of you." He noted how her hair had silvered, but her posture was still straight and her movements steady.

He let her lead him into the kitchen and sit him down at the table in the spot where his father always used to sit. All the while, thoughts about Jacob raced through his mind. It seemed his cousin had taken his place in many areas—his career, his duties as a son, and even his role as Abigail's future husband. He tried to squelch the jealousy that sprang up, forming a crushing weight on his chest. It was only the closeness of the room, he told himself, and the smoke from the fireplace and the cooking smells within the confined space that made him feel ill and claustrophobic.

His mother tied a calico apron over her gray skirt and pulled two kettles away from the fire.

"I hope you were not overset by the news of my return," he said.

143

She bustled about, filling a plate for him. "It was a shock of the best kind. I fell into my chair when I first opened your note, but Jenny Hapworth was here—she does the housework for me now. She brought me tea and let me dither on. I'm afraid I was overly exuberant for a woman my age."

He smiled and captured her hand as she set the plate before him.

"I should have come to you first."

"No, no, I understood perfectly. You had another errand that couldn't wait." She eyed him closely, her mouth drooping in an anxious frown. "How did you find Miss Bowman?"

"She. . .was a bit more distraught than you and perhaps not so exuberant."

His mother eyed him with compassion, then nodded. "I'm sorry. Well, I set about cooking and airing your room as soon as I got the news. I hope you haven't eaten."

"No, I had a glass of cider while at the Bowmans', but beyond that, I've had nothing since breakfast."

"My poor boy! I hope you still like roast mutton. We've no potatoes left, but there's plenty of biscuits and applesauce and a pudding for after."

He surveyed the plate. "I doubt I shall be able to eat all this. I'm not used to such bounty."

Tears sprang into his mother's eyes, and she ruffled his hair before hurrying to the fireplace to remove a steaming kettle of water.

"Tea or coffee?"

"Coffee, please, if you have it. I spent many evenings in my exile trying to recall the smell and taste of the brew."

He bowed his head and offered a silent prayer of thanks for his food and his homecoming.

The first bite of his mother's biscuit put him in euphoria. The outside was golden brown, the bottom firm, and the top soft and flaky. The inside was pure white and separated into tender layers. The wholesome, nutty flavor answered some craving he'd had for four years. Bread! So simple yet so exotic. During the last two months on shipboard, he'd had hard, crumbling biscuits with traces of mold. He'd gone ashore briefly in Boston a week ago, but the bread in the tavern he'd patronized was almost as dry as the sea biscuit.

He chewed slowly, looking at the hole he had bitten from the side of the biscuit. None of the shipboard food had come close to this. And a platter full of them awaited his pleasure, if he could hold them.

"Don't you want some butter?" Mother asked. She pushed the blue china butter dish closer to him, but he shook his head.

"It's perfect. Perhaps tomorrow or next week I'll put butter on one."

She smiled, and he was glad to see the old look of affection and satisfaction she'd habitually worn when watching her menfolk eat.

"If only your father had lived to see this day."

He searched her eyes and saw that her grief was well banked.

"On the last leg of my trip home, from Boston up to here, the ship's captain told me Father had died."

"I'm sorry you learned it that way."

"Oh, he was good about it. He'd known Father for years. In fact, I had met him before at the warehouse. They'd done business together for a long time. Captain Stebbins, out of Searsport."

"Of course." His mother took the seat beside him. "He's dined in this house."

Edward nodded. "He expressed his condolences to you as well. When did it happen, exactly?"

"Last July. Your father collapsed at the office. Jacob sent for Dr. Bowman right away, but it was too late. His heart, the doctor said."

"I'm so sorry. If I could have done anything to get word to you, I would have."

"Of course you would. Your father was crushed when we heard that you were dead. We both were, if the truth be told. Jacob came to visit us as soon as he returned home from the voyage and shared his memories of the time he had on shipboard with you before the storm."

Edward nodded. "We got along well. I was glad Jacob was on the ship. We spoke many times of how things would be when we came home. But we thought we'd sail back to Portland together on the *Egret* with a huge profit for Hunter Shipping."

"I. . .blamed your father for sending our only son off on a long voyage like that." She reached toward him quickly. "Please don't despise me."

"I never could, Mother."

"I admit that when we got news of your death, I was bitter toward him at first. But after a while, we worked through our sorrow, and I asked your father to forgive me. He was always a generous person, and so, of course, he did."

He patted her hand. "That's like Father. Your reaction was natural, I'm sure."

She rose and refilled his coffee, and he sipped it, savoring the rich flavor. "Mother, I've been told that Jacob is running the company now."

"Well, Mr. Daniels is still there. He heads the accounting department. Has three clerks under him. And your uncle Felix runs the warehouse. But yes, Jacob has been invaluable to Hunter Shipping."

Edward nodded. "I'm glad he was there."

"When your father died, he helped make a smooth transition in the management of the company." She sat down opposite him and held his gaze. "You see, we believed you were dead, son, so your father took Jacob into the office and mentored him in the trade. He'd decided to let Jacob take over the company when he was too old to run it anymore. Felix Price was agreeable, and it seemed the best your father could do since his only son was gone."

"I understand." Edward took another sip.

"But then, last year your father's heart gave out and he died. No one expected him to go so soon." She blinked at tears, and her voice trembled. "He was only fifty."

"So. . .what is the status of the company now?"

She sniffed and went on with a steadier voice. "Your father signed paperwork before his death, allowing me to own it. I'll be honest with you: I encouraged him to leave it to Jacob with the provision of a lifetime allowance for me. But your father wouldn't hear of it. He had the papers drawn up all legal about three years ago, after we'd given up hope you would ever be found. He told me that when he was gone I could do as I wished, but he wanted to keep the company in the Hunter name while he lived."

"And you didn't change that after he died?"

"No. I do respect Jacob, but somehow I just couldn't do it. I kept putting it off and thinking I'd take care of the transfer a little later."

"I'm surprised you were allowed to own the business."

"Well, your father made sure it was all legal. He left 10 percent to Jacob, and 5 percent to Mr. Daniels. He's been a good and faithful employee for more than forty years."

"And you hold the rest?"

"Yes, but I shall transfer it to you tomorrow. You must take me around to the office, and we'll see about the papers. There's a lawyer in town now. If you think it best, we can ask him to draw them up."

"There's no rush, Mother."

"Yes, there is. I want things as they should be. I know it has irked Mr. Daniels that technically I have the final say in business decisions. He and Jacob have to come here and tell me everything they plan to do before they can execute an idea. Jacob has been very courteous. Well, they both have, but it's been awkward."

"I'm not sure I'm qualified—"

"Now, don't start that, Edward."

"But I didn't finish the training my father sent me to undertake."

"Nonsense. You've always had a good head for business. You spent years in the office with your father before you went away. You practically apprenticed in the warehouse. You'll take your proper place in this company. Period."

Edward managed a smile. "All right, Mother. I shall do my best and pray that you won't regret your decision."

"Now tell me about Abigail. You said you saw her this evening."

He sat back and drew a deep breath.

"Yes, I saw the whole family."

"And what did she tell you? Did you know that she was affianced to Jacob when you saw her?"

He bit his upper lip and picked up his spoon. "No. But I learned it soon after."

"I assume you want to claim your right as her betrothed. What did she say?"

"She didn't say much of anything. I believe she was in shock."

His mother clucked in disapproval.

"I shouldn't have gone there today." He sighed and put his hand to his forehead. "I ought to have come directly here and sent word there, instead of the other way around. Then she would have had time to compose herself."

"Was it very awful?"

"Frustrating. I had to give her father an account of my whereabouts for the last four years, since the *Egret* sank."

"That's a tale I want to hear soon but not tonight," his mother said.

"It's soon told. I was on a small, isolated isle in the Pacific. Dr. Bowman found it fascinating. And Deborah!" He looked up at her and smiled involuntarily. "I was overcome by the change in her. She was just a child when I left, but now she's—"

"A woman."

"Yes, indeed."

His mother nodded. "A stunning woman, though I don't believe she knows it yet. One of these sailor boys will steal her heart soon, I'll warrant."

"Oh, I doubt Dr. Bowman would allow a common sailor to call on her. He would have to be a boatswain, at least."

"Or a second mate?"

Edward chuckled. Second mate had been his rank on the *Egret*. "Ah, well, a captain wouldn't be too good for her. She's very outspoken. Not at all pretentious, but with a bearing that's almost regal. In the best sense of the word, of course."

His mother said nothing but got up to serve the dried plum pudding.

Chapter 4

The next morning, Edward walked to the graveyard near the church, accompanied by his mother. She had given away most of his old clothing, but she'd kept a few things that had belonged to his father. He wore a hat that he'd often seen his father wear and a suit that hung on him.

"You'll need to have some new shirts and drawers," his mother murmured. "Perhaps I can find some muslin and linen this afternoon."

Edward felt the blood rush to his cheeks. She was his mother, but still. One thing it would never be proper to discuss with her was his island wardrobe. Hearing her plan what he would wear for linens and woolens here in Maine would be embarrassing enough.

"Don't overdo, Mother. I'm not used to a large wardrobe."

"I'll have Jenny help me. You'll be going to the office and meeting lots of businessmen. You look as peaked as a crow's beak, and you can't impress clients if you're wearing clothes two sizes too large. Perhaps I can take in that suit, but that black wool is too hot for summer. It will do in the fall, but you must have something decent to wear now."

Edward didn't argue. It was just nine in the morning and only mid-June, but already the sun beat down on them, making him sweat beneath the layers of wool and linen. He'd supposed the northern climate would seem cool and refreshing to him after years in the tropical sun, but already he was finding the summer uncomfortably warm. Besides, his mother would undertake assembling a new wardrobe for him whether he liked it or not.

He opened the gate to the churchyard, and they walked between the monuments, mostly flat slabs of slate or granite standing in the turf. Each of the families associated with this church had an area where their dead were buried. Some had one large family marker with smaller stones delineating the individual graves.

The Hunter family plot was dominated by a big, rectangular granite stone. Several generations were buried near it, from the first Hunters who had settled in colonial times to the most recently departed. Deep purple violets grew at the foot of the stone in a hardy bunch, and the name HUNTER was deeply graven on it.

His mother led him beyond the older graves to a marker that read JEREMIAH HUNTER, 1769–1819, BELOVED HUSBAND AND FATHER.

His father's grave. Edward bowed his head for a moment in silent anguish, then stepped closer. His heart lurched as his gaze caught the line chiseled lower on the granite slab.

EDWARD HUNTER, 1796–1816, PRECIOUS SON.

He gulped for air and felt his mother's strong hand grasp his elbow.

"Are you all right, son?"

"Yes. It's. . .a bit unnerving to see my own name there with Father's."

"I'm sorry. I had that done after your father died, in memory of you. There's nothing buried there for you, of course. I can ask the stonecutter to chip it off."

"No, just leave it, and someday someone can change it to the proper date."

Edward took off his hat and fell to his knees. He placed his hand over the letters that formed his father's name. *Dear Lord, thank You for the parents You gave me. Help me to live up to their dreams.*

Edward took his mother home and left her in the care of Jenny, the hired girl. In the short time he had been home, he had learned that Jenny expected to be married at harvesttime, and his mother would once more have to find and break in new household help. Already she was putting the word out at church and throughout her social circle. Edward doubted it would take her long to find another maid. His mother was not demanding, and the chores of the small household wouldn't overtax a woman.

He was glad she had the sturdy house his grandfather had built. It was not as grand as some built by sea captains and shipping magnates, but it was comfortable. The two-story building was sided with pine clapboards, and two masonry chimneys flanked the small observation deck on top. Like many a seafaring man, Edward's grandfather had spent much time watching the harbor, and Grandmother was often found on the deck, gazing out toward Casco Bay when the captain was at sea.

Edward walked toward the shipping company's headquarters near the docks. When he was a block from the building, a chandler paused in unloading a pile of merchandise and stared at him.

"Edward Hunter. Is it you, lad, or am I seeing a ghost?"

Edward laughed. "It's me, Simeon. I've returned from the sea."

"But I attended your funeral several years past. You can't say nay to that."

"Yes, I've been told I was mourned and missed, but as you see, I was never buried."

A small crowd gathered as more men heard the news or came to see what the ruckus was about.

"Please excuse me," Edward said. "I'm glad to see you all again, but I've business to attend to at Hunter Shipping."

He pushed through the knot of onlookers, greeting the men he recognized, shaking a few hands, and murmuring, "Thank you so much. Good to be back."

The company's offices were on the far side of the warehouse, and he entered through the loading door, then stopped to sniff the air. Tea, lumber, tar, molasses, apples, and cinnamon. Now he was really home.

"Mr. Edward." One of the men recognized him and stepped toward him, grinning.

Edward smiled and clapped the older man on the shoulder. "Yes, Elijah, it's me."

"Mr. Price told us you was back." The laborer shook his head. " 'Tis a marvel, sir."

"Yes, indeed. Praise God, I'm alive and I'm home. Someday soon I'll come down to the dock and break bread with you all at nooning and tell you of my adventure."

"You do that, Mr. Edward."

Two other workers stacking bags marked RICE stopped to stare. Edward waved, then turned toward the doorway that led to the offices.

A large man hopped down from a crate and blocked his path.

"Edward, my boy!"

"Uncle Felix!"

Edward submitted to a hug from Jacob's burly father, then pulled away, fighting for breath.

"My son told me last night you were alive and well." Uncle Felix slapped his shoulder and grinned. "A wondrous sight you are."

"Thank you, Uncle. I'm glad to see you're still here and carrying on."

"Oh yes, I'm fine. Fifty-three years old and still strong as an ox. Now, Jacob, he's a different sort than me. Started out down here with me, but you know, he's not made for hauling truck around the docks. He can do it, but he's made for higher things." Uncle Felix touched his temple and nodded. "Your father saw that, he did. Put my boy over in the office clerking, then sent him to sea. And now he's wearing fine clothes and keeping your inheritance safe for you. Don't forget that, boy."

"I won't." Edward eyed his uncle, wondering if he'd just received a warning to take care of his family. Uncle Felix had lived his life as a laborer, first as a fisherman. After he married Ruth Hunter, Edward's father had employed Felix at the warehouse for his sister's sake but had privately opined that Aunt Ruth had married beneath her. Still, love is love, and Father had always managed to get along with his brother-in-law. Ruth was happy to see her husband with a job safe on land.

Felix was a hearty, jovial man and a hard worker. He had risen to the overseer's post on merit, not just because of his marriage to the owner's sister. His wages had allowed him to buy a small clapboard house in the better part of town, and Aunt Ruth was content. Her three daughters had all made respectable marriages and provided the Prices with an assortment of grandchildren.

"Have you seen your sister's new babe?"

"Not yet," Edward said. "I sent Anne a message, and the family's coming to the house this evening."

"Ah, she must be pleased her brother's not drowned and dead."

"I'm sure she is. It's great to see you, Uncle Felix." Edward shook his hand and headed for the office.

"Bring your mother 'round for Sunday dinner!" his uncle called after him.

As Edward left the warehouse and stepped into the outer room where the clerks had their desks, he stopped. Several doors led off the main room, and one of them led to the private office that had long been his father's sanctum when he was owner and head of the company. But now the door stood open, and coming out of that office was his cousin, Jacob Price.

"Edward, I was hoping you'd come down today."

Jacob's greeting seemed a bit stilted, but Edward stepped toward him.

"Thank you. I hope I'm not intruding."

"How could you intrude in your own office?"

Edward said nothing but couldn't help looking beyond Jacob to the open door.

Jacob followed his gaze. "I was gathering up a few papers. You'll want this office, of course. Your father's desk and all." He stopped and pressed his lips together.

Edward glanced around and saw that the nearest clerk, while not looking at them, had paused with his pen hovering above the ledger on his desk, as though waiting to hear what would happen next.

"Could we have a word in private?"

"Of course." Jacob gestured for Edward to precede him into the inner office.

Edward stepped to the threshold and paused, taking a slow, deep breath. Memories of his father deluged him: the double window where his father had often stood looking out over the harbor to see which ships were docking, the shelves of ledgers that held the business records of Hunter Shipping for nearly a hundred years past, the large walnut desk his grandfather had brought from England—it was all just as it had been five years ago when his father had wished him well on the voyage.

He could almost see Father sitting behind the desk, sharpening a quill with his penknife. Displayed on the wall behind the desk were an old sextant and spyglass, mementos of the past captains Hunter, and a large chart of the New England coast.

It was all precisely the way he had remembered it. Except. . .

He turned to face Jacob. "I don't recall that painting over there."

Jacob looked where he nodded. "Oh yes. The winter landscape. It came on a ship from France, and I liked it. I thought it would look nice in here."

Edward took a few paces closer to examine it. He didn't recognize the artist's name, but the composition attracted him with its subdued purple and blue shadows in the snow. He kept silent, wondering if the painting belonged to Jacob or to Hunter Shipping, and at what cost. That led to the question of what Jacob was receiving as salary. Could the company afford to pay them both?

Jacob closed the door softly and stepped toward him.

"Edward, I want to assure you that if I'd known you had survived I never would have made myself at home in this room."

Edward turned and eyed him once more, searching his face for deceit or malice but finding none.

"You were within your rights. It's my understanding that my father asked you to take on a major role in the firm, as a replacement for me."

Jacob coughed and turned to the window. "It was something of the sort, yes." He shoved his hands into his pockets.

Edward stared at his back. Jacob's broadcloth coat hung perfectly from his shoulders, and his posture was straight. His blond hair curled against his collar, a fashionable length for the merchant class. He looked the part of a shipping magnate. But Jacob's head began to droop, and his shoulders slumped.

Edward walked over to stand beside him and placed his hand on Jacob's shoulder. "I've been told the business is running smoothly."

Jacob's gaze flitted to his face. "Yes, everything's fine. Of course, the company was hit hard when the *Egret* sank with her cargo four years ago, but your father was canny and made some good investments on the next few voyages with the other two ships. And I've been thinking for some time now of purchasing another vessel."

"Funds are available for that?"

"Well, yes. Daniels tells me they are. I've pretty much left the accounts to him, but we seem to be doing all right, Ed. Some of our enterprises are more profitable than others."

"Naturally."

Jacob's eyes picked up the glitter of the sunlight streaming through the window. "It was my thought to buy a ship before fall if profits continued this summer as they've been for the last year or so. Another schooner, perhaps. We purchased a small sloop before your father died that we use in coastal trade, but I think we're ready for another vessel with the tonnage of the *Egret* or larger."

Edward nodded. "I know nothing of the company's state at the moment. I'd appreciate it if you'd tutor me a little."

"Of course. Edward, I hope—" Jacob studied Edward's face with anxious blue eyes. "I hope you'll keep me on."

"I have no intention of turning you out, Jacob. I regret that my return is displacing you to some extent, but I see no reason why we can't work together."

"Are you certain?" Jacob's brow wrinkled, and his mouth held an anxious crook.

He's thinking of Abigail, Edward realized. Would the fact that they both loved the same woman come between them?

He walked to the bookshelves and gently touched the binding on his father's copy of Bowditch's *The American Practical Navigator.*

"We've always gotten on well, Jacob."

"So we have. And I'm delighted that you've returned."

Edward felt a tightness in his throat and gave a gentle cough. "I'm sure we'll work something out so that we can both earn our living here. As I said, you've proven your worth in the company. I have my mother's word on that, and I expect I'll have Mr. Daniels's confirmation soon."

"He'll show you the books, Edward. Anything you want to see. It took awhile for business to pick up after the peace was signed with England in '14, you know. Sometimes money was scarce, but we've pretty well recovered. Your father was pleased with the way our trade was going last year. If his heart had been stronger, he'd be here now to tell you this."

Edward raised one hand to curtail his cousin's words. "I'm sorry, but I'm feeling a bit emotional today, seeing my father's office and all for the first time since. . ." Edward swallowed hard, then brushed his grief aside, determined to get down to business. "You know, I think I'd benefit by a short tour of the wharf."

"Of course." Jacob hurried toward the door. "We've expanded the store on the wharf, you know."

"Oh? I came in on Richardson's Wharf yesterday, and I didn't get a good look at ours."

"Well, our chandlery is twice as large as it was when you left, and I've leased space on the wharf for several other small shops. I hope you don't mind. Most are one-year leases, and it's good for business. Draws more people to our store."

"I'm sure it's fine, so long as we're doing well in the ships' supplies."

"Last year was our best year ever. And I've worked out a deal with Stephens's Ropewalk. They make us eight sizes of cordage, and we sell all we can get, both here in our store and in the West Indies trade."

"Rope." Edward nodded. "It's a good, sound product." His mind was racing. It seemed the company was doing better than ever under Jacob's supervision. He knew it was partly due to the general economic climate of the day, but it sowed a riot of thoughts and feelings. How could he take over when Jacob was doing so well? But this was still the shipping company his father and grandfather had built. Could he do as well as Jacob was doing? What would it mean to Jacob, financially and socially, if Edward demoted him? And would it make a difference to Abby? Should he base his business decisions on what she and, yes, even her father would think?

"Of course, lumber is still our mainstay," Jacob said. "But we've been shipping a larger variety of goods in the past two years. I'm telling you, Ed, having England off our backs has opened up a lot of new markets."

Edward smiled at his cousin's enthusiasm. "Well, if you have time this morning, why don't you walk over to the wharf with me and point out the improvements? Afterward, perhaps I can sit down with Mr. Daniels and get an overview of the financial end of things."

"I'd be pleased to do that." Jacob reached for the doorknob. "And, Edward, whatever you decide you want me to do for this firm, I'll accept your decision."

"You've worked hard, Jacob. I'm not sure what our course should be yet, but I won't forget that."

Jacob nodded, but his troubled frown told Edward his cousin was not so settled as his words implied. Edward followed him out into the bright June sunlight. The thought was unspoken, but he inferred that, while Jacob might feel obligated to relinquish the management of Hunter Shipping, he would not so willingly give up his claim to Abigail.

~∞~

"I don't want to see him."

Abigail sat before her dressing table, her back turned to Deborah, stiff and unyielding, while Deborah sat on her sister's bed, attempting to count the stitches in her knitting.

"Let's not go through this again." Deborah turned her knitting at the end of the row. She couldn't knit anything required to fit someone—no stockings or gloves. Her stitches were much too tight, throwing the gauge off. But she could knit mufflers and rectangular coverlets for babies, and she was working on one for Frances Reading, whose husband had been killed in an accident at the distillery on Titcomb's Wharf a month ago. Deborah had bought the softest wool yarn she could find and dyed it a pale yellow with goldenrod. The blanket was turning out surprisingly well.

"You were less than courteous to Edward last night," she reminded Abigail. "Go down and be civil."

"Must I?"

"Oh, Abby, is this simply embarrassment over your behavior last night?" Deborah watched her sister's downcast eyes in the mirror. Getting no answer, she laid her yarn and needles aside and walked over to touch Abigail's shoulder. "It's not like you to be unkind."

Abigail's mouth clenched for an instant. "All right, I'll talk to him, but only if you promise to stay with me. Don't leave me alone with him."

"Why ever not?"

"I don't know. He seemed a bit. . .savage, I thought."

Deborah shook her head. "You're imagining things."

"But he was out there alone for years with nothing but seabirds and wolves."

"Wolves? Who said anything about wolves on his island?"

"Cannibals, then."

"Nonsense. I've always liked Edward and thought you were marrying the finest man on earth. I doubt he lost his good sense during his ordeal, though he was forced to give up many refinements."

Abigail wrinkled her nose at her reflection in the looking glass. "Oh, Debbie, I liked him, too."

"You told me then that you loved him."

"So I did." Abigail sighed. "I was thrilled that he'd noticed me and that he chose me from among all the other girls. But he's been gone so long, and he's changed."

"Give him a chance, dear. Have you made up your mind to marry Jacob? I don't want to see you discard Edward lightly. He's a wonderful man, and he's been through more than we know, though I'm quite sure we can discount wolves and cannibals."

"I know it, and I don't want to crush his spirit. I'm just not sure I can ever recapture the feelings I had for him five years ago."

"Well, he's been waiting fifteen minutes already. I do think you ought to go down without further delay."

"Come with me."

Deborah frowned. "I hate this chaperone business. It's not in my nature."

"Oh yes, I know. You're the free spirit of the family. But I don't wish to be alone with him."

"All right. But you must make a promise in return."

"What?"

"Treat him decently, as you would any nice gentleman caller."

"I'll pretend he's one of Father's friends."

It wasn't quite what Deborah had hoped for, and she laid a hand on her sister's sleeve.

"Well, keep in mind that whichever man you marry, Edward owns the business concern that will support your family."

Abigail's eyes widened. "I'm always civil, I hope."

Deborah scooped her knitting off the coverlet and shoved it into her workbag. She was longing to hear more of Edward's tale and decided to make the most of this encounter. The idea of his fighting for life against nature in a beautiful but terrible setting intrigued her. She hoped that this afternoon he would reveal more of his adventures.

They walked down the oak stairs together, their full skirts swishing. Abigail looked lovely in the pale blue gown that matched her bright eyes. Deborah was certain Edward would appreciate her beauty. Her cheeks were slightly flushed, and her golden hair shimmered. If only she wouldn't leave the room precipitately again.

At last Edward heard the sisters coming down the stairs. He jumped up and met them as they entered the parlor. Abigail smiled at him and let him take her hand for a moment. That was an improvement over their meeting last night.

In fact, she seemed much calmer, and she even murmured, "Edward, so kind of you to come this afternoon."

"It's a pleasure. I hope we can come to an understanding about. . .things."

He couldn't help staring at her. She was more beautiful than his most accurate mental images of her. While on the island, he had wondered if his mind exaggerated her charms and if he would be disappointed on his return to find that she was quite plain. But that was foolish. He'd known from the first time he set eyes on her that she was among the fairest of the city.

The blue of her gown enhanced her creamy complexion, and her hair, pulled back in honey-colored waves, enticed him to brush it with his fingertips to see if it were truly as soft as it appeared.

"Hello, Edward."

Deborah stepped forward and held her hand out to him, and he released Abigail's and focused on the younger sister. He noted anew that Deborah had become a well-favored woman, and he smiled at the gawky girl turned graceful beauty. No doubt most men would find it hard to choose between the two if asked which sister was lovelier.

"What are you grinning at, if I may be so bold?" she asked with a playful smile.

"I'm sorry. I just can't get over the change in you, Debbie—or Miss Deborah, I suppose I ought to call you now."

She waved that comment aside and sat down on the sofa next to Abigail.

"Nonsense. I grew up calling you Edward, and you always called me Debbie. We needn't commence using formalities now."

He laughed. "Thank you. That's a relief."

He settled into his chair greatly eased. Deborah, at least, was willing to see this interview run smoothly, and Abigail seemed to be in a better humor as well. The shock of his survival and return to Maine had dissipated. He hoped she was ready to discuss their future.

When he smiled at Abigail, she tendered a somewhat timid smile in return and clasped her hands in her lap. Her lips parted as though she would speak but then closed again, and she looked away.

"Well, ladies," Edward said, glancing at Deborah and back to Abigail, "I do apologize for any abruptness, but I think we all know it's important for me to understand your intentions, Abigail."

Abigail's eyes widened, and she turned toward her sister in dismay.

"Dear Edward," Deborah said, patting Abigail's hand, "you are rather forthcoming today. I was hoping, and I'm sure Abby was, too, that you'd tell us a bit more about your travels."

He swallowed hard. So, they were not going to make this simple.

"Deborah, Abigail, please forgive me for being so frank, but surely you can understand my anxiety. I spent some time with my cousin at the wharf this morning, and I must know...." He left his chair and went to his knees at Abigail's side, reaching for her hands. "Dearest Abby, I simply have to know whether or not you still intend to marry me."

Chapter 5

Abigail pulled back and jerked her hands away, looking frantically to Deborah. Edward saw at once that he'd been too aggressive. He stood and walked to the empty fireplace, leaning on the mantelpiece and mentally flogging himself for being such a dolt.

"Edward," came Deborah's tentative voice, "perhaps we could come at this topic more subtly."

He blinked at her. Deborah was stroking her sister's hand and gazing at him with such an open, accepting smile that he suddenly wanted to do whatever he must to please her.

That wasn't quite right. He ought to strive to please Abigail, no matter what Deborah thought.

He brushed his hair off his brow. His mother had offered to cut it. Perhaps he should take her up on that this evening. It was shorter now than he'd worn it in solitude but was still long enough to annoy him when it fell into his eyes.

"Please sit down," Deborah continued. "I'm sure Abby is willing to discuss the agreement she made last evening with Mr. Price."

Abigail caught her breath and looked down at her hands once more, her face flushing a rich pink. Once again Edward found his gaze flickering from Abigail to Deborah and back. Abigail, the older sister, so self-assured and cordial to him in the past, seemed terrified of him. Deborah, the lively, teasing younger sister, had assumed the role of the placid peacemaker.

He hesitated, then went to his chair and sat facing them, his nerves at the breaking point. Sweat broke out on his forehead and his back. He wasn't used to being confined in layers of clothing, and the tense situation combined with the warm weather had him perspiring profusely.

"I'm sorry," he said. "If you please, Abigail, we shall proceed with the topic at the speed you wish."

"You said. . . ." Abigail's voice quivered, and she began again. "You said you spent the day with Jacob."

"Part of it. I had a tour of the company's wharf with him this morning, looking over the expansion of the store there and some repairs done to the mooring slips. Then Captain Moody hoisted a flag indicating that a ship was entering the harbor."

"We heard the commotion about noon," Deborah said. "Was it one of your ships?"

"No, it was a schooner from Liverpool, docking at Long Wharf. Jacob decided to go down there and see if she'd brought anything we'd want to purchase for our store. I went back to the office and had a session with Mr. Daniels, our chief accountant. Jacob had told him this morning that I was back, and he had the books all laid out for me to examine."

"And were things in order?" Abigail asked.

"Well, I've only had time to give the ledgers a cursory look at this point, but yes, I'd say Hunter Shipping has been under good management these last few years." He wondered suddenly if Abigail thought he might doubt Jacob's capability, and he knew that, whether she chose to marry him or not, he must put that question to rest. "Of course, my father ran things right up until his death last year, but since then, all indications are that Jacob and Mr. Daniels have done a fine job."

She nodded and lowered her eyes. He decided to leave it at that, though one small item he'd noticed during his quick glance at the books had prompted him to make a decision. He would go through all the financial records thoroughly, especially those of the last year, as soon as he had the opportunity.

"It must have been an emotional day for you," Deborah said.

Edward nodded. "Yes. Seeing all of the fellows I used to work beside, and of course noticing that some I used to work with are missing."

"Will you go to sea again?"

He paused, wondering just how to answer that question. Abigail also seemed to take an avid interest.

"I might. I'm not angry at the sea. God determines if a man will be safe or not, whether he's walking a cobbled street or an oaken deck. But if I were a married man, I doubt I would make another long voyage. Perhaps I would sail as far as the Caribbean if the business required it, but I wouldn't want to. . .be away from my family longer than that."

Abigail flushed once more, and he felt the blood rush to his own cheeks. Perhaps a change of subject was in order.

"I saw Henry Mitchell in the warehouse today. When I left, he was only a boy. Twelve years old then, he told me. Now he's a laborer for Hunter Shipping."

"His father was one of those who didn't return from the *Egret's* voyage," Deborah said.

Edward nodded and bowed his head for a moment. "I know. Amos Mitchell was in the longboat with me and the others. But he. . .didn't survive our journey to the island."

"I'm sorry," Deborah said. "That must have been a terrible time."

"It was. We started out with eight, but only four of us made it ashore. Captain Trowbridge died soon after. He's buried there." Edward ran a hand through his hair. "I must go around to see his widow soon."

"Mrs. Trowbridge seemed despondent at first," Deborah said. "She knew one day her husband wouldn't return from a voyage, she said. But after the first year, she regained her vim. Her daughter Prudy and her family live with her in the big house now."

A sudden thought disturbed Edward. "I hope my returning hasn't given anyone false hope for their loved ones."

"No, I'm sure it hasn't."

"I must visit her tomorrow," he said, more to himself than to the ladies. How awful for the captain's wife to resign herself to her husband's death and then, four years later, to hear that one of the men she thought drowned with him had survived. For four years, Edward had lived with his failure to keep Captain Trowbridge alive. He'd respected the man and wished he could have done more to help him, but by the time they reached the island and fresh water, it was too late.

After a moment of heavy silence, Edward wondered if he ought to leave. It seemed every conversation led to depressing memories. He didn't want to throw the household into gloom, but neither did he want to make his exit without learning how Abigail felt toward him.

Deborah shifted and smoothed a ruffle on her skirt. "If you mind my asking, do say so, Edward, but I've been wondering. . . ."

"Yes?" He met her rich brown eyes and saw a twinkle there not unlike the expression she used to don when he teased her.

"Whatever did you eat on that island?"

He laughed. "At first, we thought we'd starve. But there were shellfish, and we caught some other fish. Gideon Bramwell became quite good at killing birds with a slingshot."

"Young Gideon was with you on the island?" Abigail stared at him in surprise.

"Yes, for the first two years. I. . .regret to say that he fell from a cliff while trying to raid a plover's nest for some eggs." He sighed and closed his eyes against the image of the plucky boy's mangled body lying in the surf below. Making a mental note to visit Gideon's mother as well, he strove for a more cheerful note. "We landed there in midsummer, and soon the fruit began to ripen. That was providential. And we found a few roots we could eat, and the leaves of one tree made a passable tea."

"So you weren't starving," Deborah said with a satisfied nod.

"No, although sometimes our rations were short. But as soon as we saw that we had fresh water and could find enough nourishment, we knew we could live there until a ship found us."

Abigail's brow furrowed. "Why did it take them so long?"

"From what I've heard, the first search was arduous but didn't extend to beyond where we'd actually drifted in the storm. They didn't think we could have gotten so far, but we had a sail. After we rode out the gale and had better weather, we made good headway. Even so, we were off the usual shipping routes by several hundred miles. No one would ever go to that island on purpose."

"But it had fresh water," Deborah mused.

"Yes, and that's exactly why the *Gladiator* came there and found me a few months ago. She had run into some corsairs and taken some heavy damage. Afterward, her captain didn't think he could make it to the next port, Santiago. So he consulted his charts for a place to drop anchor, do some repairs, and re-stock the water supply. I thank God he chose my island."

"But you were alone by then," Deborah said softly.

Edward nodded. "Yes. Captain Trowbridge was feverish when we landed, and he didn't last more than a few days. John Webber, Gideon Bramwell, and I kept each other company for more than a year. Then John cut himself badly while skinning a shark. His wound became infected. We tried everything we thought might help, but he died a few weeks later after much suffering."

"Such a pity," Abigail murmured.

"Yes. And then last year, I lost Gideon." Edward sighed. "That was my darkest hour. I thought I would die there as well, and no one would ever know what became of us. Our struggles in the storm and survival for so long were in vain. I fully expected to meet my end alone on that desolate shore."

"Did you remain in such low spirits for a year?" Deborah asked.

He recalled the turmoil and despair that had racked his heart, and the manner in which God had lifted it. "No. God is good, and He did not forsake me. He brought me another friend."

"A friend?" Abigail asked, and Deborah's eyes glittered with anticipation.

"Aye. His name was Kufu."

Both young women leaned forward, eager to hear his explanation.

"A native man?" Abigail asked.

"No."

"A monkey?" guessed Deborah.

"No, Kufu was a seagull. He arrived with a storm, and from how far he came over the sea, I've no way of knowing. His strength was spent, and he flew into my hut for sanctuary. He startled me, but when I saw that he was about done in, I let him rest and offered him some fish entrails and fruit. Before long, he was eating out of my hand."

"He stayed there with you?" Deborah's eyes lit up in delight.

"Yes. I gave him a name I'd heard a sailor call his parrot once, and Kufu was my constant companion from then until the *Gladiator* came."

"Why didn't you bring him home with you?" Deborah asked.

"Alas, he made the choice. He rode out to the ship with me in her longboat, riding on my shoulder. But once we were aboard and the crew raised anchor, he left me and flew back to the island."

They sat in silence for a moment; then Abigail asked, "Do you miss him?"

"I did at first, but now that I'm home again, I can't help feeling it is for the best. No doubt he will find others of his kind. He's strong again now. He has probably already left the island and flown back to wherever he came from. But I can't help believing God sent him to me when He did as a distraction and an encouragement. You see, Kufu needed me at first, so I fought to live. I had no idea how long I'd remain there."

"Four years," Deborah said.

"Yes. Well, close to that. More than three and a half years on that little piece of earth. And the last year alone, save for Kufu. But with God's help, I could have stayed there longer if necessary. So long as I remembered His goodness, I was willing to wait."

"That's a remarkable tale," Deborah said.

Abigail nodded. "Thank you for telling us. I. . .feel I understand things a bit better now."

Deborah stood. "Let me bring in some refreshment. I think we could all use a cup of tea."

"Not for me," Edward said quickly.

"Sweet cider, then?" Deborah asked.

"Yes, thank you." That sounded much better than anything hot. Edward leaned back in his chair and watched her bustle out the doorway.

It took him a second to realize that at last he was alone with Abigail.

As Deborah opened the kitchen door, her mother looked up from pouring hot water into her teapot.

"Time for a bit of refreshment in the parlor," Deborah explained.

"You've left them alone?"

Deborah chuckled at her grimace. "Yes, but both were calm when I made my retreat. I hope Abby is sensible enough to use this time to tell Edward what transpired between her and Jacob last night."

"Well, here, you can have this tea."

"No, Edward's feeling the heat, I think, though Abby might welcome a cup. I'll take some cool cider with Edward."

"There's a jug in the washroom."

Deborah opened the back door and stepped down into the cool, earthen-floored room at the rear of the house. Here was where the Bowman women and Elizabeth, the hired girl, did the family's laundry. Dug down into the ground two feet and well shaded, the washroom stayed a bit cooler than the kitchen on hot summer days, and Mrs. Bowman stored her milk and butter here, along with any other foods she wanted to keep cool.

Deborah found a jug of sweet cider nestled between the butter crock and the vinegar jug and carried it back into the kitchen.

"Take some of this gingerbread, too," her mother said. "I'll cut it for you."

Deborah brought dishes and forks to add to her tray. "Be sure to save some for Father."

"I will."

"Father's not home yet?" Deborah asked as she worked.

"No."

"He missed luncheon."

"Yes. He sent Peter round to tell me Mrs. Reading delivered a son, but the doctor was called almost immediately after the birth to the Collins farm, where one of the children met with an accident."

"Oh, dear. I hope it's not serious."

"That is my prayer," Mother said. "Do you suppose Abigail has made up her mind?"

"If so, she hasn't confided in me." Deborah carefully poured two glasses of cider and corked the jug. "I don't mind admitting that I hope she'll choose Edward. He has first claim, after all, and I always found him great fun."

"Hardly a reason to marry a man," her mother said. "Edward's a good lad. He's a hard worker, too. But then, so is Jacob. Your father's come to like Jacob a lot. He's steady."

"Edward's steady."

"Well, he was," she agreed, "but is he still? We don't know, do we?"

"Oh, come now, Mother. You know he was always a true friend and faithful in churchgoing. His father was training him in business, and he always obeyed and treated his parents with respect."

"That's true. They say a man will treat his wife the way he treats his mother, and I've no complaints about how Mrs. Hunter's son treated her before he. . . went away."

Deborah looked into her worried eyes and smiled. "Awkward, isn't it?"

"Yes, a bit. And if I'm having a hard time coming to terms with his being dead, then alive again, I guess we can't blame Abby for needing some time to settle her mind."

"Well, I have nothing against Jacob. He's a fine man, too. But Edward is different. I always thought he was special."

Her mother shot her an inquisitive glance, and for no reason, Deborah felt her cheeks redden. Her laden tray was ready, and she picked it up and escaped into the hallway. She paused at the open parlor door, hearing Abigail's soft tone.

"And so, I honestly don't know yet what I shall do," she said, a catch in her voice. "It's true I loved you dearly, but it's been a very long time; it's also true that I've developed feelings for your cousin. At first I thought it was wrong, but Mother and Father both assured me it was not sinful to. . .find love again after. . .losing the one I. . ."

She faltered, and Edward's low voice came. "I'm sorry I put you in such distress, Abby."

"I beg you to be patient, Edward, while I seek God's will in the matter."

"I shall," he replied. "And I'll pray for your peace where this is concerned."

"Thank you."

Abigail choked a bit on the words, and Deborah stepped forward. She hated to break in on them, but the weight of the tray was causing her wrists to ache.

When he spied her, Edward leaped up from the sofa where he'd been seated beside Abigail and took the tray from her, setting it on the side table. Deborah noted his grave expression as he looked to her for direction.

"Thank you. Abby, I brought you tea; I hope that's your preference."

She handed Edward his cider and gingerbread and settled back on the sofa with Abigail, placing her own cup and dish close at hand.

"Father's been called out to the Collins place," she announced. "The boy studying medicine with him brought Mother a message. I doubt he'll be home before evening."

Abigail's taut face smoothed into serenity. "Poor Father. He works too hard."

"He thrives on it," Deborah said.

"Your father is a remarkable man." Edward took the chair he'd occupied earlier and sipped his cider, then placed the cup on the table. "Won't you tell me about the folks in the neighborhood? Is Pastor Jordan still at the church?"

For the next half hour, they brought him up to date on the doings of their mutual acquaintances, and Deborah was pleased to see Abigail join in with a few anecdotes. She even laughed once, a musical chuckle, and Edward's eyes sparkled when he heard it.

Deborah longed to learn more about his exile on the distant island, but since she knew reverting to that subject would upset Abigail again, she tucked her questions away. Someday she would have a chance to talk to Edward privately. She had no doubt he would reveal the details of his sojourn to her. But for Abby, the topic was best put aside. Her quiet, well-ordered life had become chaos, and Deborah knew her sister needed time to sort it out.

Chapter 6

Four days later, Edward felt easier in his new role at Hunter Shipping. The men of the warehouse and docks, along with the sloop's crew, all seemed happy to have a Hunter once more giving the orders. The clerks in the office appeared to be a bit more unsettled by his reappearance, but he'd taken a few minutes to thank each man for his service and assure him that, so long as he continued to do his tasks well, his position was secure. Edward had no intention of making any sweeping changes in the office.

Mr. Daniels brought him the ledgers for the previous year on Monday morning, slipping quietly into the private office and laying them on a shelf near Edward's desk.

"The books you wished to look at, sir."

"Thank you." Edward glanced up from the correspondence he was reviewing. "Mr. Daniels, you saw this letter that came in from the shipwright in Bath?"

"Yes, sir."

"And you think we are in good shape to meet his needs?"

"Oh yes, sir. We've done quite a lot of business with him the last couple of years. Masts and spars for a small trading vessel he wants, and sails and cordage. Not a worry there, sir."

"Good. And the extra barrels of tar he asked about?"

"We have plenty."

"Excellent. Perhaps we should send the sloop up there this week, then."

Daniels ducked his head. "Very good, Mr. Hunter. Will you speak to Captain Jackson?"

Edward eyed the stack of ledgers on the shelf. That job would be less interesting and more exacting. Still, he needed to do it as soon as possible. He looked up at Daniels.

"Mr. Price can handle that, I think. I'll speak to him if he's in the office."

"I believe he stepped over to the wharf, sir."

Edward nodded. "Then I'll send a note over by one of the clerks. He can tell Captain Jackson to alert his crew and prepare to load the supplies for the shipwright." He reached for a quill and a scrap of paper.

An hour later, he was immersed in the ledgers, flipping back and forth between the accounts. Twice he went to the door and called for Daniels to come and explain an entry to him. The older man seemed a bit amused by his intense interest in the ledgers. Edward had studied accounting only in passing during his office training as a teenager and then only at his father's insistence. He'd been much more eager to get out on the wharf and sail up and down the coast on short trading voyages. But he knew his father had gone over the books closely at the end of each month and had spent several days at the close of each year reconciling all the accounts.

Once again he called Daniels to his side. "Did Mr. Price examine the books this year?"

"Oh no, sir," the older man replied, removing his pince-nez from the bridge of his nose. "Mr. Price is very good with the customers and the sailors, but he's not much for figures. He signs off on the payroll each month, but he's left most other matters in my hands."

Edward frowned. "My father always prepared a summary of the previous year's business in January."

Daniels cleared his throat. "Well, sir, I totaled things up and reported to Mr. Price on the year's income and expenses, and he seemed to think that was sufficient."

Edward wondered. He found nothing amiss as he scrutinized the columns of figures, but something still seemed the slightest bit out of order. He couldn't put his finger on it. Cargoes brought in on the sloop and the two schooners, the *Prosper* and the *Falcon*; wares bought from other ships that landed in Portland; goods sold in the chandlery and from the warehouse on market days; wages paid out to the men—the notations seemed endless.

At last he put the ledgers aside. He wondered if he could secure an interview with Abigail tonight. The week she'd told him Jacob had given her to make her decision was scarcely half over, yet he couldn't help feeling she was close to knowing her mind. He'd stopped by the Bowmans' modest brick house for a few minutes last evening, but he'd only had his fears confirmed. She was polite, not encouraging.

On the other hand, if he let her continue thinking it over, would his chances of coming out the victor be any better? His spirits were low, and he realized the shock of having to deal with all the changes at hand weighed heavily on him. He'd expected to come home and find his father here to guide him and Abigail ready to marry him. Instead he was bereft and lonely, and his future seemed bleak. He folded his hands on the top of the glossy walnut desk and bowed his head to pray.

He felt better when he had once again committed his future to God. Rising from the desk, he decided to amble across the street to the wharf and see if he could find Jacob.

Edward had spent the weekend visiting with his family. His sister, Anne, and her family had driven up from Saco in their farm wagon and spent a night at the Hunter house. Edward had made the acquaintance of his two-year-old nephew and Anne's new daughter, a babe of three months. On Sunday they had all taken dinner with Aunt Ruth and Uncle Felix Price. Jacob had excused himself shortly after the meal, and Edward had no doubt he headed to Dr. Bowman's residence. Perhaps it was time to speak openly about Abigail.

Edward didn't want to avoid his cousin. They worked at the same business, and he couldn't see any sense in not speaking to each other. So far they had kept any necessary communication brief. But Edward's hopes of being welcomed into the Bowman family circle decreased with each day, and there was no sense in not acknowledging that.

He found his cousin at the chandlery, helping the man who managed the store for them. The chandlery specialized in ships' supplies, and several of the warehouse laborers were carrying goods from the store out to the sloop.

"Jacob, could I speak to you?"

"Of course." Jacob handed the list to the chandler and followed Edward outside. The wind whipped their coats and the rigging of the sloop that lay secured at the side of the wharf. Edward took Jacob around the corner and into the lee of the building, letting it shelter them.

"What is it?" Jacob asked.

Edward sighed and leaned on a piling, looking off toward the next wharf. A brig was docked, and men scrambled over her decks, laying in supplies by the look of things. "We need to find room for an office for you."

"I'm getting along fine."

"No, you're not. I saw you bending over the apprentice clerk's desk to work on an order yesterday. You need your own desk and space to lay out your work. I've displaced you."

"Edward, there's no need—"

"I say there is." He turned to face Jacob. "You're a 10 percent partner in this company, and a valued member here. You're much better at some aspects of the business than I am. There's no reason we can't work together. We'll partition off some space at the end of the front room. It won't be as large as my office, but I daresay we can make you comfortable."

Jacob pursed his lips for a moment, studying Edward's face. "I won't say no to that proposal."

"Good. That's one thing we agree on."

"What do you mean by that?" Jacob leaned forward, frowning. "Ed, we've been friends since childhood, not to mention our blood ties. Can't we be frank with one another?"

"Yes, of course." Edward walked over to a stack of crates piled against the back wall of the store and sat down. Jacob hesitated a moment, then joined him.

"You want honesty?" Edward asked. "All right, I'm getting tired of this game we're playing with Abigail, and I expect you are, too."

Jacob ran a finger around the inside of his collar, not meeting Edward's gaze. "Well, cousin, you know she's promised to give me her decision by Friday."

"Yes, well, we both know what she's going to say, don't we?"

"Do we?" Jacob stared at him, an open challenge charging the air between them.

Edward jumped up and strode to the edge of the pier. He shoved his hands into his pockets and stood still for a moment, then exhaled deeply. "This is difficult for me, but I've got to face facts. She loves you. She no longer. . ."

He clamped his lips together and stared out at the waves troubling the harbor. "She no longer feels about me the way she did five years ago. That much is obvious to me."

He heard Jacob's footsteps and knew he had come to stand just behind him.

"Edward, I never. . . Please, you've got to know I didn't intend to spoil anything for you."

"I know, I know." Edward swung around and forced a smile. The pain he had expected wasn't in his heart. Instead, he felt chagrin. Jacob's face bore a bulldoggish look that Edward had often seen Uncle Felix wear.

"I've seen it coming," Edward said. "I just didn't want to admit it. She loves you. And you'd better love her as much or more, because if I find out you don't. . ."

Jacob's lips drew back, and his brows lowered in a good-natured wince. He extended his hand, and Edward shook it.

"I love her," Jacob assured him. "I would do anything for her. You know I love sailing, but I shall never sail again unless it's a short hop up the coast on business. No more voyaging for me."

"That seems extreme."

"It's not. I'll never do to her what you did. Oh, I'm not blaming you for getting shipwrecked—it could as easily have been me on that island. But knowing Abigail as I do now, I can see that the mere prospect of me not returning from a voyage would kill her. I'm staying ashore for the rest of my life, Ed. For her sake."

"Does she know that?"

"Yes."

Edward drew in a deep breath. *Dear Lord, should I just give up altogether? If I promised to stay on land, would she change her mind? Should I even attempt to find out? God, give me wisdom.*

He walked once more to the edge of the wharf and leaned on the piling.

"I think Deborah is getting tired of it, too. Last night she made no secret she despises chaperoning her sister."

Jacob laughed. "Yes, she made her father supervise Abby and me on Sunday. But if Abby affirms that I'm her choice, I should get more private time with her soon."

Edward nodded and managed a feeble smile. His disappointment ached in his heart with a dull, constant throb. *So be it, Father in heaven. Give me Your peace, and bless their union.*

"I've made up my mind," Abigail announced at breakfast Thursday morning.

Deborah's stomach twisted, and she laid down her fork.

"About time," her father said, not looking up from his copy of the *Eastern Herald*.

Mother was more sympathetic. "And which young man can we anticipate becoming our son-in-law?"

"Jacob, of course," Deborah muttered.

"You needn't scowl at me." Abigail broke a small piece of crust off her toast and tossed the morsel across the table, hitting Deborah's shoulder.

"Abby!" their mother scolded.

Abigail turned back to her mother. "Deborah thinks she knows what is best for me, but this is something I must decide for myself."

Deborah felt the accusation was somewhat unjust. It was true she had hoped her sister would choose Edward, but she had never tried to persuade Abigail to do so.

"I haven't attempted to influence your decision."

"Haven't you? You're always telling me how fine and upstanding Edward is."

"I just think you need to consider all aspects of the two gentlemen's characters."

"I have," Abigail said. "And I have made up my mind. Both are admirable, but Jacob is more. . .civilized."

"That's ridiculous."

"Here, now," their father interrupted. "You sound like a gaggle of geese fighting over a handful of corn, not two genteel ladies."

Deborah sank lower in her chair. It wasn't easy to disturb her father's placid nature. Abigail's turmoil must have bothered him these past few days, no matter how calm he appeared.

"And when will you tell the favored gentleman?" their mother asked, smiling. Deborah imagined that in her mind she had already resumed the wedding plans interrupted so rudely a week ago.

"This evening. And I've asked Edward to come by this afternoon if he can get away from the office long enough." Abigail glanced at Deborah. "I thought I should give him a private audience before my renewed betrothal to Jacob becomes public."

It was less than Deborah had hoped for, but more than she'd feared.

"Do treat him gently. He's loved you for such a long time, Abby." Annoyed with her own tender emotions, Deborah blinked rapidly and succeeded in keeping back tears.

"I shall. Of course, you understand that when I say 'private,' I mean that you shall be present as a chaperone."

"Never."

"What?" Abigail's rosebud mouth hung open.

Before her sister could wail to their mother for support, Deborah said, "I've sat by and listened to both these poor men lay their hearts at your feet. I do not wish to be present when you dash Edward's hopes."

"But—"

"Surely you can do this one thing on your own."

Abigail frowned. "Perhaps Father will tell him for me. I could send him around to your surgery, Father."

The newspaper shivered, and a deep, foreboding voice came from behind it. "I shall do no such thing."

Abigail looked to the other end of the table.

"Nor I," said her mother.

Tears streamed down Abigail's cheeks. "You all think I'm horrid, don't you?"

"No." Her mother rose and began to stack the dishes. "Jacob is a splendid young man, and we shall be proud to have him in the family. But you must do your own work with Edward, Abby. Don't send him away thinking you are a coward."

Abigail inhaled and looked at Deborah.

Deborah tried not to return her gaze, but the sound of Abby's shaky breath pierced her armor.

"Please?" Abigail whispered.

Deborah threw down her napkin.

"All right, but this is the last time. I mean the *last*. Don't come looking for me tonight. I intend to be far away when Jacob reaps the reward of his persistence."

"Thank you, dear sister."

Deborah stamped her foot. "Abby, you aggravate me so. If I ever ask you to chaperone me, please remind me of this moment and say no."

"In order for that to happen, you must stop ignoring all the young men who hover around you after church every Sunday." Abigail's watery smile was as exasperating as her comment.

As Deborah stomped from the room, she glanced at her father, not trying to suppress the resentment she felt. Hiding behind that newspaper! He ought to have interfered. Sometimes she thought he used his medical practice as an excuse to avoid the feminine intrigues that seethed at home.

She was startled when his complacent voice came once more. "Perhaps she will do that when she finds one who matches the young man she's been defending so passionately."

Deborah stopped even with his chair and stared at him.

As he folded his newspaper precisely, his eyes turned her way, and he threw her a conspiratorial wink.

Chapter 7

For once, Abigail was waiting in the parlor before her guest arrived. She sat on the sofa, twisting her handkerchief.

Deborah stood at the window, watching for Edward. The sooner this was over with, the better.

"Do you hate me?"

Deborah sighed and let the sheer curtain fall back into place. "No. But I shall be disgusted with you if you're not frank and to the point with him."

"I'll try."

"Oh, Abby, pretend you are Father doing surgery. This is a necessary procedure. Make it clean and quick, will you?" She plopped down on one of the velvet-covered side chairs.

"Do you think he knows why I've invited him here?"

"Of course."

Abigail's eyes widened in surprise. "Really? Oh dear."

Deborah threw her hands up in resignation. "You love Jacob. That settles it. It would be wrong for you to accept Edward now. You can't marry a man you don't love."

"Well, yes." Abigail wiped an errant tear from her cheek. "So. . .you think it's all right?"

Deborah was glad her sister could not see the chaos in her heart at that moment. "I know you've thrashed this out with God."

"Yes, I have."

"Are you at peace with your decision?"

"I am."

Deborah moved to the sofa and slipped her arm around Abigail's shoulders. "Then this is right. Thank God, and carry it through."

Abigail squeezed her in a suffocating embrace. "I love you, Debbie."

"I know."

They leaped apart as the thud of the knocker echoed through the house.

"Oh, he's here." Abigail dabbed at her face with the wilted handkerchief.

"Calm down," Deborah advised. "Deep breaths. Elizabeth is getting the door."

A moment later, Edward stood in the doorway. He nodded to Deborah with a slight smile, then centered his attention on Abigail.

"Thank you for inviting me," he murmured as he advanced.

Abigail shoved her handkerchief up her sleeve and extended her hand to him.

"It was kind of you to come, Edward. Please, sit down."

She resumed her place on the sofa, and Deborah tiptoed to the window, where she sat down on the cushioned window seat.

She couldn't watch, and she wished she could plug her ears and not hear without being outrageously rude.

Abigail cleared her throat. One quick glance showed Deborah that Edward had sat down beside Abigail on the sofa but was keeping his distance.

He still has hope, Deborah thought. *This will crush him. And how will he feel toward Jacob now? They've been inseparable since boyhood. Will this drive them apart forever?*

She considered her closeness to Abigail. The events of the last week had tested their loyalty, but Deborah knew she would always love her sister. She hoped Edward and Jacob's bond was firm enough to take them through this and bring them out still friends on the other side.

"Edward, I. . ." Abigail cleared her throat.

Deborah stared out the window at the sunlit garden. How she wished she were the little phoebe perched on the syringa bush, chirping in blissful unawareness.

"Edward, I am ready to give you my decision."

Abigail's voice had an icy touch, and Deborah winced. She knew her sister found her task excruciating and had retreated into coldness to make it easier. Tears were no doubt lurking, and she wanted to complete the interview without breaking down.

"I'm ready." Edward's voice was as stony as hers, and Deborah's heart ached for him.

"I. . ."

The pause was too long, and Deborah gritted her teeth, eyes closed. *Tell him! Just tell him.*

After another long moment of silence, Edward's voice came, quiet and gentle now.

"Perhaps I can help you, my dear. You wish to say that you've decided to marry my cousin."

Abigail sighed and whispered, "Yes."

"And you. . .regret any pain you have caused me."

"Very much."

"But you feel this is the only true and honest thing you can do."

"Stop being so. . .so good!"

"How would you have me be?"

Something like a hiccup came from Abigail, and Deborah couldn't resist turning her head ever so slightly and peeking.

Edward was drawing her sister into his arms, but it was not an embrace of passion. Abigail laid her head on his strong shoulder and let her tears flow.

"It will be all right, you know," he said.

"I hope so."

"It will, dear. If God had wanted us together, He wouldn't have kept me away so long."

"Really?"

"Really. I think I saw that when I first came home. I simply didn't want to admit it. But there's no denying it. You love Jacob, and you were meant to be his wife."

He stroked Abigail's hair and leaned back against the sofa with a sigh.

More than ever, Deborah wished she were not in the room. Yet she was glad in a perverse way that she was allowed to see the true mettle Edward was made of. His heart was breaking, yet he was comforting the one who'd delivered the blow.

She turned back to the window view. The phoebe was gone, but a chipmunk was scurrying about the garden. She felt a tear slide down her cheek and brushed it away with her sleeve.

"So. . .you aren't angry with me?" Abigail asked.

"All is forgiven," he said.

"And Jacob?"

"There's no bitterness between us, nor will there be."

"Thank you, Edward."

The sofa creaked, and their clothing rustled. Deborah turned to see that both had risen.

"Would you please excuse me?" Abigail asked.

"Of course, my dear."

Edward bowed over her hand, then watched her leave the room.

Deborah wondered if he remembered she was there. Should she jump up and offer to fetch his hat? What was the etiquette for ushering out rejected suitors?

He turned slowly, and his thoughtful gaze rested on her in the window seat.

"It seems your duties are ended."

"Oh, yes." She hopped up, her face flushing. "I'm sorry, Edward. It was not my choice to witness that."

"I know." His smile was a bit thin, but even so, it set her pulse tripping. "I believe her declaration was final."

Deborah nodded. "I'm afraid so. She won't change her mind."

They stood for several seconds, looking at each other. At last, Deborah said softly, "My condolences."

"Thank you. Perhaps you'll be kind to me at the wedding, and we'll laugh together about this. That way, maybe folks won't gossip about my despair and desperation."

"Is that what you're feeling now?"

"One thing I learned in my long exile, Deborah, is that God alone controls my destiny."

"So. . .perhaps even this is a part of His providential plan for you?"

"I must say yes to that, decidedly yes, or deny the faith I've gained. It is disheartening now, but I'm sure God can use this disappointment to prepare me for a different future, just as He used the shipwreck to prepare me for this."

Deborah eyed him for a moment, gauging his mood. "Do you have to go back to the office right away?"

"No, I've nothing more exciting than a stack of ledgers to draw me."

"Would you care for lemonade? I'd love to hear more about your experience—if I haven't badgered you enough about it already."

He smiled and nodded. "Lemonade sounds refreshing."

The next hour flew as Deborah plied him with questions about the men who fled the shipwreck with him and about his life on the island. He brought her near weeping again, telling how they had drifted for days in the longboat. Three of the men in the longboat had died and one was lost overboard before they reached the island. He then changed his tone and recounted humorous incidents that he, Gideon, and John went through as they became accustomed to their island home.

"They wouldn't leave off calling me 'sir' at first," Edward said. "Finally I told them, 'Listen, fellows, if we're still here fifty years from now, with our gray beards down to our belts, are you still going to dodder around calling me "sir"?' And Gideon said, 'I'm not sure we'll have belts by then, sir. We may have to eat them if we don't find a way to catch more fish.'"

Deborah shook with laughter, then sobered. "When you were alone after Gideon fell off the cliff, how did you go on? You told me about Kufu, the bird that came to you, but still. . ."

Edward settled back in his chair and sighed. "It was very difficult at first. I thought I would go mad, being alone there. I kept repeating scripture portions to myself and composing imaginary letters to my parents and my sister. And of course, to Abigail."

"That helped you?"

"Yes. I pretended to write long letters, detailing my daily life. Gathering food, improving my shelter against the rainy season, climbing the hills to scout for sail." He shot her a sidelong glance. "I even wrote to you once."

"You did?"

"Yes. I thought it might amuse you. I drew a picture of my hut on a piece of bark, too, then tossed it in the surf, pretending it would float to you, along with my latest letter to. . ."

She smiled. "You must have floated a lot of letters to Abby."

"Hundreds. And later I'd find them washed up on shore down the beach."

He sighed and pulled out the pocket watch that had been his father's. "It's getting on toward supper time. I must leave you."

"Won't you—"

He held up one hand to silence her invitation. "I don't think this is the night, but thank you."

She walked with him into the front hall and handed him his hat. It was new, she noted, not his father's old one. His fashion consciousness was probably linked to his hope to win Abigail's hand, but she didn't mind. She only knew that he would hold his own in looks and good manners if dropped in the middle of a group of businessmen and statesmen. And in a roomful of eligible women? Abigail was probably the only woman who wouldn't find him magnetic.

He stood before the door, looking down at her with a half smile on his lips, and she realized she had been staring at him again. Bad habit. She'd have to train herself out of it.

"I wonder, Deborah. . . ."

"Yes?"

His smile spread to his gleaming brown eyes. "I wonder if you and your mother and sister would care to tour Hunter Shipping tomorrow if the weather is fine."

She swallowed a lump that had suddenly cropped up in her throat. Had he not taken Abby seriously? She was sure he had.

"I. . .must discourage you, if you think my sister is not adamant in her choice."

"I'm sure she is. But I mentioned to your mother not long ago that we have some fine fabrics in the warehouse. I thought perhaps you ladies would enjoy coming to the office, and Jacob and I could show you about."

She stared up at him for a moment, amazed at his calmness. He bore his cousin no malice. Could she be as generous to Abby? Her heart fluttered, and she knew that her professed forgiveness of Abigail was genuine. She could give thanks to God for this turn of events. Surely this resolution was part of His greater plan.

Chapter 8

It was a bright, sunny day, and the breeze that fluttered in from Casco Bay kept the temperature comfortable. Edward rose early, unable to sleep well, and arrived at the office shortly after seven. He huddled over the ledgers, frowning and trying to find the elusive inconsistency he felt sure was there.

At five minutes to eight, he heard Daniels and the clerks enter the outer office, and a moment later he heard Jacob's brisk step. Edward opened his door, and Jacob came toward him, grinning.

"Still friends, Ed?"

"Of course." Edward grasped his hand. "Congratulations."

"Thank you. I can't tell you what it means to me that you're taking it this way."

Edward smiled. "I shall endeavor not to diminish your joy, cousin. What would you think of inviting all the Bowman ladies down here this afternoon?"

"I like it, but what for?"

He shrugged. "A tour of the place. Another chance to see your fiancée and to let her see you in your place of business. Let them look over the dress goods in the warehouse before we sell them all."

"Splendid idea! Will you make the arrangements?"

"Yes."

Jacob nodded. "Then I'll be in my office." He headed for the far corner of the large room, where two workmen were erecting a wall to enclose a cubicle for his new oak desk. He swung around, still smiling. "I don't suppose this will be finished by the time they get here? And decorated?"

Edward laughed. "Hardly. Would you rather wait until it's done?"

"No, no. Let's invite them today."

By way of an apprentice who swept the floors and sorted bins of hardware, Edward sent a note around to the Bowman house, asking the ladies if they would care to see the improvements at Hunter Shipping, in company with the owner and Mr. Price, and take tea afterward in the office.

The boy came back forty minutes later with a brief but courteous reply. Both the misses Bowman would await him at one o'clock. Their mother was otherwise engaged.

Edward hired a hack after lunch. He and Jacob arrived at the Bowman residence to find the ladies waiting. Abigail was dressed in a burgundy silk walking dress with a feathered hat and white gloves. Deborah's dress was a plain, dark blue cotton, topped with a crocheted shawl and a straw bonnet. Edward was not sure who was prettier—the elegant, refined lady Abigail or the wholesome, restless Deborah. Abigail seemed pleased that they would not have to walk all the way to the docks and back. Although it was a swift twenty-minute stroll for Edward, the commercial district near the harbor was not one that ladies frequented on foot.

"Riding will save you ladies from wearing out your slippers and making the strenuous uphill walk on the way home," Jacob said as he handed Abigail up into the enclosed carriage.

Deborah smiled at that, placing her sturdy leather shoe on the step and hopping up beside her sister, barely putting pressure on Edward's hand for assistance. He could almost read her thoughts: She was not one to glide about in delicate slippers and tire from a brisk walk.

As they rode slowly along the streets, Edward commented on how much the population and commerce of the town had increased during his five years' absence. He was glad he'd worn the new suit he'd had made at his mother's insistence. His hair was neatly trimmed now, too. Still, he could see that Jacob outdid him so far as Abigail was concerned. The greater part of her attention was devoted to his cousin.

When they reached their destination, Edward learned that Abigail had never been onto the wharf. Deborah, it seemed, had ventured there under escort. By whom, Edward did not ask. Abigail shrank from the edge, preferring to be safely flanked by Jacob and Deborah as they walked out past the tinker's shop and the dry goods, hardware, and candle shops to the company's large store. Edward followed a step behind. Sailors and stevedores passed them and stared. The ladies flushed, and Abigail clutched Jacob's arm.

Edward stared down the worst of the oglers and stepped forward to touch Deborah's sleeve.

"Miss Bowman?" He offered his arm. She hesitated only a moment, then laid her hand lightly in the crook of his elbow.

"Thank you," she whispered.

It felt odd having a lady other than his mother on his arm once more, but Edward decided it was pleasant. Deborah's eager anticipation spilled over in her face, and he knew few women he would rather squire about Portland.

As soon as they were inside the store, she pulled away from him, apparently feeling secure on her own now, and wandered about, examining everything. Abigail, however, clung to Jacob's arm and looked about timidly.

Deborah's fascination with the chandlery pleased Edward. She was a practical girl, and her face brightened as she surveyed the mounds of rope and canvas, piles of bolts and pins, and barrels of victuals suitable for ships' crews.

"Your father was a man of great foresight to build his store right on the wharf," she said.

"Actually, my grandfather started the chandlery here with a little shack that offered the most basic supplies. Father improved the establishment, and I have to give my cousin credit for the latest expansion. This entire section is new." He stretched out one arm, indicating the wing Jacob had added to house a wider selection of foods, containers, tools, and hardware.

"Do lots of people come here to buy?" Abigail's voice squeaked. She squeezed nearer to Jacob as a burly seaman pushed past them, nodding and eyeing the ladies.

"Yes," Jacob told her. "The store was begun to outfit Hunter ships and any others that docked at this wharf, but we're open to all customers."

Edward nodded. "That's right. We've built a reputation for offering a wide variety of goods. Of course, we're competing for the business of ships that aren't owned locally. When a vessel comes in from another port—say, Buenos Aires or New York or Amsterdam—we hope it will choose Hunter's Wharf for unloading and selling its cargo."

They left the store and ambled along the wharf toward the city. Abigail seemed more at ease and chatted quietly with Jacob. As they approached the street, Edward pointed up the hill toward the distant observatory tower, built a dozen years previously in Captain Moody's sheep pasture on Munjoy Hill.

"Look! See that flag? There's a ship coming in to dock."

"Is it one of your ships?" Deborah asked.

"I don't know yet. I hope it's the *Prosper*. We'll find out soon enough."

They crossed the busy street that ran along the waterfront, then entered the warehouse.

"This is where we stow outgoing cargo until it's loaded, and incoming until it's sold." Edward guided them out of the way of two men rolling casks down the aisle of crates and barrels. The containers were piled high, and he felt a little claustrophobic when walking between them. He glanced anxiously at Deborah, to see if she was feeling the closeness, but she took in the scene with glittering eyes.

"Well, now. If it isn't my beautiful future daughter-in-law."

They all turned and saw brawny Felix Price approaching with a grin splitting his tanned face. Beads of sweat stood on his brow, and he wiped his hands on his homespun trousers.

"Oh, Mr. Price." Abigail's breathless words were lost in the cavernous warehouse. She ducked her head in acknowledgment of Felix's boisterous greeting.

"I broke the news to my parents last night," Jacob said, his cheeks nearly as red as Abigail's.

"Afternoon, Uncle Felix," Edward said easily, but he kept a sharp watch on the man. Uncle Felix was rough enough that he wouldn't care whether he'd embarrassed his son and his employer or not. That didn't bother Edward, but he was concerned that his uncle had mortified Abigail by calling out such a teasing declaration before the workmen. Several of the laborers paused in their work and cast glances their way but turned back to their tasks when they saw Edward's stern gaze upon then.

"Hello." Abigail's face was by now crimson, but she took the meaty hand extended to her and dipped a curtsy.

Deborah greeted Felix with a charming smile. "Good day, Mr. Price."

"Well, Miss Debbie. What are you doing here? It's not Thursday."

Edward wondered what that meant, but Deborah merely told him, "We're touring Hunter Shipping."

"Well, now, ain't we grand?"

Deborah laughed, but Edward saw Jacob wince as Abigail squeezed his arm. He wondered if her fingernails were digging through Jacob's sleeve into his skin. Felix Price frightened her with his loud, breezy manner, it seemed. Edward wondered what that would bode when Abigail married Jacob.

It was true that his uncle was unpolished. Felix had been known as a ruffian in his youth. He'd fished for years, hauling a living from the ocean by brute force, and was known in those days for drinking quantities of ale when on land and occasionally using his fists in blustery tavern brawls. But Aunt Ruth had fallen in love with him. Though her social status and manner of living were lowered considerably on her wedding day, she still appeared to love him thirty years later and put up with him when his coarseness flared up. Somehow she'd maintained her gentility and was so well liked that Portland's most prestigious women still welcomed her into their parlors.

Felix was another story, and his friends were for the most part fishermen and dockworkers. His employment at Hunter Shipping for the past ten years gave him limited approval. Of course, he was always welcome in the Hunter home, but Felix did not presume on his in-laws' goodness and, for the most part, kept to his own circle. He was good at his job in the warehouse, the men respected him, and he kept the vast quantities of supplies in order.

"We're heading over to the office for tea, Uncle Felix," Edward said.

"Ah, tea for the ladies. I expect you gents have peppermint cakes and gingersnaps with your drinkables." Felix turned to the expanse of the warehouse and shouted, "Come, lads, clear the floor there! We've a ship docking in an hour's time! Look lively!"

They hustled Abigail and Deborah toward the steps leading up to the office, and Edward was thankful to shut the door and the noise behind them.

"You see that little room a-building over there?" Jacob asked Abigail, pointing to the far corner.

"Y—yes."

He smiled down at her. "That, my dear, is my new office. In a week or two when it's finished, I'll bring you down here again to see it."

"It's. . .awfully small, isn't it?"

Jacob laughed. "Well, yes, but it's more than Mr. Daniels, the accountant, has."

"What does he have?"

"A desk over there between the clerks and the record files."

Edward said nothing but caught Deborah's troubled glance. He wished he could reassure her, but he could only smile and lead them into his own office.

In the private room, one of the young clerks laid out tea for four on a small table opposite his desk.

"Abigail, would you mind pouring?" Edward asked.

"Not in the least, thank you."

There. This was going better. While outgoing Deborah might have felt at ease among the workers, Abigail could not hide her relief at escaping into the quiet, well-appointed office. He began to tell them about the nautical artifacts displayed on the walls, and soon she seemed to have regained her composure.

"That's a lovely painting," Abigail said, eyeing the winter landscape.

"Thank you." Edward glanced at his cousin. "I believe that belongs to Jacob and will find its home in his new office when it's finished."

"No need, Ed. Keep it in here if you like it. I only paid a few dollars for it, and it was company money."

Edward smiled. "We'll discuss it later." *After I look up the amount you paid for it,* he told himself. He did not doubt Jacob's word but felt he ought to go slowly in financial matters and verify what the staff told him. If all was as Jacob represented it, he would be glad to let his cousin have the pleasure of hanging the painting on the wall above his desk.

Deborah carried her cup and saucer to the window and peered out.

"You have a splendid view of the wharf and the harbor, Edward."

"Thank you. You've never been here before?"

"Not in the office."

"But you've seen the warehouse."

She smiled at him over her shoulder. "Yes, but Abby hasn't until today."

He smiled and turned to Abigail. "What did you think? We're a rough lot, I'm afraid."

She stirred a spoonful of sugar into her tea and glanced up at him from beneath long lashes. "It's. . .exciting, but I'm afraid I'm not used to such hubbub."

"No, I thought not. I hope our outing didn't unsettle you."

Jacob pulled his chair close to Abigail's. "Edward suggested you and Deborah might want to look over the fabrics we have on hand. I can ask my father to send some boys up here with the bolts if you wish."

"That might be nice," Abigail said, glancing at her sister.

"By all means," said Deborah. "I'm sure Abby will be needing some new dresses soon."

A few minutes later, two of the laborers came in with several bolts of material. They spread them on Edward's desk, and Abigail smiled at them.

"Mr. Price says that's the best of 'em, sir."

"Very good." Edward herded the men out the door.

"Thank you," said Abigail. "I didn't expect this privilege."

Edward shrugged. "You are welcome anytime, Abigail. Jacob can tell you if we get something in that he thinks you would like. When the *Falcon* returns from France, I expect there will be a great number of fancy goods on board."

"Debbie, look at this rose silk."

Deborah set her teacup down and went to join her sister at the desk.

"Edward. . ." Jacob was eyeing him uncertainly.

"Yes?" Edward matched his low tone.

"What do I do if she finds something to her liking?"

He shrugged. "Send it home with her, and send the bill to Dr. Bowman."

Jacob seemed a bit relieved, and Edward wondered, not for the first time, how his return was affecting Jacob's salary. He would have to go over the last few payrolls in detail.

A discreet knock sounded, and he went to the door.

"We've a ship docking, Mr. Hunter," said Daniels.

"We saw the flag before we came in. Is it the *Prosper*?"

Daniels frowned. "No, sir, it's the *Annabel*, out of Philadelphia. She's bringing textiles and wheat, and she hopes to take on lumber. The master's mate came ashore a few minutes ago in a boat. The ship will moor at our dock."

Edward rose. "Shall we take you home, ladies?"

"I'd love to see the ship dock." Deborah's eager brown eyes darted from him to the scene beyond the window.

"I told Mother we'd be home early," Abigail said with a note of reluctance. "Elizabeth was ill this morning, and we need to help with the dinner preparations."

Deborah sighed. "All right. I'd forgotten."

Edward went to the door and told one of the clerks to run out and secure a carriage for them. When he turned back, he saw that Jacob was gathering up the bolt of rose-colored material and smiling at Abigail. Her face bore the most serene expression Edward had seen her wear since his return. Instead of allowing pangs of jealousy or depression to assail him, he sent up a quick prayer of thanks.

"Jacob, perhaps you'd like to see the ladies home," he said. "I'll head for the wharf, and you can meet me there when you return."

"If you're sure you won't need me for half an hour."

"I'm sure."

Edward walked with them out the front door and around to where the hack was waiting. When Jacob and both ladies were aboard, he shut the door.

"I'll be back soon," Jacob said through the window.

"Fine. We'll go over the manifest together." Edward tipped his hat to the sisters and stood back. The driver flicked the reins and headed away from the harbor.

Edward stood still for another moment, trying to analyze his feelings. Why wasn't he upset today? The woman he'd loved for years had jilted him last night. He could only conclude that God had answered his prayers for peace.

As the coach turned out of the yard, Deborah leaned out the window and looked back, waving at him. Her hair had escaped the straw bonnet and flew about her rosy cheeks.

Edward couldn't help smiling. He lifted his hand and waved back.

⊗

Late that evening, Edward bent over the ledgers in his father's study at home. No matter how many times he went over the accounts, he could find no fault in Daniels's bookkeeping. Even the price of the painting Jacob had purchased was as he'd represented it. Still, something was amiss. Edward was sure of it. The *Prosper* had brought a good income to the company on every voyage until his father's death. Then she had made a run to the Caribbean that should have been profitable, but instead the goods sold barely covered the expenses for the voyage. Edward totaled the sales three times, then compared his figures to those of the schooner's previous voyages. Perhaps it was poor judgment in the goods purchased in the islands.

The next voyage had brought in a little more but was still far below the amount the *Prosper* usually earned. He then laid the figures side by side with the earnings of the *Falcon* and found that the European trade was far outearning the Caribbean voyages.

Edward ran a hand through his hair and looked at the clock. It was late, and he was tired. Perhaps things would make more sense in the morning.

But the next morning, he saw no more logic to the figures than he had the night before. The custom at Hunter Shipping was for the office staff to work a half day on Saturdays unless a ship was docking. Edward carried the ledgers back to the office and called Mr. Daniels into his private room.

"I see what you mean, Mr. Edward," Daniels admitted after Edward had carefully pointed out the troublesome amounts to him. "I did notice that the last couple of voyages were not so good for the *Prosper*, but I thought it was just one of those things that happens occasionally."

Edward shook his head. "I'm at a loss, Mr. Daniels. But I'm not sure the company ought to consider buying another ship if profits are falling."

"They've increased in other areas."

"Yes. The *Falcon* and the sloop have both done very well on their recent voyages." Edward leaned back in his chair. "I just don't understand it. The Caribbean trade has been our mainstay, and those cargoes were all good products."

"Not as much coffee as we like to get," Daniels mused. "Less of the high-profit items, more of low-profit goods like rice."

"Perhaps you can get me the copies of the *Prosper*'s manifests from these voyages," Edward said. "Now that you say that, I'd like to compare the percentages of different goods she brought back."

"Yes, sir. Perhaps it's just a matter of instructing Captain Stuart on what merchandise you want him to trade for."

Edward flipped the pages of the latest ledger once more. The arithmetic was flawless. Daniels supervised his clerks so closely that Edward was sure they wouldn't make a mistake or change the figures without the accountant noticing it. Daniels was past sixty years of age, and Jeremiah Hunter had treated him well. He earned a good salary and was now a part owner in Hunter Shipping. Edward decided that Daniels had little motive to cheat the company. But wouldn't a man of Captain Stuart's experience know what cargoes to buy? He'd made eight voyages for Hunter Shipping, and up until the last two, he'd seemed to know how to buy goods in high demand at a low price. Was it just a coincidence that the *Prosper* had barely made a profit on its last two voyages south?

Chapter 9

Deborah opened the Bowmans' front door a week later and found Edward and Jacob waiting on the doorstep. She had half expected Jacob to come around looking for Abby that evening, but it surprised her to see Edward with him. Of course, they had behaved cordially toward each other the day she and Abby toured the shipping company with them. Now Jacob was laughing at something his cousin had said, and they both turned to face her with smiles on their lips.

For the first time, Deborah saw a family resemblance. Edward was taller by two inches, and his hair and eyes much darker than Jacob's. But the nose was the same, she realized, and both had a somewhat obstinate set to their chins. Jacob's form was more compact, and his legs were shorter, like his father's. But both had broad, muscular shoulders and were clean shaven, though Edward had admitted to her and Abigail that he had worn a beard of necessity for nearly four years. She tried to picture him in a bushy, untrimmed beard, and that set her off in a chortle.

"What's so funny, miss?" Jacob asked, taking a stern posture and stiffening his back.

"Nothing you need to know. Won't you come in?" She forced her mouth into a more serious line as she took their hats. "Unfortunately, Abigail has gone with my mother to call on Mrs. Jordan. But they should be back soon, if you'd care to wait."

"Only if you'll join us," said Edward, and her heart lurched, though she knew he meant nothing special by it.

"What?" Jacob asked in mock horror. "Deborah sitting with us when she doesn't have to? Unheard of."

She showed them to the parlor, then hastened to the kitchen to fix tea. Hurrying back to her guests, Deborah paused in the front hall to glance in the looking glass. Edward had come back, even though Abby had turned him down. Her pulse surged. Did she dare think he enjoyed being here in spite of the blow he had recently received?

Although Edward was still reticent about some aspects of his voyage and sojourn on the island, Jacob was more than willing to talk. He was an excellent storyteller, and Deborah suspected that Abigail had not let him tell as many tales of the sea as he would have liked.

She listened avidly as Jacob recounted the damage sustained by the *Egret*.

184

He coaxed Edward to tell his part of the story, claiming he'd been wondering about certain points.

"How did you find Spring Island? Was it by accident, or did you make for it?"

"It was the captain's choice," Edward said, settling back in his chair with a steaming cup of tea. "He'd brought a compass and a quadrant with him when he climbed down into the boat, as well as a chart and a copy of Bowditch's navigation tables."

"Ah!" Jacob eyes gleamed. "We had a compass, but that was the extent of our navigating tools."

"The winds weren't right for us to head for the Society Islands or the Marquesas," Edward said. "I suggested Hawaii, but Captain Trowbridge said it was more than a thousand miles away. We were much closer to this little island in the middle of nowhere. He wasn't sure we could fetch it, and it would have been disaster if we'd missed it. We all would have died of thirst in another day or two. But through God's grace and the captain's knowledge, we made it."

"It's too bad our boats were separated," Jacob said.

"Yes, but that was part of God's plan, too. I believe that now. He wanted me there with Gideon and John, and at the last of it, by myself for a good long while."

"It's hard for me to fathom why God would want that to happen," Jacob said. "Do you think He wanted the others to die like they did?"

Edward hesitated. "I don't know. He took them home, one by one, and each passing left a deep impression on the rest of us. The two fellows who were with me the longest didn't hold much with prayer and faith at first. John Webber was cocky and proud. He ran wild whenever we touched port. But the captain's testimony before he died influenced John to believe in Christ."

"Praise God," Deborah murmured.

"And when John cut his arm and began to get feverish, Gideon tended him like a baby. During that time, John urged Gideon to turn to the Lord. Afterward, Gideon came to me and told me he'd had a long talk with the Almighty, and he was a child of God from then on. We had precious fellowship together, Gideon and I."

"What a wonderful blessing." Deborah set her china cup down and folded her hands in her lap, ready to hear more.

"Yes. God used the storm and the wreck and all that happened afterward to draw those two men, at least, to Himself."

"I guess I can see that He brought good from it," Jacob said. "I'm glad they believed. It's still hard for me to thank God for letting the ship sink, though."

Deborah smiled at Edward, and he answered her, his eyes full of understanding. Their gazes locked for a long moment, and she felt warmth flooding through her chest and up to her face as the blood went to her cheeks.

Edward was such a dear brother in Christ. If only God would bring a man like him to love her the way Edward had loved Abby. She would not, could not, allow the thought to reach beyond that. On other occasions, she'd felt the flutter of longing in her heart when she and Edward conversed. They comprehended each other perfectly. Hadn't Abby felt that when she talked to him? How could she not yearn to be with him?

Even these thoughts made her feel uneasy, as she vaguely discerned an uncrossable line. Edward loved Abby. She could wish for a man like him, and she could wish for his future happiness, but she could not meld those two wishes into one. It would be scandalous.

She broke the stare with regret and caught Jacob's eye. He was settling against the back of his chair with a contented smile that she hoped wasn't a smirk.

Oh no! He's imagining things between Edward and me. Or was it her imagination? The sudden prospect that she had betrayed her sister by developing strong feelings for Edward slammed Deborah's heart. She was fooling herself if she refuted it.

What had Jacob seen, exactly? Worse yet, what did he think he had seen? She could not deny the undercurrent that had surged between her and Edward. But it wouldn't be proper to act upon it. Would it? Abby had definitely put an end to Edward's hopes and was planning her wedding to Jacob. It was wrong for Deborah to feel an attraction for her sister's rejected suitor. Of course, Edward didn't feel anything of the sort for her. Did he? And if he did, he was too much of a gentleman to do anything about it so soon. But Jacob's perception of what occurred was another matter entirely.

"Edward is considering sailing down to Portsmouth in our sloop soon to look at a ship for sale there," Jacob said.

Edward's features sobered. "Yes, we're thinking of adding one more vessel to our fleet. I'm looking over the accounts to be sure we're in good enough financial shape for that."

"I thought it was settled," Jacob said, turning toward him with his eyebrows arched. "You said you would go and size up the ship we spoke of."

Deborah saw Edward's troubled frown, but she decided this topic was a good distraction for Jacob. It was much better than the flutter of guilt she'd felt a moment ago. "When are you going?" she asked Edward.

"I'm not sure."

Jacob said, "We're waiting on our schooner the *Prosper*."

"We don't want to lay out any large sums of money until she brings in her cargo," Edward explained. "But Jacob expected her back several weeks ago. We've been watching for her since I returned."

"Where did she sail?" Deborah picked up the teapot, and Jacob held out his cup for her to refill.

"To the Caribbean," he said. "Captain Frost of the *Eden* brought me a packet of letters two months past. Said he'd met the *Prosper* a hundred miles north of Havana and exchanged mail with her. The report I received from our captain indicates the *Prosper* was doing fine at that time, but we've heard nothing since."

"Perhaps she's waiting on her return cargo," Deborah said.

Jacob winced and shook his head. "I wish I knew. If she's been pirated or sunk—"

"Let's not borrow trouble." Edward threw Deborah a reassuring smile.

"How many men aboard?" she asked.

"Twenty-four," said Edward.

Jacob sighed. "Both the Ramsey brothers are part of the crew, and Ivory Mason's son. Lots of local boys. The company can't afford to lose another ship, but beyond that, the loss of the crew would devastate this town."

"Then we must pray for the best," Deborah said.

"Yes." Edward gave his cousin a slight nod, as though he'd reached a decision. "As soon as she docks and the cargo is unloaded, I will run down to Portsmouth and look at the *Resolute*." He swiveled toward the hall, and Deborah heard the sound of the front door opening.

She jumped up. "That must be Mother and Abby."

Mrs. Bowman and Abigail joined them in the parlor, and Deborah hurried to the kitchen to get a fresh pot of tea and more cups. When she returned to the front room, all four were engaged in lively conversation about the choosing of Portland as the new state of Maine's capital and the preparations underway to celebrate statehood.

Deborah poured tea for Mother and Abigail and sat on a Windsor chair tucked near the hearth and watched them all. Edward and Jacob did not seem to compete for Abigail's favor. Both participated in the discussion equally, with courteous but opinionated contributions.

Edward turned to Deborah after a few minutes. "What do you think, Debbie? Should the people be taxed to build new government buildings?"

"Well, why not? We begged for statehood. We must bear the consequences."

She wondered if he was just being polite, including her in the conversation. But his smile made her feel that it was more than that. Edward cared what she thought. The idea that a man she esteemed found her thoughts worth considering brought on a surge of pleasure that was followed by a confusing blast of self-recrimination. She could not, must not consider Edward as anyone more than a friend at this time. It would shock society if he took up with the sister of the girl who had so recently rejected him. But the very idea made Deborah's chest tighten. If Edward *should* think of her in that way—it was too intoxicating to contemplate.

Edward turned his attention to her mother as she inquired about his family, and Deborah shrank into her corner and watched the others. Jacob was fully engrossed in Abigail. He even chatted with her for several minutes about the style of gown she was sewing for the new governor's upcoming ball.

Deborah searched Edward's profile for signs of jealousy but found none. He conversed with Deborah and her mother while Jacob and Abigail continued their chat in low tones, with eyes for no one else in the room. Deborah drew in a long, slow breath. Edward had not come here to pine for Abby or to torture himself by watching his cousin court the one he loved. And she doubted he found her mother's prattle about the neighbors overly absorbing.

She peeked at him. His attention to her mother's small talk was flawless, yet. . . He threw a quick smile her way, and Deborah's lungs suddenly felt too small to hold the same air he breathed.

∼∞∼

Ten days later, Edward put on his hat and headed for the front door of his family home. He stopped with his hand on the marble knob.

"I hate to go off to the office and leave you alone, Mother. With Jenny away this morning—"

"What claptrap! Do you suppose I've never been alone before?"

"Well, no, but. . ." He looked her over and saw a capable, healthy woman with graying hair, a figure leaning toward stoutness, glinting brown eyes, and a determined scowl.

"Besides, I shan't be alone. You'll come home for dinner, and I expect Jenny to come soon after. And I shall have company for tea at half past three."

"Oh." Edward was taken aback by his gentle mother's spirited declaration. He supposed she had grown more independent of necessity since his father's death.

"Yes, and good company, too."

She seemed to be dangling that morsel in front of him, teasing him to jump at it, so he said rather cautiously, "Anyone I'm acquainted with?"

"Deborah Bowman comes to tea once a fortnight. She's more entertaining than a gossip, and more sympathetic than a parson. Today is Debbie's Tuesday, and there's no one I'd rather share a pot of tea with."

Edward smiled, wondering how this bit of information had managed to elude him. "You make me wish I were invited."

"Well, you're not."

He left the house, still savoring his mother's roguish behavior. She was back to her old self. Or perhaps not. This was a new self. She'd gained a verve that assured him she would be all right now, no matter what God placed in her path.

Her delight at the prospect of tea with Deborah was comforting, too. It told him she'd been enjoying the young woman's company for some time. Since his father's death, perhaps. Deborah was a good listener with an unfailingly cheerful outlook. Only once or twice had he seen her frown over Abigail's standoffish behavior toward him, tiny wrinkles in her smooth disposition. In fact, during the three weeks since Abigail had freed him of his need to look only at her, he'd been

188

taking some rather long looks at Deborah and had decided that her character was altogether pleasing. She matched him in intellect and energy. The idea that Deborah had been bringing sunshine and friendship to his widowed mother brought a warm feeling to his heart.

It also reminded him of his duty to the families of the men of the *Egret*. He'd been to visit the captain's widow a couple of days after he arrived home. Several days later he called on Amos Mitchell's family, and yesterday morning he'd been to see Gideon Bramwell's parents. Those visits were difficult, but the appreciation showered on him told him those interviews had been essential. The parents and wives of the sailors wanted to know how their men had fared to the end.

Gideon Bramwell's mother wept openly when Edward told her about the young man's valiant struggles for survival and their camaraderie on the island. His father shed tears as well when Edward got to the recounting of Gideon's death. He didn't suffer, Edward assured them. His fall from the cliff was unexpected and swift. He died at once on the rocks, and his last act was one of trying to provide food for himself and Edward.

He would try to get to the Wilkes farm tomorrow. It was several miles out of town, but he could borrow a horse and ride out there. Davy's death must have been a severe blow to his parents and the other children. Edward had already discussed with Jacob and Mr. Daniels giving a sum of money to the families of the men who had died when the *Egret* foundered. He himself wanted to take to the Wilkeses the amount allotted to them and tell them how bravely the boy had met his end. It wouldn't be easy, and he wasn't sure how much to tell them about Davy's suffering after he shattered his leg while escaping the *Egret*. Best wait and see what their mood was, he decided. It had been four years, but they might still be angry or bitter toward the company. If the mother seemed resentful or distraught, he would keep to himself the details of the boy's infection and lingering death.

He sighed, knowing he must take a day from his arduous work at the office to accomplish that errand. For the past week he'd given all the time he could spare to his scrutiny of the company's records. It relieved him in some measure, as he'd concluded that Daniels was trustworthy beyond a doubt.

But his study had also given him cause for further dismay. Something was definitely odd about the *Prosper*'s recent record. The ship had been a gold mine for the past two or three years, but since his father's death, she had been marginally profitable. Since Jacob had taken the company's helm, something had gone amiss in the Caribbean trade. Edward didn't like to think his cousin was directly responsible, but he had to eliminate the possibility. He weighed the option of a frank confrontation with Jacob against waiting for the *Prosper* to come in and assessing her performance on the most recent voyage. The longer the ship was delayed, the darker his thoughts were running.

"Edward! Good morning!"

He looked up to see Pastor Jordan approaching him.

"May I walk with you?"

"Certainly. I'm only going to my office."

"I'm heading for a house down past the wharves," the pastor said. "An old salt who lives down there is ill, perhaps dying. Micah Carson."

"I know him," Edward said. "He worked for my father at one time."

"And how are things going with you?"

Edward gritted his teeth. "Well, you made the announcement in church on Sunday, so you know Miss Bowman has set her heart on another."

The pastor nodded, his features schooled to neutrality. "Yes. I wasn't surprised when Dr. Bowman came to see me and asked me to announce Abigail's upcoming marriage to Mr. Price, but I was concerned about you. How are you holding up?"

Edward sighed and looked at the kindly pastor. "The first time I saw her, several weeks ago, I thought I couldn't go on living if she wouldn't have me."

"And now?"

He shrugged, looking down the street toward the harbor. "Well, I'm still alive."

The pastor laid a hand on Edward's shoulder for a moment. "It's a difficult situation, son. I've been praying for you."

"Thank you. I believe the Lord has brought about what is best. I bear Jacob no malice."

"That's good. Look to God for guidance and keep a forgiving spirit."

"I believe I'm more than halfway there."

"Good. This is a time of transition, then, in your mind and in your heart."

"Yes. We are all sifting the meal, so to speak, trying to get the lumps out. Jacob and I had a long talk when I first got home. I've accepted this as God's will for all of us. Now I'm concentrating on the business."

"A big responsibility with your father gone."

"Yes. I'm going over all the records to make sure I know everything that's happened at Hunter Shipping since I went away. I'm afraid our accountant, Mr. Daniels, finds me a bit tedious with all the questions I've been asking him this last month."

"Ah, well, hard work can be a blessing in times of emotional turmoil."

"Would you keep praying for me, Pastor? There are a couple of matters giving me some anxiety."

"Oh? Anything I can help with?"

Edward thought for a moment about the discrepancy in the Caribbean trade. That was strictly a business affair. But the other—an image of Deborah listening avidly as he related his adventures—flitted through his mind. Her smile was so genuine, so yearning that he couldn't help being drawn to her. Just thinking of her these days caused his pulse to jump. Yes, the second one was a matter of the heart.

"Not specifically," he said, "but knowing you are praying for me will be an encouragement."

"Then rest easy," said the pastor. "I've been praying for your peace and a bright future for you ever since I learned you'd come home."

They had neared the harbor, and Edward looked out over the calm water of the estuary. The morning mist was disappearing off the sea. He drew a deep draft of the salty air. His problems with Abigail had dissipated much like the fog, and a new anticipation gripped him. What would God reveal for him, now that the future he'd expected was gone?

Chapter 10

Deborah climbed the attic stairs in the Hunter house, preceding her hostess to the door at the top. It opened onto the roof, where a small platform was enclosed by a decorative white railing. She looked out over the town, which in recent years had burgeoned into a city. The cupola on top of the new courthouse caught her eye. So many buildings that hadn't been there when Edward went away. And now the new statehouse was under construction next to the courthouse. Portland must seem huge to him.

When he'd left, the businesses were still reeling from the economic blow dealt by the recent war with England. But now Exchange Street bustled with new shops, the wharves were crowded with stores, and dozens of brigs and schooners filled the harbor. The fledgling legislature was putting the new state constitution in place. Manufacturing was booming—foundries, ropewalks, soap and candle works, and mills and builders. Everywhere one looked, an air of prosperity hung over Portland.

Mrs. Hunter came behind her, puffing up the last few stairs, and stepped up onto the widow's walk with Deborah.

"You have such a lovely view of the city and the harbor." Deborah turned to the west and leaned on the railing, letting the wind blow against her face, tugging and teasing at her hair and her straw bonnet. "You must be able to see almost as far as Captain Moody can."

"Oh no, the observatory is much higher than we are." Mrs. Hunter chuckled. "Have you ever been up there?"

"No."

"My husband took me up soon after it was built. We could see the White Mountains of New Hampshire. The captain said he can spot ships forty miles out to sea with his telescope."

Deborah turned and looked east toward the conical building that towered over Moody's homestead. Built on a rise that was one of the high points of the area, it rose majestically over the town, like a lighthouse that had given up the sea, wandered inland, and settled on a farm.

"It is a lot higher," she conceded, "but I like your house best. I can see all the church steeples, the courthouse, and the river and the back cove. Even the cemetery. But I'm right here in your peaceful house."

"Thank you, dear. It's been a snug home for many years. My husband's father saw that it was well built, and I've not had much trouble with it, though

I expect Edward will need to have it reshingled before too many more years pass. You can see down there on the gable where the shingles look a bit ruffled."

Deborah squinted down at the edge of the roof. "Yes, I see the spot."

"If we get another bad storm with a high wind from the east, he may need to do it sooner," Mrs. Hunter said with a resigned smile. "But that's the way it is when you live near the sea. Wind, wind, wind."

Indeed, the gusts were pulling at Deborah's bonnet so sharply that she untied the wide strings that anchored it under her chin and took it off, holding it down against her skirt.

"Now you'll lose your hairpins." Mrs. Hunter raised her voice against the stiff breeze, but she was smiling.

"That's a lovely idea." Deborah reached up and probed her coiled hair, extracting several polished wooden pins and slipping them into her pocket. Her long brown locks tumbled about her shoulders and swirled around her face, tossed about by the restless air from the bay.

Mrs. Hunter laughed. "Ah, to be young again."

"Are you cold?" Deborah asked, noting that the older woman pulled her shawl tighter about her.

"Perhaps a bit."

"Then we must go down. I'm sure our tea is ready." Deborah took her hostess's arm and guided her back to the entrance.

Passing through the attic, Deborah noticed chests and disused furnishings crowding the room.

"The castoffs of many generations," Mrs. Hunter said with a smile. "I suppose I ought to go through it all and dispose of half of it, but it seems such a lot of trouble. I believe I'll let Edward do it one day."

Deborah smiled and ran her hand over a smooth old wooden frame. "Did you ever use this loom?"

"No, not me. That belonged to my late husband's grandmother. Lucy Hamblin Hunter, she was. They say she wove the finest linen in the province. Of course, there weren't too many weavers in Maine then to compete with her."

Deborah laughed. "I admire her patience. It's all I can do to crochet a doily."

"Sometime I will show you the table linen she wove. I have several pieces she made. Why, it must have been almost a hundred years ago now. They say she married her husband while he was in prison."

Deborah stared at her in the dim light, wondering if Mrs. Hunter was teasing her. "In prison? What for?"

"Murder. Nothing less. But he was acquitted, and he and Lucy lived a long and happy life together in a little cabin not many miles from here. It was their son who went to sea and became the first Captain Hunter."

"I like that story." Deborah took Mrs. Hunter's hand and walked slowly down the steps with her. When they had descended into the upstairs hall and the attic door was shut behind them, she said, "Thank you for taking me up. I do love it on the widow's walk."

Mrs. Hunter smiled and patted her arm. "It's a joy to me when I see your face light up. I don't go up so much myself. . . not since Jeremiah died, God rest his soul."

"You do miss him a lot, don't you?" Deborah walked slowly with her toward the main staircase.

"Every minute I miss him. I used to go up there and look over at the docks. I can see the warehouse from up there. Sometimes I would see him turning the corner of the street on his way home. I'd wave to him, then rush down the stairs to meet him." Her dreamy smile told Deborah she was off in another, more pleasant time. "But then, with him and Edward both dead, as we all supposed, I stopped going up to the roof. It seemed too morbid. I didn't want folks saying, 'There's the widow mourning her menfolk' and pitying me."

"People don't pity you," Deborah assured her. "You're far too alive. You don't mope about."

"Don't I?"

Mrs. Hunter's eyes twinkled, and Deborah laughed.

"No, you most decidedly don't."

"Well, in any event, climbing those stairs is getting to be quite an exertion for me."

"Come," Deborah said. "I smell something tasty."

A few minutes later, they were seated in Mrs. Hunter's cozy sitting room. Deborah much preferred it to the larger front parlor. This small, paneled room was full of bright cushions and enameled boxes of many colors and designs. She knew that Mr. Hunter had presented the boxes to his wife one at a time, either when he returned from a voyage or when a ship docked after a long trading excursion, laden with exotic wares. When Deborah visited, her hostess let her handle and admire them as much as she liked. She fingered the brightly painted ones from the Orient as the maid laid out their refreshment.

After Jenny had left the room, Deborah sat down and Mrs. Hunter poured out their tea.

"Quite an announcement after church on Sunday."

"Yes." Deborah busied herself with the sugar tongs, not sure she could meet the lady's gaze without bursting out in either laughter or tears. The public reading of the marriage intentions of Mr. Jacob Price and Miss Abigail Bowman had left her torn.

"You don't seem elated at the news. But then, neither do you seem dismayed."

Deborah couldn't help smiling then. "You must understand my mixed feelings. I'm happy for my sister, but only because she is happy."

"Tut! My nephew Jacob is a good lad. He's risen above his father's humble station. He has his mother's wits."

"It wasn't my intent to disparage Jacob," Deborah said. "I believe he will make Abby a good husband."

"But?"

"But I feel disappointed for Edward."

Mrs. Hunter snorted and set her teacup down. "Edward is not weeping. Neither should you be."

Deborah blinked. It was an alien concept that Edward might be pleased with Abby's rejection of him. Was he relieved to be freed from their engagement? She wondered what he had told his mother after Abby revealed her decision to him. Was it possible that in time he might think of courting another? Of course, that would be the natural course of things after his wounded heart had healed, but how feasible was it that he would be captivated by a woman he considered an adolescent tomboy? Deborah shoved the thoughts away. She didn't dare hope that he might turn his affections her way. He was a family friend now. That was all. It meant nothing, and she mustn't read too much into the recent visit he'd made with Jacob.

She reached for a raisin cake and smiled at her hostess. "All right. I shall cease mourning the rift between him and Abby."

"As is proper. This is a time to rejoice with your sister."

Deborah bit into the cake, considering that. For the past few days, she'd felt more like rejoicing than she had since the day she first saw Edward returned from the deeps. But she was afraid to let her heart run too far astray. Every time she thought much about Edward and her growing feelings for him, she felt guilty. And when she considered whether or not he might ever return them, she felt obliged to quickly stifle that train of thought. She would only lay herself open for disappointment if he did not reciprocate. Time to change the subject.

"Mm, this cake is delicious. Did you make it, or did Jenny?"

"She did," Mrs. Hunter said. "I'm lucky to have that girl. She has a proper touch with the bake oven. But neither she nor I can wait to try cooking on the new stove my son has ordered for me."

"You are getting a cookstove?"

"Yes, I am. It will be prodigious fun. Would you like to come round when it's here and practice with me?"

"I'd love to."

Mrs. Hunter nodded. "We can make a huge pot of chicken stew without stooping over a hearth or catching sparks on our skirts. We'll do it on a Thursday, and you and Abigail can take it around to the widows and orphans."

"That would be wonderful. Some of them are so poor they rarely have meat on their tables."

"Then we'll do it and bake a basket full of biscuits from white flour to go with it."

"That will be a scrumptious treat for them. Does this mean you will share with me your secret for making biscuits?"

Mrs. Hunter paused as if it were a novel thought, then smiled. "I believe I shall. But you must be careful whom you share it with."

"I shall indeed."

They shared a smile of conspiratorial friendship.

"Of course," Mrs. Hunter said primly, "if Edward had married your sister, I'd have told her."

The implications of this were not lost on Deborah, and she felt her face flush.

"Abby didn't mean to be unkind to him."

"Of course not. But my Edward was always adventurous, perhaps more than she realized. And I'll not deny his experience of the last five years has changed him. He's more passionate now, more eager to make his mark on the world. I suppose that's because he nearly lost the chance."

Deborah tilted her head to one side, mulling that over. Everyone had agreed that Jacob had done fine while he was in charge of the business, and Mrs. Hunter had no complaints about his management. But Edward would do better than fine. His plans for the company, which he'd discussed with her father after the service on Sunday, were ambitious and bold. He would put his heart into the business and run with it, making Hunter Shipping even greater if God would allow it.

"Perhaps you are right," she said to his mother. "His new passion is an extension of his fight for survival on the island."

"You see that, don't you? But your sister feels safer and more at home with Jacob's more placid nature." Mrs. Hunter nodded and raised her cup to her lips. "I expect they'll make a good match."

"I do hope so. I was a bit put out with her when she turned Edward down."

"No need of that. This is well and good."

"You believe that?"

"With all my heart." As the lady reached for a cookie, Jenny Hapworth hurried into the room, her eyes downcast.

"I'm sorry, ma'am, but one of the clerks just came up from the office with a note for you."

She held a slip of parchment out to Mrs. Hunter. Deborah used the interruption to pour more tea into her thin china cup.

"It's a ship." Mrs. Hunter's merry brown eyes filled with anticipation. "Edward sent this to tell me."

"One of their own ships?"

"He's not certain yet."

"Let's pray that it is the *Prosper*." Deborah set the teapot down with care.

"Yes, indeed."

Mrs. Hunter reached out to her, and they clasped hands.

"Father on high, smile upon us today and bring the wayward vessel the *Prosper* safely to port."

Deborah added her own quiet plea. "Dear Lord, please allow us to rejoice in the homecoming of the *Prosper* today. And if this is not that ship, then, Father, we beg You to keep all the men aboard her safe, wherever they be now, and draw her swiftly back to these shores."

They raised their heads and smiled hopefully at one another.

"Why don't you run up to the widow's walk?" Mrs. Hunter suggested. "I'm not up to making the climb again so soon, but you can go and watch."

"How will I know if it's the *Prosper*? She's probably still far down the bay."

"Here." Mrs. Hunter rose and took a small brass spyglass from the cherry sideboard. "You'll be able to see her when she rounds the point and enters the river, but before that, Captain Moody will know. He's already raised the flag for Hunter Shipping, letting the merchants know, so he's identified the vessel. Either he knows her by her lines, or she's hoisted a signal for him."

"That seems promising, doesn't it?"

"Yes, it does. Run along up, dear."

Deborah seized the spyglass and dashed up the two flights of stairs. The wind was worse than ever, and she hadn't bothered to put her hat or her shawl on. Her skirt billowed behind her as she faced east, and her hair whipped about, stinging her cheeks.

She turned to the sea first and tried to see what Moody had seen, but the headland opposite the town, across the Fore River, obstructed her view. So she trained the glass on Moody's observatory. Three banners were flying, but she picked out the one for Hunter's easily. Everyone in town knew the flags of the big shipping companies.

A sudden fear that it was not the long-awaited ship came over her, and she closed her eyes, sending up a frantic petition.

Father, please don't let them lose another ship. There's been enough grief and loss. Please!

Far in the distance, the prow of a ship rounded the cape and entered the river. She held the spyglass to her eye. The national flag flew from the mainmast—and below it the banner of Hunter Shipping!

She turned and ran down the stairs. Jenny and Mrs. Hunter stood in the front hall, where the stairs came down, and a thin boy was with them. Deborah's heart lurched with joy as she heard his pronouncement.

"She's the *Prosper*, all right! Mr. Edward's dancing a horn-pipe on the wharf, ma'am."

Chapter 11

Edward carried a sack of sugar up the companionway to the deck of the *Prosper* and heaved it onto the stack near the gangplank. He went back to the hatch and watched two stevedores climb up and deposit their burdens on the pile.

That was it. The ship's cargo was unloaded. All of the previous day and most of this morning, his men had labored at stripping the hold. Under Uncle Felix's exacting command, they'd filled the warehouse and stacked hundreds of barrels and crates in the warehouse yard and along the wharf.

Now the merchants of Portland would swarm to the yard and the wharf to look over the goods and speak for those they wished to purchase.

Edward retrieved his jacket from where he'd hung it on a peg over one of the scuppers but didn't put it on. He was sweating and filthy from his effort. He knew Jacob was on the wharf checking off the manifest that listed the cargo. And Jacob was, without doubt, cool and neat, impeccably attired for a businessman.

That was all right, but Edward preferred to get in among the men and put his back into it. That gave him a better understanding of the men's work and boosted the laborers' opinion of him. It also made the ridiculously generous check Mr. Daniels had written him last week for his monthly salary more acceptable.

Had his father drawn that much from the company every month? His mother assured him that his father had when things were going well. In tight times, such as during the war with England or in the months following the loss of the *Egret* and her cargo, he took less. He always made sure the employees were paid first, from the dockhands to the ship captains. The clerks, the sailors, and the boy who swept the warehouse floor were paid before Mr. Hunter drew his check. That knowledge gave Edward a new appreciation for his responsibility as head of the firm. Scores of families depended on him and Hunter Shipping.

More than ever, he knew he must uncover the mystery of the *Prosper*'s lagging profits. He'd handled the cargo himself and watched every cask and bundle brought up from the hold. If all was not as it should be, now was the time to discover it.

He slung his jacket over one shoulder and headed down the gangplank. The men worked about him in an orderly swarm, toting the sacks, rolling the casks, piling crates on small carts, and pulling the carts along the wharf toward the warehouse.

Jacob called to him as he approached his post near the store.

"Well, Mr. Hunter, you've been exercising your muscles, I see!"

Edward flipped the dripping hair out of his eyes. "To the point of soreness. I've only been back in the office four weeks, and already I'm getting soft."

"Well, I can put you in the warehouse under my father if you wish. That used to be your position, did it not?"

"Yes, before I went to sea as a cabin boy at fourteen."

Jacob nodded with a wry smile. "I had much the same experience, as you know, and I can tell you I prefer the deck to the warehouse floor. Of course, the office is better than either."

Edward laughed. "It wouldn't hurt you to rub shoulders with your old cronies now and then."

"Probably not, but I have a dinner engagement later. I can't see a lady receiving a gentleman in your condition." Jacob's nose wrinkled as he eyed Edward's sweat-drenched shirt.

"That bad?" Edward pulled his chin in and looked down at his clothing. "You're right. Perhaps I'd better go home to wash up and change my clothes."

"Commendable idea," Jacob murmured. "I've put the word out that we'll be open to buyers at noon. Several well-placed merchants will wish to greet you this afternoon as they do their business, I'm sure."

Edward nodded and glanced about to make sure none of the workmen were near enough to overhear. "There's something we need to discuss later, Jacob."

His cousin's eyebrows shot upward. "Anything serious?"

"Perhaps."

Jacob nodded. "At the close of business, then."

Edward bypassed the office and went straight home. He'd have to start taking an extra shirt to work with him to have on hand for such occasions. One of the clerks could fetch him wash water; they heated tea water on a small stove. Yes, he would implement the plan at once. That way he could take all the exercise he wanted and not embarrass Jacob or Mr. Daniels when the upper-class customers came around.

Was this the day his mother had said Deborah would visit? No, that was Tuesday. Time blurred with the hectic unloading of the ship, but he was sure this wasn't the day. Still, he half hoped he would run into Deborah at the house. Looking down once more at his soiled clothing and realizing how filthy he was, he cringed. No, it would not be the best time to meet the woman he hoped most to impress.

The thought startled him, but at once the sharpness of it softened. Why hadn't he seen earlier what a wonderful person Deborah was? Not that she needed impressing. She would scoff at that idea. She didn't judge people by appearances. That first afternoon, when he'd gone to the Bowman house fresh off the ship, she'd welcomed him joyfully, bedraggled as he was.

The image of Deborah's subdued beauty leaped to his mind, her lovely brown eyes and gleaming mahogany hair. She didn't play up her attributes, and many people probably would say she was not as pretty as her sister. Edward had thought so, too, at one time. Now he was beginning to revise that opinion.

His mother thought she was beautiful, and she was a good judge of such things. "Deborah has looks that will last," she'd said just the other day. He hadn't told his mother about his newly kindled feelings for the younger Miss Bowman, but somehow she seemed to know. Deborah's name came into the dinner conversation almost every evening at the Hunter house.

Yes, she was lovely. On Sunday she had sat between Abigail and her mother in the family pew. Jacob sat with the family on Abigail's other side, but Edward didn't mind. He took his place beside his mother, but he had eyes only for Deborah, two rows ahead of them that morning. Her green gown was plainer than Abigail's flounced and frilled blue, but it enhanced her creamy skin and dark eyes. And he noticed that while Abby fidgeted during the sermon and cast veiled glances at Jacob throughout the hour, Deborah sat still and seemed to give her undivided attention to Pastor Jordan.

Traits he used to find amusing in Abigail—her flickering attention, her interest in fashion—he had attributed to her immaturity in the old days. But she was a grown woman now, and she had not changed. Deborah, on the other hand, seemed to have grown into a mixture of practicality and playfulness. She appeared to be unconcerned about her appearance beyond neatness and appropriate attire. He knew her to be loyal—look at the way she'd insisted Abby not slough him off. She was industrious, too; she often brought needlework with her to the parlor while entertaining guests when she could have sat idle, and on several occasions he'd seen her jump to aid her mother with some household task. If his mother's words were any indication, she was a reliable and sensible young woman.

As he approached his home, he tried to squelch all thoughts of Deborah. They still felt wrong somehow. For more than five years he'd dreamed of a future with Abigail. But the Abigail of his daydreams didn't match up with the Abigail he knew now. Was it possible that the Abigail he'd longed for during his years of exile was more like the actual Deborah?

In confusion, he bounded up the steps and into the house to greet his mother and explain why he had come home. He was grateful it was not Tuesday, after all. He wouldn't have the slightest idea what to say to Deborah.

⁓⊗⁓

An hour later, Edward was back at the warehouse, watching the commotion from the top of a loading platform as buyers thronged the premises, touching the fabrics, sampling the molasses, and sniffing the fruit. Market days at the warehouse were a jumble of colors and scents. When a ship docked, word spread in a flash through the town, and the buyers awaited word that the unloading was

200

completed and the newly arrived wares were available for sale. The merchants hurried in to speak for quantities of goods for their stores, but individuals were just as ardently in search of a bargain at a low price.

His uncle came to stand beside Edward.

"There's your fortune, boy. Your ship came in at last, and all your financial obligations are met and then some."

"Yes," Edward agreed. "God be praised. She was delayed for loading and revictualing, and then she ran into muddy weather in the Caribbean and had to replace torn canvas."

Felix nodded. "Two days ago we feared she was lost—but she's here now, and all is well."

Edward nodded. He'd read Captain Stuart's report of the voyage, but even with the foul weather and other obstacles accounted for, the *Prosper* had made poor time. She'd brought back a full cargo, which seemed to make everyone else happy; however, the month lost on what should have been a quick run had cost the firm plenty, and Edward was not entirely satisfied with the list of products she'd delivered. He had already asked to have the ship's log on his desk by close of business today.

"Mr. Hunter!"

He turned toward Jacob's voice. His cousin always addressed him formally when employees or customers were listening. Jacob was below him on the floor of the warehouse, holding a long sheet of parchment and beckoning for him to join him and the two men with him.

Edward nodded to Uncle Felix and headed for the steep steps. Just as he was about to descend, he glanced out over the warehouse and halted.

A woman in a brown and blue plaid dress was making her way through the barrels of food and piles of bulging sacks near the door. It couldn't be—

She turned, and the sunlight streaming through the open door glinted on her rich, reddish brown hair. A young man was with her, a gangly, teenaged boy he didn't recognize, carrying a large basket. As he watched, Deborah began taking yams from a barrel and loading them into the basket.

"Edward? Are you coming down?"

Jacob had come to stand just beneath him, not quite masking his impatience. Edward hastened down the steps.

"I just saw Deborah."

Jacob swiveled around to look but seemed unconcerned.

"What's she doing here?"

"She often comes when we hold open market." Jacob turned and pushed people aside to reach the two men he'd been dealing with, and Edward followed, losing track of Deborah. Ladies didn't venture into a crush like this where bankers and dockhands mingled.

"You know Mr. Engle," Jacob said.

"Yes, hello." Edward shook hands with the gray-haired owner of a sawmill on the edge of the river.

"This is his supervisor, Mr. Park, who is in charge of the lumbering operation. They are interested in sending a load of lumber and barrel staves to St. Thomas."

Edward nodded. "The *Prosper* will put out for the Caribbean and Rio again in two weeks."

"Yes," Jacob said. "If you can have it on the wharf next week, we'll make room for it."

"What about your bigger ship?" Engle asked.

Jacob ducked his head in acknowledgment. "The *Falcon* will be in soon, but she plies the European trade for us. We've new cargo lined up for Amsterdam, LeHavre, Bordeaux, and Lisbon."

"Ah, then the *Prosper* it is. We've a large order. I hope you can take it all at once."

"Mr. Engle has shipped lumber with us before," Jacob said, and Edward nodded.

"Well, then, perhaps you could take these gentlemen into the office and arrange the transaction," he suggested, looking toward the front of the huge room, hoping to spot Deborah again.

"We hope to add a third schooner to our fleet soon," Jacob said to Engle and Park. "If that purchase works out, we'll add the *Resolute* to our West Indies trade."

"You boys are doing well," Park said. "When will you have the new ship?"

"If we decide to buy her, we should have her here inside a week," Jacob replied. "Mr. Hunter leaves tomorrow for Portsmouth to examine the vessel."

"Yes, but we're not certain yet we want to buy her," Edward said, scanning the crowd. "If we do, it will likely take us several weeks to refit her before she's ready to take on cargo."

His mind was only half on the conversation, and then only because he was afraid Jacob would promise cargo space where there was none as yet. He spotted the plaid material of Deborah's dress as the people close to her separated and surged around her.

"Could you gentlemen excuse me, please? There's someone I must have a word with."

He made his way as quickly as he could through the throng, but when he got to the crates of tea where he'd last seen her, she was gone. He gawked about, feeling foolish, but soon located her and the boy a few yards away.

"Deborah!" he called as he strode toward her, afraid he would lose her once more.

She turned toward him, and her face lit with pleasure.

"What a surprise to see you here."

"Hello, Edward. I'm often here of a Thursday."

"Indeed?"

"Yes. I would like you to meet Thomas Crowe. He assists me." She turned to the boy. "Thomas, this is Mr. Hunter."

The boy stared at him as Edward held out his hand and said, "Pleased to meet you." After a moment, Thomas shook his hand, then quickly withdrew it.

"Er. . .assists you with what, if I may ask?"

"With making my purchases."

Edward frowned and eyed the basket on her arm, then studied the larger one the boy was carrying. Surely the Bowmans had servants to do their shopping for them, and he doubted their household would need yams and tea in such quantities.

"This is a rowdy place for a lady, especially when a ship has newly docked. We get all sorts of people in here, Deborah."

She smiled. "I know it. That's part of what Thomas is for. Mother forbade me to come by myself."

"I still don't quite. . ." He looked pointedly at her heaped basket. "I mean, that's a lot of tea."

"Yes, it is."

He was at a loss for words, and she laughed at his expression.

"I see I shall have to educate you about my Thursday outings. But it's noisy in here. Perhaps you can visit the house another time, and we can discuss it."

Delight sprang up in his heart at her suggestion, but it was quickly followed by a thud of disappointment.

"I'm afraid I must decline that enticing offer."

"Oh?" She was clearly disappointed as well, and he was somewhat gratified.

"Now that the *Prosper* is in, Jacob wants me to leave immediately for Portsmouth to see about buying that other ship we mentioned."

"The *Resolute*," she said.

"Yes." It shouldn't surprise him that she remembered. "Please believe me, I would much rather spend the time in your parlor discussing your Thursday schedule or any other topic to your liking, but Jacob is right; if we don't act quickly, we'll lose this chance. In fact, we've already delayed action several weeks on this matter, and the *Resolute* may already be sold to someone else."

"Of course you must go," she said.

He nodded. "Thank you for understanding. I shall leave at high tide in the morning, and I expect to be gone several days, perhaps a week."

Her eyes seemed to lose a little of their glow, and he knew he had let her down. But she shook her head and smiled up at him. "Then we shall have to meet when you return. I'll pray you have a safe journey."

"Thank you." He hesitated, then looked at the boy again. "Er. . ."

"Oh, the provisions. You see, a couple of years ago, I began a service of sorts that occupies me on Thursdays."

"A service?"

"Yes. In the past, your father always allowed me to buy a few staples at wholesale each week or anytime a ship came in."

Edward was puzzled by this, but by now he knew that, Deborah being Deborah, she probably had a good reason.

She laughed. "I see that I shall have to tell you my secret in full. Just, please, don't spread it about, will you? It threatens their dignity."

"Whose?"

"The sailors' wives. Or widows, I should say."

"You are taking food to sailors' widows?"

"A little food and a great deal of conversation and company. That's what I do best."

"And my mother is one of your ladies?"

Her merry grin at that warmed him to his toes.

"No, your mother is in a special class by herself. She often helps me in my cause by donating clothing and foodstuffs. But you see, by obtaining food, clothing, and other goods at wholesale prices from the city's traders, I am able to help several families. . . . Well, to be plain, I help them survive."

Edward drew a deep breath. Deborah *would* undertake a cause like that. She saw a need in the seaside city, and instead of petitioning the community's leaders to meet it, she endeavored to help those she could.

"How many families?"

"I've given small aid to about a dozen so far."

"And the boy is part of this?" he asked.

Deborah flashed her smile toward Thomas. "He is the son of a brave man who died at sea."

"I'll soon be old enough to sail myself, sir," Thomas said. "But my mother wants me at home for now."

Edward could understand that. If the husband was lost, the wife would be slow to let her children take up the sailor's life.

"Each week he helps me carry the goods I buy to his mother's house, where I distribute them," Deborah said.

Edward nodded. He was seeing a new side of Deborah, and his impression of her sweet compassion combined with her energy and practical good sense only grew more defined.

"I'm glad my father promoted your efforts."

"Thank you. Your uncle let me continue to come here after Mr. Hunter died. I hope you don't mind. I probably should have asked you."

"No, that's fine. In fact. . ." He glanced toward where he had left Jacob, but his cousin was gone, no doubt into the office to set up the delivery and fees for transporting Engle's lumber. "In fact, I'd like to give you a load of provisions for these families. Just tell me what is needed, and I'll have a wagonload delivered."

Deborah opened her mouth, swallowed, then found her voice. "Thank you, that's very generous. But you can hardly do that every week, or you would lose money. What I usually do is go around and solicit private donations from my friends and some of the business owners in town. If you are willing to let me continue buying at wholesale, that is enough."

"But surely you have ladies who need more than tea and"—he peered into Thomas's basket—"and sugar. Let me this once give you a wagon full."

"Well. . ." She tilted her head toward her shoulder, considering.

Edward's heart leaped, and he longed to throw his arms around her. In that moment, he knew that life without Deborah would be boring and flat. In her world, there would never be a day without some joy, or at least the satisfaction of a worthy effort completed. That was a life he wanted to share.

"Perhaps a few things," she agreed. "Mrs. Lewis has a baby and could use some soft flannel. I hadn't looked at the yard goods yet."

"Yes! You shall have a bolt of flannel and one of calico. And some rice and coffee and all the salt fish and molasses you can use. And from now on, when you come to the warehouse to buy for your ladies, you will buy at cost."

"At cost?"

"My cost, not wholesale."

"Oh, Edward, you'll bankrupt yourself."

"Nonsense. You won't put a nick in all this." He waved his arm, encompassing the whole warehouse and almost hitting a merchant who was passing.

She hesitated, then nodded. "I shan't say no. Thank you."

He smiled. "That's fine. Pick out what you want today. And fill the wagon. I mean it. This day's goods are my gift to you and the families. I'll have one of the men drive the wagon around to the place where you distribute the lot."

"That would be the Crowe residence." She named a street in the poorest section of town.

He nodded, keeping his face straight so as not to embarrass the boy, but the thought of Deborah going there appalled him.

"I'll send a good man to drive the wagon and help unload when you get there. Will you ride on the wagon seat with him?"

"Oh no, Thomas and I shall walk."

"Do you. . .walk down there often?"

"Every week unless Abby goes with me. Then we take a hack."

He stood speechless for a moment. The thought of Abby joining this enterprise shocked him, but with persuasion from the earnest Deborah, he supposed even that was possible. His admiration for Deborah and his longing to be with her urged him to make a further overture. He drew a careful breath and reached for her arm, turning her slightly away from the boy.

"I was wondering," Edward said.

"Yes?"

"When I come back from Portsmouth, may I call on you?"

"You can visit my family anytime."

"No, I mean *you*, Deborah."

She caught her breath and looked away, staring off toward the open door o the warehouse, where clerks were totaling up a buyer's purchases and accepting payment.

"Deborah?"

"Mm?" Her face was crimson, but she turned toward him and raised he chin until her melting brown eyes looked into his face.

"If you'll permit it, I'd like to come next week to call on you. What do you say?

She opened her mouth, but nothing came out. Was she wondering wha Abigail would say? Or perhaps what her father's reaction would be?

She swallowed and tried again. "I would be delighted."

Edward smiled. "Then I shall look forward to it during my voyage t Portsmouth. Now, speak for your merchandise, and I'll arrange for the wagon."

She thanked him again and turned away. Edward watched her for a momen as she headed for the bolts of material in search of soft flannel for babies' diapers He ought to insist that she stay out of that part of town.

He almost laughed at himself. She'd been doing this for two years while h had been off digging clams and carving sticks to kill time on Spring Island. An Abigail sometimes went with her! Unbelievable! He still couldn't picture Abb entering the humble huts of the sailors' widows. But Deborah. . . Yes, he coul see her doing it.

Suddenly he wanted to hurry through the rest of this day. He wanted t put the voyage to Portsmouth behind him and come home quickly. Home t Deborah.

Chapter 12

I t's got to be the tonnage," Edward said, frowning over the mass of papers he had spread across his desk. "Nothing else makes any sense."

"How so?" Jacob asked. He shuffled through the manifests, logs, and sales reports, looking a bit lost.

"On her last few voyages, the total cargo on the *Prosper* was a lower volume than capacity."

"Really? I didn't notice that." Jacob pushed aside one of the ledgers and picked up another sheet of paper.

"It wasn't much off, but on her first voyage last year, the cargo totaled up less tonnage than you'd expect. Then, on the second trip, when she docked last fall, there seems to have been a shortage again, unless I'm missing something. Take a look at the manifest. They could easily have loaded more coffee or molasses in the Indies."

Jacob sat down and puzzled over the papers Edward had indicated.

"But this doesn't prove that anything's amiss."

"Not in itself," Edward agreed. "But this latest cargo. . ."

"Oh, really, Ed." Jacob looked up at him with troubled eyes. "You helped unload her yourself. They had that ship filled to the gunwales."

He nodded, mulling it over in his mind. "Yes, but with what? You've told me several times you expected several tons of coffee to come in. Stuart brought us only a small supply. We could have sold ten times as much coffee today. But this cargo was heavy on rice and raw cotton, Jake. Products we don't make much on when we resell them."

Jacob pressed his lips together and inhaled, looking down at the papers once more. "Captain Stuart told me he got all he could. Should we have him in tomorrow and question him further about this?"

Edward frowned and sat on the corner of his desk. "I'm not sure. I've read his log, and though there's nothing obviously wrong there, it seems a bit vague in spots. He said they turned back for repairs at one point, but the time spent on what should have been a minor job doesn't fit." He stood up. "Let's talk to some of the other men."

Jacob smiled. "Jamie Sibley. He was on the *Egret* with us, remember?"

"Aye."

"He was always a good lad. I put him on the sloop last year, but for this current voyage, I made him the *Prosper*'s second mate."

"Perfect," said Edward. "He was with you in the *Egret*'s yawl."

"Yes. I wouldn't question his loyalty to me or Hunter Shipping."

Edward nodded, liking it more and more. "Let's go."

As they walked the quiet streets of the harbor, Edward's mind surged with questions. They came to the corner of the street where the Sibley family lived, and he paused.

"Jacob, I hope you'll forgive me, but I had to start at the top on this. I've been looking pretty hard at you and Mr. Daniels the past few weeks."

"At me and—oh, Ed."

"Yes, well, I had to be sure. At first I wasn't even certain anything was going on. But I'm sure now. You had nothing to do with it, though."

Jacob's hurt expression pierced him.

"Can you forgive me for doubting you?"

"Well, I suppose you had to. I mean, it's your company and your family. Abby, too. You had to be sure she wasn't marrying a rapscallion."

"Yes. But still. . . Well, I never really thought you could do something like that to Hunter Shipping. Why would you, after all, when it looked as though you'd end up with the whole business? But there were enough indicators to make me look over all the men in the office."

"Father, too, I suppose." Jacob bowed his head, and Edward wished he could deny it; however, the truth was he'd thought of Uncle Felix, too, and whether or not there was some way he could have shorted the company when cargoes came into the warehouse.

"I. . .decided he wouldn't do that, and anyway, the discrepancies originate with the bills of lading and manifests, I believe. This thievery has taken place before the ship docks; that's my belief."

Jacob nodded.

"I'd have taken you into my confidence sooner, but. . .well, as you say, I had to be certain." Edward extended his hand. "We're in this together now, and it feels good to have an ally at my back."

Jacob grasped his hand. "I'm here for you. Let's see what Jamie has to say."

The *Prosper*'s second mate left his family at dinner and joined them in the yard of the small house.

"Mr. Hunter. Mr. Price. How can I help you gents?" He eyed them uneasily.

"We're sorry to disturb you, Jamie," Jacob said with a smile. "My cousin and I just had a few questions we'd like to ask about your voyage. Nothing to worry about."

"It's my fault," Edward said. "As you know, I've been away for a while."

"Yes, sir," Jamie replied. "And glad I was to hear you was alive."

Edward nodded. "Thank you. Mr. Price has told me how you helped the men of the *Egret*'s yawl survive, and I believe he used good judgment in promoting you."

Jamie glanced at Jacob, then shuffled his feet, looking down as he pushed a pebble about with his toe. "Thank you, sir. I was glad for the opportunity."

"Well, I'm leaving tomorrow on a short trip in the company's sloop," Edward said. "Going to Portsmouth. You wouldn't like to go along, would you? I'll be looking at another schooner we're thinking of buying."

Jamie's face lit up. "Oh, yes, sir, I'd be privileged to make that run. And say, if you's buying another ship, will there be berths on her for a new voyage?"

"Tired of the *Prosper*?" Jacob asked.

Jamie looked down at his feet again. "She's a good ship, sir, but. . .I'd just as soon try something new."

Jacob reached out and touched the young man's shoulder. "Jamie, we've been through a lot together, and I know you'll be honest with me. Is something slippery going on with the *Prosper*?"

Jamie exhaled sharply and glanced Edward's way, then looked back to Jacob. "It started with the coffee."

"Coffee?"

Edward kept quiet and let Jacob continue the interview, since Jamie Sibley obviously felt more comfortable with him.

"Yes, sir, we took on a prodigious supply in Jamaica. Finest Brazilian coffee, they had. More than half our cargo."

Jacob cocked his head to one side. "But, Jamie, when we unloaded yesterday and today. . ."

Jamie nodded, his forehead furrowed with wrinkles. "I know, I know. But Captain Stuart. . ."

"What?" Jacob asked.

"Well, sir. . ."

They waited a long moment.

"We went to St. Augustine and off-loaded most of the coffee, sir."

"You sold the coffee in Florida?" Jacob shot Edward a glance, but Edward kept still.

"Y–yes, sir. I wasn't sure what was going on, but I supposed the captain had orders from you. After that, we headed south again, and that's when I heard him telling Mr. Rankin—"

"The first mate," Jacob said to Edward, and Jamie nodded.

"Yes, sir. I heard him tell Mr. Rankin we'd run back down there quick and fill up with coffee again, and. . .and none would be the wiser, sir."

"Meaning me, I suppose." Jacob shook his head. "It's true, then. Ed, I'm not as sharp as you are with figures, and the whole thing slipped past me. He's selling off part of the cargo and reloading afterward. That's why it took Stuart so long to get back here this voyage."

"Aye," said Jamie. "But when we got back to Jamaica, they had hardly any coffee left. The captain was in a black mood. We pushed on to Havana, but he couldn't get any there, either. We couldn't go all the way to Rio for it, so we took on cotton and rice and whatever else he could get."

Edward took a deep breath. "I suppose something similar happened on her two voyages last year?"

Jamie shrugged. "I wasn't on board then, sir, but yes, from what the other fellows have told me, I'd think so. They sold off a bit of the most expensive goods at some other port."

"And the captain thought they'd all keep quiet?" Jacob asked.

Jamie hesitated. "Well, sir, he gave out there'd be something extra in it for them, and he told me. . . . Well, he told me he'd give me something later, but I must keep mum about the extra dealings." He threw an uneasy glance at Edward. "I'm sorry. I been fretting on it these two days since we docked, thinking I ought to come and tell you gents. You coming here. . . Well, that tipped it for me. I should have come to you sooner."

Jacob clapped his shoulder. "All's forgiven, Jamie, so long as you understand you're siding with us now."

"We'll turn this over to the law," Edward added. "You might be needed to testify."

Jamie swallowed hard. "It won't sit well with the men."

"We'll get you out of here tomorrow on the sloop with Mr. Hunter," Jacob said. "I'll go to see the magistrate, and I won't mention your name unless it's necessary. When you come back from Portsmouth, you might need to write out a statement or some such."

"Somebody'd have to write it for me, sir."

Jacob nodded. "Yes, well, don't you worry, Jamie. When we're done, Captain Stuart won't be able to get another ship, and any man who's been in this with him will face the law as well."

"That amounts to the whole crew, sir." Jamie seemed appalled at what his confession had put in motion.

Edward said, "We'll bring the men in and question them, and any who own up and give evidence against the captain will be kept on."

Jamie sighed. "Thank you, sir. There's some as weren't even smart enough to catch on, and then there's some who was just scared of the captain and Mr. Rankin."

Edward nodded. "We'll take that into consideration. Now go back to your family and rest easy tonight, Jamie. Be on the wharf at dawn, and we'll sail for Portsmouth."

Edward and Jacob walked silently up the street and out of the harbor district.

"Can you handle things tomorrow?" Edward asked at last.

"I believe I can," Jacob said. "I'll take Mr. Daniels into my confidence and go around to the magistrate first thing."

Edward nodded. "Perhaps your father could help you question the sailors.

They're all afraid of him, and he could put the fear of the law into most of those boys."

Jacob smiled. "That's a thought."

"If you want me to stay. . ."

"No. You take Jamie and go see about that ship. Now that we know what's been going on with the *Prosper*, there's no reason we can't add the *Resolute* to the fleet and press forward."

∞

Deborah knocked on the door of the Hunter house and looked around as she waited. The garden was a riot of color. She knew Mrs. Hunter employed three servants to keep the house and grounds in order. It was the Tuesday between her usual visits for tea, and Deborah wondered if her hostess had invited her so she could show her the lovely gardens in bloom.

Jenny opened the door and smiled. "Hello, Miss Deborah. Mrs. Hunter has a lady with her in the sitting room."

"Oh, I beg your pardon," Deborah said. "I'll come back another day."

"No, no. She insisted I bring you right in." Jenny opened the door wide and motioned her inside, so Deborah entered and handed her a basket.

"A few late strawberries for Mrs. Hunter."

"Oh, she'll be pleased. Go right in, won't you?"

Deborah removed her gloves, wondering if she'd been invited on purpose to meet the other guest. Timidly she peered into the small room. Mrs. Hunter spied her at once and stood to greet her.

"Come in, come in." To the other woman in the room, she said, "This is Miss Bowman, the physician's daughter, an old acquaintance who has lately become a good friend of mine."

The other woman did not stand but accepted Deborah's hand. She was about fifty, Deborah supposed, and elegantly dressed in a tan silk day dress edged in deep, ruffled flounces. The lady looked her over sharply, giving her the feeling that she was under inspection. Her feathered hat drooped over one ear and set off her stylishly curled hair.

"How do you do," Deborah said.

"Bowman," the woman murmured. Louder, she said, "Are you the young woman who threw Edward Hunter over for his cousin?"

Deborah felt her face go scarlet. Mrs. Hunter also flushed. Her only aid to Deborah's discomfiture was an apologetic smile.

"Actually," Deborah said, releasing the lady's hand, "that would be my sister, Abigail. I am Deborah."

The lady nodded. "I see."

"Deborah, this is Mrs. King," Edward's mother said.

"Mrs. . . . ." Deborah gulped and used her selection of a chair as an excuse not to meet the lady's eyes for a moment, while she grappled for her composure. *I've just been introduced to the governor's wife. Was I rude? Oh dear, I hope not! But she was rude first.* She swallowed again, gathered her skirts, sat down, and smiled.

"Let me give you your tea." Mrs. Hunter poured out a cup for her, and Deborah accepted it, suddenly conscious of the dark stains under her nails left by the many strawberries she'd hulled that morning for her mother's preserve making.

"Thank you."

"So your sister is the foolish chit who gave young Mr. Hunter the mitten?"

Mrs. Hunter smiled at her guests. "It's really for the best, you know, Ann. They were so young when Edward went to sea, and then he was away for five years. They both had time to mature while he was gone. And when he came back, they found they'd outgrown their childish infatuation."

Deborah tried to hold her smile but felt it slipping. This was too humiliating.

Mrs. King didn't seem to think so. "Well, I still say she missed a good opportunity. Of course, I haven't met her new intended groom. But I have met Edward, and any girl who would—"

"I'm surprised you heard about it all the way up in Bath," Mrs. Hunter said.

"We hear everything," Mrs. King stated. "Of course, my husband is in Portland much of the time now. We're taking a house here until his term is up. That's why I'm with him on this trip, you know. We're only staying at the Robisons' home until the place we're leasing is cleaned and our baggage arrives."

"How lovely," said Mrs. Hunter. "Your husband does need to be here in the thick of things just now."

"Yes. He's had many social invitations and no way to return them, so I'll be setting up housekeeping and scheduling some affairs."

"I'm so pleased that you had time to come and spend the afternoon with me," Mrs. Hunter said.

"Well, I enjoy getting out and about, and I always make time for old friends. I was hoping to see Edward, though. We've heard so much about his death-defying feat. Do you expect him home today?"

"I'm not sure." Mrs. Hunter glanced at Deborah with an inclusive smile. "Edward ran down the coast in the company's sloop a few days ago, but he should be back soon. I've asked the gentlemen at the office to send me a note the minute he returns."

"How do you dare let him go off again so soon?" Mrs. King shook her head and sipped her tea.

"It's only to Portsmouth, and I'm not worried about Edward. He's proven himself well able to survive even the most unfavorable circumstances. Isn't that right, Deborah?"

"Oh. . .yes, certainly. He's a very capable sailor."

"I suppose you have a point," Mrs. King said. "I'm so glad my husband doesn't sail on his ships, though. William sends them off full of apples and potatoes and lumber, and they come back filled with cotton and coal."

"How expedient," Mrs. Hunter said.

Deborah was startled when her hostess winked at her. Apparently Mrs. Hunter had the same thought she did—that the life Mrs. King led must be boring.

"Yes, well, the general has enough to do without floating around the globe. He was hoping to see your son, though. He tells me he's been meaning to call here since he heard of Edward's return but hasn't found time. So busy, with the new legislature meeting and all."

"Your husband is welcome anytime," Mrs. Hunter assured her. "Of course, Edward would be happy to see him and tell him of his misadventure. Perhaps we can have dinner here once we know what Edward's schedule will be."

"Good, good. That would be most pleasant. I hope to arrange some small dinner parties in the new house. It's a bit cramped, so large gatherings would be awkward. But there are a good many statesmen and merchants who've entertained General King over the past few months, and I simply must reciprocate to them and their wives. That will be my first order of business once we're settled."

"I'm sure the entire city looks forward to it," her hostess said. "Your affairs are always delightful. Now, Deborah, I do wish you'd tell me about your Thursday project. How are things going, dear?"

Deborah had relaxed, glad to be ignored, and she flinched when Mrs. Hunter drew attention to her again. "Very well, thank you."

She saw Mrs. King's inquisitive look and was about to explain her widows' aid endeavor when Jenny appeared in the doorway.

"Yes, Jenny, what is it?" Mrs. Hunter asked.

"The apprentice brought a note, ma'am, from the office."

"Oh, thank you."

Jenny handed her a folded sheet of paper, and Mrs. Hunter quickly opened it and scanned the contents. Deborah watched her face, unable to suppress an anxious stirring in her stomach. Had she been truthful when she agreed that she did not worry about Edward?

His mother smiled. "Captain Moody has raised a flag indicating he has spotted a vessel flying Hunter Shipping's colors approaching the harbor. This note is from Mr. Price, saying they are preparing a berth on the wharf."

"The *Resolute*?" Deborah breathed.

"I don't know, dear." Mrs. Hunter's eyes glittered with inspiration. "Say, why don't we go down to the wharf and see?"

"Go to the docks?" Mrs. King's arched eyebrows and shocked tone told Deborah the governor's wife did not approve of the enterprise.

"We'll take a carriage," Mrs. Hunter went on. "If Edward has come home again, this time he shall have folks to welcome him when he steps ashore."

"Marvelous!" Deborah clapped her hands together, glad that Mrs. Hunter was undaunted.

"But the docks," Mrs. King said. "Is it safe, my dear?"

"Of course." Mrs. Hunter reached for the bell pull. "The men on Hunter's Wharf all know me and respect my husband's memory."

As Jenny came to the door, Mrs. King stood and reached for her reticule. "I fear I must go back to the Robisons' house. We'll be dining out tonight, and I must catch a nap. Our journey here quite fatigued me."

"We'll drop you off on our way to the wharf." Mrs. Hunter's animated face fed Deborah's excitement. Edward was returning, and she would be on hand to greet him. Her parents would not object since she would be in the company of his mother.

"Jenny, send Mercer to bring a hack. We three ladies are going out."

Chapter 13

Aunt Mary! So glad to see you today." Jacob opened the door of the hired carriage and gave Mrs. Hunter his hand. "And Deborah! Welcome."

"Thank you," Deborah said as she lifted her skirt and stepped carefully down.

"Come. I've brought my spyglass, and we can walk out past the store and have a good view down the river."

"Do you know yet what vessel it is?" Mrs. Hunter puffed as they walked the length of the long pier, but she would not allow Jacob to slacken the pace.

"Not for certain, but I think it's still too early for the *Falcon*."

They stood together waiting. Jacob turned his spyglass toward Captain Moody's tower.

"One of our ships. I haven't called many laborers in because we're not expecting to unload a cargo today. Although Edward might have picked up a few bundles in Portsmouth."

A sharp-eyed lad gave a whoop and waved toward the mouth of the Fore. Deborah squinted and saw a vessel pull out from behind the headland of Cape Elizabeth. It was too small for the schooner they'd hoped to see.

"That's our sloop." Jacob's voice drooped in disappointment. "Well, Edward's likely on board, so your trip is not wasted."

"I did hope we'd get a first glimpse of the company's new ship," Mrs. Hunter said. "Ah well, perhaps it wasn't all we'd hoped, and he passed on buying it."

"Or perhaps she was already sold." Jacob held the spyglass out to Deborah. "Would you like to take a look?"

"Thank you." She trained the lens on the distant sloop, searching its deck for a tall, broad-shouldered man whose dark hair whipped in the wind. None of the sailors she saw had Edward's stature or bearing.

She offered the glass to Mrs. Hunter. "Would you care to look?"

"Oh yes. Thanks, dear." Mrs. Hunter scanned the sloop. "I don't see Edward."

"Nor did I," said Deborah.

His mother turned and studied the observatory tower through the spyglass. "Jacob."

"Yes, Aunt Mary?"

"Captain Moody's run up another signal."

"Oh?"

Mrs. Hunter handed him the spyglass, and Jacob turned to look toward the tower on Munjoy Hill.

"You're right!" Excitement fired his voice.

Deborah shaded her eyes with her hand and tried to make out the distant flag.

"It's our colors again. Either the *Falcon*'s come home in record time, or Edward's bought the *Resolute*."

They all waited as the sloop drew nearer, the wind carrying her against the current. As the vessel came in closer, Deborah could make out half a dozen men on the deck, bustling to make the mooring.

"Ahoy, Sibley!" Jacob cried to the man who seemed to be directing them. "Where's Mr. Hunter?"

"Yonder!" Sibley motioned behind him, down the river.

Deborah could hardly contain her excitement. Jacob handed her the spyglass and scurried to help tie up the sloop. She put the brass tube to her eye and focused on the point of land where the sloop had first appeared.

Empty water lay restless between the shores.

Suddenly a dark bulk poked into her circle of vision.

"There she is!" Mrs. Hunter cried.

Deborah lowered the spyglass. Far away but coming about toward them, a majestic ship under sail hove into sight. Deborah drew a sharp breath. "She's beautiful!"

"Magnificent. Larger than Mr. King's flagship, too."

Deborah chuckled at Mrs. Hunter's satisfied smile. She handed over the spyglass and watched the ship as the crew went aloft, ready to take in canvas.

"I see him!" Mrs. Hunter bounced on her toes. "He's standing amidships just under the mainsail. Look, Deborah! He's waving his hat."

The next half hour sped past as the *Resolute* settled into her new berth at the outer end of Hunter's Wharf. The gangplank was put in place, and Jacob led the ladies onto the deck.

Edward met them at the rail, grinning like a child who'd found a half dime, and assisted them in descending to the deck.

"Do you like her?" he shouted to Jacob, who hopped down on his own power.

"She's perfect! Everything Smith told me and more."

"And the best part is she's in wondrous shape. There's hardly anything to be done before we can put her to sea. She handles like a dream, Jake!"

Edward smiled down at Deborah, and she realized he was still holding her gloved hand. She pulled it away reluctantly.

"Oh, Ed, about that matter we discussed the evening before you left," Jacob said.

Deborah watched curiously as Edward sobered. "All went well?"

"Yes, things are in hand, and when the sloop docked, I told Jamie he has no cause to worry."

"And Stuart?" Edward asked.

"Justice is in motion. I'll tell you all about it later, but things are proceeding as we hoped."

Edward nodded. "That's good, then. Well, Mother, what do you think of the *Resolute*?"

"Makes me wish I were younger," Mrs. Hunter said, surveying the deck and the rigging. "I'd ask you to take me on her next voyage and relive the old days."

"You've been to sea?" Deborah asked.

"Oh yes. When my husband and I were first married, I took two voyages with him. It's something I remember fondly, though there were frightening moments. All in all, being with the captain and understanding his love of sailing was valuable to our marriage. And seeing other places and people so different from us New Englanders opened my eyes. I've never looked at folks the same since."

"I should like to make such a trip." Deborah sighed, then realized Edward was watching her.

"Perhaps you shall someday," he said.

She felt her face color and was alarmed when he took her arm and led her a few steps away from the others.

"I should like to come round this evening to call on you, if I may."

"Of course." A thought suddenly struck her. "Oh, Edward, I haven't told Father."

He sobered. "Do you think he'll object?"

"Why, no, I don't think so."

"Fine, then, I'll ask him. When will he be at home?"

She glanced around him and saw his mother carrying on a spirited conversation with Jacob as they walked toward the stairs leading up to the quarterdeck.

"By six, if his patients don't keep him. He's usually home for dinner."

"Good, I'll take dinner at home, then come around and see your father. If all is to his liking, we'll have some time together afterward."

Deborah felt her mouth go dry. She'd never been courted before, but she had no doubt that was Edward's intention.

"I. . .we. . ."

"Yes?" Edward's eyes twinkled as he gazed down at her.

"We may have to compete for space in the parlor with your cousin and Abby."

Edward laughed, and her heart lifted. "Have they set a date yet?"

"Yes. The eighteenth of August."

"Well, we'll turn the tables on them. You chaperoned your sister many an evening, and now it's her turn."

Deborah's heart skipped. Never in her life had she been in need of a chaperone, but a quick glance at Edward's gleaming dark eyes told her the time had come. Perhaps her mother would stop despairing of ever seeing her married.

That thought was enough to send an anticipatory shiver through her.

Edward reached for her hands and squeezed them. "You blush most becomingly. Come. I'm supposed to be showing off my new schooner, and poor Jacob has had to haul Mother off so I could have a private word with you."

"Is that what he's doing?"

"Of course. But we'd better relieve him and let him get on with his official duties. He and Mr. Daniels will have some paperwork to do. We'll have to register the ship and decide what we want for crew and cargo for her first voyage under Hunter Shipping's colors." He pulled Deborah's hand through the crook of his arm and took her toward the companionway that led above, where Jacob and Mrs. Hunter were now inspecting the tiller.

"Where will she sail?" Deborah asked.

"To the Indies, I think, unless Jacob has a full cargo waiting to be taken to some other place. Oh, they're coming down. I'll show you all the captain's cabin. It's quite spacious for the size of the ship."

"Would you captain her yourself?" Deborah asked.

"I might. Bringing her up from Portsmouth was a joy. I wouldn't mind going out again on her."

"What?" his mother barked, descending the last steps. "Did you say you're leaving again?"

"No, Mother. I merely said that with a deck like this one under his feet, a man feels like sailing."

"You're not going to hire a captain to handle this ship for you?"

"Of course we are," Jacob said, scowling at Edward. "I have several names. There are good men out there waiting for a ship."

Edward smiled. "Then I expect we'll get someone, Mother. We haven't had time to discuss any of that yet."

She looked at him, then down the length of the main deck. "She is a lovely vessel. I wouldn't blame you a bit if you wanted to sail her. But don't forget your family."

"I won't. Now come and see the captain's quarters. Whoever he may be, the master of this ship will be quite comfortable."

Deborah sighed as she viewed the neat cabin. Mrs. Hunter spun round on the carpeted floor, exclaiming over the polished wood of the built-in cupboards and drawers, the folding table, the curtained bunk, and the mullioned window in the stern of the ship.

"Oh, if we'd had a cabin like this on the *Hermia*, I'd have been the happiest bride on earth. As it was, we had a tiny room one-third this size, and your father insisted on keeping his trunk in the cabin. We could barely turn around and were always tripping over that chest."

Edward laughed. "I'll keep that in mind, Mother, if I ever ask a woman to share a cabin with me." He winked at Deborah, and she felt her blush shoot all the way to the tips of her ears.

∽⊗∼

"What shall I do if Father isn't home before Edward arrives?" Deborah threw an anxious glance at Abigail in the mirror as her sister brushed out her thick, dark hair.

"We'll just have a pleasant evening with two gentlemen callers, and Edward can speak to him tomorrow. Don't fret so."

Deborah smiled at Abby's reflection. "I'm not fretting."

"Yes, you are. You haven't been still for ten seconds since you sat down."

Deborah was surprised that her wayward tresses were obedient to Abby's gentle coaxing and lay in gentle waves about her forehead.

"Do you like it?" Abigail asked.

"I'm not sure. It doesn't look like me."

"Well, it's time you started paying more attention to your looks. You're very pretty, you know. If you'd dress up a little and guard your complexion from the sun, the young men would hang about our doorstep in droves."

"Not true."

"Well, at least half true. You'd have to stop treating them like chums as well."

"And how should I treat them?"

"Like fascinating men."

"Most of them are boring."

"You seem to find Edward interesting."

Deborah whirled around in dismay. "Does it upset you that he asked to come calling on me so soon after. . .after your decision?"

Abigail smiled and shook her head, patting at a stubborn strand of hair over Deborah's ear. "Why should that bother me? I have the man I want."

"Oh, Abby, it wasn't my intention to attract him."

"I know."

"Then why do I feel so awful?"

"No reason. You should feel pleased and honored. Edward is a fine man, as you've told me many times."

Deborah puzzled over her sister's serenity. "You seem so calm now, but a few weeks ago you were overwrought."

"Because I knew I loved Jacob and couldn't bear to hurt Edward. I couldn't help but wonder if it was my duty to marry him, even though it would rip my heart to shreds. But now, seeing that he's accepted the outcome, I feel much easier."

"You don't think it's horrid of him to want to pay attention to me so soon?"

Abigail's smile had a wise twist that Deborah had never seen before. "I expect that if I hadn't become attached to Jacob before Edward came home we still would have found eventually that we were not perfectly suited to each other."

"Really?"

"Yes. It might have taken us months to discover that, however. You see, God works things out."

Deborah nodded. "I'm sorry I was cross with you."

"You had a right to be. I didn't behave very well at first. But I also think that you and Edward have an admiration for one another that transcends the years of his absence."

"You do?"

Abby reached for a hairpin. "Mm-hmm. You know you've always adored him."

"Yes, I have. But he only saw me as your bother of a little sister."

"Perhaps, but he commented to me several times in the old days about how clever you were and what a beauty you would make some day."

The air Deborah gulped felt like a square lump.

"I never, ever thought he'd think of me as. . .a woman."

Abigail laughed and squeezed her shoulder. "You're so droll, Debbie. It's quite a relief to me that Edward's not crushed. It would have been miserable to see him at church and social functions for the rest of my life, with him slouching about and staring at me with those huge, dark eyes."

"Edward wouldn't do such a thing."

"Perhaps not, but he does have a melancholy tendency. You are just what he needs. I predict you'll keep him in high spirits. I never should have accomplished that."

Deborah started to protest, but Abigail picked up another hairpin. "Turn around and let me finish.

The image in the mirror stared back at Deborah with dark, anxious eyes. Her sister's skillful ministrations had brought her hair into a soft, becoming style. Would Edward think she was pretty?

"Thank you, Abby. I confess I'm a bit nervous."

"Well, you shouldn't be. You're much more suited to him in temperament than I ever was." Abigail tugged at her sleeve. "Stand up now. I think the red shawl will set off that white gown splendidly."

"Oh no, the red is too bright." Deborah already felt misgivings at wearing the new white dress. The neck, while not daring, was lower than she was accustomed to, and she feared her blush would become perpetual.

"It is not," Abigail insisted, holding up the shawl in question. "Red is all the fashion, and it goes very well with the delicate flower pattern of your gown."

"No, I think I'd better wear my gray shawl."

"Impossible. I'm wearing it." Abigail seized Deborah's usual dove gray wrap and threw it over her own shoulders. "It goes well with my green dress, don't you think?"

"Well. . ."

"Come on." Abigail took her hand and sidestepped toward the door. "I heard the knocker. Jacob's probably cooling his heels and waiting for his dinner."

Chapter 14

Edward arrived at the Bowman house amid a gray drizzle that brought an early dusk. The family was just leaving the dinner table. They had delayed the meal, hoping Dr. Bowman could join them, Deborah told him.

"Father was detained with a patient this evening," she explained.

Edward's disappointment at being unable to settle his business with the doctor was short-lived. The shy, hopeful smile she bestowed on him made all obstacles shrink.

"Ah. Then we shall pass a pleasant evening in spite of his absence, and perhaps I can have a word with him tomorrow."

Mrs. Bowman carried into the parlor a tray bearing coffee and a bowl of sugared walnuts. The young people settled down, with Abigail and Jacob on the sofa and Deborah and Edward in chairs opposite them, while Mrs. Bowman sat in the cushioned rocker near the hearth.

"It's chilly this evening," she said. "This rain."

"Would you like a fire, ma'am?" Edward asked. "I can kindle it for you."

"A fire in the parlor in July?" Mrs. Bowman shook her head.

"Must we be so frugal, Mother?" Abigail asked. "It's cold, and the fire's already laid for just such a night."

"All right, then." Mrs. Bowman edged her chair back to give Edward room to work. He pulled the painted fire screen aside, and soon a comforting blaze threw its warmth to them all.

They spent two hours in enjoyable conversation, mostly concerning the new government and the upcoming wedding. Mrs. Bowman seemed hesitant to discuss the latter topic when Abigail first brought it up, casting worried looks in Edward's direction.

He smiled, hoping to put her at ease. "My cousin has invited me to stand up with him for the ceremony. I'm looking forward to performing that duty."

After that, Mrs. Bowman relaxed and brought out her sewing. Deborah began to knit, glancing up only now and then.

"And Deborah shall have a new gown as well," Abigail said. "Lavender, I think. We're going to shop for material tomorrow."

"The one she's wearing now suits her admirably," Edward said.

Abigail smiled. "Isn't it lovely on her? But I want her to have something a little fancier. Mother, too."

Deborah stared at her knitting, her lips firmly closed. He supposed that hearing her appearance discussed was not at all to her liking, though he was pleased he'd had a chance to let her know he approved. Her hair was different tonight. Softer somehow, and it suited her sweet features.

"Really, dear. People don't make so much of a wedding," Mrs. Bowman said.

"No, but it's for the party afterward." Abigail laughed. "All the best people will come, and the women, at least, will be lavishly turned out. Why, Father said we may even invite Governor and Mrs. King."

"Oh dear," Deborah muttered.

"And, Edward," Abigail went on, turning a brilliant smile on him, "you must know your mother has offered her garden and parlors for the affair."

"Very gracious of her," said her mother. "We haven't much space here, but Mrs. Hunter insisted we hold a reception there for the young people."

"So she's told me," Edward said. "After all, Jacob is her favorite nephew."

Jacob chuckled. "Aunt Mary is quite excited about it. She and Mother are having a grand time planning the menu."

"She wanted to serve dinner for forty, but we told her that was too much for her," Abigail said.

"Oh, I don't know. She surprises me with her energy these days." Edward shook his head. "I think she does more entertaining now than she did when Father was alive."

"Her gardens are so beautiful that I could not refuse," Mrs. Bowman told him. "Most kind of her. Abigail and I are going over tomorrow afternoon after we finish our shopping to make plans with her and Mrs. Price."

Deborah's ball of yarn dropped to the floor and rolled a few feet. Edward stooped to retrieve it and held it loosely in his lap, letting slack out as she tugged the yarn. She looked at him, and he smiled, raising his eyebrows. Her dark eyes flashed gladness, then were hidden once more by her lowered lashes. She went on with her knitting, saying nothing but with the faint smile lingering on her lips, and he was content to hold the yarn and watch her.

At last, Mrs. Bowman rose, remarking on the lateness of the hour, and Edward looked to his cousin. Jacob seemed to be making preparations to leave, so Edward rose and offered to carry the tray to the kitchen. His hostess thanked him and went with him to show him where to place it.

When he came back into the front hall, Deborah stood by the stairway alone, and he guessed she had left the parlor to allow Jacob a moment alone with his betrothed. As he approached her, Deborah took a breath and smiled at him a bit shakily.

"Thank you for coming," she said, an unaccustomed crease marring her smooth brow.

"It was a pleasure, and I've thanked your mother for a stimulating evening."

"Discussing wedding plans?" Her doubt colored her tone. "My mother isn't used to entertaining on a large scale, and she's in a dither about this. I'm sure that wasn't the most fascinating conversation you've ever engaged in."

"I don't mind. I shall doubtless see some people there whom I haven't seen in five years or more. Now, if we can only keep Uncle Felix sober that day."

Her eyes widened in alarm, and he bent down to whisper, "Don't worry. Jacob and I have discussed it. We're hiring half a dozen of our strongest men to keep an eye on him the night before and make sure he stays clear of the taverns."

"What about the day of the wedding?"

"Mother won't allow a drop in the house, but even so, I'll detail several men to guard the punch and watch him."

"Thank you. It's not that I don't like him. . . ."

"I know," Edward said. "I like him, too, but I don't entirely trust him in matters of this nature." He reached for her hand, and Deborah turned her eyes upward and looked at him. "I will speak to your father tomorrow. Nothing shall prevent me."

Her lower lip quivered. Then she nodded. "Thank you."

A flood of longing came over him, and he considered for a fleeting moment pulling her into his arms.

No. Not yet.

He smiled and lifted her hand to his lips. "I spoke the truth when I said I enjoyed the evening."

Her luminous smile rewarded him, but at that moment, Abigail and Jacob emerged from the parlor. Abigail's face was flushed, and Edward was satisfied to note that her beauty no longer affected him. A spark of grateful gladness sprang up in his heart as he noted the happiness on his cousin's face.

"Ready to go, Edward?" Jacob asked. "I believe it's still raining, and I thought I'd hail a hack."

"Yes, I'll share with you."

The two young men said good-bye to the ladies, and Edward found himself whistling softly as he and Jacob strolled toward the corner in the drizzle.

"Feeling blithesome tonight, Ed?"

"A bit. And yourself?"

"Euphoric."

"Ah."

They spotted a horse and carriage a short distance down the cross street, and Jacob whistled and waved his hat. The driver pulled the horse around toward them.

"It does my heart good to see you and Abigail so happy," Edward confided when they were in the carriage.

"Thank you. Sometimes I still wonder if you truly don't mind."

"I don't."

Jacob smiled at him in the dim interior of the vehicle. "I'm beginning to believe that. You know, Ed, I never meant to be an interloper."

Edward smiled. "Of course not."

"But I wasn't about to give ground to you, not after. . . Well, my heart was hers already when you came back. Can't undo something like that."

"You can rest easy. I believe God has another future for me."

"Ah, yes. And not an unpleasant one, I think."

"You'll be married in a month," Edward said. "Where will you and Abigail be living afterward?"

"I've something in mind."

"Not with your parents, I hope."

"Oh no," Jacob said quickly. "I couldn't subject Abby to that, although Mother would love to have us there."

"I should say not. Your father scares her."

Jacob gritted his teeth and shrugged. "Not surprising. He scares me sometimes, too."

"Well, I only ask, because. . ." Edward swung round to meet his eyes. "Jacob, Mr. Daniels dropped your salary when I came home."

Jacob opened his mouth, then closed it and fidgeted with his watch fob. "Let's not get into that. I've found a modest house to lease for the next year, and Abigail is agreeable."

"But before I came back, she must have expected something much more lavish."

Jacob shook his head. "It doesn't matter."

"Yes, it does. When we left five years ago, you were first mate on a trading ship. You had the expectation of a nice salary with the firm when you came home and a profit from your private venture."

"So I did."

"But it was nowhere near what you were paid after my father named you his heir apparent."

"Edward!"

"Hear me out. I've looked at the books. I know you were paid considerably more last year than you were before. If Father had left the company to you outright instead of to my mother, you'd own Hunter Shipping now. You'd be taking home what I am now. Instead, I came back and usurped your place."

"I would hardly call it that."

"Fine, but at least admit that on your salary before I disappeared you never could have hoped to support a wife of Abigail's class."

Jacob's face colored. "It's true I'd have thought her beyond my reach in the old days. But—"

"I don't want you and Abby living in a hovel." Suddenly he realized that Jacob must have expected to inherit the Hunter home, too. When Jacob had first proposed to Abigail, he'd probably planned to live with her in the roomy and comfortable house where Edward and his mother lived.

"Really, Ed!" Jacob said. "My salary this past month was cut back to what I earned two years ago, it's true, but it's enough. I'll be able to maintain a respectable household."

"Respectable. Small, plain, not to say stark."

"Yes. And Abigail is not greedy. She understands that things will be a bit more spartan than we'd at first planned. She doesn't care, Edward."

"That's remarkable."

"Isn't it? But it's true. If she did care that much about money, she'd be marrying you instead of me."

Edward took a long, slow breath and sank back. He stared out the window at the dark, wet street and realized they were almost to his aunt and uncle's house.

He was glad Abigail had risen to the occasion and shown her willingness to accept a lower standard of living than she had anticipated. That fit in with the Abigail he remembered. He'd always found her amiable and supportive in the old days. Now she would fulfill that role at Jacob's side.

The driver stopped the hack before the Prices' small clapboard house.

"Look, Jacob, we'll speak more about this later," Edward said. "You've done admirable work for Hunter Shipping, and I expect you'll continue to do so. I doubt I could get along without you now, with the increase in trade we're seeing. With the *Resolute*, our profits will rise, and—well, when it comes right down to it, I'm willing to take less than Father was."

"No, Edward, stop being noble."

"I'm not. I had no idea how much Father drew for a salary. Mother tells me now that he invested much of it, and that kept them going during the war years, when shipping was at a standstill. But so long as Mother is comfortable now, I'd like to see the company pay you a salary that's commensurate with the work you do."

Jacob opened the door of the hack. "Thank you for saying that, but I won't hold you to it. We'll talk again, as you say."

"Fine," said Edward. "Now, quick, before you go, tell me what happened with Captain Stuart."

"They jailed him overnight, but he's engaged an attorney from Boston and is out on bail. I expect he'll be tried when the judge comes here next month."

"And the rest of the crew?"

"Most of the men admitted they knew about it but felt they had no choice. I'll go over the roster with you tomorrow. There are a few I think we'd be better off without, but most of the fellows are probably all right. However, Mr. Daniels agrees we should prosecute Stuart and Rankin to the fullest."

Edward nodded. "Good. We'll talk about it in the morning." He saw his stocky uncle Felix silhouetted in the doorway of the house, seeming too large for the little dwelling.

"Whattaya doin', wastin' money on a hack?" Felix roared.

"Tell him I'm paying!" Edward called to Jacob through the window.

Jacob turned back and grinned at his cousin. "Been at the ale, I'd say." He faced his father and shouted, "Hush, Father! It's Edward's money. Now, let's get inside."

Chapter 15

Edward walked from the harbor to Dr. Bowman's surgery the next morning. The small building on Union Street had been erected as a wheelwright's shop, but after the owner's untimely death, the doctor had bought it and refurbished it as a place to attend his patients. He'd kept the wide double door, but instead of wagons and buggies, it now admitted the injured and ill people who sought his services.

Edward entered, pulling off his hat, and looked around. Two women sat stone-faced on a bench near the door, one of them holding a fretful infant. A curtain of linen sheets stitched together stretched across the room, and from behind it, he heard the murmur of voices.

"Is the doctor in?" he asked the older woman, and she nodded toward the curtain.

Edward hesitated, then sat down on the far end of the bench.

A moan came from behind the sheets, followed by Dr. Bowman's hearty, "There, now, that's fine. Just keep the bandage on until you see me again. Come back Friday."

A man in tattered sailor's garb appeared from behind the curtain, holding his left forearm with his other hand. His dirty shirt was stained with blood, and he walked a bit unsteadily. The woman with the baby stood up and walked with him to the door.

A gangly young man who seemed hardly out of his teens poked his head from behind the curtain and looked at the other woman. "Dr. Bowman's ready to see you, mum."

The doctor appeared next, carrying a few instruments and some soiled linen. He dumped the linen into a large basket in the corner and set his tools on a small table, then poured water from a china pitcher into a washbowl and immersed his hands in it.

As he dried his hands, he looked around and saw Edward sitting on the bench.

"Well, lad, this is a surprise. Not ill, I hope."

"No," Edward said, rising. "I only wanted a word with you, sir."

The young man who assisted the doctor was taking fresh linen from a cupboard. Dr. Bowman glanced at the middle-aged woman who was waddling toward the curtained area. "I'll be right with you, Mrs. Atfield."

"I'm next in line, Doctor," she retorted.

"Yes, I'm well aware of that. I shan't be long." He smiled at Edward and whispered, "Here, let's step into my private office."

He opened a door in the side wall, and Edward chuckled, stepping out into a tiny backyard.

"Mrs. Atfield comes at least once a week for her dyspepsia," the doctor said. "It will still be there after we've had our say. How can I help you?"

Edward drew a breath; the tangy salt air seemed inadequate, and he felt a bit lightheaded.

"Sir, I came to ask permission to court your daughter."

Dr. Bowman stared at him, and though Edward feared for a moment he was going to be censured, slowly the man's mouth curved and his eyes began to dance.

"I've heard that from you before."

"Yes, sir, you have. I was sincere then, and I am sincere now."

"Well, since you know I've promised my elder daughter to your cousin, I suppose there's only one conclusion for me to draw."

Edward's smile slipped out of his control. He was sure he looked the buffoon, but he couldn't help it. "Yes, sir. It's Deborah I'd like to court."

"Well, now. Sensible lad." Dr. Bowman slapped him on the shoulder. "I almost felt the family had taken a grievous loss last month when Abigail chose Jacob. But I see I was early in my conclusion. We get to keep both you boys." He nodded. "I'm pleased. So will Mrs. Bowman be."

"Thank you, sir."

"And I don't have to ask how Debbie feels."

"You don't, sir?"

"No, she's championed your cause from the start."

"That means a lot to me. We've been friends a long time, and I see a staunch loyalty in her, not to mention she's a lovely young woman now."

"Just don't ever let her feel she's your second choice, son."

Edward nodded. "I shall endeavor to let her know that she will be first in my heart from here on."

"Good. Very good." The doctor sighed. "And now I suppose I must get back to Mrs. Atfield. Why don't you join us for dinner this evening?"

"Thank you very much, sir." Edward shook the doctor's hand and watched him go back through the door. He walked around the corner of the building and headed for the harbor, smiling.

He had been thinking on and off for a week about Deborah's charity for sailors' widows, and his mind returned to it as he walked toward the wharves. He'd seen some of the poverty in the shabbier parts of town. Deborah didn't despair about it. She set about to alleviate the worst of it. Through careful inquiries, he'd learned that she not only gave food to those in need, but she also helped the women learn new skills and had even found jobs for a few.

She was like the biblical Ruth, he thought, who gleaned grain for the widowed Naomi. Willing to work hard to help others.

He'd intended to visit the widow of Abijah Crowe, one of the men who fled the *Egret* in the longboat with him and the only one whose family he had not yet contacted. To his surprise, he had heard Deborah mention the name Crowe the day he'd given her the wagonload of provisions, and now he wanted to learn whether Abijah Crowe's wife was one of the women to whom Deborah ministered. He decided the staff at Hunter Shipping would not miss him if he stayed away another hour.

He recalled the directions Deborah had given the day she collected her goods at the warehouse. By asking about in the neighborhood, he soon found the Crowe house. The humble cottage looked in need of repair; however, the front stoop was neat, and bright curtains hung at the window that faced the street. He knocked, wishing he had dressed differently—not in the tailed coat he wore to the office most days. But it was too late. The door creaked open, and he looked into the face of a thin woman with dull brown hair. Her cheeks were hollow and her hands bony.

"Hello," he said.

"What do you want?" Her eyes narrowed as she looked him over.

"Mrs. Crowe?"

"I be her."

"I'm Edward Hunter."

She stared at him blankly, and he thought she did not recognize the name. He said, "I heard your name mentioned by Miss Bowman. Deborah Bowman."

The woman drew her shoulders back and scowled at him. "And?"

"Well, I wondered if you were possibly related to Abijah Crowe."

Her gaze pierced him, and he stared back.

"He were my late husband."

Edward sighed. "I was with Abijah on the *Egret*."

"I know it. I heared you came back after all this time."

He nodded. "After our ship sank, Abijah was with me and a few others in the ship's longboat."

She said nothing but continued to watch him, unblinking.

"I...meant to come and visit you earlier. I've tried to visit the families of all the men who were in my boat."

"Nancy Webber told me you came to see her."

"Yes. Her John and I were together on the island for quite some time, and we got along well. I was glad I could tell her what her husband meant to me in those days." Edward removed his hat and wiped the perspiration from his brow. It was nearing noon, and the sun's rays made him uncomfortably warm.

"Do you want to set a spell?" she asked.

"I should be glad to if you've no objection."

Mrs. Crowe turned and shuffled into the cottage, and he followed. Two children about five and seven years old scuttled out of the way and tumbled onto a bunk, where they crouched and stared at him.

Edward took the stool the woman indicated near the cold hearth, and she sat opposite him.

"Thought you weren't going to come here," she said.

"I'm sorry I put it off, ma'am. It took me awhile to get used to being home again, and I've been back at work the past few weeks. But I believe I've gotten round to all the other families. I'm sorry it took me so long to find you."

She nodded once and reached behind her for a ball of yarn and a carved wooden hook. As she began to crochet, Edward studied the yarn. It looked very familiar.

"My Abijah died in that boat," she said.

"Yes, ma'am, he did. I'm sorry. He was a good man and a good sailor."

She frowned but kept on hooking the yarn through the endless loops.

"He spoke of you and the children."

Her hands stilled, and she sniffed. "What did he say?"

"He asked the captain, at the end, to remember him to you. And he said he didn't want the children to grow up fatherless."

"The captain died, too," she said, not looking at him.

"Yes, ma'am, he did. Several days later. But I tried to remember all the messages the men had given him in case I ever made it home."

"How did he die?"

"Abijah?" Edward asked.

She nodded.

"I'm afraid it was lack of water, ma'am. We started out with very little, and we all suffered from it."

"It's a terrible death." Her ball of yarn dropped from her lap and skittered across the floor, and Edward jumped to catch it.

He took it back to Mrs. Crowe and handed it to her. "Deborah Bowman brought you this yarn."

Her eyebrows drew together. "You're the man who owned the ship. The man Miss Abigail was going to marry."

"You know her?"

"Surely. She comes here with her sister and helps with the sewing and tells stories to the kiddies."

He sat down again. "My father owned the *Egret*. And yes, I was betrothed to Abigail Bowman when I left here five years ago."

"But she found some other fellow she liked more." She shook her head. "I thought better of her than that."

Edward cleared his throat. "It wasn't quite like that, Mrs. Crowe. You see, my cousin was also on the ship with your husband and me, but when the *Egret* went down, he was in the other boat. His boat was picked up, and my cousin Mr. Price came home thinking I was dead. After several years of believing I had perished, Miss Bowman agreed to marry Mr. Price."

"She shouldn't, though. Not now that you're here."

"Well, I thought so myself at first, but God has shown me a better plan."

"A better plan?"

"Yes. I believe our heavenly Father brought them together in their grief and that He has another woman chosen to be my wife."

"Oh?" She looked doubtful, and he smiled.

"Yes, ma'am. This morning I've been making arrangements to call upon another young lady. Someone I think you'd approve of."

"I?"

He nodded.

"Not Miss Debbie?"

"Yes."

Mrs. Crowe began to smile at last. "She be a fine young lady."

"Indeed she is."

"She gets victuals for those as can't buy them, and she sews togs for the little ones. She even brought me fine cotton for curtains." The woman nodded toward her small window, and Edward turned to observe the red calico fabric that hung there.

He smiled at her. "She told me that she had friends down here."

Mrs. Crowe's chin came up several inches. "She does. And she ain't ashamed to claim them. Miss Debbie says anyone who believes in Jesus is her sister."

Edward nodded. He could almost hear her saying that. "I'm so glad she is your friend, and I wanted to bring you something." He reached into his coat pocket and brought out a small pouch of coins. "Mrs. Crowe, Hunter Shipping has made a gift to the family of each man who died when the *Egret* sank."

"Don't want no gifts."

"But, ma'am, your husband served the company well."

"Don't need no charity. Now Miss Debbie, she comes down here, she shares with us, and she sits and stitches with us. She shows us how to do things. She taught me to spin raw wool, she did. The food she brings is for them that's starving. This family's not starving."

"I'm glad to hear that. How do you live, ma'am?"

"My older son, John, goes out with Abe Fuller fishing every day, and Thomas, the next one down, he runs errands for the haberdasher and the butcher, and sometimes Captain Moody. We get by."

"That's commendable. I'm glad your sons are able to work. But this money that I've brought you isn't charity. It's coming to you for your husband's good service. He did his job on the *Egret* until the day she foundered, and if he'd made it home, he'd have been paid for every day of that work. Hunter Shipping owes your husband money, Mrs. Crowe. But since he's not here to receive it, I would like to give it to his heirs, meaning you and the children. It's the pay he would have gotten for the days he worked, not a penny more."

She pursed her lips together. "My man was a good man."

"Yes, he was." Edward set the little pouch on the table near her, and she did not protest.

"You say he died in that boat before the captain died."

"Yes." Edward rubbed a hand across his forehead. The harsh memories deluged him once more, and he sent up a silent prayer for peace. "We were in the boat for a fortnight, ma'am. Your husband lasted ten days, I believe. Longer than a couple of the others."

"Was he in distress?" she whispered.

"We all were. I won't lie to you, ma'am. It was awful."

She nodded. "And he's buried at sea?"

"Yes, ma'am." He reached into his pocket again. "I believe this was his." He held out a small knife he had removed from Abijah Crowe's pocket before they lowered him over the side of the boat. "I used it during my time on the island and was thankful to have it. Very useful it was. In fact, I might not be alive now if it weren't for this. But now...well, I thought your older boy might like to have it."

She took the knife in her hand and stared down at it. It was a poorly forged blade with a handle of deer's antler. Tears welled in her eyes and spilled down her cheeks. " 'Twas Abijah's all right. Thank you."

Edward left after wishing her well. He walked along the shore, surveying the wharves and boats without seeing them. After ten minutes he stopped, realizing he had come to Hunter's Wharf. Instead of heading across the street to the office, he walked all the way to the end of the wharf, past several moored vessels and the shops and chandlery. At the end of the wharf, he halted and stood gazing down into the water that swirled around the massive pilings.

At last his duty to the families was concluded, though he knew he would have dealings with many of them again. Amos Mitchell's son was now his employee. He prayed he would never have to face Mrs. Mitchell again on such an errand.

He recalled Mrs. Crowe's face as she looked down at her dead husband's knife. He'd seen similar reactions when he had delivered mementos to other families. The captain's wife had accepted his compass and quadrant with dignity, but even so, her face had crumpled as she examined the items. Davy Wilkes hadn't had anything in his pockets, and Edward had sliced a button from his coat before they eased his body overboard. His mother had wept over that, saying she'd stitched it to his woolen coat a few days before he'd sailed.

For Gideon Bramwell's parents, he'd delivered the key the boy wore on a thong around his neck. Edward had thought it belonged to Gideon's sea chest, which was now at the bottom of the ocean, but his mother told him it belonged to the chest that the girl he loved had filled with household items and vowed never to open until he returned with the key.

For each one of the seven men in the boat with him, he'd managed to preserve some small item to convey back to their families. John Webber had carved a wooden chain from a piece of driftwood he found on the island. It was more than two feet long when he died. Edward had chopped off the excess wood and carried the chain home to Mrs. Webber. With Amos Mitchell, who was lost out of the small boat in high seas, Edward had only a misshapen hat left behind where he'd sat. For Isaac Towers, they'd found pinned inside his pocket a small emerald brooch he'd bought in Rio and was planning to take home to his wife.

What would they have brought home if it were me? Edward wondered. The trinkets he'd bought for Abigail and his mother were sunk and gone. His clothes had gone to rags, and the few tools he'd had on the island had belonged to others. In his excitement on being rescued, he'd brought only the grass pouch he'd woven to hold the mementos of the men. Just one other thing had made it home with him from the long adventure. He shoved his hand in his pocket and rubbed his thumb over the smooth, rounded shell he'd carried for several months now. He'd stooped to pick it up from the sand one morning, and when he straightened and glanced toward the sea, there, incredibly, was a ship under sail, making for his island. His ordeal was over. He had thrust the smooth shell into his pocket and run toward the surf, shouting and waving his arms. His isolation had ended.

He closed his eyes and inhaled the salty air, feeling the breeze on his face and the sun on his shoulders. It didn't matter that he'd lost all. What mattered was the way he handled what God had given back to him.

"Thank You, dear Father, for bringing me home. Use me in what is left of my life as You see fit."

Finally he opened his eyes and turned toward his office.

Chapter 16

Deborah's heart soared as she opened the front door to Edward.

I have the right to love him now. Thank You, Lord.

The answering light in Edward's eyes sent anticipation surging through her. Modesty said she should avert her gaze, but she couldn't look away. Instead, she smiled and reached for his hand, drawing him into the house.

"I'm so glad you're here. Abby is dining with the Price family tonight, but Father and Mother are eager to see you."

She led him to the dining room, where her parents greeted him.

"You see, I tore myself away from my patients this evening," Dr. Bowman said.

"I'm delighted, sir." Edward shook his hand and turned to his wife. "Thank you for your kind invitation, Mrs. Bowman."

"We're pleased you could come. Sit here, Edward, where Abigail usually sits. Jacob has carried her off to spend the evening with his family tonight."

A thin, sober-faced woman served them under gentle instruction from Mrs. Bowman. When the maid carried the platter of lamb in and set it before the doctor, her hands shook so that the china hit the table with a loud *clunk*, and the woman jumped, flushing to the roots of her hair.

"There, now," said Dr. Bowman. "A nice leg of lamb. Thank you, Mrs. . . . What's the name again?" He looked around vaguely toward his wife.

"It's Mrs. Rafferty, Father," Deborah said.

"Ah, yes. And is there sauce?"

"Aye, sir." The woman curtsied and dashed for the kitchen.

"Mrs. Rafferty is a friend of mine," Deborah said to Edward, hoping he would understand that she meant one of her Thursday widows. "She told me that she hopes to earn a bit of money in service, so Mother agreed to train her."

"If she works out well, I may recommend her to your mother, Edward." Mrs. Bowman raised her eyebrows. "Has she found a replacement for Jenny Hapworth yet?"

"No, she hasn't. I'm sure she'd be happy to consider anyone you vouch for."

"She's green, but she's willing to learn."

Deborah smiled at him. "We have Elizabeth in during the day, but because Mother has no one to help serve dinner, we've been letting Mrs. Rafferty practice on us this week. Usually one of us helps her, but I think she's doing splendidly, don't you?"

At that moment, the maid cautiously pushed the door open and entered, bearing a steaming dish and a pewter ladle on a tray. She inched toward Dr. Bowman's end of the table and set the tray down with a sigh.

"Thank you," he said, reaching for the gravy.

Mrs. Rafferty dipped her head, then looked toward Mrs. Bowman.

"Perhaps Mr. Hunter would like more potatoes?" the mistress suggested.

"Oh no, ma'am, I'm fine," Edward assured her. "I don't eat as much as I used to."

"Short rations for a long spell will do that to you," the doctor said.

"But it's delicious," Edward said quickly, and Deborah smiled at him. "The biscuits are very light, too. Much like my mother's."

Deborah said nothing but knew her face was beaming. Mrs. Hunter had watched her bake twenty batches of biscuits one rainy day until Deborah's were identical to her own. The children of the fishermen's shacks had reaped the bounty of her cooking lesson, with their fill of biscuits delivered and distributed by Mrs. Hunter's gardener.

But her mother was not about to ignore a chance to brag about her talented daughter.

"Deborah made the biscuits, and aren't they flavorful? She baked the pie you'll be enjoying later as well."

Edward sent a look across the table that topped approval. Deborah could only interpret it as thorough admiration, and she whipped her napkin up to hide the silly grin that stretched across her face.

Her father began once more to ask Edward about his travels, and Edward obliged by recounting tales of the sea and the ports he had visited. Deborah listened, enthralled. What would it be like to travel to such strange places? She was sure her imagination was inadequate to show her the wonders Edward described.

"Are you happier on dry land?" Mrs. Bowman asked.

"In some ways." Edward reached for his water glass and shot Deborah a smile.

"Jacob says he'll stay ashore now," Dr. Bowman asserted. "I'm afraid Abby's making a landlubber out of him."

"There, now, that's all right," said his wife. "Jacob says one shipwreck was enough for him, and he doesn't mind not sailing anymore."

"We've plenty to keep him busy at the office," Edward said. "I doubt I would undertake any long Pacific voyages again, but I might take one of our company schooners to the West Indies."

"That's a profitable destination for you, is it not?" The doctor carved a second helping of lamb for himself.

"It's the backbone of our trade. The goods are perhaps not as exotic or expensive, but we can make more trips there and back."

"Volume," Dr. Bowman agreed.

When the meal was over, Mrs. Rafferty brought the coffee tray to the parlor, where Mrs. Bowman poured and the doctor continued the discussion with Edward about trading and the outlook of Hunter Shipping. Deborah felt sure he was pumping her caller about his financial prospects, and perhaps Jacob's as well, but Edward didn't seem to mind.

At last, Mrs. Bowman rose. "I must see Mrs. Rafferty before she leaves for the night. And, my dear, you said you would get a hack to drive her home."

Dr. Bowman took his cue and stood as well. "Yes, she can't walk all that way alone after dark. There, Edward, I've kept you rambling on about business all evening. I expect you young folks have other subjects to discuss."

Edward had jumped up when his hostess stood, and once more he shook hands with the doctor.

"Thank you for having me in, sir."

Her father laughed. "I expect I shall be seeing a lot more of you. Come around my little surgery anytime you wish to talk, Edward."

"Thank you. I will."

"And don't keep Deborah up too late."

"No, sir."

Edward watched the parents leave the room, then looked down at Deborah and took a deep breath.

"It seems I am to be trusted now without a chaperone."

She nodded. "You do seem to be well favored."

"Would it be too forward of me to sit beside you?"

She felt her throat tingle and swallowed hard, then managed to say, "Not at all."

He came around to the sofa and sat on the cushion next to her, suddenly very close, and Deborah's stomach fluttered.

"You haven't said much this evening."

She smiled at that. "Well, you know Father. When he gets onto a topic, he won't let go."

Edward nodded. "I saw him this morning."

She stared at the fire screen that covered the empty fireplace. "I thought you must have."

They sat in silence for a moment, and she wondered if she ought to ask the outcome of that encounter.

"He. . .seemed a little sad at the thought of an empty house," Edward said.

"A what?" She stared at him, at his rich brown eyes and the dear, disorderly lock of hair that fell over his forehead.

"Well, if both his daughters left home, I mean."

She turned away, but it was too late. The telltale blush had returned, though she'd determined not to let it.

He grasped her hand lightly, and joy shot through her.

"I don't expect they'll go so far away that they can't visit," she whispered.

"I seem to recall you saying you'd like to sail one day."

She nodded. "So I should."

"I know you'd love it. But I wouldn't entrust you to just any ship or any captain."

Feeling very daring, she said, "And to whom would you entrust me?"

"I believe the *Resolute* will make trade voyages to the Indies soon."

"How soon?"

"Well, Mr. Price, the second officer of Hunter Shipping, tells me she'll sail within the month under Captain Redding. But this winter, that is, after the hurricane season. . ."

Deborah found enough courage to look up into his face once more.

Edward smiled and lifted a hand to her cheek. His voice cracked as he continued. "Mr. Price tells me that she'll sail again then under a different master."

"Oh?"

"Yes."

"As you say, I shouldn't want to go with just anyone."

"By then the company thinks it can spare its owner for a few months, and the ship will sail under. . .Captain Hunter."

Deborah took two deep breaths, trying to calm her raging pulse before answering. "I hear he comes from one of the oldest Maine families and a long line of sea captains and ship owners."

"I've heard that, too. Farmers of the oldest stock turned sailors."

She felt his arm warm around her shoulders, and he eased toward her. A flash of panic struck her but then was gone. She had nothing to fear with Edward. She surrendered and leaned her head against his chest, where his broadcloth jacket parted to show his snowy linen shirt. With a deep sigh, he folded her in his embrace and laid his cheek on top of her head. She heard his heart beating as fast as hers.

"Deborah?"

"Yes?"

"I love you."

"And I've always loved you."

He tilted her chin up and searched her eyes for a moment, and her heart tripped as their gazes met. He bent to kiss her, and she luxuriated in the moment, resting in his arms.

"Can you forget the past?" he whispered.

"I doubt it. Not altogether. But we learn from the past."

"Yes."

He was silent, holding her close to his heart and stroking her hair. "I shall always love you," he said.

"And I you."

He pushed away and fumbled in his coat pocket. When he brought his hand out, a round, brown-speckled shell rested in his palm.

"What is it?" she asked. "I've never seen one like it."

"It's all I have from the island. The few other things we had I gave to the men's families for remembrances. But I'd like to give you this."

She took it and ran a finger over its hard, satiny curve. "Thank you."

"And I hope we'll sail together one day and find other mementos."

He went to one knee beside her and clasped her hands, with the shell hidden between her palm and his.

"I'd like to bring you another keepsake soon. A ring, dearest. Will you be my wife?"

Deborah caught her breath. Would her father object and say it was too soon?

A certainty overcame her misgivings. This was what she had waited for these many years. This was why she had reserved her heart from loving any others.

"Yes," she whispered. "I shall be honored."

He drew her toward him and kissed her once more, and Deborah knew her own solitude had ended, too.

Epilogue

A cool October breeze blew in off Casco Bay and ruffled the limbs of the trees around them. A tall maple waved its branches, and red and yellow leaves fluttered down into the Hunters' garden. Edward seized Deborah's hand, and she smiled at him, then looked down and waved at the people below.

They were mad to get married on the tiny rooftop platform, but this was Deborah's choice. Indian summer had hit the Maine coast, and she had reveled in the warm, clear autumn days the last two weeks had brought. Edward had agreed to her suggestion for the wedding venue as he agreed to nearly everything she asked, eager to please her in the tiniest detail. Still, it was a bit cooler today, and harsh weather was not far away.

The two of them, Pastor Jordan, their witnesses and parents were all the widow's walk could hold. The other guests filled the garden and spilled over onto the walk. A few of Deborah's Thursday ladies and their children even stood outside the neat white fence, gazing up at them with awe.

Jacob and Abigail joined them at the railing. Edward's mother and Dr. and Mrs. Bowman left the shelter of the stairway and came to stand beside them. Mrs. Hunter was swathed in a fur cape and a woolen hood, but still, Edward hoped the ceremony would be short.

"Perhaps this wasn't such a good idea," Abigail said to her sister.

"I'm sorry. Are you cold?" Deborah asked.

"A bit."

Jacob seemed to feel this was license to slip his arm around his wife of two months and hold her close to his side, and Edward winked at him.

"Let us begin," said the pastor. "Dearly beloved, we are gathered here in this unusual place...."

They all chuckled, and the pastor went on with the timeless words.

Edward pulled Deborah's hand through the crook of his arm and held it firmly as they recited their vows.

As the ritual ended, they bowed their heads, and the pastor invoked God's blessing.

"You may kiss the bride."

Edward leaned down to kiss Deborah tenderly. He felt the change in wind as it rippled his hair and sent his necktie fluttering to the side. When they separated, he opened his eyes and automatically sought the observatory tower.

"A ship!"

"Hush, Edward," said Abigail. "This is your wedding day. Stop looking up there."

"You mustn't be thinking of business," Jacob agreed.

"But a ship is heading for our wharf, and it can't be one of ours."

Jacob squinted toward the fluttering signal.

"Spanish."

"You sure?" Edward frowned, wishing he had the spyglass.

"Don't worry," Jacob said. "My father's in the warehouse. He insisted on working today on the odds something like this would happen. He and the harbormaster will see to it."

Their parents stepped forward to embrace them.

"Come in out of the wind," Mrs. Hunter said, leading the way to the door. "I'll have Hannah open the front door for our guests. We're serving in the double parlor, not the yard."

"I'm sorry it turned too chilly to eat outside," Deborah said, making her way cautiously down the steep attic stairs behind her mother-in-law.

"Don't fret," Mrs. Hunter replied. "I've planned on it all along. Can't trust the weather in these parts. But I'm glad you didn't plan dancing on the wharf, Deborah."

"Dancing on the wharf?" Abigail asked as they reached the hallway below. "What a novel idea."

Edward smiled and squeezed Deborah's hand. He'd have gone along with it if Deborah had wanted it, but she'd confided that her mother would find it too raucous, and it was just as well. It would have been chaos with a foreign ship landing during the reception for the newlyweds.

The parlor was already filled with distinguished guests. Governor and Mrs. King and the state's congressmen rubbed elbows with ship owners, merchants, and Dr. Bowman's patients. Edward's sister, Anne, greeted the couple with a radiant smile, and her husband brought their two little ones over to kiss their new aunt. Deborah's widowed friends hung back in the yard, too timid to enter at first, but Edward took his bride out to stand on the front porch and urge them inside, along with most of the men employed by Hunter Shipping, where he had declared a half holiday.

"We shall cut the cake in a moment." Deborah's eyes glowed as she hugged Mrs. Crowe. "Hannah Rafferty helped Mrs. Hunter bake it, and you must have a piece. All the children, too."

The ladies came inside at last, with downcast eyes, peeking up now and then at their opulent surroundings. Abigail went around with a basket of little bags of sweets, handing one to each child. The rooms were crowded, but Edward stationed himself at Deborah's side, knowing she was determined to speak to each guest. She greeted each poor widow as graciously as she did the congressmen's wives.

At last the guests began to slip away, and only the newlyweds' families were left.

Felix Price entered, filling the doorway with his bulk.

"Any cake left?" he roared.

"Yes, Father," Jacob told him. "We fed near a hundred people, but even so, I think we'll be eating cake for a week."

Aunt Ruth hurried to fix a plate for him, and Felix sought Edward out.

"Well, now, there ye be with your beautiful bride."

Deborah smiled up at him. "Thank you, Mr. Price. It was kind of you to tend to business while Edward and Jacob were otherwise occupied."

"You're welcome, lass. But you must call me Uncle." He glanced at Edward. "May I kiss the bride?"

Before he could respond, Deborah turned her cheek to Felix, and he planted a loud smack on it, then turned to Edward with a grin.

"It's a fine Spanish brigantine at your wharf this minute."

"What's in her hold?" Edward asked.

"Olives and their oil, sugar, grain, wheat, and oranges."

"Oranges?"

"Aye. They look to be all right. A few spoiled, but I think they picked them green."

Jacob shook his head. "We'll have to have market day tomorrow. I'll send word around to all the buyers."

"Half of them were here today," Edward said. "If we'd known half an hour ago, we could have told them all at once. But you're right; unload as soon as possible. Most of it will keep well, but the fruit has to be sold quickly."

"There's cork, too," Felix added. "Big bundles of it."

"Good, we can sell that for certain." Jacob extended his hand to Edward. "Sounds like I should get down to the wharf. Abby can go home with her parents. Don't worry, Edward, we'll turn a good profit on this cargo."

"Should I come down in the morning?" Edward asked, glancing at Deborah. She closed her lips tight but made no objection.

"Of course not!" Jacob glared at him as though he had uttered heresy. "You have two weeks' honeymoon before you and Deborah sail in the *Resolute*. And you are not to show your face at the office during that time."

Deborah laughed. "Oh, please, Jacob. If you think you can keep him away for two weeks, you're daft. Besides, we'll be going back and forth to the *Resolute* while you're loading her. I expect you might see both of us once or twice during the interval."

"Yes," Edward said, patting her hand. "I insisted Deborah decorate the cabin for her comfort and bring along plenty of clothing. We'll be making a few trips to bring our baggage to the ship and get things settled."

"Fine." Jacob stepped back, looking around the room and smiling when his gaze lit on Abby. "Just don't let me see you for a few days at least, Ed. You'll scandalize the clerks if you show your face within a week."

Felix roared with laughter as his wife approached with a plate of food and a glass of punch. Edward noted Deborah's scarlet cheeks and guided her into the hallway, then, seeing they hadn't been followed, up the stairs and into the room his mother had designated as Deborah's new sitting room. The chamber adjoined the large bedchamber they would share and was fitted out with delicate cherry furniture and bright hangings and cushions.

"Are you tired?" he asked. "I thought you might want to sit for a moment, here where it's quiet."

"No, I'm not tired, but I'm glad to have a minute in private with my husband."

He swept her into his arms, blocking from his mind the preparations, the ceremony, the chitchat with the guests. This was his reward for long patience. This exhilarating moment brought him such joy that he could not speak but held her tight, brushing his cheek against her silky hair and inhaling her scent.

"Hasn't it been a splendid day?" she whispered.

"Perfect."

He kissed her then as he had longed to kiss her for months now, prolonging the interlude and relishing the light pressure of her arms as they slid around him.

When he at last released her, she nestled in against his vest, and he cradled her there.

"You know," he murmured, "I never thought I'd want to go back to Spring Island, but now I'm thinking it wouldn't be so bad, if you were there with me."

She laughed and squeezed him. "If you want to be marooned again, Edward, and live a wild life as a castaway, that's fine with me. Just do take me with you."

"No fear." He stroked her soft, dark hair and kissed her brow. "I shan't let you out of my sight now that I've found you."

THE
LUMBERJACK'S
LADY

Dedication

To my sister, Pat, *qui a le courage lire mes romans*. You helped me learn to read and taught me my first few words of French. You didn't proof this page, so if I phrased something wrong, it's my fault. I can forgive the many times you scared the wits out of me (we're talking apple-burger stand here, as well as dire predictions about Duke and Duchess eating children alive). And in case you're still wondering, the estate papers prove I am NOT adopted. As we used to say, "Sailor leave-ra." Sisters forever!

Chapter 1

Maine, 1895

Étienne LeClair bounded down the steps of the lumber camp's bunkhouse and headed for the stable. Marise, the cook, needed supplies, but the lumberjack didn't look forward to driving to the nearest town, twelve miles away. The January sun held no warmth, and the bitter-cold morning air chilled his lungs. He would rather be at his usual duty of felling trees with the other men.

However, the big boss was here, come all the way up from his fine home in the city a hundred or more miles away to inspect the operation. Perhaps it was better not to be working in the cut when Lincoln Hunter was on hand.

As he crossed the yard to the stable where the sturdy draft horses were housed, a sharp scream reached his ears.

Étienne stopped and turned toward the distant sound. In a fraction of a second, his brain registered the woman's voice. It was not the tone of the rotund camp cook, Marise. But there were no other women in the lumber camp. Or there hadn't been until yesterday.

He caught his breath. The boss's daughter!

He sprinted toward the woods behind the bunkhouse, searching for a hint of her whereabouts. Beneath the trees he stopped and listened. Over the sighing of the bare branches above, a thrashing noise reached him. He ran on, straight toward it.

"Mademoiselle?" he called as he broke through the trees to a frozen little pond in the woods.

"Here! Help me, please!"

He saw her then, at the far side of the pond, standing a little more than waist deep in a hole in the ice, the broken chunks sliding around her as she tried to climb out. Her futile movements were clumsy as she tried to raise a knee to the edge of the surface.

"Wait, mademoiselle!" he shouted, and she turned toward his voice.

Panic was etched on her face. Even from a distance he had an impression of vivid blue eyes like her father's. Wisps of light brown hair fluttered about her face. She tried once more to climb up out of the hole, but the edge of the ice broke beneath her weight, plunging her, prone, into the frigid water.

"Mademoiselle Hunter!"

He charged around the edge of the pond, not daring to trust the ice to hold him up. She surfaced and batted the edge of the ice sheet with her hands, encased in sodden wool gloves, floundering as she tried to stand. Her frightened eyes searched him out and stared toward him in mute appeal as she choked and sputtered.

When he was as close to her as he could get on solid footing, he grabbed a sapling for support and leaned out toward her.

"Mademoiselle, can you reach my hand?"

She stretched toward him, her hand extending toward his but not quite meeting it. If she didn't grasp his fingers within seconds, he knew he would have to plunge in and get her, but that would endanger them both. It might be too hard for him to climb out again carrying her, and the frigid water would sap his strength in seconds.

"Come to me, *mon amie*," he said softly.

Her pupils flared, and she took one lunge of a step and launched herself in his direction. As her body met the broken edge of the ice and once more her weight caused it to give beneath her, he grabbed for her wrist and caught it as her head went under.

He pulled her upward, holding the springy young tree with his other hand and praying it would not crack under the stress. Miss Hunter surfaced and stared at him, terror in her eyes.

With painful slowness he drew her in, but her soaked clothing dragged her down, and it took all his strength to pull her to the bank. At last she stood just below him, clinging to his arm. He stooped and lifted her, setting her down on a fallen log near the bank.

Her teeth chattered violently, and water streamed from her skirt and coat. She had no hat, or if she'd worn one, it was gone now. Her bedraggled scarf hung limp and dripping, sagging toward the frozen ground, but he knew it would freeze stiff within minutes. Quickly he unwound it so that it would not put any pressure on her neck. Then he noticed the steel skate blades clamped to her shoes.

"Here, mademoiselle." He stripped off his warm wool jacket and wrapped it around her shoulders. Even in her own wet coat, she could fit inside it, and he yanked his gloves off so he could fasten the top button, then snatched his hat off his head, pulled down the ear flaps, and settled it over her matted hair.

"Can you walk?" he asked.

She stared up at him, her eyes not quite focusing on him. That vacant gaze frightened him, and he tossed aside the reservations that normally would have kept him from touching the boss's daughter.

He bent and enfolded her in his arms.

"Place your arms around my neck."

She blinked at him. He thought she would not respond any further, but slowly she raised her hands. Her gloves were rapidly freezing, and drops hanging from the fingertips congealed into little icicles. He grabbed her gloves, peeled them from her stiff hands, and threw them to the ground, stooping for his own discarded gloves. They were drier than hers, though not much. He slid them over her hands, and she raised them to his collarbone then over his shoulders. The cold wind sliced through his flannel shirt and union suit, and when the frozen gloves touched the skin at the back of his neck, he flinched.

"Hold on now. I will take you back." His face was very close to hers, and he noticed the drops of water frozen on her dark lashes. When she blinked, the ice droplets touched her cheek, and she frowned.

He delayed no longer but lifted her bodily and strode for the bunkhouse, one long step after another. She was heavier than he'd expected. Strands of her hair escaped from beneath his cap and mingled with his beard, freezing together against his chin. He shook his head to dislodge them, but when he did it she moaned and sank lower in his arms. He gritted his teeth and hurried on, not pausing until he reached the step at the back door of the kitchen.

He couldn't knock, and he wouldn't set her down, so he raised one foot and kicked a tattoo against the lower boards of the door. After waiting a few seconds, he thumped again with his boot, and at last the door flew open.

"What is it? Étienne! That's the young lady. Oh, my sakes, what happened to her?" Marise, the foreman's wife who cooked for the lumbering crew all winter, clapped a hand to her cheek.

"She fell through the ice." Étienne grunted.

Marise sidestepped, holding the door wide. "Bring her in! Hurry."

Étienne's strength was ebbing, but he managed to lug Miss Hunter to the small room behind the kitchen that was allotted to her for the duration of her visit. It was the only private chamber away from the men's quarters overhead. Usually Marise and her husband, Robert, occupied it, but they had given it up for the young lady's convenience and were sleeping on bunks curtained off from the rest of the open barracks above, as was Mr. Hunter.

Miss Hunter's eyes were closed now. Marise tugged off the cap and gloves that Étienne had forced on her and then began to ease her out of his wool jacket.

"Oh, the clothes! Her coat is soaked. Help me."

Étienne lifted the young lady once more and helped Marise tug the saturated sleeves from her arms.

"We must get her warm," the cook muttered. She glanced at Étienne. "Yes, and you need to get warm, too. Your hands are stiff, no?"

He nodded.

"Build up the kitchen fire," Marise said. "Warm yourself and heat the kitchen. Once I get her into dry things, we will take her out there."

There was no fireplace in the small chamber, and Étienne knew Marise's plan made sense. He staggered to the kitchen, fed some sticks into the low blaze in the cookstove, and held his hands over the open cover of the firebox, flexing his fingers. When they had stopped stinging and he could function better, he built up a fire from the coals in the big fireplace of the dining hall, too, and stoked the blaze there.

The kitchen grew warmer, and his shivering subsided. His hands still ached, but he shook off the mild pain. What would Mademoiselle Hunter feel when she awoke? Her pain would be far more intense. He sent up a silent prayer for her and walked down the short hall to the door of the chamber where she lay.

Marise was shaking out a wool blanket and spreading it over the form on the bunk. "It's warm out there?"

"Yes."

The cook nodded. "You carry her then. I will drag the tick out there for her."

Étienne approached the bunk and looked down at the young woman's face, now in repose. *So beautiful,* he thought. *And so vulnerable.*

"Is she unconscious?" he whispered.

"Sleeping. She was all worn out, poor thing!" Marise had stripped the young woman's wet clothing from her and somehow gotten a dry flannel gown onto her. Although the ice had melted from her lashes and hair, the air was still chilly, and her face was marble white. He stooped to gather her in his arms, and she let out a soft moan. He lifted her, straightening his knees. Marise tucked the edges of the striped blanket around the girl, and he gathered them in.

She was much lighter than before. The sodden coat and other clothing must have accounted for much of the staggering burden that had hindered him earlier. No wonder it had been impossible for her to drag herself out of the hole in the pond, carrying that load and battling numbness in her limbs.

He carried her to the kitchen, and Marise came behind, pulling the straw-filled mattress from the bunk and placing it close to the stove, not close enough to scorch her skin but near enough for her to feel the radiating warmth.

He knelt and deposited Miss Hunter gently on top of the white linen sheet Marise had smoothed over the straw tick. She settled with a soft sigh.

"She needs her pillow," Marise said.

Étienne rose and headed back to the small chamber.

"And bring another blanket," the cook called after him.

It took him a minute to locate the cupboard where extra bedding was stored. He chose a creamy Hudson Bay blanket with red stripes along one edge because it stood out from the other plain, dark ones.

Foolishness, he thought. *What does the color of a blanket matter?*

When he returned, Marise was bustling about the cookstove. "I am making tea for her, and broth."

He nodded and knelt beside the sleeping woman again. Her damp hair was matted to her temples, but tendrils were drying and separating. He slipped his hand beneath her head and lifted it, sliding the feather pillow underneath. He and the other men slept without pillows and were thankful to have lumpy straw ticks. But this was a delicate young lady, and he supposed she needed a softer place to rest her head.

He couldn't resist brushing back a wisp of hair, dark with dampness, but lightening as it dried. She didn't look like the boss, whose shrewdness showed in his sharp nose and jutting jaw. Étienne knew she had the same intense blue eyes as her father; he'd had opportunity to stare into their depths as he pulled her from the pond. But her cold, pale face held a rounded sweetness that was more than youth. She was beautiful.

Étienne had not seen her before the encounter at the pond. Last night when the men returned from the woods after spending all day working at the cut, they had learned that the boss and his lovely daughter had arrived and would be in camp for a couple of days. Mr. Hunter had spoken to the men after supper, but the young lady was nowhere to be seen.

Now he wondered how the boss dared to bring her to his lumber camps. Hunter came around every year to take a firsthand look at operations, but he'd always brought a male clerk. Never a woman, and especially not a young, beautiful woman. The forty rough men who lived in this camp for the winter didn't see women for months at a time, other than dumpy Marise, who was nearly as tough and outspoken as her husband. Marise wouldn't take any nonsense from the crew. But a pretty young lady like this?

She stirred, and Étienne drew back, still gazing at her. Under ordinary circumstances, he would scarcely dare to look at her, and then only covertly, from a distance. He was a humble workman, and a French Canadian at that. He would never speak to such a lady, let alone touch her. Yet today he had done both, and here she was lying helpless.

He turned to Marise, a sudden panic in his chest. "She will be all right, won't she?"

"Oh, yes, she is not a weakling, this one. But she has been shocked, you know. She needs rest. And she may take cold."

"I tried to keep her warm."

"You did well. Don't fret so."

He swallowed hard and looked down at the mademoiselle's face again. Was he imagining it or was the color returning to her cheeks? Her lashes were dry now, lying soft and feathery against the light skin.

Marise came toward him carrying a steaming cup with a spoon handle protruding from it. "Her father will thank you; be sure of that."

Étienne stood up, suddenly in turmoil. "Her father! We must tell him."

"I sent Jean Charles."

He exhaled in relief. The blacksmith. Marise must have summoned Jean Charles while he was getting the bedding. He was glad he didn't have to go in search of Mr. Hunter. He didn't want to see the anger and fear in the man's eyes when he learned his daughter had been in mortal danger. And he wanted to stay beside the mademoiselle as long as he was permitted. But still, if the boss was already being told of the mishap, he would be here soon.

Dread and misgiving fluttered in his chest, and he inhaled deeply. No one liked to be singled out by the boss. Mr. Hunter was a hard man whose one passion in life was his business. It was true he admired and praised men who worked hard, but he couldn't tolerate those who were lazy or clumsy or wasteful. Was he tender toward his only daughter? He might be upset that she had come into such peril, and if so, he might look for someone to blame. Étienne did not want the man's scrutiny directed at him.

"I had better get on with my errand."

Marise went to her knees beside the young woman and set the cup down beside her. "Yes, go. I need those supplies before supper. Especially the sugar."

Étienne knew how unhappy the other men would be if they did not get the sweets Marise produced for dessert each evening. The rich foods gave them the energy they needed to perform their grueling work and ward off the cold.

"Here now." Marise stroked the young woman's cheek. "Miss Hunter, can you hear me? You need to take some tea. That's it. *Bien!*"

The young woman's lashes fluttered and rose, and Étienne caught his breath. Yes, her eyes were as blue as the eggs of the red-winged blackbird.

She looked at Marise, then shifted her gaze upward and found him.

He smiled. "Mademoiselle is feeling better?"

"You..." It was only a whisper, and her forehead furrowed.

"Here, now. Take this." Marise held a spoonful of liquid to the young woman's lips.

Étienne turned and then slipped out the door, sending a prayer of praise heavenward.

Chapter 2

Letitia Hunter woke in a small room with rough board walls. Raising her head off the pillow, she recognized the little chamber in the bunkhouse at Spruce Run Camp, where she'd slept last night. She sat up. Hadn't she been in the kitchen? She recalled the plump cook bending over her. Her hands and feet ached. With a sudden lurch of terror, she remembered the pond.

Her gaze fell on the bedside table, and there were her steel skate runners. She had clamped them to her shoes with such joyful anticipation! The chance to glide across the ice of the little wooded pond had beckoned her, and for a few glorious seconds, she had felt like a child again.

A soft knock sounded on the door, and she pulled the woolen blanket around her. "Come in."

Marise entered, carrying a steaming mug and a small plate.

"Bien! I hoped mademoiselle was awake. You feel better now?"

As the cook set the dishes down, Letitia saw that the cup held a dark liquid and the plate a pair of dainty pastries.

Marise smiled at her. "I put lots of sugar in the tea."

"Thank you." Letitia hadn't the heart to tell her she drank her tea plain. "I was foolish, wasn't I? I nearly got myself killed, and I suspect you've been tending me."

"It is nothing. But your father, he is worried."

"He carried me in here, didn't he?"

"Yes, after we knew you were warmed up and would be all right here in this cool room. And he sat by your bedside for an hour."

"Really?" Letitia had some difficulty imagining such tenderness in her father. When she was little, yes, but Mother was alive then. Lately he'd been distant and businesslike.

"He is out in the dining hall now, waiting to see the man who rescued you."

Letitia frowned. "I. . .remember. He was a big man."

Marise smiled and bobbed her head. "Étienne LeClair. He is a fine man and strong as a young ox. He pulled you from the water and brought you here."

"I must thank him."

"I'm certain you will have the opportunity. Now you take a bit of refreshment and rest some more."

Letitia picked up the tea and took a small sip. As she had feared, it was far too sweet. She set the cup down. In her mind, she saw the muscular lumberjack

251

clinging to a sapling and leaning out over the water toward her. "Come to me," he'd said, and she'd wanted to, more than anything. She'd looked up into his rich brown eyes, and for a split second she'd forgotten about her peril. She'd noticed only those wide, steady eyes.

"He had beautiful eyes." She saw the cook's surprise and laughed. "I'm sorry. It's just that when I was in the freezing water and I thought I'd never get out, he came to help me—and I thought his eyes were the most beautiful things I'd ever seen."

Marise nodded solemnly.

She thinks I'm very silly, Letitia thought. *But when I see Étienne LeClair again, I shall let him know how grateful I am. I shall never forget his kindness or his eyes.*

"Mademoiselle should rest now."

Marise padded from the room and closed the door, but Letitia knew she couldn't sleep anymore. She rose and reached for the stool beside the bed as her knees wobbled, threatening to betray her. She pulled in a careful breath and eyed her clothes hanging from pegs on the opposite wall. If she were cautious, she felt sure she could get them and dress herself.

⚬⚬⚬

The sun hung low behind the dark fir trees when Étienne returned to the Spruce Run Camp. The horses were tired from the long trip, and the biting cold air had frozen the sweat on the shaggy winter hair of their flanks. Étienne led them into the stable, and Jean Charles came to help him unharness the team.

"You had better get that sugar to the kitchen, *vite!*"

Étienne raised his eyebrows. "Marise, she is fretting?"

"Ah, you've no idea. She is making a special dish for the boss, and she is blackening your name for being so long with her sugar. Go. I will do this."

Étienne smiled. Marise's frequent tirades were meaningless. He hefted two twenty-pound sacks of sugar from the wagon bed.

"*Merci.* I will be back to unload the rest."

When he entered through the back door, he was relieved to see that Mademoiselle Hunter had been moved out of the kitchen but disappointed that he did not have another glimpse of her.

"Ah! The sugar." Marise pounced on the first sack as soon as he thumped it onto her worktable, cutting the coarse thread that bound the top closed. Étienne set the other sack down in a corner.

"The mademoiselle, she is better?"

"Yes, she is resting. But you need to go in there." Marise nodded toward the dining hall.

"I have more to unload."

"Later. The boss, he wants to see you."

A salvo of apprehension slammed Étienne in the chest. He stooped and looked through the gap above the counter where she served them their meals into the large dining room beyond. Huddled in a chair at the table nearest the stone fireplace sat gray-haired Mr. Hunter, cradling a stoneware mug in his hands.

"Go." Marise plunged a tin measuring cup into the sugar. "He has been waiting a long time. First he sat by his daughter's side, but after we moved her into the back room again and she went to sleep, he came out and stayed in the dining hall. I took him biscuits and coffee, but that is not what he needs. Go."

Étienne took off his gloves and shoved them into his pockets, then reached up and pulled off his cap. Would the boss be angry? He brushed a hand over his hair to smooth it down. Probably he just wanted to hear Étienne's account of what had happened.

Maybe he wonders why I was nearby to help her, he thought. *Maybe he thinks I was watching her, thinking to harm her.*

He gulped air that seemed suddenly thick and unwieldy. One tried not to be noticed by the boss. Not that he was harsh, but when he came out to the cut, the men were on edge as his bright, piercing eyes took in every swing of the ax, every adjustment on the harnesses and chains as the teamsters prepared for their horses to twitch the logs out, dragging them over the ground. Sometimes Hunter gave praise, and that was a good thing. But sometimes his face darkened, and he would speak to the foreman. Then Robert would curse at them and order them about with an arrogance that said, "It's not my fault, Mr. Hunter, that the men, they are so stupid. It's not my fault they are doing it wrong. It's not my fault they are slow and clumsy."

None of this was spoken, but it made the lumberjacks and teamsters feel less than men. And it made them resent Robert. It also made them wonder if Mr. Hunter had ever held an ax in his hands. He was good at running a sawmill and selling lumber, yes, but could he fell a tree on a dime or limb logs all day? Probably the boss's hands would blister in five minutes if he tried to do what they did.

The men had good times in camp, but the boss's visits were not those times. After Mr. Hunter had left, that would be the time when they relaxed in the evenings and brought out their checkerboards. Michael would play his fiddle. They would laugh and tell stories and eat Marise's doughnuts and feel happy to be here. But not while the boss remained in camp.

"Would you go?"

Marise's sharp hiss prodded him. Étienne squared his shoulders and pushed through the swinging door to the dining hall.

◇◈◇

Letitia struggled with her buttons. Her fingers still ached, but she forced them to function, determined to dress and take dinner with her father. The best way to banish his concern was to prove she had recovered from her mishap.

She probed the back of her hair and found only a few hairpins left in her tresses. No doubt the rest were at the bottom of that wretched pond. One would

253

think, with the cold weather, that the pond would have been solid ice from surface to leafy bottom. But according to Marise, it hadn't been so awfully cold until the last two days. She supposed that the evergreens had sheltered the pond from the wind and kept it from freezing clear through. She reached for her hairbrush.

Father would probably forbid her from skating again. He would certainly regret bringing her with him on his annual trip into the northern Maine woods.

He'd caught her off guard the day after Christmas when he announced that she would accompany him. She was shocked that he would take her into the seven lumber camps the Northern Lumber Company maintained.

Usually when he traveled to his far-flung camps, he took his chief clerk with him to keep records and take care of correspondence. But this year the elderly clerk, Oscar Weston, was retiring, and he had told her father with more force than he normally employed that he would not traipse about the lumber camps again this winter. His rheumatism had taken enough of that, thank you. Her father had managed to persuade Weston to postpone his retirement and run the office while he was away, and then he had told Letitia to pack her bag, as she was coming along to clerk for him.

At first she had balked at leaving the comparative comfort of home in the dead of winter, but she knew there was no getting around it. When her father made up his mind, that was that.

Of course, there had been two clerks in the Northern Lumber Company office. But the second clerk had been dismissed when her father discovered that the figures in his ledger did not agree with those in the orders received.

Rather than hire another man, Lincoln Hunter had pressed his daughter into service. She was quick with figures, patient, and able to make a decent cup of coffee to offer clients. He had assured her that the position would be temporary, but nearly two years had passed—and as far as Letitia could see, her father had made no effort to find another clerk. She had worked in the office with old Mr. Weston, learning every aspect of the business's paperwork: orders, accounts, correspondence, price lists, and shipping schedules. A sigh escaped her, and she wondered if she would ever get away from the office.

Then a smile touched her lips. This trip was a good thing, she decided, as she pulled the brush through her long hair. It gave her a chance, on the train ride and the long wagon trips between camps, to talk to her father. At home he never sat still long enough for that. She hoped he was beginning to understand that she wanted a home and family of her own one day. She did not want to finish her life as a retired spinster clerk.

Since her mother's death, Letitia's social circle had shrunk. For the most part, her father had stopped inviting people to their home. If he wanted to entertain a client, he bought him dinner at one of the town's best hotels. When she began working full time in the office, Letitia's isolation had increased. She saw only the clients, Mr. Weston, and the other employees of Northern Lumber.

Her closest friend was now Angelique Laplante, wife of the lumberyard foreman. Letitia often visited in the Laplantes' modest home on Sundays. She sensed that her father wouldn't approve if he knew, but she found the boisterous family buoyed her spirits and encouraged her in her spiritual walk.

The last button in place, she smoothed the soft skirt of her blue wool dress. There was no mirror in the chamber. Apparently Marise never needed to check her appearance. Letitia took her hand mirror from her valise and surveyed her reflection. Her face was still pale, but otherwise she looked fine.

A sudden flash of memory hit her, and once more she saw the kind brown eyes of the lumberjack looking down at her in the kitchen. She rummaged in the valise. Where was the blue ribbon that matched this dress?

She stopped and scolded herself. Vanity. Most likely she and Father would leave this place tomorrow and get on to the next camp, and then she would never see Étienne LeClair again. Why should the thought of him prompt her to rifle her luggage for ribbons? Nonsense. Besides, if she did have a chance to thank him for saving her, she would probably find him quite homely—not nearly so handsome as the dashing rescuer her eyes had perceived in that moment of panic.

Chapter 3

"You asked to see me, sir?" Étienne stood facing Mr. Hunter before the big stone fireplace. It was too warm for him with his heavy jacket on, but he didn't dare take it off. He wished he'd thought of it before he left the kitchen.

The boss stood up and looked him over, from his oiled leather boots on up. "I understand you're the one who dredged my daughter from the pond this morning."

Étienne pulled his gaze from the eyes that pierced like a blue steel dagger. "Yes, sir."

"Well, now." Hunter's voice softened, and Étienne shot him a glance. "What's your name?"

"LeClair, sir."

Hunter's brow furrowed. "And your first name?"

"Étienne, *monsieur*." He saw doubt in the boss's eyes and added, "It means the same as Stephen."

Hunter's brow cleared. "Oh, Stephen. Why didn't you say so? Well, listen here, Steve. . .you are from Quebec?"

"Yes, sir." Étienne fought back a smile. It was well known in camp that the boss spoke next to no French, and he always pronounced the foreman's name, Robert, with a decidedly American inflection.

"You speak English well."

"Thank you, sir."

"Can you read?"

Étienne flushed. The man apparently assumed all Canadians were illiterate. "Yes, sir."

"And write?"

He nodded.

"In French?"

"Yes."

"And English?"

Étienne clenched and unclenched his fingers. How long was this to go on? "Yes, sir, I learned both."

Hunter nodded. "Good, good. And how are you with figures, boy?"

"I. . .have studied the mathematics."

"Can you figure board feet?"

256

He smiled then. "Oh, yes, sir."

"Can you add columns of figures?"

"Of course." He winced as he realized the boss might take that answer as rude.

Hunter reached into his vest pocket and produced a sheet of paper. "Can you tell me what this says?"

Étienne reached for it and held it toward the firelight. "It appears to be an order, sir. Five hundred board feet of oak flooring and two hundred board feet of clear pine boards."

Hunter nodded, frowning, and Étienne wondered if he had displeased him.

"Here you go, LeClair." Hunter held something out to him.

Étienne hesitated, then extended his hand, palm up, and felt the heavy weight of a coin.

He looked down at the lustrous gold disk. An American five-dollar gold piece! He swallowed hard and licked his lips, not sure what to say.

"That's a little something extra for you. Just a token of my gratitude."

"There's no need for that, sir." Étienne held the coin out toward him.

"Keep it."

"But I didn't—"

"I know. You didn't expect a reward for your service. But I daresay you can use it, eh?"

"Well. . ."

"Sure you can. Got a wife and kiddies that you send half your pay to, back home in Quebec, have you?"

"No, sir. But there is my mother. . . ." Étienne looked down at the coin that was warming in his hand. It was true that most of the lumberjacks sent the bulk of their pay home. They spent the whole winter away from their families in hopes of earning enough to see them through to next year. If not for his widowed mother and three younger siblings still at home, Étienne would not be this far from the farm. But the wages were good here. The monthly payday made the hard work, debilitating cold, and primitive conditions worthwhile.

"There you go. She'll be proud when you send her something extra this month." Hunter clapped him on the shoulder. "It doesn't anywhere near reflect my appreciation, boy."

Étienne gulped and made himself look into the boss's eyes again. He decided Hunter was sincere, and there was no point embarrassing him by refusing his reward. "Thank you, sir."

A swish of movement at the other end of the room claimed his attention, and he caught his breath. Miss Hunter was gliding toward them across the dining hall, a vision in blue. She swept between the rough tables and smiled as she approached them. His pulse quickened. He ought to look away from her radiant face, but he couldn't.

"Well, Father, I see you've met my rescuer."

Hunter turned and stepped toward her, his eyebrows almost meeting over the bridge of his nose. "My dear, had you ought to be up so soon?"

"I'm much better, Father." She clasped his arm and flashed a smile at Étienne. "I must thank you, sir, for helping me this morning. Though I didn't say so then, I am most grateful for all you did."

Étienne felt as though all his bones had deserted him, leaving him as floppy and uncoordinated as a scarecrow. He sucked in a deep breath. "I'm glad to see you looking so well."

"I feel well," she insisted. "Might I have supper with you tonight, Father?"

"Well, yes, of course, if you don't mind forty men staring at you all the while."

Marise came in from the kitchen and began setting out the dishes for the evening meal.

"Marise," Hunter called. "Can you set a place for my daughter and me a little away from the men? Perhaps you and Robert and Steve here will join us for supper."

She inclined her head. "Of course, monsieur, but I will be serving. I am certain my husband would like to eat with you, however."

◆

Letitia felt sorry for LeClair. He sat across from her father at the table, picking at his food and fidgeting. It was obvious that he would rather be sitting elsewhere in the room, among the other men.

A twang of regret hit her. It would have pleased her if he'd acted happy to sit close to her and have a chance to further their acquaintance. Instead, he stroked his neatly trimmed beard and looked longingly toward another table where several of the fellows were chattering in French and laughing. Her French was not good enough to follow their rapid-fire banter. She almost thought she saw a flush creep up to Étienne's ears, and she wondered if the others could possibly be having fun at LeClair's expense.

She cleared her throat, and he jerked around with wide, surprised eyes.

"So, Mr. LeClair, did I hear my father say you come from Canada?"

"Oh. . .yes, mademoiselle. It is a farm close by a small village between here and Quebec City."

"I see. I expect it's much like the town where we live."

"Oh, no, I am sure it's not. It is a tiny place. You and the boss, you live in a city."

She chuckled and saw a look cross his face that made her heart skip. Was it wonder? Admiration? It certainly was not indifference. She felt a warm blush sneaking into her cheeks.

"Our town is not very large." It came out softly, and she had to look away from his eyes to regain control of her voice.

"I beg your pardon," he said. "I was mistaken."

Her father jumped in and proceeded to describe the town of Zimmerville, on the bank of the Kennebec River.

"We're near enough to bigger towns to do business," he said. "We've got the railroad and the river. That's all we need."

Once her father began talking, Letitia knew she and LeClair need not cast about for topics of interest. The boss would carry the table talk, and they need only answer an occasional question or murmur an "Mm-hmm" when appropriate.

She studied LeClair's face as he gave his attention to her father. His dark hair feathered over his forehead, where she made out a faint scar. It gave him an interesting, almost dangerous air.

She realized suddenly that she was staring at the handsome young man and looked quickly down at her plate. That was not the way a lady should behave. She picked up her knife and carefully split a biscuit down the middle.

"Will you be moving on to Round Pond Camp tomorrow, sir?" Robert asked.

To Letitia's surprise, her father hesitated. "No, I think we'll stay here one more day."

The hall was so quiet she could hear Marise clanging silverware in the kitchen.

"There are one or two things I want to accomplish," he went on, "and I think it would do my daughter good to rest another day."

Robert's expression was comical, and Letitia could almost read his mind. *Oh, no! We have to put up with the boss for another day!*

"I'm fine now, Father. Really."

He raised one hand in dismissal. "I've made up my mind. We'll stop here until Thursday. Old Guillaume tells me we may get some snow tomorrow, and if so, we'll be able to leave the wagon here and take the sled to Round Pond."

"That would be an improvement," Letitia conceded. But how would she avoid blushing every time she saw Étienne LeClair? Perhaps she would take all her meals in her room tomorrow, because she was sure that she *would* flush.

This inexplicable attraction seemed to be growing since her father had let his favor fall on LeClair. Did every woman who found herself in a perilous situation develop a fancied affection for the man who sprang to her aid? Of course, it didn't hurt that he was a muscular young man with a smile that warmed her through and through. In fact, she reflected, Étienne could probably have rescued her by simply smiling at the pond. All the ice would have melted, and she could have walked out, taken his arm, and strolled off with him in a haze of infatuation.

She glanced at him through her lowered eyelashes. LeClair concentrated on his food, as though making an effort not to look at anyone else seated near him. Again Letitia felt empathy for him. He was out of place and embarrassed to be singled out.

As if he sensed her attention, LeClair met her gaze then looked quickly away.

It struck her that she could be a major cause of his discomfiture. Unused to eating with ladies, a man of his background would consider her to be far above his station. Her presence must be excruciating for him. The only thing worse than sitting across from her would be the necessity of talking to her. She determined not to speak to him again, for his sake as well as her own.

～∞～

The next evening, Étienne put the checker set back in its little wooden box after soundly beating Guillaume at two games. He was tired, but the boss hadn't come into the dining hall since supper, so they'd had a relaxing evening. The men were yawning and heading for the stairs, though it was not yet eight o'clock. Work began early in the lumber camp.

He took the box of checkers and the wooden game board to the cupboard by the fireplace.

The room grew hushed, and when he turned around, he saw the cause. Mr. Hunter had come into the hall.

The boss smiled, spoke to the men nearest him, shook a few hands, and worked his way around the room. Most of the men escaped up the stairs as soon as they had greeted him.

"LeClair."

Étienne nodded. "Good evening to you, sir."

"Sit down for a moment, Steve."

Hunter smiled affably, but Étienne found it hard to smile back. Did the boss expect him to be his pal because he'd given him a five-dollar gold piece?

He tried to think of a logical reason to refuse but found none. The boss had seated himself on the bench nearest the fire, so Étienne dropped onto the one at the next table. Michael picked up his fiddle case and scurried up the stairs after the others, leaving them alone.

"How may I help you, sir?"

Hunter's smile became a grin. "I'll tell you, Steve. I suppose all the men have been wondering why I stopped here an extra day."

Étienne ran his finger along the rough edge of the table. "Well, sir, I know you were concerned about Miss Hunter's health."

"Oh, Letitia's fine. She's always had a strong constitution."

Étienne accepted that with a dubious nod.

"Not like her mother," Hunter added. "Sturdy girl. No, I had another reason."

"Sir?" Étienne croaked the word because the boss watched him closely, and he felt a response was expected.

"I stayed to watch you."

"Me?"

"You."

Étienne cleared his throat and looked about the room. Why had they all run off and left him alone with the boss?

"Sir, I assure you, when I heard Miss Hunter's cry of distress, there was nothing in my mind but—"

Hunter's laugh boomed out. "Don't be so timid, Steve! I didn't think you had designs on my daughter. That would be ridiculous."

Yes, wouldn't it? Étienne thought. The likelihood of the young lady noticing him was so remote that her father dismissed it without a further thought. But Étienne had been thinking about it for two whole days now, and little else. The very thought of Letitia Hunter looking his way was enough to set his heart romping. A woman like that—he couldn't even imagine being friends with her. And yet his brain insisted on imagining the impossible—being loved by her.

"But good has come from that incident," the boss said.

"It...has?" Étienne didn't like the prickly feelings that ran up his arms and down his spine.

"Yes, indeed! You see, it brought you to my notice." Hunter leaned toward him and smiled. "I guess you've seen me watching you the last couple of days?"

"I—" Étienne gulped. He had felt the boss's eyes on him more than once and tried his best to stay out of Hunter's line of vision.

"Well, I like to learn a little bit about a man before I do business with him."

What on earth? Étienne sent up a quick prayer. *Lord, please give me Your peace. This man is driving me insane with all this talk. If he's going to fire me, please let him be quick about it.*

Hunter sat back and scrutinized him with those penetrating blue eyes. "I've seen for myself that you're strong and diligent. No slouch mentally, either. And the other men like you. Robert has told me you are trustworthy. In fact, I understand that yesterday after rescuing my daughter, you were entrusted with a sum of money and drove to town for supplies."

"*C'est vrai*, monsieur." Étienne winced. He had intended not to lapse into French. "I mean, that is the truth."

Hunter nodded. "Well, Steve, it's like this: I'd like to offer you a position in my office."

Everything stopped then as Étienne stared at him. "Sir?"

"My office, back in Zimmerville. I'd like to take you back there with me. My head clerk is retiring, and I have a spot for a bright young fellow like you."

Étienne looked away, his heart racing. "I...don't know what to say, sir. What does the job entail?"

"Just what I've asked you about. Writing letters, making up orders and invoices, keeping accounts..."

"I...might need some direction, sir."

"You shall have it. I'll ask Mr. Weston to stay on and train you."

Étienne hesitated, not wanting to ask, but not wanting to agree, either, until he knew a few things. Hunter was watching him, so he inhaled and dove in. "And the pay, sir? If I may ask."

"The same as you're getting now, but a lot easier work. If you do well, I shall raise it a dollar a week this summer."

Fragments of thoughts raced through Étienne's mind. The same pay, but with a softer life. He would be in an office all day, not out in the fresh air. Would he suffocate? It was a hard life in the lumber camps, working all day in the bitter cold, and dangerous, too. He'd seen several men killed or maimed while logging. But he doubted many men died while keeping accounts.

Of course, he would not get to go home in the summer, as he did now. His mother wouldn't like that, and he would miss his younger brothers and sisters terribly, but if he could help them more, help them have a better life. . .

He would live in a town. He'd never done that before. His family scraped out a life on a small, stony farm. The nearest village had only a church and one small shop that was really a widow's parlor stocked with basic merchandise. He thought he might like to live in a real town, at least for a while. Maybe there would be a library there, or a shop that sold books.

And a bit more pay in the summer. That sounded good. Surely by then he'd be able to send more home to his family. Of course, there would be no bunk-house in the city.

"Well?" Hunter's bushy eyebrows nearly met, he was frowning so.

"What about housing, sir?"

"Of course you'd have to board somewhere."

Étienne's hopes plummeted. "Well, sir, I don't think. . ."

Hunter shook his head. "Yes, yes, I see. All right, I'll cut you a housing allowance. Not much, you understand."

"Of course."

"There's quite a French quarter in the town. I expect you can find a place to board among them."

"That would be. . .agreeable, sir."

"So you're accepting my offer?"

"I. . .yes."

It was done. He had committed himself to work in the lumber company office. At once he wondered if he was making a mistake. But he wouldn't have to stay there forever. If he hated it, he would work for six months or a year, then resign and go back to Quebec.

At that moment, Letitia Hunter came into the room, and they both stood. Etienne's pulse picked up, and he tried not to stare at her.

"Letitia! I thought you'd retired." Her father smiled, and Étienne was glad. A man who loved his child had some tenderness, some compassion.

"I'm just about to, Father. I wanted to ask you to wake me when you get up in the morning so that I don't delay the trip. With this snow and the warmer temperatures, we should have a pleasant journey to Round Pond."

"Steve here is coming with us tomorrow," Hunter said.

Letitia blinked up at her father, and her cheeks flushed. "He is driving us to the next camp?"

"And all the way back to the depot in Bangor. He's going to replace Weston in the office."

Letitia turned to stare at him; then her lips parted. She dropped her gaze after a moment, and the flush was undeniable. Étienne wondered what she was thinking.

"That is. . .good news." She stepped toward him and extended her hand. "I'm pleased, Mr. LeClair. Father has been telling me these two years he would hire another clerk. And now, with Mr. Weston finishing his tenure and business increasing, we are getting desperate. You are most welcome."

Étienne took her small, soft hand in his for an instant. Its warmth surprised and thrilled him. So different from when he'd pulled her from the icy pond.

"Mademoiselle is looking well," he said. "I am glad you have recovered from your accident."

"Thank you. And now, good night, gentlemen. I shall see you at breakfast."

Étienne watched her go, with her brown woolen skirt swaying gracefully about her as she walked. He felt the boss watching him and quickly shifted his gaze. No good. How would he ever keep from staring at her on the long trip tomorrow?

Chapter 4

The sleigh sped over the trail toward Round Pond, gliding on the new snow. Three inches had fallen in the night—not much, but enough to ease their journey and the work of the lumberjacks.

Lincoln Hunter insisted on driving the first stretch, and Letitia sat beside him. The sun rose as they left Spruce Run, sending its rays down through the frosted branches to sparkle off the pristine snow. The air was warmer than it had been for several days. The only thing that marred the excursion was her constant awareness of Étienne LeClair, sitting behind them with the bags and bundles.

He remained silent throughout the first two hours, and Letitia had to force herself not to look back to be sure he was still with them. How would she ever keep from watching him in Zimmerville, where they would be working in the same room every day? It promised to be awkward. What was her father thinking, bringing such a handsome and likable young man into the office?

Under other circumstances, she would have looked forward to becoming acquainted with Étienne. Their few attempts at conversation intrigued her. He seemed intelligent and thoughtful. Surely they could find some common ground. Since she'd begun working full time, she'd lost contact with most of her friends, and she missed having other young people to talk to. Étienne could fill that gap, in a different situation.

But her father would never sanction a friendship between her and his clerk. She practiced cordiality to all the employees of Northern Lumber in Zimmerville, but her father had made it clear that she was not to socialize with them. The one exception was her friendship with the lumberyard foreman, Jacques Laplante, and his wife, Angelique. Her father tolerated some interaction with the family, but then, he didn't know the extent of her relationship with the Laplantes. And a foreman was a foreman, after all. A clerk, however... No, Father would never countenance an affinity between his daughter and a clerk.

Instead of dwelling on her new coworker, she made small talk with her father about business—the quality of the wood his crews were producing and the likelihood of more snow to make hauling the logs to the rivers and railroads easier.

She thought he looked tired, and she was glad their circuit of the camps would soon end. His face seemed a little off color, and the lines at the corners of his mouth were more pronounced these days.

The horses slowed, and he leaned forward, squinting down the path of unbroken snow ahead of them.

"Something's in the road."

A stirring behind her focused Letitia's awareness on LeClair once more as she shaded her eyes to look ahead.

"There's a tree down, sir."

Letitia jumped. The young Frenchman's voice was very close to her, and his warm breath tickled her cheek.

Her father guided the team up close to the obstacle and halted them. Letitia stared at the huge tamarack lying in the roadway.

"Well." Her father sighed.

The sleigh frame creaked and shivered, and Letitia turned to see that LeClair had sprung out and now rummaged among the bundles. He produced an ax and advanced on the fallen tree without waiting for instruction.

Her father sank back in the seat. "Well, I'm glad we have a strong man along. If I'd been out here alone with Weston, we'd have been all day making a way past that."

Letitia felt a flush of gladness at LeClair's willingness to help out. She sneaked a glance in her father's direction, wondering if he felt poorly. In the past, she would have expected him to be the one to jump out and attack the tree trunk.

The lumberjack walked along the tree, from one side of the roadway to the other, looking it over, then climbed on it near the smaller end and began to swing his axe. Under his firm, rapid blows, limbs soon began to fall from the trunk, exposing the log. LeClair set his feet again and began to chop with rhythmic, powerful swings.

Letitia stirred and laid aside the traveling robe.

"What are you doing?" her father asked.

"I am going to help him. I can't do much, but perhaps I can drag aside the limbs he's cut off."

"Stay here."

Her father rose and began to clamber out of the sled.

"Father, you should rest. You've driven for two hours and you're tired."

"Nonsense."

Letitia gathered her skirts and climbed down on her side. If he could be stubborn, so could she.

Her father grasped the end of a large branch that lay between the team and the fallen tree. Letitia took hold of a smaller one and followed him, dragging her burden through the loose snow to one side. It was harder than she'd expected.

She and her father both stood panting when they'd finished. He looked as though he were about to speak sharply, so she hastened to haul away another, smaller limb. When she had disposed of it, her father had made his way closer to where LeClair stood on the log, chopping.

"Hey, Steve!"

The ax froze in midair.

"Sir?"

"What's the plan?"

LeClair straightened and rested his ax with the head against his boot. "Well, sir, I thought I'd leave some stumps of the branches and hitch the team to them. They ought to be able to pull that end of the tree off the road, and we'll be able to get around the bigger part. I haven't left any more than I had to, and I think they'll be able to haul that smaller end away. If they can't, I'll have to chop that part into shorter lengths. It could take some time, sir."

"How can I help?" Letitia asked.

"I think you've done all you can for now, mademoiselle. It's just a matter of my chopping on through the trunk." He smiled and lifted the ax again, hefting it between his hands as though eager to get on with the job. Letitia caught her breath. There was something in his gaze that made her feel alive and happy she had met him.

Hunter nodded and stepped back. "Sounds good to me. I guess you'd better have at it."

They sat in the sleigh, watching him. After a few minutes, LeClair unbuttoned his thick wool jacket and removed it, tossing it behind him among the tamarack limbs. He renewed his efforts, and Letitia watched speechless. His every move was purposeful but graceful. The chips flew as he raised the ax again and again, putting his considerable strength behind each blow.

She had never watched a man work so hard before. As a girl, she'd been sheltered from such scenes. Now that she worked in the office, she often saw laborers loading lumber and moving logs in the lumberyard, but it wasn't a steady, driving force like this. She wondered at his stamina and the beauty of his effort.

"Are you sure he's worth as much in the office?" she asked softly. The idea of caging Étienne LeClair seemed almost cruel, now that she'd seen his skill in the outdoors.

Her father had sunk back against the seat, his eyes closed. Alarmed, she leaned toward him and shook his arm.

"Father, are you all right?"

He jumped and opened his eyes. "What? Oh, yes, yes, I'm fine. Didn't sleep well last night."

"Are you sure you're not ill?"

He sat up straighter. "No, I'm not ill. But the meal we had last night didn't agree with me."

"The moose meat in the stew was tender," she said.

"Yes, I've nothing against moose meat. But the beans. . ."

Letitia hid a smile. When her mother was alive, he had forbidden her to ever let the cook serve dry beans, whether baked, stewed, or otherwise. Mrs. Watkins remembered, and beans never graced the table in the Hunter home.

"Well, you didn't have to eat them."

Étienne leaped down from the log and rested his ax against it.

Letitia rose. "You stay here, Father."

"I will not."

She sighed and hurried to help Étienne, who was clearing away a few more severed limbs. As he turned toward her, she could feel the warmth radiating from him, and his dark hair clung to his damp forehead. His eyes, as before, inspired confidence in her. It was like the day he pulled her from the pond; he was capable of putting all things right for her.

Without considering the propriety of it, she blurted, "I'm worried about Father, Mr. LeClair."

He frowned, and his gaze flickered past her for a moment.

"The boss is ill?"

"He says he's not, but. . ."

Étienne nodded. "Come, we can get this. Can you hold the horses' heads while I unhitch the whiffletree?"

"Here, Steve, wait for me!" Her father puffed a little as he plodded toward them.

"I think that your help is not required, monsieur." Étienne smiled at her father and walked to where the harness was hitched to the whiffletree, between the team and the sleigh.

Letitia approached the nearest horse and gingerly reached out to stroke the huge animal's nose. The horse snorted and shook his head, then stretched his neck toward her. She gasped, then laughed and scratched his forelock.

"Just hold still, you overgrown puppy."

She took hold of the cheek strap, knowing that if the big Belgian decided to move, she wouldn't be able to stop him. But the team stood patiently while Étienne unhitched the harness from the sled.

He gathered the reins and called, "Now, mademoiselle. Release them."

Letitia stepped back, and Étienne lifted the reins and clucked. The two horses moved forward, and he maneuvered them to a spot in front of the log, turning them with the ease of an experienced driver.

"That Steve's a good man," her father said.

"Yes, he is. Are you sure he wouldn't make a good foreman at one of the lumber camps?"

"He probably would. But right now I need a clerk, and he speaks French."

"What has that to do with anything?"

Her father watched Étienne attach a chain from the whiffletree around the stubs of branches on the log.

"You know we're doing business with the shingle mills in Quebec. If I've got somebody who speaks the language, I'll feel a lot better placing orders with them. I might even send him up there one day to look things over for me and make sure they're not shorting me on my orders."

Letitia nodded. Last fall her father had blustered for weeks before finally placing a large order with a Canadian mill. He'd prefer an American company but couldn't find one that produced the volume of cedar shingles his clients demanded.

"Are you still considering opening a shingle mill in Fairfield?" she asked.

"Thinking on it."

Étienne hopped over the fallen tree and stood on the other side with the reins in his hands. He clucked to the horses, and they leaned into their collars. At first the log didn't move, but he called quietly to them, his French words soft and sweet. Letitia wished she knew what promises he crooned to them.

The tree shivered and began to move. The team gained momentum, pulling the smaller half down the road, past the sleigh and off to one side.

"I'm going to help him." Letitia ran down the path the log had carved in the snow, reaching Étienne as he fumbled to unhitch the team. He straightened and grinned at her.

"Bien, mademoiselle. You can hold the reins for me, yes?"

She took them, feeling happy and hopeful as his bright smile warmed her. He removed his gloves and unfastened the chains, then let the whiffletree rest on the ground.

"Thank you." He reached for the reins.

"You're welcome."

She walked with him behind the huge horses and again held the reins while he hooked the team to the sleigh. Her cheeks must be scarlet, but perhaps it was only because of her small exertion and the crisp air. She sent up a quick prayer of thanks that they'd had such a strong and capable man along in this small crisis.

"Father, perhaps Mr. LeClair should drive now," she said. "I'll sit behind, and you can rest."

"I'm all right."

She clamped her lips tight. Her father was becoming irritated, and she mustn't imply any further that he wasn't fit.

"Fine. Drive if you want, but I'd like to close my eyes for a little while, and I thought I'd curl up in the back." She held out her hand to LeClair, and he assisted her as she climbed into the back compartment of the sleigh and settled among the bundles. She poked about and found her pillow. When she turned toward the front, LeClair held out the robe she'd tucked over her legs for the first part of the trip.

"Mademoiselle," he murmured.

"Oh, thank you. You might want it, though."

"It is warm now. I shall not need it." He retrieved his jacket and ax, placing the ax in the bed of the sleigh with her and his coat on the front seat, between her father and the empty spot where he would sit. Looking toward her father, he said, "Would you allow me to guide the team for you, sir?"

Letitia thought he chose each word carefully and pronounced it with precision, with as little accent as possible. Or perhaps for Étienne, it was with an accent—an American-English accent. He had it almost perfect when he spoke slowly. How many other things was he doing, without her even noticing, to please her father?

It unsettled her somehow, to think of him in a servile position. As a lumberjack, he was an employee, but he had his freedom. As her father's clerk, he would be at the beck and call of a moody man every minute of every workday. Could he stand that? Letitia could barely stand it herself, and the boss was her father.

Yet LeClair seemed to understand what he had gotten himself into when he accepted the job and was studying how to stay in the boss's favor. Was it purely for his own advancement, or did he truly want to do a good job for Northern Lumber? And how long would it last? She would observe his adjustment to his new duties with interest.

<hr>

They pulled into the camp at Round Pond late that evening. Étienne unloaded the sleigh, then unharnessed the horses and put them away for the night. By the time he entered the bunkhouse, the boss and his daughter had been shown to their quarters.

Round Pond Camp was larger and more civilized than Spruce Run, and the Hunters were given a small cabin a short distance from the bunkhouse. Étienne found a plate of beans and biscuits awaiting him in the kitchen and was then directed upstairs to an empty bunk. He pulled off his boots and sank onto the mattress with only time enough for a brief, silent prayer of thanks before he fell asleep.

In the morning, he rose with the other workmen before dawn and was pleased to find two, Marc and Adrian, with whom he had worked the winter before.

"You are taking the boss to the train?" Marc asked.

"*Oui*, and I am going to work in his office, doing paperwork for him."

The two stared at him. "This is unthinkable," Adrian said in French.

"Why?" Étienne laughed. "You think I cannot learn something new?"

"No, but. . ."

Marc clapped him on the shoulder. "You will die of boredom, my friend. You are not a man who will like to live in the city and do every minute what the boss asks you to do."

"He will eat you alive before spring," Adrian predicted.

Marc nodded. "His temper can be foul, they say."

A shadow of apprehension fell on Étienne, dulling his customary good humor. "I have also heard this, but I have not seen him angry. He is traveling with his daughter, and perhaps she is a good influence."

"Oh, that is why you are doing this." Adrian laughed.

"She is pretty, no?" Marc asked. "I have been told she is a beauty, but me, I have not seen her."

They went down to breakfast together, and Étienne was relieved when the cook informed him that the boss and Miss Hunter were taking breakfast in their cabin. He was to meet them in an hour.

He spent the morning touring the camp and the logging sites nearby with Mr. Hunter. After lunch the boss went over some records with the foreman and had Étienne copy statistics on dozens of aspects of the operation: hours spent on various tasks, money paid out for supplies, man-hours lost to accidents and illness, number of board feet of various species of wood originating from the Round Pond Camp, and even the number of times the traveling doctor and preacher had visited the men. Then Mr. Hunter dictated two letters, which Étienne took down in carefully scripted English. He was glad Miss Hunter was not in the room, or he would never have been able to keep his attention on the meticulous work. But the boss looked the letters over afterward and nodded his approval, much to Étienne's relief. Perhaps this assignment would not be so difficult.

At the supper table that evening, the other men reopened the topic of the boss's daughter, to Étienne's consternation. Several of them reported seeing her that day from a distance, and an argument arose as to whether or not she was beautiful.

"I saw her last night," said Richard, who had helped Étienne stable the horses. "It is hard to tell much about a person all bundled up in cloaks and bonnets. But her face, what I saw of it? Yes, *très jolie*. Very pretty."

The other men laughed, and Adrian said, "Ask Étienne if she is pretty. You have seen her up close, have you not?"

Étienne felt his face go crimson and was glad he still had his beard. He would shave once their traveling ended; he was sure the boss would want him to come to the office well groomed. But for now, the beard not only kept him warm but also hid his embarrassment.

"You ought not to speak so lightly of the boss's daughter," he said, but this only brought more laughter.

How could he make them understand that, though Letitia Hunter was indeed a lovely woman, she should not be the object of their jesting? They meant no harm, but still, it made him uncomfortable.

They all vowed they envied him, but he reflected that it was not necessarily a good thing to be thrown into close association with a lady. The past two days had been a trial for him as he strove to keep a courteous demeanor in her presence. Most of the time, he tried not to look at her unless circumstances demanded it. If he did look her way, she might see his growing admiration for her, or worse yet, her father would. And if one thing would anger the boss, that would be it.

Chapter 5

Two things brought great relief to Étienne when they stepped off the train in Zimmerville the next night. The first was the large, hearty man who met them, welcoming the boss and Miss Hunter like old friends.

He was French. Étienne tried not to show his surprise when Mr. Hunter introduced the middle-aged man as the lumberyard foreman, Jack Laplante. With him was another man, René Ouellette, younger and definitely less at ease around the boss.

The second thing was the revelation that Étienne would separate from the Hunters almost immediately.

"You will stay with René and his family." Laplante grinned and slapped Étienne's shoulder. "You will find that René's wife, Sophie, is a wonderful cook. The good luck has found you today, my friend."

The boss had sent a telegram from the railroad station in Bangor, and apparently Laplante had made this arrangement with Ouellette, who worked in the sawmill. Étienne was glad. René smiled at him when the boss wasn't looking. The young man seemed a bit timid but sprang to gather the Hunters' baggage and stow it in a carriage. Laplante instructed Étienne to go with René to his new quarters.

Étienne hesitated and looked toward the boss.

"Go on, Steve," Hunter said. "You've done well on this journey, but we'll let Jack take over now and see us safely home. You go and get settled. Oh, and bring those papers with you tomorrow. Ouellette can show you where the office is when he comes to the mill."

"Yes, sir."

Hunter turned and sought out his daughter. "Ready, Letitia?"

"Yes, Father." Before she followed Hunter, she threw a quick glance toward Étienne. He smiled and nodded, wondering when he would see her again. She returned his nod and stepped forward to allow Laplante to assist her into the carriage.

René insisted on carrying Étienne's small bag on the quarter-mile walk from the station to his home, but Étienne kept the leather writing case the boss had entrusted to him tucked firmly under his arm.

When he'd first received the case, he'd hesitated to touch the papers already inside, but Hunter had encouraged him to study them and copy the way the records were compiled at the other camps. At that point, Étienne had wondered if the boss had written them himself, but the neat, dainty script belied that. Had there been another clerk on the first part of Hunter's journey?

The tiny initials at the bottom of each page had not registered until he'd opened the case once more on the train to review his paperwork. *L.H.* The boss's initials, yet. . . . Was it possible the boss's daughter had recorded the statistics for her father until they reached Spruce Run? He wanted to ask but didn't dare.

She'd kept her distance from him, so far as possible while traveling together. She was polite and even smiled at him now and then, but it was a cool smile, not like the one she had given him when she'd held the horses for him on the road.

They were in her world now, and he suspected he would see very little of her. If they did meet again, he must not assume she would treat him as anything other than her father's man.

René Ouellette loosened up when they were away from the train depot and the boss's eye. "My wife and I are pleased that you are willing to stay with us, Monsieur LeClair. Our home is small, and with four children it is crowded and sometimes noisy. But I do hope you will find it to your liking."

"I'm sure it will be fine," Étienne said. "But are you certain you can spare the room?"

"Well, monsieur, the truth is, Sophie and I could use the extra income your board would bring. My wife, she used to do sewing for people, but with the last baby, it was too much for her. So when Jacques came to the sawmill this afternoon and told me a place was needed for the new clerk, I went home and asked Sophie. She agreed. We can put the three girls all in one room, and you shall have the front upstairs. It is small, but. . ." René shrugged and watched him anxiously.

"It sounds ideal," Étienne assured him. "But you must call me by my given name."

"But monsieur is to work in the office."

"That makes no difference. I'm a poor fellow from eastern Quebec, and I'm no better than you. Please call me Étienne."

By the time they reached the little house, Étienne felt he had made a new friend. The children were in bed, but Sophie greeted them and showed him up the narrow stairs with a candle.

"This is the room, monsieur. It is tiny, I know." She stood back from the doorway.

Étienne ducked as he passed through the low doorway and looked around. The cot was freshly made up with a cheerful patchwork quilt, and a stool and small table sat beneath the window. Pegs on the wall would easily hold his few clothes.

"I used to share a room about this size with my three brothers. It is perfect, madame."

Sophie smiled and assured him that the price he offered was agreeable. She knew he was tired. Her husband would bring him a pitcher of water and answer any questions he had.

Twenty minutes later, Étienne blew out his candle and lay back on the cot, weary but content. The specter of the office loomed in the darkness, but he refused to be intimidated by that. He rolled on his side and looked toward the small window. He could see a cluster of stars. This chamber would be more comfortable than a bunk at one of the lumber camps in a room with forty other men. God had worked this out for him so effortlessly. Surely the office was nothing to be feared.

⤜⤛

The next morning, Letitia was travel weary; her stiff, sore muscles pained her when she climbed out of bed.

Mrs. Watkins, the cook, had left sliced ham and fresh eggs in the icebox, and the scent of coffee filled the warm kitchen. In the bread box, Letitia found biscuits and oatmeal bread. As usual, she prepared breakfast, knowing Mrs. Watkins would come in later to fix luncheon and dinner.

She was beginning to wonder if her father had overslept when he came into the dining room yawning. His eyes were rimmed below with dark smudges, and she felt a pang of anxiety.

"Are you sure you ought to go to the office today, Father?"

"What kind of nonsense is that? Of course I'm going in."

"You've had a strenuous trip. Mr. Weston can—"

"Mr. Weston knows how I like to run things." Her father's stern tone silenced Letitia. "As if I would turn up late on the first day of LeClair's employment. What kind of example would that set him? As to Mr. Weston, I expect he'll be on time, don't you?"

"Well, of course."

"Of course," her father agreed. "He has never been late in the thirty years he's worked for me, and I presume he won't be during the last two weeks of his employment. After that, I expect you and LeClair to continue the custom of punctuality we hold to at Northern Lumber."

Letitia looked down at her plate. "Yes, Father." It was no use to hint that he needed more rest. Lincoln Hunter was not a man to rest when his employees were working. Suggesting that his stamina was flagging would only bring his displeasure.

When they arrived, Weston had already unlocked the office and started a fire in the stove and was showing Étienne LeClair his new desk.

"I shall stay on another fortnight to assist you, Mr. LeClair, so in the interim—" Weston broke off as Letitia and her father entered. "Ah, Mr. Hunter."

"Morning, Weston. LeClair." Lincoln Hunter nodded at the two men and strode toward his large walnut desk at the far end of the room.

Letitia stepped inside and met LeClair's stunned gaze. Obviously he had not anticipated seeing her here. She noticed then that he had shaved. His brown hair fell thick and shiny over his brow, and his firm jaw was the perfect complement to his huge brown eyes. He wore a red plaid flannel shirt, which seemed out of place in the office, but she supposed he hadn't had a chance to purchase anything else. It brought a rugged, masculine air to the usually subdued room.

She hesitated, feeling a flush work its way up her neck as their gazes locked. Father hadn't told him, then. He must have thought she only took the trip for entertainment. She decided to let Weston explain her situation to him. Smiling in their direction, she glided toward her desk with a brisk, "Good morning. Hello, Mr. Weston."

"Welcome back, Miss Letitia."

"Thank you." If only her cheeks didn't go scarlet whenever she was near Étienne. This couldn't go on. She would get used to him, and soon it would be a mundane thing to enter a room and find a fine-looking lumberjack there. She was sure she could train her pulse not to hammer so violently in his presence.

LeClair cleared his throat. He opened his mouth but closed it without saying anything and nodded.

She turned her back to the men and hung up her cloak and bonnet. Weston's quiet voice went on, explaining to LeClair that he wanted him to take over the head clerk's desk immediately.

"I will be nearby to explain anything you need help with, but I do think it's best if you take charge of the orders and correspondence right away."

"But, sir—" Étienne paused, then murmured, "As you wish, Mr. Weston."

"Very good. And if you are quick, why, then you won't need me as long as Mr. Hunter seems to think you will."

Letitia sat down and drew a stack of papers toward her. She knew Weston had done the banking and urgent accounts during her absence, but a backlog of bills to be paid had accumulated, and several orders and payments needed to be posted to the ledger.

Weston began his lesson with LeClair. "Now, we had this order come in yesterday for lumber and shingles. It's from a private individual, not a contractor. I'll show you how we write it up for the lumberyard foreman. You've met Mr. Laplante?"

"Yes, sir."

Letitia couldn't help looking over at them. Her desk was situated with one end against the wall halfway along the room. Her father's lair was behind her, and Weston's desk—now LeClair's—sat at the other end, facing the window. She had grown accustomed to seeing Weston's back all day as he bent over his work. She'd often wondered why he faced the wall and window, not the room, and had decided he disliked being distracted. When customers entered, they usually went straight to Mr. Hunter's desk or stopped to inquire of Letitia about their business. Apparently Mr. Weston liked it that way, but perhaps the young Frenchman would rather turn the desk around and face the room. But if he did that, how would she keep from staring at him? She concluded that the desk being turned the other way was a good thing.

LeClair was much larger than the elderly clerk, and when he sat in the oak chair before the desk, his bulk blocked a great deal of light from the window. He seemed too big for the desk, in fact, for the room. In spite of his quiet manner, he brought a vitality into the office that made Letitia want to shout and laugh.

Weston pulled one of the chairs usually reserved for clients over nearer Étienne's desk. He instructed the younger man in quiet tones on where to find the record books, loose paper, envelopes, and other items necessary for the job. Then he told him to take a fresh sheet of paper and prepare the order for the foreman. Letitia noted that Weston did nothing but sit with his hands folded and talk to LeClair, making the younger man think about each task and do it unassisted.

She made herself concentrate on her own work, and for the next half hour all remained quiet.

"Weston!" her father suddenly bellowed, and she jumped.

Weston turned toward the boss. "Yes, sir?"

"I've been going through this mail, and I need you to take a letter."

"Very good, sir. I'm sure Mr. LeClair can accommodate you."

"Hmph," was all that came from Lincoln Hunter's corner, and Letitia smiled to herself. Weston had always had a way of keeping her father in line, like a tutor instructing a naughty schoolboy. She would miss the old man.

Étienne rose slowly.

"Take your pen and paper," Weston said softly, "and the portable desk to write on."

Étienne gathered the supplies, fumbling a bit as he hurried. Letitia thought as he turned from his desk that she detected a slight glint of panic in his eyes. She lowered her gaze and busied herself while he went to do her father's bidding.

Was this the way it would be from now on? Two people who hardly dared look at each other working in the same room all day?

She thought much about the matter that first day, and in the days that followed. Étienne kept his place, never leaving his desk unless his job demanded it, never speaking to her unless it pertained to business.

Under the eyes of both her father and Mr. Weston, Letitia felt both men stifled the natural inclination to talk and become acquainted. But her father liked a quiet, professional office, and Mr. Weston knew that well. The influence of the two of them dulled any inclination she might feel to liven things up. She was a clerk, and she must keep her demeanor in line with her position. Étienne certainly did, and she respected him for that. She wouldn't want to embarrass him or risk causing unwanted attention to fall his way.

Still, she found she liked him more and more. Was he ignoring her only to avoid her father's displeasure, or had he decided he didn't like her well enough to take the risk? He didn't seem frightened of her father but respectful and perhaps a bit wary. She knew Étienne had seen the boss's irritable side when a customer failed to pay his outstanding bill. But was that the only reason he kept away from her, or had her own aloofness put him off? He must be lonely, so far from his family and friends. Letitia was lonely, too.

By the end of Mr. Weston's tenure, she longed to talk to Étienne and learn more about him. She saw his face brighten whenever Jacques Laplante entered the office, and she inferred that they were now friends. She wondered if they saw each other after-hours.

She determined on the second Sunday after they returned from the trip north that she would visit the Laplantes after church and see if she could coax some information from Angelique without seeming nosy.

Her father slept late on Sunday, the one day of the week that he indulged himself. Although it grieved Letitia that he no longer went to church since her mother died, she was glad he was at least getting some rest. He still looked a bit run-down to her.

She'd brought up the subject of church a few times, hoping he would attend with her, but he dismissed it brashly. So she went alone. If he asked her later how the service was—which was rare—she would give him an honest but vague answer. At this point, it seemed better not to divulge to him that she had quit attending the large, traditional church the Hunters had belonged to for years. Instead, at Angelique Laplante's invitation, she now went to the smaller, less ostentatious church the Laplantes attended on the edge of town.

She entered the little church just a minute or two before the service was scheduled to begin and looked toward the pew where Jacques, Angelique, and their children always sat.

Letitia stopped short in the aisle. Someone else was sitting with the Laplantes, and the pew was so full she doubted it would hold her as well. Was it their son-in-law? No, the man sitting between Jacques and fifteen-year-old Matthieu was broader through the shoulders than Marie's husband. In fact, that straight back and wavy, dark hair looked suspiciously like...

He turned his head slightly, and she caught her breath. Étienne LeClair was sitting with the Laplantes. And wearing a suit. Of course, he had received his first pay envelope on Friday. The coat fit flawlessly over his muscular shoulders and suited him as well as his casual work clothes.

She slipped into a pew near the back and hoped Angelique would not spot her before the service began. She couldn't fit in the row with them all if she wanted to, and she certainly didn't want to force a situation where Étienne would have to converse with her in public. That might embarrass him, and it might also start tongues wagging.

As they sang the opening anthem, her galloping pulse slowed. Why was she so tense over Étienne's appearance at church? She ought to rejoice. Did he share her faith, or had he come to please his new friends?

When the service ended, she made her way without haste to the front door. Without lingering, she walked leisurely toward the street.

"Miss Letitia! Wait!"

She turned and smiled at Angelique. "Hello."

"I did not see you before. I was afraid you were sick."

Letitia shook her head. "I saw that your pew was full, so I sat farther back."

"Ah." Angelique leaned closer. "Did you see? Étienne, the new clerk, he came with us today."

"Yes, I saw. That's wonderful."

"He is boarding with the Ouellettes, you know."

"I heard."

"Sophie Ouellette is very glad to have him. She says he is the perfect boarder—neat and quiet, doesn't go out to drink at night, and he gets along well with the little ones. He told her he has younger brothers at home, so he is used to children."

"I'm glad they are getting on so well."

Angelique nodded. "But they go to the big church—you know. Étienne went with them last week, but he told my husband it was not the same as what he was used to and he felt lost in that crowd. So Jacques, he said, 'Why don't you try our little church?' And, *voilà*! He is here."

Letitia smiled. "Did he like it?"

"I think so, yes. He is eating dinner with us now, and I will ask him this question."

Angelique's youngest daughter, seven-year-old Colette, joined them and grasped Letitia's hand. "Mademoiselle, are you coming to our house today?"

"Oh, I think not," Letitia said with a pang of regret. "You have other company. Perhaps next week."

Angelique straightened her shoulders. "You must not stay away because of the new clerk."

Letitia bit her lip, trying to sort the feelings at war inside her. "Yes, dear friend, I think I must. He would be embarrassed, you see, if I came today. He is new here, and he didn't know he would be working with me every day, and I'm sure he's glad on Sunday to be away from my father and me. This is his time not to have to think about the office, but if I am there. . ."

Disappointment registered on both faces. "Perhaps you are right," Angelique said. "But next week you must come, and I will not invite Étienne. But after he is settled here and things are not so. . ."

"So silly," said Colette, and Letitia smiled.

"I was thinking so complicated," her mother corrected. "Then at that time, we shall invite you both."

"Oh, no, you really shouldn't." Letitia glanced toward the church door and saw Jacques and Étienne speaking with the pastor.

"I shouldn't?"

"No. If Father heard, he would not understand, and I don't think—"

Étienne was about to descend the church steps. He glanced her way and froze for an instant. His eyes lit, and his lips twitched as though a smile were struggling to escape.

Letitia swallowed hard and tried to inhale without gasping.

Angelique nodded soberly, then smiled. "I see."

Chapter 6

Letitia bent over her desk, concentrating on the column of figures she was adding. As March had now arrived, she was going over the figures for the previous month, as she always did. At the far end of the office, her father leaned back in his swivel chair, discussing a large order with a local contractor. John Rawley had bid successfully on building a new courthouse for the county, and while the foundation and facade would be of stone, his lumber needs would be extensive.

Dry, planed spruce from the north of Maine was selected for the framework. Walnut would be brought by ship from Pennsylvania for the wainscoting and interior details. Maine red oak would be used for the stair treads. Her father and Rawley talked on, laying out a delivery schedule for the thousands of board feet of lumber that would be needed.

Letitia was used to mentally blocking out her father's business conversations while she worked. At first she had found it an annoying distraction, but she had taught herself to go on with her calculations while the voices droned on.

"Steve!" Hunter called, and Étienne laid aside the correspondence he was working on and rose to answer the boss's summons.

A month had passed since Étienne began working in the office, and Letitia was acclimating to the presence of the quiet Canadian. The office still seemed smaller when Étienne was in it, and even though he'd bought a conservative black worsted suit, he still carried himself like an active outdoorsman. Could he be happy cooped up in here day after day? Did he regret giving up his life in the woods?

Étienne was determined to excel, she could see that, and he appeared to have conquered his nerves. He'd advanced quickly during Oscar Weston's two weeks' mentoring, and he worked mostly on his own now, tending to all the correspondence, orders, and shipping, while Letitia handled the bookkeeping and payroll.

She'd heard her father bragging about LeClair yesterday to one of his friends while Étienne was out of the office. "He's worth twice as much in the office as he was in the woods," he'd said. She wondered about that, knowing Étienne's skill with an ax. But if her father believed that, why hadn't he raised the clerk's salary to equal what he'd paid Mr. Weston?

The small central Maine city of Zimmerville, where the office and lumber mill were located, had a high percentage of Canadian transplants. Already Hunter relied heavily on LeClair for dealing with French-speaking clients, for interviewing prospective workers who spoke no English, and for correspondence with business contacts in Quebec. He also entrusted more and more details of the technical side of the business to the young man. But Hunter insisted on using the anglicized form of the clerk's name and had no dealings with him outside the office.

Rawley's laugh reached her, and Letitia frowned. The contractor was not one of her favorite customers. When he visited the office, he always made a point of speaking to her in a manner she found far too familiar. Her reaction was to ignore him unless forced to speak to him about business.

She went on with reconciling the records for sales, wages, and expenses for the month of February. Étienne stood near her father's desk, telling him and Rawley where they could best obtain each of the materials on Rawley's list. He would draft letters to dealers in other areas for those not available locally. When Rawley had approved the list of materials to be ordered, it would come to Letitia; she would itemize the bill, finding the current prices and figuring the final cost. With this project, Rawley's account promised to be one of the company's most profitable.

"We'll have the walnut shipped directly to your site," LeClair said. "The spruce and oak we'll mill here and send down the river."

Rawley discussed at length the quality he wanted to see in the lumber for the courthouse, and Letitia sneaked a glance at Étienne. He listened carefully to both men and assented to Rawley's demands and Hunter's instructions. She was proud of him. He had taken on a professional demeanor easily, even though he kept that rugged, wild essence. Already men liked to deal with him, showing confidence in his judgment.

Twenty minutes later, Étienne was dismissed, and he went quietly back to his desk. Rawley and Hunter stood up and shook hands.

"Thank you for your business," Hunter said.

"I know Northern Lumber will get everything I need, and at a decent price." Rawley pulled out his pocket watch. "Won't you and Miss Hunter join me for luncheon?"

Letitia sat still for a moment, then made herself go on writing while she waited, as if unhearing, for her father's reply. She had planned to go home, as usual, for lunch. She didn't really want to go out to a public establishment with the men. Her hands were ink-stained, and her serviceable navy suit was not what she would have chosen for luncheon in a restaurant. Beyond that, she had no desire to spend an hour forcing herself to be cordial to the contractor.

"Why not?" Her father swung around and looked at her. "Letitia, Mr. Rawley's invited us to dine with him."

She looked up and saw John Rawley's gaze resting on her. She felt a wisp of hair, escaped from her bun, tickling the back of her neck but resisted the urge to put her hand up to control it. She didn't want him to think she was preening for him. He looked her over as he would a building site, spotting the best view, weighing the assets, and noting flaws that would require changes to meet his specifications. His smile drew his lips back in an almost canine expression that sent a sick apprehension over her.

"I ought to finish the monthly books, Father," she said as placidly as she could.

"Surely you need to eat," Rawley said, smoothing each side of his blond mustache with his index finger.

The impeccable mustache had no attraction for Letitia. "Oh, I–I'll dash home for a bite, Father. Mrs. Watkins will expect us, and she'll be disappointed if neither of us comes home this noon." Letitia dipped her pen in the inkwell. "You go on." She went back to her work, hoping Rawley could not see the flush she felt creeping up from the collar of her white shirtwaist.

"All right. I'll be back in an hour," her father said, shaking his head.

Letitia thought he was a little put out with her for snubbing one of his wealthiest clients.

"Perhaps another time," Rawley said.

His silky tone almost made her shiver, and she sighed with relief as the door closed behind the two men. She estimated Rawley to be ten years her senior, and she didn't want him or anyone else in Zimmerville to think she was interested in him. Most of all, she doubted he would meet her other criteria for a potential suitor. He lacked the quiet spirit and courtesy she looked for. Above all, a man's faith mattered to her, and she doubted they would agree on that.

But her father didn't seem to consider faith as a necessary trait in a son-in-law. At least he seemed to be seriously considering Letitia's future and looking over Zimmerville's men for a suitable match. However, the three or four men her father had so far mentioned to her as worth cultivating socially were not to Letitia's taste.

Étienne had sat with his back to the room during most of the exchange, and he kept at his work in silence for another ten minutes.

The office door opened, and the broad-shouldered foreman of the lumberyard strode in, going straight to Letitia's desk. He held out a sheaf of papers, smiling.

"Mademoiselle Letitia! Here is what you need to pay my crew." He glanced toward LeClair, "*Ça va,* Étienne?"

"Ah, Jacques." Étienne looked up with a grin. "Bien, mon ami. *Et toi?* I am well, my friend, and you?"

"Bien *aussi.*" To Letitia, Jacques said, "We've finished loading the flatcars with the order for Auburn. All the receipts are there for the railroad, and the slips for the men's wages."

"Thank you, Jacques." Letitia riffled through the papers and said, "That's fine. The men you hired just for this job can come in tomorrow for their pay."

"I will tell them."

Jacques Laplante had worked for Northern Lumber since he was a teenager, doing everything for the company that involved physical labor: stacking boards, cutting trees, moving logs with a team of oxen or horses, and sawing and planing lumber. He had proven himself dependable and worked his way up to lumber-yard foreman.

Letitia rubbed her eyes and opened the top desk drawer, placing the records inside for future consideration.

"Mademoiselle *est fatiguée*," Jacques said.

She smiled. "Yes, I'm a little tired. How are Angelique and the children?"

They chatted for a few moments, discussing Jacques's three-month-old grand-baby, and Jacques took his leave, calling good-bye to Étienne on his way out.

The door closed, and Étienne turned slowly in his swivel chair. "Would you like to go home and eat your luncheon, Miss Hunter?" he asked. "I'll stay while you do."

"All right, thank you." Letitia always hesitated over what to call him. She wouldn't refer to him as Steve, as her father did, and she thought "Étienne" would be too intimate...so she avoided addressing him by name, using "Mr. LeClair" when it was absolutely necessary.

But she thought about him much more than was necessary.

To her chagrin, he seemed to think very little about her. Though forced to work more closely with her now that Weston had retired, he ignored her most of the time. He was always polite, and occasionally she caught a smile from him that kept her hope alive. Someday perhaps they could be friends. But she felt it would be improper for her to initiate such a thing, and he seemed content to keep a cool distance.

She hurried home and ate only a small portion of the food Mrs. Watkins had ready. The cook fussed about the table, complaining that she never knew whether or not anyone would come home to eat the meals she prepared.

Letitia suspected Mrs. Watkins was lonely. Of course she missed the old days, when Mother was alive. Then the house was full of people. Friends, rela-tives, and clients were frequent guests, and the Hunters' dinner parties were famous for the fine food, exquisite entertainment, and delightful conversation. Mrs. Watkins had headed a staff of four, and the kitchen always bustled with preparations for some event or other.

Now the big house stood empty and forlorn. Mrs. Watkins stayed on and cooked but had only Letitia and her father to cook for, and so she also had time to do a bit of cleaning. Father had discharged the two maids and the cook's helper long ago, and they relied on Mrs. Watkins and another woman who came in twice a week to do heavy cleaning.

Letitia tried to soothe the cook's injured feelings by eating a dish of pud-ding, though she didn't really want it. Maybe someday the house would be happy again, but she didn't see how that could happen if she and her father spent all their energy on the lumber company.

She headed back to the office, wondering if her father had yet returned. Being alone in the office with Étienne was becoming awkward. Not that he did anything to make her feel that way—quite the opposite. She mentally ticked off his attributes as she hurried along the sidewalk. He was prompt, courteous, neat, efficient, respectful of her father, and diligent at his work. She told herself she didn't consider his looks. To her, the mental and spiritual aspects of a man took precedence over the physical.

If she could bring herself to acknowledge it, though, she would also have admitted that he was quite handsome. He was strong; she'd had ample proof of that when he carried her from the pond to the bunkhouse at Spruce Run and again when he'd cleared a path for the sleigh. His features were well defined and pleasant to look at. In fact, it was disconcerting having a man so good-looking in the office. She'd resolved from the outset not to embarrass him or herself—or her father, for that matter—by ogling him. She'd cultivated a cool but courteous manner and downcast eyes. No one else seemed to have an inkling that her heart raced whenever she thought about him. It helped that he sat with his back to the room when working. For eight hours a day she mostly saw his broad shoulders. There were worse things to look at.

She hurried along, admonishing herself to stop letting her thoughts stray into an unprofitable avenue. Even if Étienne should ever notice her the way she noticed him, her father would never consider the Canadian an acceptable suitor for his only daughter.

When she stepped into the office, Étienne turned in his chair, and she smiled at him.

"You go ahead for your lunch now, Mr. LeClair."

"Thank you, but I brought a lunch my landlady packed for me, and I ate it while you were gone. Your father will not mind that, will he?"

"Oh, no, I don't think so, as long as there were no customers in here at the time. But you are entitled to go out for a while if you wish."

He sat watching her as she returned to her desk.

"The order for the courthouse is quite complex," he said tentatively, and Letitia snapped her eyes up to his. Was he making an overture of sorts?

"Yes," she agreed. "It will take several months to bring in everything Mr. Rawley wants, I think."

LeClair nodded, his gaze not leaving her face.

It was unnerving for Letitia. During the workday, she often found herself gazing at the nape of his neck, where the dark hair was trimmed abruptly above his collar. Having the tables turned, with him appraising her, caused a slip in her usual calm demeanor. She dropped her gaze and reached for her pen.

"I suppose he will come here often to see about the lumber?" Étienne asked.

"I hope not." She realized she had spoken out of turn and added quickly,

"We will deliver it to his building site as soon as we have each load ready."

Étienne nodded, his face grave. "And Mr. Hunter, he feels better now?"

"Yes, I think so. Thank you for asking."

"His color is better since we came back here."

She nodded. "I believe the journey strained him. But he's back to his own home and the cook who knows his digestive habits well. He seems fine now."

"That is good." He stood up. "I will be back soon."

She watched him walk to the door. He was tall, and his black suit jacket, although cut from inexpensive material, hung from his shoulders with a flair. With money for the right clothes, he could be a striking figure. When the door closed behind him, she jerked her attention back to her task. *You are a foolish girl,* she remonstrated. *You have no call to think of this man in that manner.*

She took out the men's pay slips and added them, then wrote the amount on a slip for the bank. *Or any man, for that matter.*

She laid the pen down and rested her head in her hands with her elbows on the desk. She had let herself imagine something between herself and Étienne. She was lonely; she recognized that. But he must be lonely, too. Would it be wrong for a friendship to develop between them? And if it did, would she be content to keep it at that? He had begun the fragmented conversation today, while her father was out. Was it significant? Or was he merely attempting to put her at ease? Had he sensed her embarrassment when Rawley spoke to her? Or was she imagining his interest?

Did he have a sweetheart back in Quebec? Was that the reason he'd been so distant toward her all month? Had he come here to save enough money to make his marriage feasible?

Dear Lord, she prayed silently, *help me not to engage in foolish speculations. You know what is best for me. I feel such a longing for friendship with Étienne, but I don't wish to displease my father. Please take this desire away from me if it's wrong. And I do ask that You would meet Étienne's needs, whatever they are. He's so far from his family. I know he's found a church home here. He has kept a distance between us, both inside this office and out, as I have. I think that is best. I don't want to cause him any distress, and I want to please You.*

⌘

Étienne leaned against the end of a stack of lumber where René Ouellette sat, eating the lunch Sophie had packed for him in a lard pail. He would have joined René in sitting on the boards, but he didn't want to get sawdust all over his suit. The March sun held some warmth, bringing out the sharp smell of newly cut lumber and melting the little snow that lurked in the corners of the lumberyard.

He didn't always take a break outside the office at noon. Most days Mr. Hunter and Letitia went home for lunch, and he ate at his desk and reopened the office afterward. But today Letitia had returned before her father, and he'd felt just a bit of awkwardness in the situation.

She had not rebuffed him when he spoke to her, but neither had she seemed eager to continue the conversation, so he had decided to get some fresh air and give her a few minutes alone. From his post near the lumber pile, he could see almost to the door of the office and knew he could tell if her father returned or a customer arrived.

"You are getting on well in the office," René said.

Étienne nodded. "It goes fine most days. Today. . ."

"What happened?"

Étienne hesitated, realizing he did not want to discuss the feelings nagging at the back of his mind. He spread his hands and shrugged. "It is nothing. Just a client, one of the contractors who does business with Monsieur Hunter. He is a man full of himself."

"A rich man?"

"I would say so."

"What is it about him that bothers you? Does he treat you poorly?"

"Not really." Étienne thought back to John Rawley's manner when they discussed his order. "No, he did not seem prejudiced against me."

"That is good," René said. "Sometimes men like that treat us bad. They think we are stupid, and they yell at us and blame us for things that are not our fault."

Étienne nodded as he thought about that. "He was not that way."

"What about the boss?"

"No, he treats me well."

René shuddered. "I don't see how you can be in the same room with him all the time. Me, I would have a nervous condition if he stood over me while I worked."

Étienne smiled at that. "It's not like that. He lets me alone most of the time, and I write my letters and keep the records. And now I suppose I'd better get back at it."

He left René and strolled toward the office. It was not Lincoln Hunter who'd tested his nerves today. It was Rawley, but not in his manner toward Étienne. He didn't seem to care that the clerk was a Frenchman, only that he knew where to get the materials he wanted and could offer the best prices.

No, it was his attitude toward Miss Hunter. Rawley hadn't said much, but the way he'd looked at Letitia had heated Étienne's blood. One quick glance was enough; then he'd forced himself to keep his eyes on his ledger.

But he'd seen Rawley's smug, predatory appraisal of Letitia. Immediately, a protective rage had risen in Étienne's heart. But her father said nothing. Nothing!

No, that wasn't true. Her father had actually tried to coax her into going along to have lunch with the man, while Letitia was clearly uncomfortable at the suggestion.

If I could speak up, he thought as he neared the office. *If I had the right. . .*

But that train of thought was useless. He would never have that right. If he were on an equal social footing with such a lovely woman, he would never pursue her with the arrogance Rawley had exhibited. And if it were within his power, he would not expose her to such a crass man. Was her father blind? Could he not see the possessive way Rawley had looked his daughter over? Or did he simply not care?

Maybe the boss wanted to marry Letitia off to a rich man.

Étienne shook his head. If that were the case, putting her in an office day in and day out and dressing her in the plain garb of a workingwoman was not the way to entice the prey. Letitia should be at home in the fine mansion on High Street, pampered and coddled, swathed in silks and velvets, and Mr. Hunter ought to have parties and balls where the tycoons could meet her in a social setting.

Instead, her father treated her like a servant.

Last week Étienne had gone to the bank alone for the first time, to get the payroll money on Friday. Letitia had prepared the bank order, totaling the amounts on her worksheet while he watched. To his surprise, her name was not among those receiving a paycheck. Her father's draw was there, and all the names of the employees, including his own, from the sawmill and lumberyard foremen down to the boy who shoveled shavings from under the planer. But not Letitia Hunter's.

He concluded that Letitia served unpaid. She might see it as her contribution to the family. Étienne saw it as something else: stinginess on her father's part and a lack of true paternal love. She was a precious gem, and her father ought to guard her!

As he reached the office door, he saw Mr. Hunter half a block down the street, returning from his lunch with Rawley. Étienne determined to put the incident from his mind. Thinking about it would only embitter him toward the boss and perhaps cause him to say something he would regret.

He pushed open the door and stepped inside. As his eyes adjusted to the dim interior, he saw that Letitia was looking up at him.

She smiled. "Welcome back." This time she did not look away.

He returned her smile, and the errant thought whispered in his mind once more, *If I had the right. . .*

For a moment they held the pose, looking into each other's eyes across the room. There was so much he wished he could change, so much he wanted to say.

A step behind him prompted him to break the gaze and turn in the doorway.

"Good afternoon, Mr. Hunter. Let me take your hat and coat, sir."

Chapter 7

I'll be over at Mark Warren's office for the next hour or so. I need to have him go over this contract with me." Lincoln Hunter stopped by Étienne's desk. "Steve, I expect Tappy Pinkham to come in and pay his last installment today. You handle it if he comes while I'm gone." The boss breezed out the door, letting in a blast of April wind.

Étienne felt anticipation as he dipped his steel pen in the inkwell. The times when Mr. Hunter left the office during the day were a sweet torture for him.

Since John Rawley had placed his order a month ago, something had changed between him and Letitia. She greeted Étienne with a lilt in her voice each morning, and he found it more and more difficult to keep his eyes off her.

He was glad old Weston had chosen to face his desk toward the window. It was growing harder to conceal his elation when he found his lovely coworker's gaze—dare he think of it as *tender*—on him. Her smiles, more frequent now, were treasures he tucked away in his memory to be recounted and cherished later.

This wonderful distraction alternated between thrilling him and distressing him. After all, nothing could come of the feelings growing so lush in his heart. Was it wrong to let the small gestures of friendship flourish between them? He didn't think he could stop, now that he'd begun to go beyond courtesy and show her a glimpse of the esteem he felt for her.

Sundays were even worse, when he saw her at church, usually in the pew with the Laplante family. He'd taken to sitting a couple of rows behind them, where he could see the back of Letitia's head. She always sat so demurely, the picture of attentive devotion. Sometimes she turned her head a bit to share her hymnal with one of the children, and he saw her profile. That image always sent a tremor of longing through him. Night after night, his prayers ended with, "And Father, if You could send me a woman so faithful and sweet to be my wife..."

He couldn't specifically ask that God would give him Letitia. Could he? No, that was unthinkable. Knowing he thought the unthinkable brought on waves of guilt.

Even before Mr. Hunter's footsteps died away as he left for the meeting with his attorney, Étienne struggled with these thoughts, and he looked out the window in an attempt to clear his mind.

"Mr. LeClair?"

He inhaled carefully, savoring his name on her lips. Dared he ask her to call him by his first name?

"Yes, mademoiselle?" He turned and met her gaze.

Her cheeks bore a charming flush. "I am finished with these orders. Do you need to see them again?"

"Oh, I am done with those, thank you."

"Then I shall file them away." Her blue eyes met his for a long instant, and his pulse caught and then rushed on.

She rose and went to the cabinet across the room where old documents were kept. He knew it would be impolite to stare at her as she worked, so he turned back toward his desk. He'd discovered that when the light was right, he could see her reflection in the window, and he couldn't resist catching a glimpse. Even in her plain blue skirt and white blouse, she was lovely. In his heart, she was as beautiful as any princess.

As she opened the cupboard door, he remembered the day he had lifted her slender form, so heavy and cold, and carried her from the pond to the bunkhouse at Spruce Run. The knowledge that he would never again have the chance to hold her in his arms saddened him. Why were his affections fastened on this unattainable woman? Why hadn't God led him to a young Canadian woman of his own class?

The office door opened abruptly, and a tall man came in, slamming the door behind him against the wind. He pulled off his hat, exposing his blond hair, and Étienne recognized Rawley, the contractor who was building the new courthouse.

Rawley glanced at him, then turned the other direction. His gaze swept over Lincoln Hunter's vacant desk and chair, then landed on Letitia.

"Ah, Miss Hunter. Your father is not in?"

Letitia closed the cabinet door. "No, he has gone out for a while. Is there anything Mr. LeClair can help you with?"

Étienne stood quickly, but Rawley only gave him a quick glance and took a step closer to Letitia.

"No, I don't think so. But if you don't mind, I'd like to leave a message with you for Mr. Hunter."

"Of course."

Letitia's features went wooden, and she walked briskly to her desk. "Would you like to write him a note?"

Rawley followed her and leaned across the desk as she sat down behind it. "No, that's all right. It's only that he told me a week or so ago that he expected the shipment from Boston soon."

Letitia looked past him, and Étienne caught a flicker of dismay in her face as her gaze connected with his. Was Rawley's stance and his nearness to her making her uncomfortable?

Étienne hesitated no longer but strode toward Rawley.

"Perhaps I can assist you, sir. That shipment has not yet arrived, but it is true we look for it any day. We can send a boy around to tell you when it comes in."

Rawley straightened and rounded slowly to face him. Étienne received the distinct impression that the contractor was not pleased with his interference.

"Yes. That would be most helpful. Thank you, LeClair." Rawley turned his back on Étienne. "Well, Miss Hunter, now that that is settled, there is something else I'd like to discuss with you."

Étienne stood still for a moment, uncertain of how to react. The contractor had dismissed him, no question. Should he fade into the woodwork and resume his post at his desk? One more look at Letitia's tense face rooted Étienne to the spot.

"And what would that be, Mr. Rawley?" She avoided looking up at him but pulled a sheet of paper to her and began scribbling on it with a pencil.

Rawley gave Étienne a pointed look, and he gulped and stepped back, closer to his own desk.

What should I do, heavenly Father? Étienne sat down slowly. He was certain Rawley hoped he would leave the office, but it would take a locomotive to get him out of here when Letitia clearly didn't want to be left alone with the customer.

"Well, I was hoping you'd do me a favor."

"I?" Letitia's voice rose in doubt.

"Why, yes. Last month I invited you to join your father and me for luncheon, but you said it was inconvenient. I've done a lot of thinking about that, and I can see that it was shortsighted of me. Of course you wouldn't want to go out in the middle of the day in your working attire. So I thought perhaps you would make up my disappointment to me."

"Really, sir, there is no reason to feel badly."

Étienne sneaked a glance. Letitia's face was reddening, and she shook her head in protest.

"Oh, but there is. You can allow me to undo my gaffe by agreeing to have dinner with me one evening."

Étienne sat very still, holding his breath and waiting for Letitia's answer.

"Thank you, but I don't think—"

"Please?" Rawley's voice took on a soft wheedle. "It would give you a chance to dress up. You must not get out much. I never see you in any of the restaurants. I'd love to show you the new dining room at the Highland Hotel."

"Thank you, Mr. Rawley, but—"

"Wonderful!" he cried.

"No!" Her consternation caused Étienne to wince, and he had to force himself to stay in his chair and not look her way.

"No?" Rawley asked. "You don't mean that."

"I do. Mr. Rawley, I don't wish to go with you." Her voice was firmer now.

"But it will be a diversion for you. A pleasant evening."

"I said no."

"Look, Letitia, if you're worried about what your father will say, I assure you—"

Étienne sprang to his feet. "Excuse me, Mr. Rawley, but I think you should leave now."

Letitia's gaze met his with such relief that he stepped toward the contractor with confidence.

Rawley squared his shoulders and turned slowly toward him. "I beg your pardon?"

Étienne cleared his throat. "I think that the lady would prefer that you leave."

Rawley's face was flushed, and his eyes narrowed. "And I think that you've overstepped your place."

There was a moment's silence as they took each other's measure; then Letitia's gentle voice sliced the crackling air.

"I meant what I said, Mr. Rawley. I don't wish to go out, but I thank you for the invitation. Now, I've written down your message for my father, and I will let him know you inquired about the Boston shipment."

Rawley's lower jaw flexed; then he glanced at her and back toward Étienne. "Fine." He strode out the door and banged it shut.

Étienne breathed a prayer of thanks and turned to look at Letitia. She was sitting very still, her eyes closed and her cheeks nearly as pale as they were when he fished her from the pond.

"Mademoiselle," he said, "I hope I did not add to your discomfort."

"No." She opened her eyes and gave him a chagrined smile. "Not at all. Thank you."

He nodded, satisfied. No matter what future revenge Rawley devised against him, it was worth it.

"Could I get you some tea?" he asked.

Her eyes widened in surprise. "That's not necessary."

"No, but it might do us both some good."

A genuine smile lit her face. "Perhaps you are right. Thank you."

He went to the woodstove between her desk and her father's and took the teapot and a cup down from the shelf above. It took only a minute to measure tea from the tin and pour the water from the kettle they kept simmering.

When he placed her cup carefully on her desk, she again looked up at him with those startling blue eyes. "Won't you join me?"

"I...well, yes, thank you." He poured himself a cupful and took it back to his desk. Could he move his chair closer to hers? That might be presumptuous. He turned it to face her and sat down two yards from her desk.

Letitia lifted her cup to her lips. Étienne did the same. He hadn't let it steep long enough, and it was weak, but she didn't seem to care as she continued to sip the hot brew.

He smiled at her. "You are feeling better, is it not so?"

"Yes, I am. I cannot thank you enough, Mr.—Mr. LeClair."

"Please. Étienne."

She nodded, her face set in grave, almost sorrowful, lines. Should he have told her to call him Steve, as her father did? No, if they were to be friends, as he truly believed she wished to be, then she would not mind calling him by his own name.

"I—would you—?" She pressed her lips together and stared down into her teacup, then met his gaze once more and said, a little breathless, "Do you think you could call me Letitia?"

He hesitated.

"Oh, not when Father is here."

Her hasty disclaimer had him holding back a smile. This was the way it had to be, but it was a step forward. He nodded. "It would be an honor."

They sat in silence for several seconds, and slowly her lips quivered upward. Étienne inhaled deeply. In the deep recesses of his mind, it seemed there was something he ought to be doing this morning, but he couldn't for the life of him recall what it was. It couldn't be as important as watching Letitia, seeing her relax moment by moment. She lost the worried air and settled back in her chair, cradling her warm cup in her hands and looking at him.

Someone knocked, and the door opened. A farmer bundled in a wool coat and knit hat entered. Étienne set his cup on his desk and jumped up, turning his chair around quickly.

"May I help you, sir?"

"I've come to pay my bill. Pinkham's the name."

"Certainly. I have your account right here, sir." He reached for the sheet of paper on his desk.

The man settled the bill and took his leave. Étienne closed the door behind him and handed Letitia the money.

"I had better write up the invoices now," he told her with an apologetic smile.

"Yes, I have some details to attend to as well."

As he resumed his usual post at the desk, a warm contentment settled on him.

The door swung open once more, and Mr. Hunter stomped in. "Letitia, I just saw John Rawley down the street."

Étienne kept his head down and wrote the date on the sheet of paper he would use for the first invoice.

"He came here looking for you about half an hour ago," Letitia said. "I told him we would notify him when his shipment comes in."

Étienne marveled at her serene tone.

"Really, Letitia! I don't know why you continue to reject that man's advances. He's from a good family, and he has a thriving business."

"Please, Father. Could we discuss this later, in private?" Her voice was strained now, and Étienne wished that this time he had an excuse to leave the room.

"I see no reason why you can't give him a little encouragement."

"He is a client, Father. I try to keep a professional relationship with all your clients."

The boss uttered a sound somewhere between a snort and a grunt. "You need to understand, Letitia, that John Rawley is one of my biggest customers. I rely on men like him for a living. He can be difficult at times, it's true, but business with him might go more smoothly if you were to show him a sweeter disposition."

Étienne froze in his chair. His stomach churned. How could Hunter address his daughter in that manner? Was he suggesting it was part of her job to beguile the customers?

After a moment of silence, Letitia choked out, "Please, Father. I cannot abide the man."

"Oh, and why not, may I ask? He's perfectly courteous."

"I do not find him so. And if you must know, when I went to the bank last week, I saw him coming out of that. . .establishment across the way."

"What, the Loon? He probably had lunch there."

"It's a tavern, Father."

"Most taverns serve good, plain food."

"He was—" Letitia stopped, then whispered, "He was with another man, and he was rather boisterous. And I don't wish to discuss it further."

A long silence was followed by the creak of the boss's chair at the far end of the room and the slamming of a desk drawer.

Étienne realized he'd copied the figures for the invoice without thinking about them. He laid down his pen and went over the sheet to be sure he'd written everything correctly. The quiet in the office was painful. Perhaps he should have stayed in the woods.

Chapter 8

The following Monday afternoon, a merchant came in to discuss with Lincoln Hunter the materials needed for the construction of a new store, and Letitia and Étienne were left to deal with several men who came in to pay their bills as the end of the month approached.

Letitia had hoped to get away after lunch and do some shopping at the Harris Emporium. Her shirtwaists were becoming stained and frayed at the cuffs, and she hadn't had a new dress in two years. She knew she could count on Mrs. Harris, the lovely widow who ran the women's clothing shop, to help her pick out suitable wear for the office and a nicer dress for church.

Sometimes Letitia envied Mrs. Harris. She had run the business herself since her husband died two years earlier. The eligible men of Zimmerville watched her with uneasy admiration. The women loved to shop in her establishment, as she had an unerring sense of fashion tempered by practicality, but they gossiped about her independence. Mrs. Harris seemed to enjoy her self-reliance and was not yet ready to have a man take care of her again.

But today was not the day to visit the emporium. The customers continued to come and go, and several employees came in on errands from the lumberyard and sawmill.

At two thirty an errand boy from the railroad depot dashed in. Seeing that Mr. Hunter was busy, he went to Letitia's desk and handed her a slip of paper. She was used to receiving this sort of communication from the stationmaster and gave the boy a nickel and sent him on his way.

After deciphering the note, she went to stand near her father's desk, waiting for a break in his conversation.

"Yes, we can get you clear pine for that," he told his client. "It may take a few days to collect as much as you want in that quality." He glanced up at Letitia. "What is it?"

"Excuse me," she said. "Mr. Kreedle sent a note saying the large order for Mr. Rawley is at the station. He thinks it will be three wagonloads, at least."

"Fine; tell Laplante." As she turned away to carry out her father's request, he called after her, "Oh, and go round and tell Mr. Rawley, too. He'll want to be ready when our men get there to unload."

Letitia turned to see if he truly intended for her to take the message personally, but he was already listening to a story the customer was telling.

She hovered for a moment in the middle of the room, then went to the coat tree. Perhaps Jacques Laplante would assign one of his men to do the unpleasant chore for her. She reached for her shawl and spread it over her hair, tucking the ends together at her throat, then took her coat from its hook.

"Pardon me," Étienne said softly behind her.

She whirled, surprised to find him so close.

"I couldn't help but hear." He glanced toward her father. "Forgive me if I presume too much, but you might be more at ease if I were the one to carry this message to Rawley's place of business."

"Why. . .thank you. I was hoping one of Jacques's men could go."

"He will need them all at the depot."

She nodded, knowing it was true, and bit her bottom lip. "Do you mind?"

"No. At least, not so much as I would mind sitting here trying to work while I wondered what became of you on this errand."

She looked down at the bare oak floor. She could read his unspoken thoughts—her father ought not to have told her to go to Rawley's office alone. It was unacceptable, at least in the perception of a gentleman like Étienne.

"He doesn't mean to be thoughtless," she whispered.

Étienne's gaze darted past her toward the other men, and he said softly, "*Tout* est bien. . .all is well. And I shall tell Jacques first, so you need not worry about that, either."

He grabbed his hat and jacket and hurried out the door. Letitia went back to her desk with some relief. However, her father's dark scowl did nothing to reassure her.

Ten minutes later Étienne had not returned when her father saw the customer out the door. He turned around, his eyebrows lowered, the lines at the corners of his mouth deeper than normal, and fixed his gaze on Letitia.

"Why are you letting LeClair do favors for you?"

She stared up at him in surprise. "He offered to go."

"Oh, yes, he offered. I asked you to take that message. LeClair has plenty of work to do."

"Father, please." She felt the mild pain that preceded tears forming in her eyes. "You know I dislike Mr. Rawley. It baffles me why you would purposely put me in his path. You would never have asked Mother to do something like that."

Her father stood still for a moment, glaring at her, and Letitia wanted to run. Her father had disappointed her many times, but he had never frightened her before.

At last he sighed and pulled Étienne's chair out. Sagging into it, he ran his hand through his silvery hair. "All right. I give up. You don't like him."

"I don't."

Her father nodded and exhaled heavily. "I don't know what to do with you, Letitia."

"You don't?" She smiled and shook her head. "I'd say you do. You put me behind a desk, and here I've been for more than two years."

"Do you hate it?"

"No. But. . ."

"But what, child?"

She looked about the room, unsure how to begin, or even whether or not she wanted to. At last she brought her sights back to him. "I don't wish to work in this office all my life."

"So you've told me before."

"I. . .haven't meant to complain, Father."

"I don't say you have. No, what you're telling me is reasonable. It's been easy to let things go on as they have, but—" He sighed and sat back a little, eyeing her at length. "You are quite grown up, daughter."

"Yes, I am, Father. I shall be one and twenty in the fall."

"I thought perhaps you might see something commendable in a man like John Rawley."

She picked up her pen and the rag she used to wipe it with. "Must I marry one of your clients?"

"I wouldn't say you have to. It might further my interests. But, no, you don't have to."

"Thank you," she whispered.

"I suppose we ought to entertain more and give you a chance to meet prospective suitors in a more congenial setting than this." His gesture encompassed the stark office.

"You needn't do that."

"Oh? And where do you expect to find a husband, if not here?" His eyes flared suddenly and he stood up. "Don't even think it, Letitia!"

She felt the blood rush to her cheeks. "What?"

Her father walked to her desk and leaned down, gripping its edge. "LeClair is a common laborer who grew up in a hovel in some hamlet in Quebec. I plucked him out of a lumber camp." His voice grew louder, and his eyes flashed. "Do you think I would ever consent—?"

She shoved back her chair and stood facing him, her knees trembling. "He is a fine man and a good clerk. I've heard you say so."

"What, and you think I'd marry my daughter off to a clerk? You know what the man earns."

"I don't know where you've gotten this notion, Father. Mr. LeClair offered to carry out a distasteful errand for me. There has been nothing between us. Why you think he would aspire to winning my hand, I've no idea. He is a gentleman; that is all. And he is an excellent clerk."

Her father's lips pursed and the fire in his eyes died down. "He's been quick to learn his new duties; I'll give him that."

"I heard you tell Mark Warren he's invaluable to you."

"He has potential."

"You ought to pay him accordingly."

"Ha! Watch your tongue, girl! You're awfully concerned about this clerk in whom you have no interest."

Letitia sat down and covered her face with her hands, taking slow, deep breaths. *Lord, forgive me,* she cried silently. *How could I be so defiant? Father is right.*

She looked up, and he still towered over the desk, scowling down at her.

"I'm sorry."

"Hmph."

Her tears flowed freely then. "Forgive me, Father. I should not have spoken to you in that manner."

He straightened and did not meet her eyes. "Well, there now. No need to get all riled up, is there?"

She shook her head and opened her desk drawer in search of a handkerchief.

"We'll say no more about it, then. You know how I feel."

"Yes, Father." *But you don't know how I feel,* her heart cried.

"I'd say it's time we had a social event at the house."

She stared at him, unable to respond.

"Several clients have contracted large orders with us recently, and I always used to entertain them in celebration of such events."

"Are you thinking. . .a dinner party?"

"Yes. Can you arrange it with Mrs. Watkins?"

Letitia gulped. "I'll speak to her this evening. How many people?"

"Well, let's see. There's Eldon Bane and his wife, and Clive Wheaton. I assume he's married. George Young might come, but he lives over in Shawmut. And there's Rawley, and Mark Warren and his wife. How many is that?"

Letitia did a quick tally. "Ten, I think, if they all come. Mr. Young is a widower, is he not?"

"Yes, and you'd do well to buy a new dress for the occasion."

She lowered her pencil and eyed him suspiciously. "What does my wardrobe have to do with Mr. Young?"

He held up his hands in defense. "I shan't push you, but you want to make a good match, don't you?"

"And Mr. Young is your idea of a good one?"

Her father shrugged. "He's a bit older than you, but—"

"A bit? Father, he's your age!"

"Nonsense. He can't be over forty."

"That's much too old for me."

He frowned and strode toward his desk. "All right, but the least you can do is look for a husband whose business will complement mine."

"Father! I thought the subject was closed."

He frowned at her. "I shan't force you into a marriage you don't want. But you've told me you want to marry."

"I do, someday. But not just any man, Father."

"Fine. I give you leave to refuse any man who doesn't suit you. But, Letitia, if you must marry and leave me in the lurch here, lacking a clerk, you can at least look for a man with a good business head on his shoulders. And be prepared to play the gracious hostess at that dinner party!"

"Yes, Father."

She wanted to ask him if he must include John Rawley in the guest list, but their argument had left her drained, and she didn't want to take a chance on starting another.

A new customer came through the door, and she lowered her head over the papers on her desk. As she had hoped, her father greeted the man and drew him to the far end of the room. She closed her eyes for a moment. *Lord, please forgive my anger and my behavior toward my father. And please, Lord, I don't feel confident that Father will find the right man for me. I'm going to leave that up to You. It's clear I can't consider ever forming an attachment for Étienne. I must forget that.*

An ache in her chest told her that it was too late. She'd known it was impossible, and yet she had allowed the hope to grow. And after today, she was fairly certain Étienne harbored feelings for her, too. But that could never come to fruition. She would have to let him know somehow that they could never allow their friendship to blossom into anything more. Would that hurt him as much as it was hurting her? In addition to the pain of separation, she was hit with a monstrous guilt.

She had allowed his hope to spring up, too. And now she had to kill it.

Chapter 9

Letitia raised her arms and let the maid ease her new gown of orchid silk chiffon over her head. It floated down around her in a soft cloud, and she couldn't resist swirling a bit and watching the skirt billow.

The maid smiled at her. "Shall I do your buttons now, miss?"

Agnes, Mrs. Watkins's niece, had agreed to aid her aunt in preparing for the dinner party and help Letitia get dressed. Letitia had also engaged their biweekly cleaning woman to put in extra time scrubbing the house and polishing everything in sight. Her father had assured her a few days earlier that he had employed a man to act as their butler that night.

The dinner party was the most exciting event at the Hunter home in years, and Letitia couldn't deny her anticipation. Even if the guest list was not of her own choosing, she was sure she could find someone to converse with. *Even the customers' wives must have something to talk about,* she thought as Agnes fastened the buttons on the back of her dress.

Agnes turned her around and stroked a wisp of Letitia's hair into place. "You look beautiful, miss."

"Thank you." Letitia smiled and sent the girl down the back stairs to the kitchen to help with the last-minute chaos there. She picked up her gloves and fan, then paused for one last look in the mirror.

She hadn't been looking at herself much lately. On work mornings, she donned serviceable clothing for the office and took a cursory glance in the glass to be sure she looked neat and efficient.

Now she caught her breath. The gown was the perfect color, a brighter shade than she'd first chosen. But Mrs. Harris, the owner of the emporium, had assured her the orchid was more flattering than the pale lavender, and that it was all the fashion in Boston this year.

"You don't want to look dowdy," she'd said, smiling at Letitia and cocking her head to one side.

"Well, no," Letitia had replied. "But I don't wish to be. . .daring, either."

Mrs. Harris laughed, showing her even, white teeth. "No worries there, my dear. The design you've chosen is far from audacious. In fact, I was thinking perhaps we could alter the neckline just a bit—"

"No!" Letitia had winced at her own sharpness. "I'm sorry. I. . .wish to be modest, even for an evening party."

Mrs. Harris nodded, smiling. "I see that. Simplicity is definitely the look for you. But you can be both modest and fashionable. What would you say to some of this elegant duchesse lace for the collar?"

Now Letitia could see the wisdom in the widow's suggestions. The lines of the gown Mrs. Harris and the dressmaker she employed had sewn for her set off Letitia's figure and creamy complexion. Her blue eyes seemed darker than usual against the vivid orchid backdrop, and Letitia was pleased with the upswept hairdo she and Agnes had managed together. Of course, the man she cared about would not be there to see her tonight. She must put all thoughts of Étienne out of her mind and be open to the Lord's leading.

Well, at least I shan't be embarrassed about my clothes, she thought. A prayer formed in her heart, and she sent it winging heavenward. *Lord, let me please Father tonight, if possible, and let our guests be glad that they came.*

She inhaled deeply and left her room for the main stairway. The thud of the knocker resounded through the house. Below her in the hall, a man in a black suit was heading toward the front door. The temporary butler, Letitia surmised. She slipped quickly down the steps and into the parlor, where her father and several guests stood before the fireplace with glasses in their hands.

"Ah, Letitia," her father said. His gaze swept over her, and he seemed a bit relieved, bestowing on her a smile of approval. "You've met my daughter?" he asked, turning toward his guests.

"Oh, my," said a large, florid man, staring at her in wonder. "This isn't the little lady I've seen at the office?"

Letitia felt her cheeks redden but smiled and extended her hand. "Why, yes, Mr. Young. We've met several times."

"Oh, but you weren't got up like this, my dear. Why, your father shouldn't hide you away like that! Once you're seen in that gown, you'll be invited to social events all over the county."

She knew her face was scarlet now but was at a loss for words. *This is the man Father hinted was interested in courting me? Oh, no, please, Lord!* The man was as old as she'd guessed, if not older, and his nose was uncommonly large. She allowed him to grasp her hand while she sought a suitable response.

To her relief, her father said, "And you know Mr. and Mrs. Warren."

Letitia nodded and extricated her hand from Mr. Young's, then extended it to the attorney's wife. "Welcome, Mrs. Warren. Thank you for coming."

"You look splendid, my dear," Mrs. Warren said. "That color suits you."

Lincoln Hunter looked toward the doorway and cried, "Clive! So glad you could make it. And Mrs. Wheaton, I don't believe you've met my daughter, Letitia."

The Banes, who were owners of a feed and grain business, arrived next. Letitia smiled until her face ached and drew the wives away from the men, inquiring about children and grandchildren. She was soon at ease and realized the three other women were carrying at least their share of the conversation, talking about gardening, dressmaking, and the difficulty of finding household help.

John Rawley was the last to arrive, and Letitia turned away as he entered, quickly asking Mrs. Wheaton a question so that she need not meet his imperious gaze. She heard her father and the other men greet him heartily and welcome Rawley into their circle.

Her father put a glass in Rawley's hand, and he lifted it to his lips. Letitia had to hide her smile behind her fan when she saw the change in his expression. Her father had assured her that he would adhere to the family's tradition, faithfully followed when her mother was alive, of not serving alcohol in the house. Only the magnitude of her relief revealed to her how much she had feared he would change that custom. Rawley, however, seemed unpleasantly surprised.

Mr. Young soon worked his way to a spot at Letitia's elbow, and she was forced to include him in the chatter. After that, the small knots of people broke and reformed several times.

Rawley's greeting when he approached her was more subdued than usual, and Letitia wondered if he still smarted from her refusal to go out to dinner with him.

"That's a lovely gown," he murmured in her ear when the other guests were distracted.

"Thank you." Letitia took a step away from him, but he followed.

"I knew you must have something nicer than those plain duds you wear in the office."

She glared at him. "Really, sir!"

He chuckled and opened his mouth again, but at that moment Mark Warren claimed his attention, and Letitia escaped to join Mrs. Bane and Mrs. Warren, who were discussing a mission project both were involved in at the large church downtown.

Letitia felt a moment of panic. That was the church her family used to attend. What if someone asked her why she hadn't been there for the past year? This wasn't how she wanted her father to learn of her choice. Though Lincoln Hunter himself did not care to attend any longer, she felt sure he'd disapprove of his daughter leaving the big church and joining a smaller, less formal congregation.

A moment later an expectant hush fell over the company, and Letitia glanced toward the doorway. The temporary butler stood in the arch, his face impassive. As all the guests turned toward him, he looked toward Letitia's father and received an almost imperceptible nod from him.

It couldn't be.

It was.

A mixture of dismay, wonder, and rage crashed over Letitia.

"Dinner is served," said Étienne.

~⊗~

Étienne tried to keep his gaze from straying to Letitia. It was one of the hardest things he had ever done.

The rich purple silk dress she wore seemed plain at first glance, but he realized almost at once that it was not. Understated, perhaps, but the lines and flow of the shimmering fabric were anything but common.

But it was not the special dress that tempted his eyes so sorely. It was Letitia's face, and the stricken look that clouded her beautiful features when she recognized him.

Étienne watched Mr. Hunter offer his arm to one of the visiting ladies, and he knew it was time for him to go to the dining room. He took a deep breath and turned, not meeting Letitia's eyes. He couldn't bear to see the distress there.

It was crucial that he stay calm through the rest of the evening, but his heart pounded and his stomach churned. He had made a mistake. Seeing him tonight had upset her, and he would gladly have forgone the extra money he was earning to avoid hurting her.

He stood straight and still by the kitchen door, where Mrs. Watkins, the cook, had told him to, waiting for the guests to enter. Outwardly he must appear steady and emotionless, but his mind was in upheaval. Somehow, without meaning to, he had brought pain to the woman he loved.

That admission sent his pulse racing even faster. It was true, although he could never admit it to anyone or declare it to Letitia. He loved her! He watched the doorway, eager for another glimpse of her.

She entered on Mr. Young's arm. Étienne had waited on the man twice at the office. Young owned a farm south of town and had come to Northern Lumber to select materials for a large new barn. The big man could scarcely take his eyes off Letitia, and Étienne couldn't blame him. Letitia's appearance tonight was perfection, and Étienne knew that she was lovely within, too. He forced back a twinge of jealousy. He had no right to object. The widower pulled out her chair, smiling at her and saying something he no doubt thought witty. Letitia, the charming hostess, smiled back, but without a trace of coquetry. Étienne wondered if she was enjoying the party or enduring it the best she could, to please her father. Her demeanor suggested something in between, and he was relieved. Her guests could not fault her in her genuine hospitality.

Letitia sat at one end of the table, opposite her father. On either side of her were Young and Rawley. Étienne waited until they were all seated, then opened the kitchen door a crack and signaled to the cook that it was time. Mrs. Watkins carried a large, covered china dish to him. The soup tureen, she had told him earlier. It was a new word in his English vocabulary, but he grasped the handles firmly.

"Be careful now," she whispered. "Don't be spilling my onion soup on the floor in front of company."

Étienne nodded and carried the heavy dish into the dining room.

The guests looked his way in anticipation, and he walked cautiously. He mustn't stumble tonight. In most situations, the stares of the people would not bother him. They were only interested in their dinner, not in the man who carried it. But once again, Étienne saw Letitia glance his way, then quickly avert her eyes.

He should have mentioned his intention to her yesterday at the office, but there had been no chance when her father wasn't present. No, he shouldn't have agreed to this arrangement without her knowledge. He felt a flush rise from beneath his stiff collar and flood his face, but not for himself. His embarrassment was for Letitia.

～∞～

Letitia smiled and answered her guests' comments and sipped her water. She even permitted Étienne to serve her a bowl of soup. All the time, her anger against her father simmered. Her hands trembled, and she dared not look at Étienne again or she would betray her intense feelings, both her attraction to him and her abhorrence at seeing him forced to play such a menial role.

Rawley and Young vied for her attention, and she wondered if her neck would be sore tomorrow from all its turning back and forth. Mrs. Bane, who sat on Young's right, inquired about the delicate china, and Letitia was glad for the distraction.

"Yes, it was my mother's wedding gift from an aunt."

"It's very pleasing," said Mrs. Bane, holding up her teacup. "Now, your mother was a Chamberlain, wasn't she?"

"Yes," Letitia replied.

"That's right. Her father was a doctor, I recall."

"That's correct."

"And the Hunter family, they go back a long way," Mrs. Bane said.

"There've been Hunters around here for a long time," Mr. Young agreed.

"Yes," said Letitia. "My great-grandfather started the sawmill. His family had all been sailors and traders, but Great-Grandfather decided to build a career in lumber."

"Smart move," Rawley said. "This area has grown constantly in the last fifty years. Always new buildings going up."

When the main course had been served, Étienne took up his post by the kitchen door, watching the table. Letitia knew he was waiting for a signal from her or her father that something was needed.

She tried not to let her gaze linger on him but noticed that the color in his face was a bit deeper than usual. He must be embarrassed, but he was keeping his dignity.

"I hear there'll be quite a cultural program at Colby College in Waterville next week," Mrs. Bane said.

"Yes, I heard about it," said Rawley. He smiled at Letitia. "Lectures on several topics and musical performances."

"They've a pianist coming all the way from Vienna," said Mrs. Bane.

Rawley nodded. "There's even talk of the city building an opera house. That would be quite an addition for Waterville."

"Don't know as I'd care for opera." Mr. Young shook his head.

"Well, they're also having a brass quintet perform," Mrs. Bane said. "You'd like that, I daresay. Stirring music."

Letitia saw a gleam strike in Mr. Young's eyes. He opened his mouth, but before he could speak, Rawley jumped in.

"As a matter of fact, Miss Hunter, I was planning to invite you to attend the lecture series with me. Or, if you prefer, one of the concerts."

Mr. Young glared at Rawley but spoke to Letitia. "I'd take you round to one of the concerts, Miss Hunter, if you like music."

Letitia looked from one man to the other, feeling a bit like a mouse hesitating between a cat and a mousetrap. She cleared her throat.

"Thank you, gentlemen. That's very kind of you both. I. . .shall have to speak to my father and see what his plans are. He. . .may have already spoken for tickets."

Mrs. Warren, seated to Rawley's left, joined the discussion then. "Oh, I can hardly wait to hear the lecture on women's suffrage. Are you attending that one, Mrs. Bane?"

The lady opposite her coughed. "My husband prefers that we go to the talk on Amazonian explorations."

The gentlemen chuckled, and Mrs. Bane shrugged, as though she was resigned to missing the lecture that most attracted her.

At that moment, Étienne reached silently to remove Rawley's plate. Letitia caught her breath. Had Rawley even registered the identity of the butler? He began to gently tease Mrs. Bane about her desire to vote, and she replied with good humor.

Letitia swallowed hard and leaned back a little so that Étienne had easy access to her plate, although she'd eaten only half her portion of roast beef and vegetables.

"Mademoiselle is finished?" He whispered near her ear, and a tingle shot all the way down her spine.

"Yes."

She pressed her lips tightly together and stared at his big, muscular hands as he lifted the delicate china. He really was an excellent manservant. But then, he was good at anything he put his mind to. Put him in flannel and give him an ax, and he would chop trees all day. Dress him in wool serge and give him a ledger, and he became the consummate business clerk. In servants' livery. . . No! She hated the very idea of him bowing and performing menial tasks for the likes of John Rawley.

She looked up and found Rawley watching her with hooded eyes.

"Am I correct in assuming this is your first dinner party as hostess?"

She dropped her gaze to the tablecloth. "Yes. Father has not liked to entertain much since my mother died."

"It's going quite well," he assured her with a smile.

"Thank you."

"The only thing that would make it better is if you would tell me you'd accept my invitation."

"I. . .cannot promise that."

"Surely your father wouldn't reserve tickets for the entire series without telling you."

She knew it was true. In fact, her father probably wouldn't take tickets for any of the lectures or performances. He would consider it a waste of time. But she had no other excuse, and she feared it would sound scandalously rude to refuse simply because she did not want to go with the person issuing the invitation.

"I. . .shall write you a note when I know of his plans."

She could hardly wait until the dessert was served, when she could escape the dining room and avoid the men for a while.

Étienne and Agnes served the cake flawlessly, and Étienne circled the table once more to refill the water glasses and pour coffee for those who wanted it.

At last it was time for the ladies to withdraw to the parlor. Letitia knew her father and the other men would linger in the dining room over their coffee. She hoped Father wouldn't allow anyone to smoke in the house. She'd seen a cigar peeking from Mr. Wheaton's breast pocket. Her father had never taken up smoking and considered it a wasteful and dirty habit. But would he deny the privilege to guests he wanted to impress?

She stood, signaling to the women that the moment had come.

The men also jumped up and hastened to hold the ladies' chairs. Rawley shoved his chair back, perhaps farther and harder than was necessary. The resulting soft *thud* was followed by a sharp intake of breath and a crash.

Letitia stared, along with all the others.

Étienne stood a few inches behind Rawley's chair, staring downward in dismay. On the floor, in pieces, lay one of Letitia's mother's china dessert plates.

Chapter 10

Étienne glanced toward the boss. Lincoln Hunter scowled at him, and Étienne sensed mental daggers flying across the dining room.

He knelt and reached for the largest pieces of china, not daring to look Letitia's way. He'd done the worst thing possible: embarrassed her. All evening he had wondered if Rawley recognized him when he let him in the front door. Now he was certain. The contractor had timed the shove of his chair on purpose.

"Sorry," Rawley said.

"Don't mention it." Letitia's quiet reply sounded a bit strained.

Rawley chuckled. "So hard to get well-trained domestic staff these days."

Étienne continued retrieving slivers of china, not expecting Rawley to speak to him. His offhand apology was to the hostess, as was proper.

Agnes darted in from the kitchen with a small broom and dustpan, and Étienne took it from her with a grateful smile.

"Merci."

"The snobbish oaf," Agnes whispered under her breath.

Letitia left the dining room with the ladies following her. Étienne kept busy sweeping up the fragments, his face down.

When he got to the kitchen, Mrs. Watkins was waiting. "Well, now. What did I tell you?"

Étienne winced. "At least I did not spill the soup."

The gray-haired woman scowled, her hands on her hips. "One of the mistress's best plates. I expect Mr. Hunter will take that out of your wages."

He gulped. "Yes, madame. How much?"

"I don't know. That china is probably irreplaceable now."

Étienne sighed. Perhaps he would receive nothing for this evening's work and humiliation.

"Shall I see if the gentlemen want more coffee now?"

Mrs. Watkins exhaled sharply in a near snort. "Can I trust you with the good coffeepot?"

As he reentered the dining room, Étienne's eyes watered. Smoke. Several of the men were puffing on cigars. Mr. Hunter was not partaking but was leaning back, relaxed, in his chair. He beckoned, and Étienne squared his shoulders and approached him.

"We're all set, Steve. Just leave the pot and go help Mrs. Watkins clean up now.

305

And see me before you leave."

Étienne nodded and went back to the kitchen.

Mrs. Watkins frowned at him. "They want something?"

"No, madame. I am yours to command now. What would you have me do?"

She opened a drawer and pulled out a piece of white linen. When she shook it out, he saw that it was a large apron.

"The water is hot for the dishes."

Étienne nodded. "Yes, madame." He removed his suit jacket and hung it on a peg near the back door, then put the apron on, tying it behind his waist.

Mrs. Watkins turned to Agnes. "Go and check on the ladies. See if they want anything."

Étienne rolled up his sleeves, poured the hot water into the dishpan, and swished the soap into it. This was not so bad. He always did dishes at home when he was a boy. He began to hum under his breath as he eased a stack of china plates into the water.

"Be careful now!"

He nodded at Mrs. Watkins's admonition, and she smiled. "Agnes told me it wasn't your fault, but likely that won't matter to Mr. Hunter."

"It's all right."

She shook her head. "You're a good lad, and I'll tell Mr. Hunter so."

"I do not want him to regret giving me this job," Étienne said.

"There now. Just you wash up those dishes and don't drop anything more, and that will show him you're not clumsy. Mr. Hunter never could abide a clumsy person." She brought him a clean dishrag, and Étienne was ready to pitch in to his task feeling a little less an outcast.

"Oh, and we'll need more hot water," Mrs. Watkins said. "Take these two pails out to the pump and fill them, please."

He took the two buckets she indicated and went out the back door. Earlier, the cook had shown him the attached shed that housed the pitcher pump. He worked the handle vigorously, glad to have a brief physical outlet for his frustration.

When he plodded back through the kitchen door balancing the full buckets, he was surprised to see Letitia in conference with Mrs. Watkins.

"It's not a problem as far as I'm concerned, Miss Letitia. The lad is sorry he caused a scene, but it really wasn't his fault, you know. Ask Agnes. But he's willing to accept blame; he told me so himself." The cook looked at him, and he nodded gravely, then poured the buckets of water slowly into the reservoir on the stove. He could feel Letitia's gaze on him, but he didn't turn toward her. It would not bode well if the cook thought the hired servant had designs on the master's daughter.

Letitia left a moment later, casting one confused glance over her shoulder as she opened the door to the hallway. Étienne sighed and placed the last clean plate in the rack beside him. Agnes breezed in carrying a tray of dirty cups.

"Here you go! I'll dry."

She snatched up a linen towel and began to wipe the clean dishes so fast he had to hurry to keep up with her. But his every movement was precise and deliberate, and no more accidents befell the china.

∽⊙∼

When the gentlemen joined the ladies in the parlor, it was all Letitia could do to keep from glaring at her father. Despite Mrs. Watkins's reassurances, her father's arrogance appalled her. Shame on him for requiring Étienne to do this!

Rawley picked up a cushioned Queen Anne side chair and carried it over to place it by the love seat where Letitia was perched with Mrs. Wheaton.

She gave him a faint smile and returned to her conversation. Rawley soon found an opening, however, and she was forced to include him.

He leaned toward her when no one else was listening and said, "Tell me, has your father always been a teetotaler? I expected he'd bring out the brandy after dinner, but not so."

She frowned at him. "Why would you expect that? My father has never been a drinker."

"Ah. I do wish you'd go out with me, Letitia. I could show you places where we could get good food and drink. Nothing overpowering, just a fine, light wine to complement the meal. I'm sure you'd see how it adds to a special dinner."

Aghast, she watched him for a moment from beneath her eyelashes. What sort of response could she give to that? At last she said softly, "I consider that an insult to this family's hospitality, sir."

He sat back with a smile. "No offense intended."

She saw that Mrs. Bane was examining the knickknacks on the mantelpiece.

"Excuse me." She jumped up and hurried across the room. "Do you collect Dresden figures, Mrs. Bane? My mother was enamored of these."

During the next hour, she avoided Rawley as much as possible and gently but firmly told Mr. Young she was not interested in attending a family reunion with him. At last the guests began to leave. Étienne helped them with their wraps in the hallway, and Letitia stood at her father's side, thanking them all for attending and wishing them a safe journey home.

When the last one was out the door, her father turned to Étienne. "There are a few dishes yet in the parlor, Steve."

"I will get them, sir."

Étienne went into the parlor, and Letitia grasped her father's arm as he started toward his study. "How could you do this to him?" she hissed.

He frowned and eyed her hand on his sleeve austerely. "Whatever are you talking about?"

"You've humiliated Mr. LeClair."

He stared down at her for a moment. "I thought you understood my feelings about LeClair."

A huge lump popped up in Letitia's throat.

"Steve will do whatever he is paid to do," her father said sternly. "And you, my dear, should mind your own business." He turned and walked down the hallway, disappearing into his study.

Letitia stood rooted to the hall carpet. Her chest and throat ached, and tears filled her eyes. She blinked them back and walked to the stairs but stopped with her foot on the bottom step.

It wasn't right!

She raised her chin and went back to the parlor door. Étienne was about to emerge, carrying a tray with several cups and glasses on it. He stopped and stood facing her, the tray between them. His large brown eyes were cautious, and perhaps a bit sad.

"I am so sorry, Étienne! My father should not have forced you to do this. I hope you do not think that I consider you to be a servant. You are a skilled clerk, and you should be treated with more respect."

She paused for breath, and Étienne smiled. "It's all right, Letitia."

He pronounced her name with his soft French accent, giving it a gentle, flowing lilt. Her heart fluttered. She closed her eyes for a moment, unable to resist imagining what it would be like to be loved by this man, to hear him utter soft, sweet words of love in her ear.

"I do not mind being in a position of service," he went on, and Letitia opened her eyes.

"You. . .don't?"

"No. I came here to serve your father."

"In the office, yes, but after hours you shouldn't have to—"

"Uh-uh," he said quietly. "Mr. Hunter did not force me to do this."

"He didn't?"

Étienne's smile broadened, and her heart thumped.

"Not at all, so be at peace. If there is anything else I can do to make your life and your father's go more smoothly, I would be happy to oblige."

"But—" She looked down at the tray he carried. "This is not part of your job."

"No, you are correct. This is extra. But it is well, mademoiselle. Please do not distress yourself over it."

Stunned, Letitia watched him carry the tray down the long hall to the kitchen door. When it closed behind him, she strode to the entrance of her father's den. He was seated at the old oak rolltop desk that had been his grandfather's, staring up at her mother's portrait on the wall between the windows.

"Ah, Letitia, I thought you went upstairs."

"Not yet."

"Is there something I can do for you?"

"It's about Mr. LeClair."

He swung around to face her, scowling. "I told you to keep out of it."

"I know you did, but. . .Father, I thought you made him come here tonight and pretend to be our butler, perhaps to embarrass me."

"Certainly not."

"Then why did you ask him to do it? I hope it was not some haughty notion of keeping him in his place."

He barked a short laugh. "All right, missy, you sit down and listen to me."

Letitia gulped and sat down one of the comfortable, leather-covered chairs. "Yes, Father?"

"A few days ago, I mentioned the dinner party to Steve at the office. You were gone somewhere—to the bank, I think. Anyway, Mrs. Watkins needed a helper for the evening, and I instructed Steve to find someone to take the job. I asked him to find a clever fellow in the French quarter who could look handsome, be polite, and work hard one evening for some extra cash."

Letitia opened her mouth, then closed it.

Her father picked up the silver pen that lay on his desk. "Later that day, Steve approached me and inquired—a bit nervously, I admit—if I would consider him eligible for the job, as he would appreciate the chance to earn some extra money."

Letitia gasped.

"What—you don't believe it?"

"I. . ." She frowned, unable to meet his gaze.

"Steve comes from a poor family. You know that, don't you?"

She nodded.

"Letitia." Her father's voice softened. "My dear, they are poverty-stricken. But Steve is a strong and clever young man. When he sees an opportunity to help his poor widowed mother and the younger children, he takes it. And that day he saw such an opportunity. I gave him money for a new collar and tie and told him to show up early to help Mrs. Watkins set up, then show the guests in. He did very well tonight, I thought, except for that one little mishap. But you see, Steve is a working-class man. I've enabled him to rise to a clerk's position. Well and good. But he still sees a need to earn extra money, so I allowed him to do that. Do you understand, Letitia?"

"Understand what, Father?"

"He is beneath you, but he is capable of defending himself. He doesn't need you to fight his battles for him. And I do not like to see you so overset by this imagined wrong."

Letitia rose and walked to the door. She turned around and looked at her father, but his eyes were hard and unyielding. She hurried out the door and up the stairs.

Halfway up, she stopped. Her mind reeled with retorts she ought to have made. If he paid Étienne the same wage he had paid Weston, for instance, then Étienne wouldn't need to kowtow to their guests for extra money. And if Father truly valued Étienne as he said he did, he would see that such a man would be an excellent choice for his daughter. Such a man would always take care of the woman he loved.

She set her jaw, determined to storm back down the stairs and launch another argument. She would not back down. She would show him that he was wrong about Étienne's station and that people could move from one plane in life to another.

She took one step, and the kitchen door opened.

Étienne came down the hallway whistling. He stopped walking when he saw her on the stairs, and his whistle silenced. They looked at each other for a long moment, and then he smiled.

Letitia's pulse careened in her veins. She smiled back but knew she was close to tears.

"Your party went well," he said.

She winced. "I'm glad it's over. The ladies were all nice to me, but. . ." She saw that his face had taken on an anxiety, with tiny lines creasing his forehead, where she could barely see the mysterious scar. "Father explained the situation to me. I'm sorry I made a fuss about it. I hope I haven't added to your discomfort."

"I am fine, mademoiselle."

"Well, I do hope Father doesn't make you pay for the damaged plate. That was not your fault."

His expression lightened. "As a matter of fact, he left my wages with Mrs. Watkins, and she just gave them to me. The full amount he promised."

She sighed. "That's good. I was afraid. . . Oh, Étienne, I'm sorry. I was certain Father was making you do this, and I wondered if you hated doing it."

"No, no, it did not bother me one bit. And the money I earned this evening, I will send it home to my mother. That makes me very happy, to be able to help her more than usual."

Letitia nodded. "I suppose it's somewhat like the way I feel about helping Father with the business. Only better because Father doesn't really need me. He could hire someone else."

He was watching her with those large chocolate brown eyes, and she stopped, wondering if she sounded silly. She realized how tired she was. This was probably not the best time to try to analyze her relationship with her father.

"I will tell you one thing that makes me happy," he said.

"Please do." His smile sent a thrill through her.

"Seeing you, Letitia. Seeing you here in your home. You were a very good and beautiful hostess tonight, and your guests had a pleasant evening."

"Thank you. I hope I didn't embarrass you by my reaction when I saw you. . .working tonight."

"Not at all. I was afraid I was the one who brought the mortification to you."

"No, please don't think that."

He glanced down the hallway. "I'm glad we've had this chance to speak to each other."

"So am I. Perhaps sometime we will have another opportunity, and you can tell me more about your family."

He nodded. "I would like that."

A rattling of pans came faintly from the kitchen, and they both looked down the hall and then back at each other.

Étienne held out his hand. Letitia hesitated, then leaned over the railing and clasped it. She tried not to recall her father's adamant words: *I thought you understood my feelings about LeClair.*

"I must go," he all but whispered. "Perhaps I shall see you at church tomorrow."

"Yes."

They stood gazing at each other for another long moment, and her pulse cavorted wildly. Then he gave a nod, as though he completely understood her chaotic feelings, and turned to leave.

Letitia scurried up to her bedchamber, thankful that her father had not emerged from his study while Étienne stood holding her hand over the stair railing. She shut her door and leaned against it, breathing in broken gasps. She ought not to have confronted her father. Had she done Étienne irreparable harm by letting her father see her anger at the perceived slight? Could her father read her other emotions as well? Did he guess the depth of the attraction she felt for Étienne? Could he see that love was growing in her heart, and that she could not stop it?

A soft knock sounded on the door, and Letitia jumped away from it.

"Yes?"

Agnes's voice came through the panels. "May I help you with your dress, Miss Letitia?"

"Thank you. I'd appreciate that."

The stress of the party and her anxiety for Étienne had drained her strength. Having the maid on hand to assist her was a relief, and she allowed Agnes to undo her buttons, lift the dress over her head, and bring her a robe. Then she sat down and let the girl take down her hair and brush it with soothing strokes.

"Your hair is so pretty, Miss Letitia." Agnes smiled at her in the mirror.

"Thank you."

"Mrs. Watkins says two of the men who were here tonight want to marry you."

Letitia was too tired to even consider blushing. "I wouldn't say that. I hardly know them."

"Well, the blond man was handsome. I'd marry him if he learned some manners. If he asked me, of course."

"Would you?"

"Oh, yes, miss. He's very rich, I think."

"Well, money isn't everything, you know."

"Yes, I do know, but it helps."

Letitia smiled. "Did you enjoy working here today?"

"Oh, yes! I'd like to work here all the time. Was I. . .all right?"

"You did fine. I'll keep you in mind if my father is of a mind to hire anyone."

"Of course, you know who the most handsome man here tonight was, don't you?" Agnes asked with a roguish smile.

"No, who? My father?"

A laugh burbled from the girl's throat. "No, although he cuts a very distinguished figure. I was speaking of Mr. LeClair." A dreamy look came over Agnes's face. "I suppose he's too old for me."

Letitia twisted around to look at her. *Agnes mustn't be more than seventeen,* she judged. *And Étienne must be. . .what, five and twenty?* Agnes's admiration of him was slightly disturbing, but even worse was the thought that every young woman in the French quarter was probably languishing over him. "I should think he is."

Agnes sighed. "I was afraid of that. I liked him excessively."

Chapter 11

At the end of August, Lincoln Hunter announced over breakfast his intention of viewing the site of the new sawmill on the west bank of the Kennebec River in Fairfield. He would stay at a hotel and go over the new mill with the builder and the man he had chosen as its foreman.

"I'll take LeClair with me," he told Letitia as he perused his morning newspaper.

Letitia's heart caught. She wondered if she could persuade him to take her, too. But, no, he would want her to keep the office running smoothly.

"After that, we'll take the train to Bangor," her father continued, "and run up to check on things at the camps."

Her hopes plummeted. A tour of Northern's lumber camps meant that her father and Étienne would be gone for several weeks. She should have expected it; he'd been fretting over the new bunkhouse being built five miles north of the Spruce Run Camp, wondering if it would be ready for the crew who would arrive after the first hard frost. It was like her father to want to inspect the preparations personally. Letitia knew he had a reputation as an exacting employer, but one who provided good conditions for his laborers.

"I suppose this is the best time to go," she said.

"I think so. We'll be busy this fall, and I won't be able to get away. And if there's anything amiss up there, I want to know it now."

In the office, Letitia waited all morning for her father to call Étienne aside and tell him. Nearly two months had passed since the dinner party, and her friendship with Étienne had progressed gradually until the bond was stronger than any she had ever known outside family. He felt it, too; she was certain. But they both knew it could go no further, and with unspoken agreement they did not seek to change that. At church on Sundays, they smiled and spoke to each other. On the occasions when her father left the office for a short time, they had quiet, contented conversations. They were learning more about each other, and Letitia's heart leaped each day when she walked into the office and met Étienne's charming smile. Still, she knew this was as deep as the relationship could go. She would not think beyond the present.

By noon, her father still had not confided his plans to Étienne, and tension built in Letitia's heart. They walked home for lunch, leaving Étienne at the office, and sat down to the meal Mrs. Watkins had prepared.

Letitia bowed her head briefly and offered a silent prayer. She'd asked Father once, shortly after her mother died, why he no longer asked the blessing at meals, and he had replied, "If you want to pray, then pray." Since then, she had not mentioned it.

"You'd best start packing for me this afternoon," he said, cutting the slice of ham on his plate. "I expect to be gone three or four weeks."

"Have you told Mr. LeClair yet, Father?" She had taken portions of each dish but was finding it difficult to eat.

"Haven't mentioned it yet. Thought I'd tell him Monday."

"But, Father, he'll need time to prepare, too."

Lincoln held up his cup, and Letitia rose to fill it with coffee. "It won't take him long to pack a bag."

"But. . .just as a courtesy. . ."

"You tell him," her father said with a shrug. "If you think it's important, let him know this afternoon. We leave Wednesday."

"You don't want to tell him yourself? What if he has questions?"

"I'm meeting Russell Chandler at one thirty in his office. What kind of questions would LeClair have?"

"I don't know. What do you want him to take?"

"Paper and pen, the things he uses for accounting and correspondence. And his personal things, of course."

"All right. I'll tell him."

"Forgot to give you the payroll this morning," her father said. "It's on my desk. You can take it to the bank after lunch. I'm raising LeClair's salary two dollars a week."

She nodded without a word, but her heart sang.

"What?" he asked, looking at her shrewdly.

"Nothing."

"You're thinking it's high time."

"I didn't say that."

"Well, he's become very dependable, and I told him I'd raise his wage this summer."

Her father had entrusted Mark Warren, his friend and attorney, with care of Letitia during his absence before, so she wasn't surprised when he said, "If you need anything while I'm gone, see Mr. Warren. And charge your groceries and such." He pulled out his wallet and laid a five-dollar bill on the table. "That enough for your sundries while I'm away?"

"Plenty, I'm sure."

"All right. If you need more, ask at the bank. You will be in my place, Letitia. The foremen will come to you with their headaches, as they would to me. I trust you to use your judgment, and do call on Mr. Warren if an urgent situation arises."

"Yes, Father." Letitia was confident she could handle the office while he was away. Last summer, he'd taken Mr. Weston with him on a two-week trip, leaving her in charge, and she'd had no major difficulties. Of course, it was understood that she was to put off any major decisions until her father's return.

Her father left her at the corner of the street that led to the office and went on alone to his appointment. When Letitia opened the door at Northern Lumber, Étienne was speaking to the mill supervisor, Raymond Linden.

"Mr. Hunter won't be back for a while," he told Linden. "Perhaps another hour."

The man sighed. "I've got a broken belt on the saw, and I wanted to tell Mr. Hunter. We're getting it laced up as quickly as we can, but we'll run a mite behind this afternoon."

"I'll tell him," LeClair promised.

"I'll have things right again soon," Linden pledged. He nodded at Letitia and went out the door.

Étienne looked at her then dropped his gaze. "Letitia," he murmured.

"Étienne." Their quiet greetings when her father was absent always thrilled her, and she stepped to her father's desk to get the papers he had left there. She knew that if she looked Étienne in the eye again, her joy, tempered by the knowledge that he would soon be leaving for an extended period of time, would show. When she walked back to her desk, he had turned back to his own work. She sat down and cleared her throat. He swung around at once.

"My father asked me to tell you. . ."

His dark eyes widened in inquiry, and she looked away. Those beautiful, sympathetic eyes were far too distracting.

"He'll be leaving on a business trip next Wednesday, and you will accompany him."

"Where are we going?"

"To Fairfield, where the new mill is under construction. Father may have lined up some other appointments as well in the Waterville area. He wants you to do the accounting and correspondence for him."

Étienne nodded.

"And after that—" His eyebrows arched, and she broke off, dismayed as her pulse rate increased.

"After?"

"He plans to tour the lumber camps up north."

"And. . .I'll be with him?"

"Yes." She wondered what was going through his mind, behind the dark eyes. He lowered his gaze to the floor, and she noticed that his dark lashes lay against his cheek. She turned away quickly.

"Have you taken your lunch yet?" she asked.

"No." He stood up and turned toward the door, then paused.

"Do you suppose—?"

"What?" she ventured.

"It was just a thought. That I might be able to visit my family."

"Perhaps," Letitia said. "You could ask him."

He nodded and strode toward the door with a new purpose in his walk.

When he was gone, she felt apprehensive. She would be alone in the office for up to a month. Étienne would go with her father to act as his secretary and handle the details of his travel. But he was homesick and would soon be on the Quebec border far to the north, closer to his homeland than to Zimmerville. Lincoln Hunter had brought Étienne back from the camps on his last trip. Would he come back alone this time?

∽⊗∾

In the first four days of the journey, Étienne's list of new experiences grew rapidly. After their tour of the half-finished sawmill, he drove on to the city of Waterville with the boss, where they stayed in a hotel. Mr. Hunter took a suite on the ground floor, and Étienne expected he might be billeted in a small room on the third story, or even at a boardinghouse in a poorer section of town. But, no, the boss informed him that the second bedroom of the suite was for him. He was to stay nearby so that he would be handy to write a letter anytime Mr. Hunter took a notion to dictate one.

The room's opulence shocked Étienne. It was three times the size of the one he occupied in the Ouellettes' home, and the curtains and linens were the finest quality he'd ever seen, outside the Hunter home. The paintings on the walls and matching china pitchers and bowls in the bedrooms must have cost a fortune.

After luncheon in the hotel dining room, the boss visited an architect and a contractor, and Étienne took notes and wrote out a large order for the contractor. When they returned to the hotel, Mr. Hunter instructed him to prepare the envelope for the order and mail it to Letitia.

"Do you wish me to write anything to Miss Hunter?" Étienne asked.

"Oh, whatever you think is appropriate." Hunter took out his pocket watch. "I'm going to stop by city hall and see an old friend for a few minutes. I won't need you. You can catch up on your paperwork while I'm gone."

Étienne sat at the walnut secretary in the suite's sitting room to prepare the letter. He addressed the envelope first. *Northern Lumber* would do, he knew, but it pleased him to commit her name to paper, so he penned *Miss Letitia Hunter* above the company's name. He said it aloud. "Miss Letitia Hunter." It almost hurt to say it. He finished the address and took a sheet of paper.

Dear. . .

Just writing that one word and knowing to whom it was going set his heart tripping. He took a deep breath and continued writing.

316

Dear Miss Hunter,
Enclosed is the order Mr. Hunter procured from Mr. Orcutt of
Waterville Builders. I trust you and the staff will have no trouble in fulfill-
ing this order and having the lumber delivered by rail to Mr. Orcutt.

He hesitated then concluded the note:

Very truly yours,
Étienne LeClair (for Mr. Hunter)

He decided it would do. Businesslike. A touch more cordial than was absolutely necessary, but not so much that it would raise the boss's eyebrows if he
should see it. How he wished he could set down his true feelings for her to read.

My dearest Letitia,
We have been several days on the road, and already I miss you more
than I can say. My thoughts are with you, my darling, as I picture you sit-
ting at your desk, so poised and competent, yet so lovely, with your vibrant
blue eyes and—

The door opened abruptly. "Say, Steve."

He jumped from his chair. "Yes, Mr. Hunter?"

"When you go out to post that order, perhaps you should shop for another
suit. It's been uncommonly hot this week."

Étienne swallowed hard. He'd sent most of his last paycheck to Quebec and
had brought along only a couple of dollars for pocket money on the trip.

"Sir?"

Mr. Hunter shrugged. "Up to you, but that black must be stifling in the sun.
There's a decent haberdashery down on Water Street that could probably meet
your needs. Something lighter. A linen jacket and trousers, maybe."

Étienne couldn't help staring as the boss opened his wallet and extracted a
ten-dollar bill.

"Here. We're having lunch tomorrow with the mayor and his wife. I told
him I have a bright young man in my employ with me, and he said to bring you
along. You'll have a chance to meet a young fellow who's just taken a seat on the
city council. Educational for you."

"Yes. . .sir."

Hunter held out the money. "Well, take it. It's a business expense."

"Thank you, sir." Étienne wondered if this would be deducted from his pay
later, but Mr. Hunter hinted at no such thing.

"If you have any change, put it toward socks and collars and such. A man in
business has to dress the part."

Étienne nodded and folded the bill into his breast pocket.

"If you look successful, men expect you'll give good service and help them be successful."

"Yes, sir."

Hunter nodded. "Good."

"Did you. . .wish to see the letter, sir?"

"Letter? What letter?"

"To Miss Hunter."

"Oh, no, that's all right. Just send it right out so she'll get it tomorrow. Orcutt wants that order in a hurry, and I assured him we had everything in stock. Linden can have it to him in two days, I'd say."

"Oh, yes, sir, I think so."

Two hours later, Étienne returned to the hotel wearing a new suit and a hat much the same style as the one Mr. Hunter wore. He felt overdressed, but none of the gentlemen in the hotel lobby stared at him.

The suite was quiet, but the door to Mr. Hunter's room stood partway open. Étienne approached it and peeked in. The boss was stretched out on the bed, snoring softly.

For two more days they stayed in town. Mr. Hunter seemed to do more socializing than business, yet each day he gleaned one or two large orders for the firm. Étienne gained a new respect for the boss. He'd half expected Mr. Hunter to cut up when out from under his daughter's eye, but the boss maintained his conservative routine: early to bed, early to rise, a brisk morning walk, three square meals a day, and no alcohol or tobacco, though his friends and clients offered them routinely.

On the fourth day, they took the train north. Étienne sat upright in the seat, alert to the swaying sensation, the warm breeze flowing through the windows, the smoke that hung in the air, and the people around him. It was only his second railroad journey, and he found it slightly scary but exciting. Mr. Hunter sat by the window and was already slumped in his seat with his eyes closed, but Étienne knew he could not sleep as long as the train was moving. The trip to Bangor would only last two hours, and he didn't want to miss anything.

He wondered what Letitia was doing. No doubt she was at the office by now. Would the boss make any appointments in Bangor, or would they head right out to the lumber camps? Étienne hoped he would see a few businessmen so there would be another order to send to Letitia that afternoon. The notes he enclosed with those orders were the high point of his day. Knowing she would read them in a day or two was better than lunch at the mayor's house, better than fancy new clothes, better even than feeling that the boss was pleased with him.

The train began to slow, and the conductor came down the aisle.

"Bangor! Next stop Bangor!"

Étienne closed his eyes for a moment. He was perhaps fifty miles away from her now and would soon be farther. The trip was exciting, and the possibility of visiting his family was sweet. He'd dared to mention it to the boss this morning, and Mr. Hunter had not said no. He'd only said, "We'll see how things are when we get to Little North Fork Camp." Étienne knew that was the camp closest to the Quebec border.

But, as much as he longed to see his mother and siblings, already he was looking forward to returning to Zimmerville. His heart lay southward, with Letitia.

Chapter 12

The day following Mr. Hunter and Étienne's train ride, Letitia received a thick packet of papers from Waterville along with the regular daily mail. She sat down to open the envelope addressed in Étienne's hand. On top was a note in her father's scrawl:

Met with Langley & Fortin today. They want 5,000 bd. ft. pine. LeClair will write it up for you. Add another 500 ft. red oak to Orcutt's order. Saw the mayor yesterday. Hope all is well at the office.

Yr loving father,
LH

Letitia sighed. Her father was no doubt widening his circle of political acquaintances. He believed in the power of lobbying for the lumber industry. She set the note aside and examined the papers that came with it. In Étienne's neat handwriting were the new orders. There was also a new schedule of lumber prices. At the bottom he had written:

Miss H.,
I hope this information will aid you in preparing the orders. It came this morning from New York.

Wishing you good health,
E. LeClair

Letitia couldn't help comparing the two messages. Despite his affectionate closing, her father's note seemed less empathetic than Étienne's.

She looked bleakly across the room at his empty chair and longed to see him sitting there once more. But he and her father must be on their way to the lumber camps already.

The door swung open, and Jacques Laplante entered.

"Bon matin, ma petite. Comment vas-tu?"

"Bien, Jacques." She smiled up at the big man, knowing that if she had a real emergency she would run to Jacques long before calling on Mark Warren. *"J'ai une lettre de mon père,"* she said, gesturing toward the papers on her desk.

"Bien."

"I'll send him a note at Little North Fork to let him know how things are going here."

"I came to tell you we have exceeded our goal for production this week, and I am calling for the bonus your father authorized."

"What bonus?"

"He tol' me before he left that if the Henshaw order was finished before Friday to give the men two dollars bonus. They have been driving themselves hard all week."

"He didn't tell me."

Jacques frowned. "He should have. Maybe he didn't think they could do it. Is it agreeable?"

"Well, if Father said so."

"It was Étienne's idea. He tol' your papa a fortnight ago that to get the men to work harder he needs to promise them something extra. And your papa really wanted that order out of the way. My crew is loading it on the cars now."

"Fine. If you tell me it's so, I believe it."

Jacques nodded. "You are lonesome while your papa is away?"

"No more than usual," she said, wishing she hadn't let slip that insight into her inner life.

Jacques looked closely at her. "You come to supper with Angelique and me."

"Oh, that's all right. I'm fine."

"No, you come. You haven't been to the house for a while. We will tell stories and drink tea and talk."

She smiled. With people like Jacques and Angelique nearby, loneliness was a choice. "All right. I'd like that."

She wrote a letter to her father after lunch, detailing the business that had come in and noting that she had authorized Jacques to pay out a bonus to the crew. If her father didn't like it, it was too late, and she would bear his wrath.

After some consideration, she took another sheet of paper.

Mr. LeClair,
    I hope you don't mind I rifled your desk today for the address to
Adirondack Lumber. It was urgent, or I would not have done so. I trust
your trip has been comfortable so far.

She hesitated then wrote:

    I do hope you are able to visit your family.

                                                    Sincerely,
                                                Letitia Hunter

She sat looking at the paper for several minutes, then folded it with shaking hands, sealed it, and wrote on the front: *Mr. E. LeClair.*

After a moment's thought, she took the letter to her father and at the bottom wrote: *P.S. If it is convenient, I believe Mr. LeClair desires to visit his family in Quebec when you are near the border.*

She didn't know if she would hear from her father again, as mail was sporadic at best north of Bangor. She posted the letters before the afternoon train left for Bangor, including a couple of business documents in the packet, then plunged back into her work, trying not to think about the note she had sent LeClair. Would he think her forward to send him an unnecessary personal note?

∞

Just three days later, she sat staring at a letter in Étienne's handwriting. She put off opening it, trying to calm the jitters that seized her every time she looked at her name, *Miss Letitia Hunter,* written in his neat script on the envelope.

It's only business, she told herself, but as long as she didn't open it, there was no proof of that. She recalled their talks on the few occasions when they'd been alone in the office and the smiles that were meant only for her.

She waited until the lunch hour, locked the door, and slit the envelope. The first sheet was a full-page letter, not a hasty note.

> *Dear Miss Letitia,*
> *I hope I do not offend by addressing you thus.*

Letitia's heart lurched. This was more than a business letter.

> *Your father requests that I inform you he is in good health and has had a profitable journey so far, as the enclosed orders will attest. Production for these orders may begin as soon as Mr. Linden is prepared.*

She ruffled the enclosures, noting three new orders. Apparently her father had stopped over a day in Bangor and made good use of his time. She turned back to the letter and sat very still, looking at the words, so neat, so ordinary—to her so significant.

> *I have broached to your father the subject of visiting my family. He seems open to this, so long as I swear to rejoin him quickly. I think perhaps he fears I will not want to return to Zimmerville. I assured him I will not desert him, and he has given me permission to take three days leave while he is at Little North Fork Camp, if all goes smoothly.*

Letitia smiled. Trust her father to leave himself a loophole.

I write this in the train station at Bangor and have only a few
minutes before we go beyond frequent mail service. I hope you do not take
offense if I say I think of you and pray often for you, for your safekeeping in
the absence of your father.

Sincerely,
Étienne LeClair

Letitia closed her eyes and breathed deeply. Before opening them, she prayed, *Lord, thank You. Keep them safe. And if it is in Your plan, please allow this friendship to continue to grow.*

Raymond Linden came to the office that afternoon, and she gave him the specifications for the new orders.

"We might need to hire a couple of extra men to get these out before we finish the Rawley order," he said, eyeing the paper.

"Fine. I know Father wants the entire mill's production available for Rawley when the oak arrives."

"Well, we've put through the spruce," Linden said. "It's in the drying shed. But when the rest comes in, we need to concentrate on that."

She nodded. "There should be men looking for work now."

"All right. I'll put one crew on this Hatcher order tomorrow."

Letitia worked in solitude through the afternoon, interrupted occasionally by customers. At five o'clock she closed the office and went home. It was hot, and she opened the windows. Mrs. Watkins had left her supper in the icebox, but she wasn't very hungry. She stood before the open parlor window, overlooking the town that sprawled between the house and the river. The wind lifted strands of her dark hair, and she began taking out the pins that held her bun firmly on the back of her head.

If she were truly an independent businesswoman, she would change into a fashionable dress and go out to eat supper at a restaurant. That was what Mrs. Harris, the owner of the emporium, did. The people of Zimmerville watched her in confusion. The matrons asked each other why Mrs. Harris didn't take another husband. Any one of a number of well-off bachelors or widowers would be happy to take care of her.

Letitia's ideas of being cared for were nebulous. Her father took care of her; at least, he provided for her needs. But she knew there were deeper needs that he could never meet.

In her imagination, there was somewhere a man who would want her to make a home for him, to be waiting for him in the evening when he left his work. He would love her deeply and would strive to keep her happy, not just well fed and clothed.

As she took the letter out of her pocket and sat down with it by the lamp, Letitia realized that for the past few months, the imaginary suitor had dark eyes and hair, and the solemn expression of Étienne LeClair.

He was beyond the railhead now. If she sent a letter, it might never reach him. She knew they would be at Little North Fork for several days; her father had granted him three days' leave there. Perhaps if she addressed a letter to him there, it would catch up with them before they went on.

She prayed before she began to write. *Lord, am I putting too much store in this? Please help me not to be indiscreet.*

She sat with the pen poised over the blank paper. The greeting would set the tone. *Dear Étienne?* No, she had been trained to write letters in a more formal style. He had addressed her as Miss Letitia, and she did not want to seem forward.

> *Dear Mr. LeClair,*
>   *I received your letter from Bangor with pleasure and have attended to the business referred to therein.*

It sounded stiff, but she let it stand.

> *I am pleased to hear you will be able to visit your home, and I hope this letter will reach you at Little North Fork. Please give my regards to my father, and tell him all is well in the mill and lumberyard.*

Now what? The letter was too short, but she couldn't fill it with empty drivel. She thought back over the last few days, how she had missed his presence in the office and at church.

> *I visited with the Laplantes a few days ago. Friends like Jacques and Angelique are a true gift from God.*

She hesitated then decided to step off into more personal matters. If she did not hear from him, she would know she had probed too deeply.

> *I am wondering, and I hope you do not mind my asking, how you came to know the Lord. Are your family believers as well? If my inquiry is too direct, I beg your pardon.*

Stilted, stilted, stilted.

She reviewed the list of camps her father would be visiting. He would spend only a night or two at most of them.

> *If you receive this, you will be nearly halfway done with your journey. I pray daily for you and my father, and trust to see you again soon.*
>   *Yours truly,*
>   *Letitia*

She paused, debating on whether or not she could be casual enough to omit her last name, but lost her courage and penned *Hunter* at the end.

Her heart raced as she addressed the envelope in care of the boss at Little North Fork Camp. She would take the letter to the post office early the next morning and send it off with a prayer, entrusting its delivery to God.

❧

Étienne settled into the rustic traveling life with ease. He drove Mr. Hunter from one lumber camp to the next and wrote up a report at each, detailing the provisions needed, crews expected to sign on for the season, and preparations for the winter's logging enterprise. He wrote letters to the foremen and cooks for each camp, asking them to confirm their intentions to work for Northern Lumber this year, and he totaled up the many lists of supplies purchased.

Mr. Hunter seemed uncomfortable while the warm weather lasted. A few days after they left Bangor, however, the temperature began to drop and the nights were chilly. The boss regained some energy then, but still Étienne thought he looked drawn. His face had the same grayish cast it had taken on the previous winter. When he wrote to Letitia, as instructed, that her father said he was well, Étienne felt he was not being entirely truthful. He tried to spare Hunter any exertion.

Étienne's quick visit home was bittersweet. His mother and younger siblings were overjoyed to see him but couldn't understand why he had come all that way if he could only stay a short time with them.

He brought them a small sum of money and a couple of books he had purchased in Maine. His mother was proud to hear how highly the boss praised Étienne's education, though he had gotten most of it at the little village school.

"Won't you ever come home to live?" his fifteen-year-old brother, Paul, asked.

"I. . .don't know," Étienne admitted. "Mr. Hunter has raised my wages, and I like what I'm doing now."

"I want to go into the lumber camps this year," said André, who was eighteen.

"Me, too," Paul added.

"Not you," their mother protested. "I need you here, Paul."

Two of Étienne's sisters were married and lived nearby, and they brought their babies over to see him.

In the morning he was sad to leave them all but glad he'd seen with his own eyes that they were doing all right. His mother admitted that without the money he sent regularly, she and the three children left at home would be hard-pressed.

"But if I am hired this fall," André said, "we won't need your pay anymore. You can come home."

His mother said softly, "Perhaps it is time your brother thought of having a family of his own."

Étienne said nothing, but he couldn't quite meet his mother's penetrating gaze. He pulled her in for a hug, then set on his way. He would walk five miles to the next village, where a farmer had promised him a ride to the next town.

As he walked, his thoughts flew to Zimmerville. How was Letitia faring? Would there be a letter from her awaiting him at the camp? He prayed for her as he traveled, longing for the day when he would see her again.

Chapter 13

The saws and planers roared without pause, and Letitia was busy in the office every day. She visited the post office each morning, trying to push down the hope that rose repeatedly, until she saw that there was nothing from the north.

By the end of the week, she was certain that she had, after all, been too candid in her last letter. She wished desperately that she had not written it.

By the following Wednesday, she was depressed. If Étienne felt she was pursuing him, he might change his mind and resign. He wouldn't want to work every day with a girl who lacked discretion.

Woman, she told herself. *Not girl.* She was twenty-one, her birthday passing in the middle of the week without remark from anyone. If her father had been at home, she would have made sure they marked the day somehow, even if she had to instigate it. Her mother had always prepared a special meal for birthdays, and her father always brought her something, a trinket, even since her mother's death.

She had spent the evening of her birthday alone, sitting at home with a book—a collection of short stories by Robert Louis Stevenson called *Island Nights Entertainments*. She had seen it in the window of Mrs. Harris's store that morning and had rationalized that if Father were home he would surely buy it for her as a birthday gift.

On Saturday she made her usual trek to the post office, carrying a sheaf of bills to mail. She had given up on hearing from Étienne again. Maybe her letter had missed him at Little North Fork. . . .

"Miss Hunter!" the postmaster exclaimed when she entered the tiny post office. "I've been looking for ye. I've got something interesting for ye, sure, this morning."

Letitia's eyes widened as the rotund, white-haired man brought a flat box from beneath the counter and set it down in front of her.

" 'Tis not for Northern Lumber, no, no," he said jovially. " 'Tis addressed to yourself, Miss Letitia Hunter. Now, what do ye think?"

She smiled and handed him her outgoing mail.

"I think it is very exciting, Mr. Donnell. Thank you very much."

He handed her the regular mail, and she gathered it up with the box and walked quickly down the street to the office. A flush had spread to her cheeks, but perhaps she could blame it on the warm morning rather than the mysterious box addressed to her in the hand of Étienne LeClair.

She had ten minutes to spare before opening time. Letitia locked the door behind her and set the box on her desk. It was very light, and she shook it, but it gave only the tiniest rustle. With a trembling hand, she took scissors from her drawer and cut the string that bound the parcel. Then she carefully removed the brown paper.

She lifted the lid and found two folded sheets of writing paper on top of crumpled newsprint. She opened the letter and read:

Dear Letitia,

Mr. Hunter has asked me to prepare a parcel for him in celebration of his daughter's birthday, which he regrets missing. He is hopeful this will reach you on the auspicious day or soon thereafter. Your father has been very busy inspecting the camps, making sure they are ready for the season ahead. He is also checking to see if they have the supplies of food and animal fodder spoken for and if the equipment is in working order. We were longer than expected at Spruce Run and the new camp above it, as Mr. Hunter wanted to see completion of the chimney and walls before he left.

Letitia plopped down in her chair, breathing raggedly, and read on.

He asked me to purchase something suitable for the occasion when I went to Quebec a few days ago, as there is no place on the Maine side of the border with merchandise to please a lovely young lady.

She wondered if Étienne were quoting her father, or if those were his own words.

So, you see, if this does not please you, it is not your father's fault. The guilt is mine, and I beg your indulgence. The towns I passed through were very small and the choices limited. However, I thought this might be acceptable. The old woman who made it is very skilled, having learned her craft from her grandmother, who came from Chantilly.

Unable to stand the suspense any longer, Letitia parted the layers of newspaper and drew out a delicate table runner of intricate lace. She gasped and took it to the window, holding it up to the light. Never had she seen such fine work. She went back to the desk and picked the letter up again.

It is my hope that this token will brighten your home and you will remember your father's love for you each time you view it.

Letitia knew it was not her father she would be thinking of when she saw the lovely lace gift. It was the man who had chosen it for her, who had sensed that she craved beauty and femininity.

There was more to the letter, and eagerly she read on.

> *I was able to visit my old home and was glad for the chance to see my family once more.*
>
> *You asked me a question, and I would like to answer it now. I came to know Christ three years ago, at one of your father's lumber camps, the one at Flood Pond. Every year a preacher comes to the camps in winter and preaches God's Word to the men. Some of them, or us, I should say, listen, and some do not. That year, I listened. It was with great wonder that I realized I was a sinner in need of redemption. I will always be grateful to Mr. Hunter for allowing the missionary to visit the camps. My mother is also a believer in Christ, and one of my brothers, but I continue to pray for the rest. Perhaps you would join me in this prayer.*

She bowed her head at once, breathing out both gratitude and supplication. The privilege of praying for Étienne's family warmed her with an inner joy. And Étienne had rejoined her father! He would be back in a couple of weeks. Her prayers had been answered, and their friendship was no longer tentative, but solid, and she knew it would last. If this was to be the extent of it, she would be satisfied.

Her stomach fluttered as she turned to the second sheet. At the bottom was a tiny but lifelike drawing of a man cowering in the branches of a spindly tree, while a moose snorted menacingly below. She plunged eagerly into the letter once more.

> *Your father and I will move on in the morning to French Joe Camp, but I will entrust this package to a man going south, and I will pray that it reaches you safely. The men have had encounters in this area with l'original, as we call the moose. It is my hope that the messenger will not be chased up a tree and left clutching your birthday gift as l'original paws angrily below.*
>
> *And now, Miss Letitia, if you do not mind, I would like to wish you a happy birthday, and it is with anticipation that I consider our return.*
>
> Sincerely,
Étienne

There was a knock at the door, and Letitia jumped, realizing it was well after eight o'clock. She should have opened the office. She thrust the letter into her desk drawer and hurried to open the door. John Rawley stood on the stoop.

"Ah, Miss Hunter."

Letitia shrank back, hoping her serviceable work clothes were plain enough to snuff any admiration he might otherwise feel for her.

"Mr. Rawley," she said evenly. "My father is touring his lumber camps. May I help you this morning?"

"Yes, I wanted to see if my lumber has been sawn yet. Your father promised last spring that it would be dry when I needed it."

"We have the native spruce in the drying sheds," Letitia said, moving back into the office. "The other woods are being brought in. If you would like to speak to our mill supervisor, Raymond Linden, I'm sure he can give the exact status of each component of the order."

Rawley eyed her with mild surprise. "And when do you expect Mr. Hunter to be back?"

"Not for at least two weeks," she replied. "If there is anything you wish to communicate to him, I will be writing to him today."

"No, no, that's fine," Rawley said. "I'll step over to the mill and see Linden." He walked toward the door, and Letitia reflected that the handsome man, with his broad shoulders and luxuriant mustache, still held no appeal for her. He swung around at the door, with his hand on the knob, and appraised her again.

"I would offer you lunch, Miss Hunter, but I suspect you would turn me down flat."

Flatter than a pancake, she thought. "I try to stay near the office these days, but I thank you for your kind invitation." She smiled cordially.

He nodded, his eyes thoughtful, then went out and shut the door.

Letitia turned her attention back to her package and folded the lace carefully. When she was ready to place it back inside the flat rectangular box, she noticed another sheet of paper in the bottom and lifted it out.

Dear Letitia,
> *My heartiest wishes for a happy birthday. I regret I was not there to celebrate with you.*

> *Your fond father*

She smiled. So he hadn't left the entire process to his assistant, after all.

∽∽∞∽∽

Letitia went about her duties that day with a light heart and allowed herself three times to take out Étienne's letter and read it over. By the end of the day, she knew its contents by heart and savored its nuances. She had not offended him with her letter, and, most telling of all, he was looking forward to his return.

She decided to send one more missive to her father, and also one to Étienne. Their final stop before coming home would be a farm on the edge of the northern forest, where a middle-aged farmer raised Belgian horses. Lincoln Hunter bought horses from him each year for the lumber operations. His loggers used the massive animals to haul logs out of the forest on the smooth snow to the river.

> *Dear Father,*
> *Thank you so much for your birthday greetings and the lovely gift. It was with great surprise that I opened the package and discovered the beautiful lace runner. I have never seen anything of such fine workmanship. It is incredible to me that I have reached the advanced age of one and twenty, but here I am. All is well at the office. Mr. Rawley was here today, and I sent him to Mr. Linden for a report on his order. I look forward to your return.*
>
> > *Your loving daughter,*
> > *Letitia*

That out of the way, she settled down to the demanding but more pleasant task of framing her reply to Étienne. Her heart hammered as she carefully penned:

> *Dear Étienne,*
> *It is my hope that this letter will reach you at Turnbridge Farm and that you and my father are in good health. The box indeed arrived, so you see, the messenger had no untoward encounters with l'original or other menacing creatures. My father's birthday gift is lovely, and I appreciate the thoughtfulness with which it was chosen. I tremendously enjoyed your drawing. I hope you have not been among those who have faced an angry moose.*
> *I do not think you have been able to attend services on your journey north, and I think of you each time I go to church. I pray that our heavenly Father will bless you from His Word and that you will have fellowship with other believers.*

I sound like a schoolmarm, she admonished herself. She strove for a more friendly touch, without sliding too far into intimacy.

> *I also pray for you and your family each day, and I accept your birthday greeting with pleasure. I'm glad you were able to make the journey to your family home.*
> *If you are able to wire me from Bangor, it would please me to meet you and Father at the station when you return. I look forward to having you both back here. The office seems very empty these days.*
>
> > *Sincerely,*
> > *Letitia*

She reread the text and paused, uncertain whether to let the letter leave her hands or not. When Étienne returned, she was sure they would be more than coworkers. She rejoiced in that, and mailed the letter.

❧

The next morning she was startled when John Rawley appeared once again at the office.

"Miss Hunter, I have some concerns about the lumber for the courthouse. Since your father is not available, may I discuss it with you?"

Apprehension settled over Letitia. She swallowed and dredged up all the courage and confidence she could find deep within her. "Of course. Won't you sit down?"

Rawley pulled a chair over and sat facing her. "I spoke with Linden yesterday."

"Yes. Is there a problem?"

"For starters, I'm concerned that the lumber is not all in hand yet."

"Father has ordered everything you requested. We have approximately half your requirement in the drying sheds, I believe, and the rest will be shipped all sawn or will come here as logs to be sawn within a month. When you need your finish lumber in the spring, it will be delivered in good time."

"It must be fully dried."

"I'm sure it will be." She kept pasted on her face what she hoped was a confident smile.

"Perhaps we should discuss other options." Rawley looked sharply into her eyes.

"Other options?" Letitia barely escaped stuttering. If she botched the order for her father's largest client in his absence, the fur would fly when he returned. "Would you please explain yourself, sir?"

"I need to be sure that lumber will be ready, and dry, when I need it."

"But you don't need it until next spring."

"April first."

"I see no problem in Northern Lumber delivering it by then."

He stared at her, and she felt uneasy. She knew he had discussed the delivery date with her father the day he placed the order.

"Perhaps you would have lunch with me a week from today and apprise me of the situation," he said. "If the operation is on schedule, I'll feel much better."

"I will send a report around to your office that day," she countered.

"No, I need the assurance only the owner can give me, in person."

"The owner, as you know, is still out on business."

"But you represent him."

"Yes."

"Then I would like to make an appointment. At noon next Friday, at the Maplewood. I will meet you there promptly at twelve, and you will have the facts ready," Rawley said firmly as he rose.

Letitia cast about in her mind for a retort that would put him in his place without jeopardizing his business with her father but could think of none. A flush crept into her cheeks as Rawley strode to the door. She couldn't just let him walk out. *Father, this is not right!* she prayed silently. *Make me wise.* She jumped to her feet.

"You would not speak so to my father," she called after him, and he stopped in the open doorway.

"Perhaps you are right. Your father is not a pretty girl who holds men at arm's length. He is a rational man who knows business. If you are going to represent him, you must learn to think like a man."

He went out the door.

Letitia was furious. She stood shaking for a moment, then sank into her chair. She certainly was not a man, but that did not mean she was irrational. Was Rawley sneering at her or pursuing her? Perhaps they were the same for him.

One thing Letitia knew: She would not have lunch with John Rawley the following Friday.

⤜⧉⤛

Over the weekend, Letitia pondered Rawley's visits to the office. She had known he was attracted to her. Perhaps he was trying to press the issue in her father's absence and her recalcitrance had pushed him to speak in anger.

She prayed a great deal and took solace in the church services on Sunday. Her battered spirit found rest and peace in worship. She would survive this test by relying on God.

If Rawley withdrew his order in retaliation for her coldness, she would stand before Lincoln Hunter on his return and tell him exactly what had happened. She was sure he wouldn't like it, but she thought he would take her side. This clash with Rawley would never have happened had her father been home. And she wished Étienne were there. She felt somehow that his piercing brown eyes would cut through Rawley's pretense and unmask his true motives.

The more she thought about it, the more she was certain she had heard a threat in the contractor's words. Was the proposed luncheon an ultimatum, with loss of the contract the consequence of defying him?

She worked hard all week, keeping close tabs on the mill's production. The smaller orders were filled, and oak logs came in. Linden turned once more to sawing Rawley's required boards. They were a week into September, and the nights were chilly. In a few more weeks the lumberjacks would return to the camps and begin the winter's harvest.

Letitia did not confide in Linden about Rawley's visit, but the supervisor became edgy whenever she walked over to the mill. She realized she was checking on him two or three times a day, which would make any employee nervous.

On Thursday she tried to stay out of the mill. Linden was competent and had assured her several times he would move the job along as fast as could be done safely. She worked over her accounts and dealt with clients. Two young Frenchmen came to inquire about work, and she sent them to Jacques to see if he needed more hands in the lumberyard. She realized she was fretting, partly over Rawley and partly because she had had no word from the travelers for a week.

Late in the afternoon, Linden came into the office.

"Miss Hunter, I thought you would be over to see how we're doing," he said with a strained smile.

"No, Mr. Linden. I know you're doing a good job, and I decided not to hound you about it."

He smiled. "Well, thank you. Things are going forward."

"The Rawley order is on schedule, then?"

"Yes, or a little ahead of what we expected."

"So I can send word to the client that all is well?"

"Yes, if you think that is necessary." Linden looked keenly at her.

Letitia returned the look. Her father trusted Linden, she knew. He had been with Northern Lumber for more than twenty years, and mill supervisor for ten.

"Miss Hunter," he ventured, "is there a problem with the Rawley order?"

"I. . .don't think so," she faltered.

"You seem anxious about it."

She looked down at the open ledger on her desk. "Well, Mr. Rawley seems anxious about it."

"Did he complain to you last week after he came to the mill? I showed him what we've done and assured him we would have the lumber in plenty of time, to his specifications."

"He expressed concern about the lumber being dry in time."

Linden nodded. "I went over the timetable with him. There's nothing to worry about. It's fine."

Letitia frowned. "Then why did he—?" She broke off. Rawley had come to her the next day and intimidated her, implying that things were not moving along as they should. It occurred to her that perhaps she should call on Mr. Warren, her father's lawyer.

"Is everything all right, Miss Hunter?" Linden asked.

"Other than Mr. Rawley, everything's fine," she assured him. "And Father ought to be home in another week, two at the most."

He nodded. "I expect the last of the red oak to come in soon. We'll saw it out when it arrives."

Letitia sat at her desk after he had gone. She wished she had a way to reach her father, but she couldn't be sure where he was now. Maybe at Turnbridge Farm, maybe still at one of the lumber camps. She might send a wire to the farm, but she didn't know if it would be delivered. Turnbridge was a good twenty miles beyond Bangor. Her father wouldn't want her to send for him unless it was an emergency.

Should she go to Mr. Warren? She balked at that. Mark Warren would make a fuss and probe into the matter and embarrass her. This wasn't a legal matter. It was a business matter, between her and Rawley. Or was it a personal matter?

She sighed and closed the office for the night.

Chapter 14

On Friday morning Letitia paced nervously across the office to Étienne's desk, then turned and walked back to her own. Noon at the Maplewood. She wouldn't do it.

At ten o'clock she went to the lumberyard and asked Jacques for a man to run an errand for her. He gave her a twelve-year-old boy whom he had employed short-term to help stack the boards for the large Rawley order.

"What is your name?" Letitia asked as they walked toward the office together.

"Pierre Levesque, *ma'm'selle.*"

"Pierre, I need for you to take a message to a gentleman for me. Come into the office and I will give you the message."

At her desk, she picked up the report Linden had sent over from the mill half an hour earlier. It stated that all of the spruce lumber for Rawley's order was sawn and drying nicely and that three-fourths of the red oak was sawn. The rest was in production.

On a sheet of paper she wrote:

Dear Sir,

From this report by my mill supervisor, you can see that your order is in good hands. Things are progressing nicely, and I am sure the service afforded by Northern Lumber will please you. I see no need for us to meet to discuss the matter.

Sincerely,
L. Hunter

"There now." She entrusted the note and the report into Pierre's hands. "Here is the address. If you deliver this to Mr. Rawley personally, I shall give you a bonus."

"Oui, ma'm'selle." His dark eyes glittered. *"J'attendrai la réponse?"*

Letitia considered. Should she have him wait for an answer? "If he tells you to wait, then do it; but if he says nothing, just come back and report to me."

He sped out the door, and Letitia couldn't help but smile at his eagerness. She began writing a letter to a supplier of exotic woods and tried to forget about Rawley.

Fifteen minutes later he marched into her office, slamming the door in the face of the French boy, who was panting at his heels.

"Miss Hunter, what is the meaning of this?" He held up her note.

Letitia took a deep breath and stood. "The meaning is good news, sir. Your lumber is going to be just as you ordered it. I'm confident it will be premium dry lumber. End of discussion."

"End of nothing," he roared. "We have an appointment in exactly"—he pulled out his pocket watch—"one hour."

Letitia tried to speak soothingly, although she was trembling. "Sir, I see no need for that. There is nothing to discuss."

"Nothing except your pride!" he shouted.

Letitia took an involuntary step back.

"You have rebuffed me time and again." Rawley's face reddened and his eyes snapped with anger.

"I—"

Letitia cringed as he roared, "I demand to know what you have against me! You surely cannot think I'm not good enough—"

The street door swung open with a crash, and Letitia jumped.

Étienne filled the doorway, looking first at her, then at the raging contractor.

Rawley rounded on LeClair. "Get out!" he shouted. "I am speaking with Miss Hunter!"

Letitia's heart pounded. What was he doing here? And was her father on his way as well?

Étienne held up his hands, palms outward. "Be calm, *m'sieur*. Mademoiselle does not wish you to shout, I believe."

Letitia's shock at seeing him gave way to pride and gratitude for her champion.

Rawley glared at Étienne. "This is a private conversation!"

"*Non*, m'sieur, *pardonnez-moi*, but this is not the conversation. It is what we call the shouting match. I will not permit you to abuse Miss Hunter."

Letitia's empathy swelled when she heard Étienne's lapse in grammar. She knew his English was flawless except when he was agitated.

She stepped forward. "Mr. LeClair is right, Mr. Rawley. I do not put up with shouting in my office. No *man* would, either. If you wish to discuss business, please sit down and speak calmly, but I contend there is nothing to discuss."

He stood facing her for a moment, his lips twitching slightly.

"If I prefer to not continue doing business with Northern Lumber, then what?"

Letitia hoped her dismay did not show on her face. "Then I will tell my father that the order is withdrawn, sir." Unable to stand any longer because her knees were wobbly, she sat down, hoping it looked intentional.

"Sir, you cannot do this," Étienne said.

Rawley whirled toward him. "Who says I can't?"

337

"Does not m'sieur have a contract? Mr. Hunter's advocate will say this."

Letitia regretted not going to Mark Warren, after all. She said shakily, "Yes, that's right, Mr. LeClair. Mr. Warren will discuss the matter with Mr. Rawley, I'm sure. I can send the boy around to ask him to see Mr. Rawley today." She glanced toward the doorway, but the boy had disappeared.

Rawley stepped closer to her desk and stood looking down at her. For five seconds he neither moved nor spoke. Étienne stayed solidly in the doorway. Letitia tried to return Rawley's stare without flinching.

"*Pardon!* Everything is all right?" said a deep voice, and Letitia darted a glance toward the doorway. Jacques Laplante loomed on the doorstep, addressing Étienne. The boy peeked around his elbow.

"Everything is fine," Étienne said. "Miss Hunter is having a discussion with a client."

Rawley cleared his throat. "Forgive me, Miss Hunter. I am not accustomed to losing my temper with ladies."

She returned his gaze. "And I am not accustomed to being browbeaten by our clients."

He sighed. "Please accept my apology. The lumber order stands. It is fine, I'm sure. Your father is a shrewd man. It. . .surprised me that he left his business in the hands of a novice."

Letitia said quietly, "I am competent, sir. I don't see why you should wish to punish my father because of your dislike of me. However, if you wish to discuss transferring your order to another firm with my attorney. . ."

"No," Rawley said firmly. "That would set me back months. It wasn't my intention to renege on the agreement."

"Then what was your intention?" she asked, surprised at her own boldness.

He hesitated, then glanced toward Étienne and Jacques still towering in the doorway. "Could I have a word with you alone, Miss Hunter?"

Spending another moment alone with John Rawley was the last thing she wanted, but she didn't want to humiliate him before the men and Pierre when he seemed ready to reason. She looked toward them. "Mr. LeClair, if you and Mr. Laplante would be kind enough to wait outside, I will call you if I need you."

"*Certainement*, mademoiselle," said Étienne. He went out, and Jacques pushed Pierre gently before them. The door closed, but Letitia was confident her protectors were only inches from the door.

"What is it you wish to say?"

He sat down, his face set in contrition. "I did not set out to alienate you and disrupt our business agreement. Quite the contrary, I. . .was hoping for an opportunity to further our acquaintance."

Letitia swallowed and tried to quell the distaste that filled her heart. "Mr. Rawley, I will be frank. I have no desire to further a personal acquaintance with a man with such a temper as I have seen displayed here today."

"I understand. Please believe me, I regret this scene, and if you change your mind—"

"I won't change my mind. Sir, you have called me a novice and implied that I am too feminine in my thinking, whatever that means. These are insults, and it seems a strange way to attract a woman, if that was indeed your design."

He sat silent a moment. "I cannot fault what you say. I will take my leave, Miss Hunter, and perhaps we would best forget this exchange. I will not bother you again about the lumber but will do business with your father when he returns."

She sighed with relief when he left. Étienne, Jacques, and Pierre came into the office.

"Mademoiselle is all right?" Jacques eyed her anxiously.

"Yes, thank you. But, Étienne, where is my father? I didn't expect to see you here—and without him. What has happened?"

The lines of his face went flat and grave. She noticed as he came toward her that he had not shaved that morning, and dark stubble shadowed his face.

When he reached her side, he startled her by dropping to one knee beside her chair and reaching for her hand.

"Letitia, it grieves me to tell you this, but apparently I have outdistanced the telegram I sent you from Bangor. You did not receive my message?"

She stared at him in confusion. His gentle touch thrilled her, but his words and his troubled demeanor frightened her.

"What is it?" she gasped. "Please tell me."

"Your father is ill." He paused, gazing into her eyes as though to gauge her distress. "He is still at Turnbridge Farm. I left him there at dawn and rode as fast as I could to the train station. I sent a telegram, and I hoped it would reach you before I did, but apparently it has miscarried."

Letitia felt her lips tremble, and she put her fingers up to still them. "How bad is it?"

"We had the doctor come yesterday, and he did not like what he saw. He came again early this morning, and he advised me to fetch you. That is why I am here, mon amie. I will take you to him. Come, we will go first to your house so that you can pack whatever you need."

"Oh, yes. Thank you."

"We have an empty wagon in the lumberyard, all hitched up," Jacques said. "Take that."

"Thank you, I will," said Étienne.

Letitia stood and glanced uncertainly around the room. "Should I just close the office?"

Étienne's brow furrowed. "You may be gone several days, I fear. Perhaps while you are packing, I can step around to Mr. Weston's house and see if he would be willing to come in and keep things going during this crisis."

"Yes, thank you." She noticed Pierre then. The boy stood near the door, his lips twitching. "*Mille mercis*, Pierre."

"I met him at the corner as I came from the station," Étienne said. "He begged me to help you. He said the rich gentleman was yelling at mademoiselle."

"And he ran into the yard a few moments ago," Jacques added. "He told me to come quick; mademoiselle needed me."

She smiled. "I promised Pierre a bonus for delivering my message to Mr. Rawley, but he deserves far more for fetching the two of you."

She opened her desk drawer and took out the two one-dollar bills left from the five dollars her father had given her nearly a month earlier.

"Voilà, Pierre," she said, holding the two dollars out to the boy. His eyes grew round, and he looked up at her with distress on his face.

"Non, non, ma'm'selle! C'est de *trop*!"

"It *is* too much," Jacques agreed.

"Far from it," Letitia replied. "Pierre, you must keep the money, young man. You have earned it."

Pierre turned his huge brown eyes on Jacques, and the big man laughed. "Keep it."

The boy smiled in adoration at Letitia. "Merci, ma'm'selle."

He dashed out the door.

"Come, now," Étienne said with a gentle smile. "I will escort you home, then go and see Mr. Weston. If he cannot help us, I will see if Mr. Linden has a trustworthy man who can keep the office open for a few days. I need to inform him of your father's illness anyway."

"I can tell Linden," Jacques said. "And I am very sorry about your father, mademoiselle." He left the office with a sympathetic smile.

Letitia stood and straightened her desk, then walked to the coat tree where her bonnet hung. As she reached for it, the door opened, and a strange boy entered the office.

"Telegram for Miss Lettie Hunter."

Letitia grimaced at his pronunciation of her name and held out her hand. "Thank you." She looked toward her desk but realized she'd given Pierre the last of her cash.

Étienne reached in his pocket and handed the boy a coin.

"My message, no doubt," he said as the boy left.

Letitia nodded, but she opened it anyway.

> *LH very ill. I will arrive Zimmerville 11 a.m. and bring you to him.*
> *E. LeClair*

As she stared at the bleak words, tears welled in her eyes, and the gravity of the situation hit her with the force of a hurricane. Her father's condition must be severe indeed for Étienne to leave his side to get her.

He touched her elbow lightly. "Come, *ma belle*. I will take you home."

A sob shook her, and she felt her courage splintering. Étienne wrapped her in his strong arms and held her against his chest. She crumpled the telegram in her hand and leaned against him. His warmth comforted her, and for a moment she wished she could stay forever in his embrace and not face the sorrow that surely awaited her at Turnbridge Farm.

Slowly she slid her arms around him, and he stroked her back. His cheek came down gently against her hair, putting a warm pressure on her head, and she closed her eyes.

"Letitia," he whispered, "I will do everything in my power to help you. We must hurry, though, *ma chérie*. We will take the 1:35 train."

"Can we make it?"

"I think so. Come."

Chapter 15

An hour later, Étienne knocked on the door of the Hunter mansion. Mrs. Watkins opened it, her face pinched and pale.

"Come in!" she cried. "Tell me about the master. Miss Letitia says he's very ill and you're carrying her off to the north lands."

"Yes, it is true. We have not much time to reach the station. Jacques Laplante has brought the wagon to carry our bags, and we must hurry."

Letitia came down the stairs carrying a satchel, and he stepped forward. His heart wrenched at the sight of her blood-shot eyes. But she had changed into a dove gray dress and bonnet and held her back straight.

"I'm ready," she said.

"Come, then." He took her bag and offered his arm.

"Mrs. Watkins, thank you for agreeing to stay here," Letitia said.

"Oh, that's nothing. Don't you worry about the house. Everything will be fine."

Étienne escorted Letitia down the wide steps. Jacques leaped forward and took her luggage while Étienne assisted her onto the wagon seat.

On the short ride to the station, Jacques reached over and squeezed Letitia's hand.

"Angelique and I, we will pray for you and the boss."

"Thank you." Letitia turned to Étienne, who sat on the other side of her. "Did you see Mr. Weston?"

"Yes. He will go in this afternoon. And Mr. Linden said he would send Marston, one of his foremen, if needed. He's not trained in accounting, but he can deal with clients who come in. Between him and Mr. Weston, all should be well."

"Thank you so much," Letitia said with a sigh. Her eyes clouded with anxiety. "Oh, the payroll! I left the account and payroll ledgers in my desk."

"Do not worry," Étienne said gently. "Mr. Weston assured me he will handle the payroll and other financial accounts. Do not distress yourself, mon amie."

She settled against the seat. "You're right. Thank you."

He wished he could offer her more comfort, but under Jacques' sharp eye he didn't dare touch her. She had allowed him to hold her briefly at the office, and he sensed that she understood how deeply he cared about her. Being here beside her was the right thing for this moment.

"Do you expect to be gone long?" Jacques asked, looking at him past Letitia.

Étienne hesitated. "I do not know what we shall find at Turnbridge, but I will try to get word to you soon."

Jacques nodded and turned the team in at the depot.

～✦～

The train was boarding, and Jacques walked briskly with them to the platform and handed their luggage to the porter.

He took Letitia's hand. "*Bon voyage*, mademoiselle. Your papa will be happy to see such a pretty thing come to cheer him."

She gulped, hoping she could avoid weeping.

"He will mend," Jacques assured her.

"I don't know, Jacques. It sounds very serious." She shot a glance toward Étienne, who waited for her a pace away.

"Ah, well. Many will be praying."

"Thank you."

"Étienne will take good care of you, *mon enfant*."

"Yes, I think he will. *Au revoir*, Jacques. Merci, mon ami." She smiled at him a little shakily.

Étienne extended a hand to help her mount the steps of the passenger car. Even though she wore cotton gloves, his touch exhilarated her. The prospect of being alone with him on the train ride after being apart for a month unnerved her a little. Their relationship had changed since he left with her father. His warm embrace at the office after he broke the news to her was proof of that. Her face colored as she remembered that moment, and she paused in the aisle.

"Sit here, mademoiselle, if it is to your liking," Étienne said softly from behind her.

She sank gratefully onto the seat and slid over near the window. Étienne placed his hat on the overhead rack and settled beside her with a mournful smile.

"What will happen when we reach Bangor?" she asked.

"I left Mr. Turnbridge's team at a stable in Bangor. He is very concerned for Mr. Hunter and has great respect for him. Yesterday he sent me for the best physician to be had."

"That is good to know." She realized that he'd had no time to rest during his brief return to Zimmerville.

"Did you have dinner?" she asked.

"Jacques gave me a sandwich from his dinner pail when he brought the wagon back. How about you?"

"I—yes—well, of sorts. You know Mrs. Watkins."

"Ah, yes. You were too nervous to eat, but she insisted."

She couldn't help but smile. "You are right." The train began to move. She inhaled sharply as her thoughts once more reverted to her father. "Étienne?" she whispered.

"What, mon amie?"

"What exactly is wrong with my father?"

His eyes filled with compassion, and he covered her gloved hand with his. "I am afraid it is very bad. He seemed fatigued all through the journey, once we left Bangor. I thought when I returned from Quebec that he looked more rested. But when we got to Nine Mile Camp, he was exhausted. We rested there, and he seemed better, but I think the horseback trip we made to the new camp took a lot out of him."

Letitia sucked in a breath. "It was hard traveling?"

"Yes. The road was in very poor shape. He was tired and dizzy the night we arrived at Round Pond. I urged him to stay an extra day, but he wanted to push on to Turnbridge Farm. By the time we arrived, late that afternoon, he could barely stand up." His eyes were troubled. "I apologize, Letitia. I should have insisted he wait at Round Pond. But your father. . .he is very. . ."

She smiled ruefully. "Yes, I understand. Father is the one who gives the orders."

"Exactly. I thought if he rested a few days. . ."

Letitia nodded.

"The next morning I could see that he was very ill, and I urged him to stay in bed. When he did not disagree, I knew it was bad." Étienne hung his head. "He. . .complained of a pain." His look of distress raised her apprehension. "Mr. Turnbridge told me where to get the doctor, and I went immediately. Letitia, I fear it is very serious. The doctor says it is his heart. That is why I made the decision to come for you."

"I'm glad you did." She squeezed his hand, and he sat looking down at their clasped fingers.

"When I left this morning, he seemed a little easier. The doctor could not stay, but he promised to call again later today. There may be some word when we reach Bangor."

"And how long will it take us to reach the farm?"

"Several hours, depending on the roads and the horses, but Turnbridge's teams are fast. Perhaps three or four hours."

She nodded, meeting his gaze soberly. "I'm glad you are with me, Étienne."

"Oh, ma chérie, if I could—" He broke off and stared forward, his mouth in a grim line.

Her heart fluttered at his endearment and also at his evident distress. "Do not blame yourself," she said.

He sighed deeply and settled back against the seat cushion but kept her hand clasped in his.

After a few minutes, the conductor came down the aisle, and Étienne released her hand to reach into his pocket for their tickets. She had noticed his new suit earlier, but she observed him closely while the conductor distracted him. The suit was well cut but not tailor-made. She wondered if her father had a hand in the increase of his wardrobe. Or was Étienne using money he would rather send home to his mother in order to dress in a manner that would please his boss?

She untied her bonnet and removed it. When the conductor moved away, Étienne asked, "May I take that for you, mademoiselle?"

"Yes, thank you."

While he stored her bonnet above and opened the side window, she removed her white gloves. It was a warm day for mid-September, and the air in the car was nearly stifling. Étienne dropped the window sash, and a cool breeze flowed in and ruffled her hair.

"Too much?" he asked.

"No, it's heavenly."

He smiled and settled back beside her.

Letitia folded her hands in her lap and wondered what the proper etiquette was for traveling with a man. She had made a few trips with her father, but this was different. Should she try to keep the conversation going, and if so, what topics were deemed suitable?

She darted a glance toward him and found his warm brown eyes were resting on her. She caught her breath and looked away. The rhythm of the wheels quickened as the train left the city.

"Letitia." He had leaned close to be heard above the noise of the train.

She turned toward him and was startled at his nearness. "Y–yes?"

He drew back a little. "I am very sorry your father is ill, but it does not completely outweigh my delight in seeing you again." He watched her steadily, as though trying to gauge her response.

Letitia found it hard to breathe steadily. Yes, everything had changed. She had wanted this, but now that she faced the reality, she wasn't sure she was ready. She swallowed hard.

He glanced around, and she looked, too. There were perhaps a dozen other passengers in the car, spread out over its length. None were immediately behind or in front of them, though there was a gentleman across the aisle.

"Your letters . . . ," he said, leaning close.

She nodded.

"They gave me hope."

Again she nodded.

"Letitia . . ."

She looked up into his handsome, strong face. His kindness warmed her, but she also caught a touch of insecurity in his wrinkled brow. After his first uneasy day in Zimmerville last winter, he had given her the impression of quiet confidence as he adjusted to his new surroundings. Now he seemed once more slightly at sea.

"I—you—" She gave up and turned away, reddening.

"What is it?" he asked, near her ear.

She stared out the window. They were passing a lake edged with hardwoods, and the leaves were beginning to turn crimson and gold. She soaked up the beauty of the afternoon light on the trees and water.

She took a deep breath and turned away from the window and faced him. "I've prayed so hard that we could be friends. The Lord seems to have answered my prayers."

"Yes." It was almost a question.

Letitia felt she had said the wrong thing. Would he take it to mean she wanted only to be friends, nothing more?

He put his hand on hers. She slowly turned her palm upward and grasped his fingers. He glanced at the man across the aisle, who seemed oblivious. Étienne drew her hand through the crook of his arm and covered it with his warm fingers, stroking it and not looking at her. She sat very still, thinking, *I'll become accustomed to this. I will.*

They sat without speaking as the miles passed beneath them and lay in neat lines behind them. Her heart raced faster than the train. Gradually it slowed, and her stomach stopped churning. Only now and then a jolt of joy shot through her, even as concern for her father caused sorrow.

Étienne leaned toward her. "You could sleep, perhaps."

"No," she replied. "I certainly could not."

He squeezed her hand and sat back beside her as the miles passed by.

༺꧁༻

They reached Bangor just after four o'clock, and Étienne claimed their luggage.

"Are you sure you don't want to rest here until morning?" he asked, stooping a little to look down into her blue eyes beneath the brim of her bonnet.

"No, I'd rather get on to Father. That is, if you're not too tired."

"I am ready to go if you are certain," he replied.

"I am."

"Come, then. We must go to the stable."

Étienne found a hack just outside the depot and instructed the driver to take them to the livery stable. The sprawling city of Bangor still made him a little nervous, but he was beginning to feel comfortable getting back and forth from the station to the stable. He was sure he would get lost if he ever had to venture off that short route.

She smiled at him, a timid but hopeful smile that told him she was still as uncertain as he what the future held for them. The rattle of wheels and the clop of horses' hooves camouflaged the beating of his heart.

When they reached the stable, he helped harness the horses to Turnbridge's farm wagon and placed their luggage in the wagon bed. He helped Letitia onto the seat and climbed up beside her, taking the reins from the ostler.

It took all his concentration to guide the team until they struck the road that would take them north, away from the hubbub of the city and into the quiet countryside. The horses fell into a brisk trot, and he sighed and settled against the board seat's back. After several minutes' consideration, he shifted all the reins into his left hand and reached for Letitia's hand once more. She glanced up at him, a smile on her lips.

"If I do not offend you," he murmured.

"You do not."

He nodded, and they sat in silence for a few precious minutes, while he regained control of his heart, which was doing cartwheels and backflips a circus performer would envy.

"I suppose it will get dark before we are there," Letitia said.

"Yes, I fear you are right. But we have a lantern in the back, and some traveling robes if you get cold."

"The road is not bad so far," she said.

"No, it is good near the city. But the farther out we get, the worse the ruts. Still, it is not so bad this time of year as it will be next spring."

He watched her face as new scenery spread before them: fields of dry cornstalks, bathed in late afternoon sunlight; orchards heavy with fruit; and a large stand of scarlet sugar maples, with a little cabin nestled among the old trees. She seemed to take delight in every new vista. At last they entered the forest, and he could barely make out the road ahead in the shadows. But the team knew the way home and went rapidly along.

"So, three or four hours?" she asked timidly.

"If we could keep up this pace, we'd be there in two hours more," he said. "But I came over this road yesterday, and I know it gets worse."

The wind increased, and Letitia shivered. Étienne reached behind him and pulled a lap robe from the wagon box.

"Put this over your knees, chérie."

He had not meant to let the sweet name leave his lips again, but when he glanced at her face, she did not seem displeased.

"You must be chilly, too," she said.

His linen jacket was not as warm as the woolen one he had put away in Waterville. He considered stopping to open his bag and take out the black jacket.

"Perhaps you could share a corner of the robe," Letitia said softly.

She moved closer to him in the twilight, and he pulled the edge of the lap robe over his knees. He drove on, very happy. He longed to take her hand in his again, but he must preserve propriety at all costs. After all, it was getting dark, and she was a lady, and one in a sorrowful situation at that. This was not really a proper time for courting, even if he had her father's consent, which he did not. He decided he would do better to give his attention to the horses.

Soon the big Belgians slowed to a walk, and Étienne barely guided them, letting them choose their own path in the roadway.

"Sleep if you can," he said.

"I can't. I keep thinking about Father."

"He is in my prayers constantly," Étienne said.

"Mine, too. Thank you for praying for him. It is my wish that God will spare him. But if not, what then, Étienne?" In the dimness, he could not read her expression, but her voice told him much about her sorrow. "I can't bring myself to think what I would do if Father were incapacitated or—or worse."

"If that time should come, the Lord will guide you." As he said it, he realized he believed every word. "Your father has friends who would be competent to advise you. And this month you have proven yourself able to run the business."

"Oh, but that was only temporary until Father and—you—returned."

"I am but a cog in the wheel," he said. "A very small, insignificant, replaceable cog."

"Don't say that. My father has come to depend on you."

"Well, I don't say he hasn't, but we have been beyond civilization. When we return to Zimmerville, he may forget the things he said to me in the north woods."

She was quiet for a moment then asked, "What sort of things did he say to you?"

"He mentioned a trip he planned to make to Philadelphia after Christmas. He...said he might send me in his place."

"But, Étienne! That's wonderful. It means he trusts you as Northern Lumber's official representative."

"Well, I don't know. He did not say for sure that he would do that. It was only a possibility, if..."

"If what?"

"If I do well between now and then. He said he would educate me further and see that I had time to study accounting and economics. He mentioned several times sending me out on business for him. He said—" He stopped abruptly. Some of the things the boss had said in his moments of pain were not meant for Letitia's ears.

"What?" she asked softly.

"I do not wish to distress you."

Immediately he heard alarm in her voice. "What is it, Étienne?"

He sighed and flicked the reins to keep the horses at a trot. "Your father said he is getting too old to travel. When he first became ill, he complained a bit. Not much, you understand."

"Oh, I understand." Letitia smiled. "You should have seen him two winters ago, when he had influenza. I know what a difficult patient he can be."

"Well, he said that he ought to quit traipsing about in the winter and send a younger man to tour the camps and be sure all was well."

"Meaning you."

"So I understood. And then he began talking of me going to Philadelphia."

"My father does not speak rashly of things he doesn't mean to follow through on."

Étienne fell silent, thinking about the things Mr. Hunter had said to him in private. The horses pulled steadily on, snorting now and then.

"Letitia?" he began cautiously, eyeing her in the deepening darkness.

"Yes?"

He drove on for a minute, wondering whether it was wise to speak again. "I wanted to write to you and share my hope that your father would. . .permit me to. . .be a friend to his daughter."

"Did he give you reason to think so?" she asked. "That would be good news, indeed."

He laid his hand once more over hers and squeezed it.

"You are cold," she whispered. "You should have gloves."

He shifted the reins to his left hand, and she lifted the edge of the robe. He allowed her to pull his hand beneath it, and they sat with fingers clasped between them, beneath the thick covering. Slowly his hand began to warm. He knew that after a few minutes he would have to switch hands again, although it would mean relinquishing the sweet contact.

He thought back to his early days in the Northern Lumber Company office. She had sat all day, so prim and proper, not speaking to him; he'd known she was conscious of her father, yards away behind his massive walnut desk. Étienne had kept diligently to his paperwork, longing to speak to the beautiful Miss Hunter, or even just to glance at her now and then, but fearful of upsetting the stern owner.

"My father can be intimidating," she said.

He laughed. "You minimize the effect of his presence."

"Yes, perhaps that is so."

"He seemed to be. . .arranging suitors for you, or trying to. But you—you kept them all at a distance."

"The men he brought around did not seem right for me."

"I was glad," he admitted. "When you put Mr. Rawley aside, I was very glad. He would not have been a good match for you."

"Oh, yes, John Rawley," she said with distaste.

"Can you tell me why he was at the office today?"

She frowned. "May I tell you everything?"

"But yes."

She smiled, and he realized he'd lapsed in his syntax again. If he truly wanted to please her father, he would have to stop letting his French roots show through his speech.

"You'd better warm your other hand."

He squeezed her fingers and took his right hand out to hold the reins, shoving his left hand into the pocket of his jacket on the other side.

The horses came out into an open stretch, and the moon shone down on them, striking golden highlights in Letitia's hair and gleaming off the harness buckles.

"It's so bright," she noted. "How can it be so cold?"

"It is the time of year. I think it will freeze tonight. We are far north of Zimmerville now. The frost comes earlier here."

He reached into the wagon bed and pulled up a woolen blanket.

"Wrap this around your shoulders."

She complied and settled again beside him, her shoulder almost touching his.

"Now, then, you were going to tell me something," he said.

Letitia sighed. "John Rawley insisted that I meet him for lunch today, to tell him how his order was coming along. I refused to go, but. . .Étienne, I was afraid he would cancel his order if I defied him. I sent Pierre Levesque with a message saying the lumber was well into production and that the meeting was unnecessary."

"You sent Pierre? Rawley must have loved that!"

"Yes, he came storming into my office and slammed the door in Pierre's face."

"And the boy saw me coming up the street and ran to fetch me, then got Jacques from the lumberyard."

"Yes. Pierre was quite heroic. I'll always be glad he was there." Letitia was silent a moment; then she turned toward him in the moonlight, her face lined in thought. "I couldn't decide why he had spoken to me so rudely. Was it because he disdains women who aspire to commerce, or because he—?" She pressed her lips together and looked forward, toward the horses.

Étienne tried to reach beyond her words and catch her thoughts. "Yes, that was it, ma chérie."

Chapter 16

Letitia whirled and peered at him. "How do you know what I was going to say?"

"What *were* you going to say?"

"Well, I—" She paused once more, and he smiled.

"Your modesty will not let you say that he was angry because you showed no interest in him. I'm glad you refused to meet him."

"Yes," she admitted. "And I'm glad you came when you did, although the reason for your arrival saddens me. But if you had been there all along, perhaps Rawley would not have spoken as he did."

"Perhaps not."

She looked up into his eyes. "Why do you suppose he did that, when Father was away? He must have known the lumber would be good and that it would be ready on time. Do you suppose he mistrusts women that much?"

"No, I don't think he doubted your competence. And he knew you were only your father's proxy."

"Why then?"

"It is as we said. He has been attracted to you for months. Perhaps he thought he could break through your reserve when Mr. Hunter was out of the way."

"Perhaps. He was so angry."

"He had been denied the object of his ambition."

"Ambition? I would hardly call myself an object of ambition."

"Why not? You are a wealthy young woman."

She laughed. "I haven't a penny to my name. My father doesn't pay me for my labor. I had to go to the bank this afternoon for money for this trip."

"But, you see, you could do that. You could walk into the bank and ask for cash, and they would give it to you without question."

"Well, yes, because my father has authorized me. . ."

"Exactly, and you are his only daughter. Letitia, you are his heir."

She sat still. "You don't think—"

"Oh, don't I?"

"But. . .Étienne—"

"This is why young men like me must remain silent when they admire you."

"Because my father would think you—oh, no." Her upper lip quivered.

"Oh, yes, my dear Letitia! In your father's eyes, I am not a worthy man for you. He has said as much, has he not?"

She would not meet his gaze.

Étienne could not keep back a wry chuckle. "Perhaps I am foolish even now, thinking we can be friends. What is friendship when I desire so much more, and what hope have I of ever being suitable, so far as your father is concerned?"

Once more, she scrutinized his features in the moonlight, and his pulse raced. He longed to sweep her into his arms and kiss her, but what would that tell her, hard on the heels of their conversation about fortune hunters? She would think him no better than Rawley, who had tried to force himself on her.

"Perhaps I overstep the bounds even now," he said regretfully. "Letitia, I cannot speak. I have not the right."

They rode on over the rough road, and the silence between them lengthened. When his right hand was cold, he wanted to swap the reins to his left and reach for her warm, gloved hand beneath the robe again, but he didn't dare. He should not have set her thinking about men who aimed to marry for gain. She was pondering what he had said; he could tell. The chill deepened, and she pulled the blanket tight around her. Étienne drove on, deep in thought.

An hour later he said, "We will soon be there. I cannot tell you how much I have enjoyed being with you this night. Were it not for your father's need of you, I would not wish it to end."

Letitia smiled and said gently, "Nor would I."

His wayward pulse throbbed once more. It was no use. Even though he knew it was pointless, he could not deny his love for her.

The huge horses neighed and quickened their steps.

"We are close now," he explained. "They smell their home."

It was after eight o'clock when they trotted into the farmyard. Étienne stopped the team before the house and hopped down. Before he had tied them and helped Letitia down, the door opened and a white-haired man came out.

"LeClair?"

"Yes, sir, it's me."

"You brought Miss Hunter?"

"Yes, sir, here she is." He put his arms up to Letitia and swung her lightly to the ground.

"You must come in, young lady," the farmer said.

"How is my father?" she asked, stepping quickly forward.

"Not good. The doctor was here earlier and thought he was somewhat improved, but he's had a turn this evening."

Letitia walked quickly toward the lantern light spilling from the farmhouse's doorway.

"I'll put the horses away," Turnbridge said, going toward the team.

Étienne handed over the reins. "I thank you for the use of them."

"Well, your employer buys from me every year. I could not do less in his time of need."

Étienne followed Letitia into the kitchen of the farmhouse, where she removed her bonnet and coat.

"Let me take you to the room where your father is staying." He took a candle, lit it from the lantern on the kitchen table, and led her down a short hallway to the stairs.

At the top of the staircase, he turned to the left and showed her the door of a snug room. Another candle burned on a small table. The whitewashed wall sloped to meet the ceiling on one side, and a dormer window jutted from it. The room was dominated by a maple bed covered with several colorful, pieced quilts. Under them lay Mr. Hunter, very pale and thin.

Letitia gasped at the condition of her father. She stepped quickly to the bedside and lifted his hand. "Father!"

Étienne stood beside her. "He is sleeping now."

"He has lost weight," she said. "He looks gray."

"Yes," said Étienne. "He needs our prayers."

He pulled forward a chair with a padded tapestry seat. "Mr. Turnbridge must have been sitting with him. Do you wish to sit?"

"Yes, thank you." Letitia sank onto the chair, rubbing her father's hand.

He moaned, and his eyelids fluttered open. "Steve?" he called.

Étienne stepped close to the bedside and bent down so he would be within Lincoln Hunter's vision. "I am here, sir. May I help you?"

"My girl—"

"She's here, sir. I brought her." He stepped back, nodding at Letitia.

"Father! Father, I'm here with you now. You will be better soon, and I will take you home."

He squinted at her. "Letitia?"

"Yes, Father."

"You look like your mother."

She sat speechless, tears coursing down her cheeks.

Étienne drew a handkerchief from his pocket and handed it to her.

"Letitia, listen to me," her father said, struggling as if he would sit up.

"Take it easy, sir." Étienne placed his hand firmly on Lincoln's shoulder. "Just lie back and speak to your daughter. She will hear you."

The older man sank back on the feather pillow and lay breathing loudly. "Letitia, don't sell."

"I beg your pardon, Father?" she asked, her eyes widening.

"Don't sell the company."

"I—I won't, Father."

"Have to keep it in the family."

"Yes." She looked beseechingly up at Étienne, but he shrugged, feeling helpless.

"Northern Lumber will support you all your life if you're careful."

"Certainly, Father."

Lincoln closed his eyes and seemed to drift off. Letitia sat alert, stroking his hand.

"He may rest now, just knowing you are here at last," Étienne said.

"I will stay with him in case he wakens again. What did he mean?"

"Just anxious about the business, I suppose. You ought to rest."

"No," said Letitia. "It is you who needs to rest. You have traveled twice as long and hard as I. Just let me sit with him. If he is no worse by dawn, I will perhaps lie down."

Turnbridge appeared in the doorway, his head nearly scraping the lintel.

"He spoke?"

"Yes," Étienne replied. "But he seems to be sleeping now."

Turnbridge nodded. "Can I bring you anything to make you more comfortable?"

"No, thank you. I am fine, sir," said Letitia.

"All right. We've fixed a room for you. Down the hall, last on the right. When you wish to rest, my wife or I will relieve you, and you can get some sleep. If you think he is worse, I'll send for the doctor again."

"Thank you, sir," she said.

Turnbridge nodded and left the room.

Étienne hated to leave her, but he knew the wisdom of taking some rest. He'd slept little the night before and traveled all day. He took an extra candlestick from the dresser and paused by Letitia's side.

"*Bon nuit*, mon amie," he whispered.

"Good night. And thank you for everything."

She looked up into his eyes, and he saw tears threatening. One spilled over and trickled down her cheek, and he could not stay his hand from reaching out to her. He touched her face gently with his palm, brushing the tear away with his thumb.

"Pray, my love." Instantly he knew he had again said too much, and he drew back his hand. "Forgive me. This is not the time."

She grasped his hand and brought it back to rest against her cheek. "We disagree. Can you forgive me for that?"

They looked into each other's sorrowful eyes for a moment, and Étienne swallowed hard. "Always," he said. "And I stand corrected."

⌘

Letitia sat watching her father's face. His breathing seemed too rapid and shallow, but she couldn't detect any signs of pain. She sat for hours, and her eyelids drooped. There was no clock in the room. How far away was dawn?

She jerked awake, thinking she must soon call someone to spell her or she would fall off the chair and end up asleep on the hooked rug.

"Letitia."

"Yes, Father." She went eagerly to her knees beside the bed to get closer to him.

"Mark will help you."

"Mark? No, Father, you don't understand. I'm here with you at Turnbridge now. When you are better, we'll go home."

"Mark Warren knows. He will help you. If you don't wish to marry—"

"Father, don't concern yourself about such things now. Be at peace. You need to rest and get your strength."

"No, I sent Steve for a reason." He tossed fitfully beneath the red and white flying geese quilt.

"You sent him to get me. I am here now."

"Yes, daughter."

Letitia stroked his hand.

"Talk to Mark," he said a moment later, without opening his eyes.

"All right, Father. I will."

A growing unease filled her. Her father was worried about something specific. She stayed on her knees on the rug, holding his hand and leaning her head against the side of the bed, where the quilt hung down.

She jerked awake some time later and realized Étienne was kneeling beside her.

"Letitia, dear," he said softly, "Come, ma chérie, you must rest. I will take you to your room."

She stared at him blankly then shifted to look at her father. His breathing was softer, but still rapid, and his face was ashen.

"But Father—"

"Yes, darling," Étienne said. "He is the same."

She turned toward him, unable to stop her tears, and he put his arms around her.

"What time is it?" she asked in a small voice.

"After two o'clock. Dearest Letitia, you need to sleep. I will watch him." He held her head against his shoulder and stroked her silky hair.

Letitia let out a tremulous sigh. Never had she known that a man's strong arms could bring so much comfort. "C–could we pray?"

"Of course." Étienne bowed his head and began, "Our dear Father in heaven." He paused, took a breath, and then hesitated again.

Letitia opened her eyes a crack and peeked up at him.

"I am sorry," he whispered. "I am not accustomed to praying in English."

"Pray in French, then. God will understand you."

His smile all but melted her heart, and he stooped to brush his lips across her forehead. "Thank you, my love, but He will understand my poor English as well." He took a deep breath and closed his eyes once more. "We beg Your healing for this man and Your strength and comfort for his daughter."

She relaxed against him. His cotton shirt smelled fresh and clean, and a trace of the odor of soap lingered where he had obviously shaved earlier.

After his brief prayer, she smiled up at him. "Please don't make me leave, dearest."

Étienne frowned and glanced toward her father's form once more. "If it were my father, I would not want to leave either," he conceded.

When Mrs. Turnbridge came to the door two hours later with a tray of tea, bacon, and biscuits, she smiled at Étienne. He knew it was because he, the lumberman's clerk, was sitting on the rose trellis rug covering the hardwood floor, holding his employer's beautiful daughter, sound asleep, in his arms.

Chapter 17

The physician returned to Turnbridge Farm just before noon, and Mrs. Turnbridge brought him up to the patient's room, where Étienne was keeping watch. Mrs. Turnbridge had put Letitia to bed hours before, and Étienne had stayed with her father, promising to call her if there was any change.

"He seems feeble, Dr. Bowles," Étienne said, as the man bent over the bed, counting Hunter's heartbeats.

"Yes, he's weaker than he was yesterday."

"Do you think he has a chance of recovery, sir?"

The doctor shook his head. "His heart has betrayed him, young man. You went for his daughter?"

"Yes. She spent the night at his side and is resting now. Do you want to see her?"

"I think she must be prepared," said Bowles.

"Yes, sir."

"I will fetch her," said Mrs. Turnbridge from the doorway. She turned and went down the hallway.

Ten minutes later Letitia appeared, freshly attired, but with a cast of fatigue still on her face.

"Miss Hunter?" asked the doctor, rising from his chair.

"Yes, sir." She trembled as she stepped forward, and Étienne went to her side.

"You must not have too much hope, my dear," the doctor said. "Your father is very weak, and I cannot say he will rise from this bed again."

Letitia stood still for a moment, then reached out toward Étienne.

He grasped her hand. "Sit down, Letitia," he murmured and drew her to the chair.

When she was seated, she looked up at the doctor. "Do you think, sir, with extended rest. . . ?"

Bowles sighed. "Anything is possible, if you believe in God Almighty."

"Oh, I do, sir."

He shrugged. "I do not wish to give you false hope. You cannot move him. That is certain. If he hangs on, he might strengthen; but it would be a matter of weeks, perhaps a month or more."

Letitia turned toward the doorway where Mrs. Turnbridge, in her apron, still hovered.

"Could you keep us, ma'am? I will pay you well for your hospitality."

"Of course," she said. "You may stay as long as there is need. My daughter and I will help care for him. You mustn't trouble yourself about that."

"You understand it's unlikely?" the doctor persisted. "I do not think he will live much longer, though it pains me to be so blunt with you."

"I understand." Letitia turned once more to gaze on her father's ashen face.

"I can do nothing for him. He could slip away anytime."

"Or he might get better?" Letitia asked hopefully.

"Do not hope too much."

"But if I don't—" She sobbed, and Étienne placed his hand on her shoulder.

"I'm sorry I can do no more," said Bowles. He picked up his medical bag. "If he rallies, send me word. If he is worse, well. . .if he is worse, there is nothing I can do, and it will be too late by the time I get here. I'm sorry."

"I understand." Letitia pressed a generous fee on him, and the doctor went on his way.

She stayed in her father's room, and Étienne found another chair in his bedroom and brought it so he could sit with her. The farmer's daughter, Mrs. Clark, brought lunch up for them a short time later, and he urged Letitia to eat, knowing she had taken little in the past twenty-four hours.

Lincoln Hunter lay unmoving, his eyes closed, his skin as pale as the white patches between the triangular red flying geese of the quilt.

"He spoke to me about his lawyer last night," Letitia said, glancing toward Étienne.

"What did he say?"

"Just that I should talk to Mark Warren. Étienne, I felt he was trying to tell me something particular. You were here when he said, 'Don't sell,' and then later he started to say something about my marrying."

"He is concerned for you, in case he is not here to take care of you."

"No, it was more than that. He urged me several times to talk to Mr. Warren."

"Then you should do it."

"Yes, when we go home."

An hour later, Étienne urged her to nap again while he stayed with her father.

"No, I can't bear to leave him now," she said. "You go rest, and I will wake you when I can't keep my eyes open."

"You said that last night," he replied. "If it does not distress you, I will stay awhile."

"Thank you."

He saw relief in her eyes, and he pulled his chair closer to hers and reached for her hand.

"Perhaps I should write a note to Mr. Weston," she said.

"If you wish. It sounds as though you might be here for some time."

"Yes."

"Let me make a proposal," said Étienne. "If in a day or two it looks like your father will have a long convalescence here, I will bear your news to Mr. Weston and Mr. Linden, and I will stay in Zimmerville as your agent."

She looked at him in alarm. "I should hate to see you go. How would I manage without you?"

"I should hate to leave you, too, but one of us needs to be there to watch the business your father has built so painstakingly."

Mr. Hunter moaned, and Letitia flew from her chair. "Father! I am here. Can you hear me?"

"Water," he whispered hoarsely.

Étienne held a glass to Hunter's lips, raising his head and shoulders with a strong arm.

"Daughter."

"Yes, Father." She squeezed his hand and knelt again on the rug, her face inches from his own.

"Letitia, if you don't want to marry him..."

"Who, Father?" she cried.

"If you don't like him, don't sell out to him. And you must rely on yourself to find a husband. God knows I've tried."

Letitia sniffed. "I'm sorry, Father. You've always let me refuse any man I didn't care for."

"I don't want to see you unhappy, my dear. But I thought I would see you married. You need a man who—" He closed his eyes and breathed with effort.

"Just rest now. We'll talk about this later," Letitia said quietly, stroking his forehead.

He opened his eyes again. "No, child, there's not time. Northern is a very valuable company."

"Of course, Father."

"It is yours now."

"No, Father, you can't—"

Étienne's hand came down once more on her shoulder, and she looked up at him.

"Let him speak," he said gently.

She turned to her father and whispered, "All right. Dear Father, what is it you wish to tell me?"

Lincoln drew a deep breath. "He spoke to me in April, when he brought the order."

"Who, Father?"

"John—" he gasped.

"Not John Rawley?" Letitia's distress wrenched Étienne's heart.

"Yes. When we went to lunch that day. He asked if he might court you, and I told him he would have to win your affections, because. . ." Hunter's breath was more ragged. "I will not marry my girl to a man she cannot love."

"Oh, Father, thank you." She buried her face in Étienne's handkerchief and sobbed.

"You didn't like him?" It was a whisper.

"No, Father. He came while you were away. He insulted me. I could never love him."

"Ah, well." He was quiet a moment, his eyelids fluttering down then opening again. "I told you, you may refuse whoever you will. Don't let anyone push you into a marriage you don't want."

"You'll get better," she insisted. "And I won't marry anyone unless—Father, you've said I may refuse anyone I choose."

"Yes, child."

"But may I accept the man of my choosing?" Her face flushed scarlet, and Étienne tightened his hand on her shoulder.

Hunter's breathing was more labored, and confusion crossed his face.

"What?" he gasped. "You have picked a suitor without my help?"

"Y–yes."

Étienne felt her tremble. He dropped to his knees beside her. "Sir, it is me. May I speak to you?"

"Steve?" Hunter blinked at him.

"Yes, sir."

"Help Letitia. You have a good head, Steve. Help her with the business. I'm giving you a raise. Now. Today. You'll be her right hand. But if she marries, her husband will take over."

Étienne hesitated. "Yes, sir, but I have something else to say."

Hunter looked into his eyes then, his breath short and wheezing.

"Speak."

"Sir, I love her. If you would consent, I would take care of her for the rest of my life." He stopped as the older man's eyes flared and his face convulsed.

"Father!" Letitia pushed Étienne aside and stroked her father's brow. "Father, it is enough talk for now. Please don't leave us. Just rest. Don't be upset."

His eyes closed, and each breath seemed a Herculean effort.

"Oh no, oh no." Letitia laid her cheek on the quilt and wept. "I should have kept quiet. Étienne, I shouldn't have said anything, but I love you." Her sobs racked her.

Étienne put one arm around her and smoothed her hair with his other hand.

"Ma chérie, I am sorry. I will do anything for you. I'm so sorry."

"He told you to speak," she quavered.

"Yes. He knows now." Étienne's heart ached with guilt and sorrow. "I don't think he was pleased."

She sobbed once, then took a deep breath. "It is in God's hands."

They sat together for several hours, until the sun dropped low in the west, sending brilliant orange rays through the dormer window onto the white wall beyond. Letitia shifted her position several times, from the rug to the chair to the far edge of the bed. She was sitting in the chair with Étienne beside her when Lincoln's eyes opened again.

"Letitia."

"Yes, Father." She jumped eagerly closer.

"You choose your man. Rawley wants the company, but. . .you must have a man. . .who loves you."

"I do, sir!" Étienne said firmly.

Hunter looked up, searching for him.

"Steve—"

"Yes, sir."

"Don't sell out, Steve."

"Never."

"Then marry her. It is. . .right."

Étienne slipped his arm around Letitia as her father turned his troubled eyes on her.

"I should never have turned away from God. But He knows."

"Yes, He knows and forgives," Letitia whispered.

"I love you, daughter." His eyes closed. He breathed again, then sighed, and the room was still.

"Father!"

"He is gone," Étienne said softly.

Letitia touched her father's cheek then turned slowly. "Étienne."

"Yes, my love."

She put her arms out to him, and he pulled her into his embrace.

"I will take care of you," he promised.

"I know."

She looked up at him, her eyes full of hope and trust; and he bent toward her, his lips meeting hers in the kiss he at last had the right to give. She trembled and slid her arms up around his neck. He held her tightly for a long moment.

At last he said, "I will go tell Mr. Turnbridge, ma chérie, and tomorrow we will take him home."

Epilogue

Étienne guided the team toward the Zimmerville train station through the lightly falling snow.

"I'm so glad your mother and the boys could come before Christmas." Letitia scooted over closer to him on the seat, took her hand from her fur muff, and slipped it through his arm.

He smiled down at her. "You get your wish, and we can be married Christmas Eve."

"Do you think Richard and Jean-Claude will be all right alone in the office this afternoon?" she asked. "I'd like it if you could stay at the house with us for a while, but if you think they'll need you. . ."

"Those boys will be fine," Étienne said. "Jacques will no doubt look in at least twice to make sure his son is not misbehaving while the boss is out."

Letitia smiled. Training Jacques and Angelique's oldest boy to replace her as clerk, along with Richard Shelby, had been a joy. Every day as she and Étienne tutored the two young men in the office routine, they knew the day of Letitia's freedom and their wedding was coming closer.

The train arrived in a flurry of noise and smoke. Étienne scanned the windows anxiously, then touched Letitia's arm and pointed. Soon a small, middle-aged woman and two half-grown boys were climbing down from the passenger car.

"Étienne!" the younger boy cried, running toward them. "You should have been on the train! We went so fast!"

Étienne laughed and stepped forward to assist his mother. Letitia waited for him to greet her privately, but when he turned and beckoned to her, she joined him, glad to meet his mother at last.

"My dear," Madame LeClair murmured with tears in her eyes.

Letitia bent toward her and kissed her cheek. "I'm so happy that you are here, madame."

Étienne's mother turned to him. "*Elle* est belle!"

He chuckled. "Oui, très belle, *Maman*." He quickly introduced his two youngest brothers, Paul and Denis.

"Will André be able to come?" his mother asked him.

"Yes," Étienne told her, "I've written to his foreman at Nine Mile Camp and told him to give André next week off."

She nodded, content. "I wish your sisters could come, but it is just too far."

Letitia smiled. "We wish they could be here, too, but we're overjoyed that

362

you and all the boys will be with us for the ceremony."

Madame LeClair looked anxiously at Étienne. "And after? I did as you said and sold the farm to Elaine and her husband."

"Do not fear, Maman," he told her. "Letitia and I have looked about the town for a small house for you and the boys, and we have made a decision."

"Oh?"

He glanced at Letitia, arching his eyebrows.

Letitia stepped forward and took his mother's hands. "Étienne and I have decided to keep my parents' house. We thought at first we would sell it, as it is very large. Perhaps too large. But then we thought, why sell this big place and buy two smaller houses, one for you and one for us? Why not have you and the boys stay with us?"

"Oh, we do not wish to impose," Madame LeClair said. "You will be newly-weds, after all."

Étienne laughed. "Maman, wait until you see the house. It is so large we will not even know you are there unless you want us to. And besides, I am taking Letitia away for two weeks after the wedding. We need someone to be there in the house and to welcome us when we return."

Madame LeClair looked from him to Letitia, her forehead wrinkled and her brown eyes anxious. "Well, if you are sure."

"We're sure," Étienne said. "But if you try it for a while and you don't like it, we will make other arrangements in the spring."

"Well, I suppose I can help Letitia with the cooking," his mother said.

"We have a cook, Maman, but don't let that scare you. I'm sure Mrs. Watkins will let you into the kitchen if you want to bake an apple tart."

The boys came down the platform hauling several satchels.

A half hour later, they all stood in the parlor of the Hunter mansion. Étienne watched as his mother stared about her. Even Paul and Denis were silenced by the grandeur of the house.

"It is too much," Madame LeClair said.

"But this is Letitia's home, and she loves it very much," Étienne said.

His mother shook her head, staring at the paintings and velvet draperies. "It is so—" She swallowed hard and looked at Letitia. "I am sorry, my dear. It is wonderful. It is just—we are not used to such—"

Letitia touched her sleeve. "I understand. I hope that you will grow to love this home as I do. But if not, we will find you a little house of your own, I promise."

"Come, boys, I will show you your rooms," Étienne said.

"We get our own rooms?" Denis asked. He and Paul stared at each other.

"Yes, but they have a door between," said Étienne.

"And I will take you up to your room, dear mother," said Letitia. "Agnes will bring your bags and help you unpack."

"Wait," said Madame LeClair. "I have here a box for you, Letitia."

She held out a parcel tied with string.

"Why, thank you." Letitia took it, and Étienne brought out his pocketknife to cut the string.

She laid the box on a cherry side table and opened it, lifting out a filmy shower of ethereal lace.

"Oh, it's lovely!"

Madame LeClair smiled at her oldest son. "I went to Madame Rousseau, as you instructed me."

"The same lady who made the table runner you sent for my birthday?" Letitia asked him.

"Yes. I asked Maman to see if she would make you a wedding veil."

"It's the most beautiful creation in the world," Letitia said.

❦

On Christmas Eve Étienne paced a small anteroom in the little church. His brother André, who had arrived on the Bangor train the night before, slouched in a chair, watching him with glittering eyes. Jacques Laplante and René Ouellette straightened each other's neckties.

"What time is it?" Étienne asked.

"Relax, mon ami," said René. "They will tell us when it is time."

At that moment the pastor entered. "Come," he said to Étienne. "It is time."

André went to escort their mother to the seat of honor, and Étienne and his friends stood at the front of the church.

The pews were filled with the church members, the employees of Northern Lumber, many of the company's customers, and the Hunter family's old acquaintances. Étienne felt sweat beading on his brow, although the sanctuary was cool.

The organist began to play, and all eyes turned to the back of the church. Sophie and Angelique entered, walking slowly the length of the aisle. Jacques and René beamed at their wives, who wore the simple but lovely gowns Letitia had ordered sewn for them. Finally came Letitia, on the arm of attorney Mark Warren.

Étienne caught his breath. Through the sheer lace veil he could see her bright eyes on him and her radiant smile. At last she was by his side, and Mr. Warren gave her over into his care. With her hand cradled in his, he faced the pastor, ready to conquer the world.

He repeated the simple vows looking into her eyes, knowing that finally he had the right to say them and to claim her. "I, Étienne, take thee, Letitia, to be my lawfully wedded wife."

Her voice breathless, she took her vows, and he slipped the plain gold ring onto her finger. Angelique stepped forward and laid back the intricate lace veil.

Étienne stooped to kiss his bride. If not for her joyful smile, he would have thought this moment an impossible dream.

She clung to him for a moment and whispered, "I love you."

He smiled down at her. "*Je t'aime*, ma chérie."